DARK CORNERS
in SKOGHALL

by

ALIDA WINTERNHEIMER

The Skoghall Mystery Series,
Book Two

This is a 28.5press book.

Published in the United States by 28.5press
Minneapolis, Minnesota

1. Ghost—Fiction. 2. Murder Mystery—Fiction. 3. Midwestern Gothic—Fiction. 4. Service Dog—Fiction. 5. Writer—Fiction. 6. Illustrated Novel—Fiction. I. Title.

ISBN: 978-0-9912923-5-6

Cover design by Daria Brennan.
Cover photograph by David W. Nance.
Illustrations by Mad Scientist.
Graphics by Catherine Bychkova.
Title fonts by Gluk.
Isabella's font by Lee Batchelor
Grace's font by Artimasa Studio

Please support independent authors and artists.
Don't be a pirate.
Aaargh!

for Seva

and service dogs the world over
who truly change people's lives

10% of proceeds from this book will be
donated to Helping Paws of Minnesota

Seva's story is at
www.alidawinternheimer.com/servicedog

Helping Paws is at
www.helpingpaws.org

DARK CORNERS
in SKOGHALL

Prologue

DAN SWUNG VIOLENTLY, grabbing at her hair. What was her name? She had told him in the bar. June. Or April. Or August. It was a month. It hardly mattered now, because he wanted to kill her.

The girl bent backwards, reached for something on the table to her side. A pile of 45s slid to the floor, some of the thin, black discs coming free of their paper sleeves. He lurched after her, his foot landing on the records, snapping several in half with a satisfying *click click click* as he shifted his weight and they yielded. That copy of "Great Balls of Fire" would never play again. What was the B side? It's the sort of thing he would have known if he were himself. Dan liked rock and roll and had a fully catalogued collection of vinyl filling the shelves of his rec room. Other people collected model airplanes or trophy kills they stuffed and mounted over their console television sets. Not him. His prized possession was a 1973 Wurlitzer jukebox, model name, "The Nostalgia," because it had been styled after the classic consoles of the 1940s. For him, it brought back nostalgia all right, but not for a bygone era, for his childhood in Milwaukee. While his friends pedaled down to the comic shop and spent their allowance on Clark Kent and Double Bubble, he wasted entire afternoons in Mick's Record Shop. Mick had one of these jukeboxes and loaded it with all the newly released singles—his version of try-before-you-buy. He also kept his favorites in the record carousel, and it wasn't uncommon to hear Pink Floyd after Duran Duran after Buddy Holly.

Dan had rescued the Wurlitzer and restored it with his own two hands. That was the sort of thing a man could take pride in.

His own two hands. There was a lot he could do with his hands.

The girl backed herself into a corner. The shelves she pressed against, as though if she leaned into them enough they would yield her escape, were crammed with all the discarded, disused detritus of people gone or forgotten. Garage sales, foreclosure auctions, abandoned storage units had all contributed to the junk surrounding them. The man who had collected it all had a mental illness, or, at the least, a lack of self-control. March put her foot on an overturned steel pail and pushed herself up, twisting to grab at the shelves and attempting to climb to safety the way a kitten might scale a curtain. Her miniskirt rose enticingly up her thighs, up her ass, revealing the twin rounds of young buttocks—she wore a thong if she wore anything under that skirt. *That,* he thought, *is proof. She's a whore.* She sobbed a terrified plea that never left her throat and he felt a throbbing down low.

He could have caught her already, but Dan was enjoying this part, the… what was it called?…*chase.* He grinned as he reached out a hand. She got a toe on the edge of a shelf and pushed upwards. Her grasping brought a stack of yellowed pamphlets advertising a sanitarium on the shore of Lake Superior cascading to the floor, and she sobbed again. Dan slid his hand between her thighs, a laugh of mischievous glee on the verge of erupting from his lips.

April screeched at the touch and came down from the shelves, a crack emanating from her ankle when she not so much landed as crashed. She spun around, her face a mess of running mascara, mousy hair teased out of its clip, lipstick smeared onto her lower lip from their kiss. It had been the kiss that triggered something in him. March swung both arms together in a wide arc from her hips upwards toward the dark ceiling, connecting with his head. The thud of a heavy amber glass ashtray—the kind people kept out as a coffee table centerpiece, an objet d'art to collect their butts—striking his skull, fracturing the bone beneath his eyebrow, sent him reeling backwards. Dan tripped over a crate of Life Magazines and landed on something that made his tailbone sear.

May stood over him, the ashtray streaked with his blood still gripped tightly in her hands. Her top had twisted with all the activity, and a breast thinly veiled by a red lace bra showed itself. His wife always insisted it was tacky, the way girls today showed off their bras.

Now he was going to kill her.

Chapter One

JESS COULDN'T REMEMBER the last time she'd run like this. And here she was in August, out on some county road, sweat pouring off her head and trickling down the small of her back into her running shorts. Even with sunglasses, she found herself squinting. "Chandra," she called, "wait."

Chandra, her best friend, had finally made it down from Minneapolis for a visit, packing a bottle of tequila and pair of running shoes. She slowed and made an easy U-turn on the narrow gravel shoulder and came back to Jess. Jess stopped running, put her hands on her thighs, and considered throwing up for a moment, then decided not to. "Damn, woman," she panted. "I can't keep up with you. You're barely sweating, too." Jess pushed her damp hair away from her brow. "What the hell? You're like a frickin' gazelle."

"My mom *was* born on the African savannah."

"Really?"

Chandra shook her head with a look full of pity. "She was born in Chicago, which you already knew."

Jess grabbed Chandra's wrist. "You can't expect my brain to work after eight miles of torture."

"Two," she looked at a workout tracking device on her wrist, "and this isn't even fast."

"Two! Two miles! You mean we have to go another two miles to get home?"

"Do you know a shortcut?"

Jess looked around them in every direction. County Road QQ ran east between rolling fields of corn tucked and folded into the bluffs that surrounded the Mississippi River valley. Occasional gravel roads intersected the county road, leading into either farms or forests. From within the tall leafy corn stalks, grasshoppers played their leg fiddles. She shaded her eyes and looked toward the perfectly bright and empty blue sky. "Come on." Jess turned the way they'd come and started walking. At least the sun was behind them and the way home was slightly downhill.

Chandra threw an arm over Jess's shoulder. "I'm a gazelle, huh?"

Jess grumbled. "Since when have you run like this?"

"I'm training for a half-marathon."

"Really?" Jess squinted up at the tall blonde, her mass of spiraling curls bouncing around her head like an overly cheerful halo. She flung Chandra's arm off her shoulder. "You could have warned me."

"If we jog, we'll get back in half the time."

Jess picked up her feet and began a slow jog. "When did you become such a big runner anyway?"

"Peter's a runner. I took up running for him." She shrugged. "I decided just because I gave him up doesn't mean I have to give up the running."

"Lose a guy, take up a marathon?" Jess panted as Chandra began to stretch her legs. "Hey, we're taking this slow." Chandra slowed again. "So when are you going to tell me about the break up?"

"Now, I guess." Chandra sighed and looked at Jess. "Thanks for giving me some time to just hang out." She had turned up the day before in a sleek, yellow convertible, her curls tied under a lime green scarf, oversized sunglasses hiding her doe eyes. She honked and waited for Jess to come outside, like some 1950s starlet posing for the paparazzi. "I thought he might be the one, you know?"

Jess nodded.

"I mean, I don't know that I was thinking of marrying him or anything like that, but I wasn't *not* thinking of it. The fact that we lasted nine months is huge. I know when a guy is wrong for me and I don't stick around. Know what I mean?"

Jess did know. Chandra's dating track record was impressive for quantity, if not quality. Most men were in and out within a month or two, long enough to measure compatibility and no longer. What exactly Chandra used for a compatibility scale, Jess had never been able to figure out. "You dumped him, right?"

"It was more of a mutual thing. He got transferred to Austin, Texas. A pretty big promotion. And he wanted me to move with him." Chandra pushed sweat away from her brow. "I didn't want to move."

"Yeah, but…" Jess huffed, "there's more to the story or you wouldn't be here. I hope you'd be here to visit me, but you wouldn't be here to recover from Peter's leaving."

"He thought I should move just because I can. He argued that as a graphic designer I can work anywhere I want to. 'It's all digital these days,' he said, like my career was the only factor to my quality of life."

"Ouch."

"Yeah. I have friends and family here. I love the Cities. Why would I leave all that behind? Besides, *Austin*. I detest humidity, and it's humid there like eleven and a half months out of the year."

Jess waited a moment before venturing to state the obvious. "Maybe he thought you'd move for him."

"That is precisely what it came down to…and I picked me." She stopped running and stood on the blacktop, scanning the horizon where the land merged into a vertical line of trees. Chandra looked at Jess, her face unusually pained. "Am I a fool? Did I let the best thing in my life walk away?"

Jess put her arm around Chandra's shoulder and drew her in for a supportive squeeze. "No. I'm standing right here."

Chandra chuckled and pushed Jess away. "Yeah, and you're dripping sweat."

"So are you." She wiped her palm on her running shorts. "If you aren't ready to move to Texas, it means he's not the one, but you got closer this time." Chandra didn't seem convinced. "There *are* other men out there," she added. They started moving again. After only a few yards, Chandra stopped. Jess turned back to face her. "What is it?"

"About that other men thing."

"Yeah?"

"You're going to hate me for this."

"Chandra?" They'd been best friends for a decade, and Chandra was not one to apologize. She hardly ever found fault with herself, which, she claimed, left nothing to apologize for. "What is it?"

"I slept with Mitch."

"*What?!*"

"Oh shit, I knew it." Chandra pointed at Jess's face and circled her finger. "You've gone red. Well, redder. You hate me."

Jess spun away from Chandra, then turned on her. "How? Why?"

"The day Peter left for Austin, I decided to go out drinking." Chandra shrugged like every girl parties to mend a broken heart. "I decided to go to Liquor Lyle's and I ran into Mitch."

"And that was all it took?"

"I was sad and lonely and kind of drunk."

"Right. That's all it took."

"Jess!" She threw her hands up. "Be nice."

"Nice? You slept with the enemy. You slept with my *ex-husband*. You of all people know what he put me through. You know everything about my divorce and what a jackass he is."

"I know. I know. I wasn't right in the head. I can't explain it any other way, Jess. He was there and he was looking good..."

Jess made a disgusted sound and folded her arms over her chest. "I do not want to hear that anything about him was good. He's a bastard, and you know that."

"I'm sorry."

"What?" Jess stared at her intently. "Say it again."

"I'm sorry?"

Jess almost smiled.

"I'm sorry. Jess, I am truly sorry."

"My god, Chandra Bjornson actually apologized for something. I didn't think I'd live to see the day."

Chandra rolled her eyes. "All right. *Mea culpa.* Should I beg?"

"You slept with Mitch, so...yeah."

"Jess, I would never jeopardize our friendship. Especially over a man. Peter leaving totally messed me up."

Standing under the sun wasn't doing them any good. Jess tilted her head in the direction of the house. They began walking again and she wished a breeze would come out of somewhere to dry some of the sweat rolling down her body.

"I think," Chandra continued, "I was punishing myself a little."

"By getting laid?"

"Ouch."

Jess met her friend's eyes. "Yeah, okay, that was harsh."

"By pretending Mitch was all that was left for me, was all I worthy of, or something like that. I don't know. I'm pretty together now, Jess, but I was a wreck last week."

"I don't think I've ever seen you messed up over a guy."

They came to the T-intersection where the county road met Haug Drive. To the south, fields and forests as the road dipped and rose, curving up into the hills. To the north, Jess's driveway, then the road banked west and sloped downward into Skoghall, turning into Main Street once around the bend.

"It wasn't pretty," Chandra said. "Do you forgive me?"

"I don't have a choice if I want to keep my best friend, but I'm pissed about this." She stopped to look Chandra in the eye. "You know that, right?"

"I know. It was an asshole thing to do and I am sorry." Chandra turned her face to the sky and sighed, then brought her gaze back to meet Jess's. "I don't grovel and I don't do punishments, but you have a big fat pass in my book. If you ever screw up with me, you're ass is covered."

"Fine. I won't punish. A little groveling wouldn't hurt, though." She shoulder bumped Chandra as they started down her driveway.

"I'll see what I can do about that." Chandra shoulder bumped her back and they stumbled forward.

An old red barn, the paint peeled and boards faded, stood nearest the road. Jess had dreams for the barn, but for now she was content to lend it to the critters who found it a convenient shelter. Across the drive, the ring of an old smokehouse reminded Jess of the difficulties she'd faced when she first moved here not that long ago. She believed in recycling, not bad memories, and figured one day it would make a nice fire pit. Jess's house, a beautiful foursquare ordered from Sears Roebuck in 1921, sat back on the tree-ringed property. She'd fallen in love with it the moment she saw it.

They sat on the porch with tall glasses of water, letting the sweat dry on their skin, while Shakti, Jess's eight-month-old Golden Retriever sniffed her way through the yard. "I can't believe you slept with Mitch." Chandra didn't say anything. "I can't believe I ever married that jerk." Jess pushed herself up to standing. "Can you watch the dog while I go shower?" Chandra nodded and Jess went inside.

She passed the door to the guest room at the top of the stairs and wondered what Chandra would put on today. She'd arrived with a duffel bag big enough to keep her going for a month, including a halter dress with a swinging skirt and a pair of strappy heels. When Chandra had pulled the dress from the bag, Jess asked what it was for. "A night on the town," Chandra had informed her. "Where is the closest hot spot?" Jess replied, "St. Paul." Jess had always liked Chandra's impulsiveness and the fact that Chandra got her to stretch her limits. So was she really surprised Chandra had slept with Mitch? It was hardly the first thing her friend had done in poor taste.

Jess had just about worked it out of her system by the time she got out of the shower. She stood in front of her vanity, toweling off her long brown hair, when she heard Chandra calling.

Chandra's voice rose with alarm. "Jess!"

She ran downstairs and onto the front porch. "What is it?"

"Shakti's gone."

"What did you do?"

"I didn't do anything. I sat here the whole time and she just disappeared."

Jess looked at Chandra's phone on the side table between her rocking chairs. Jess ran off the porch and called her dog. "Shakti!" No response. She circled the house, calling into the woods. The trees were thinnest to the south where a line of trees separated Jess's yard from her neighbor's soybean field. "Shakti!" The woods were dense enough to lose a young dog for days on the west and north sides.

Jess ducked through undergrowth at a small track just the right size for a dog. She called Shakti as she bush whacked her way through the trees. Less than two months ago, Shakti had run into the woods during a huge summer storm and nearly been crushed under a falling tree. Had the dog forgotten her terror already? Possibly, but Jess hadn't. Memories flooded her mind and her heart clenched in her chest, and the woods no longer seemed benign.

Jess called Shakti repeatedly. The dog did not respond and her thoughts turned panicky. She pushed her way through the scrub and brush, denser than it had been in June, and found Shakti with her nose stuffed in a hole, probably the entrance to a rabbit warren. She stood rigidly, her tail at attention. "Shakti." The dog did not respond, her senses so acutely tuned to her object of fascination that she had completely blocked out the rest of the world.

She might be too big to carry, but Jess would drag her home by the scruff of the neck if need be. Just as she reached for Shakti, the dog's head jerked up. She glanced over her shoulder at Jess and sprang away, her eyes glimmering with mischief. "Shakti," Jess complained. Her dog lapped her in a tight circle, then bounded away down the trail.

Chandra picked an anchovy off the mound of romaine in front of her and tilted her head back before lowering the small fillet and laying it on her tongue.

"Seriously," Jess said.

"Seriously. Have you ever tried one of these?"

Jess had ordered a vegetarian Caesar salad, while Chandra had requested the small briny fish be added to hers specially. The Water Wheel café had a good sized dinner crowd, which was allowing Jess and Chandra the relative privacy they needed to catch up.

"So that's the guy?" Chandra said, tilting her head toward the kitchen where Tyler was working away. "He makes a mean salad."

"You should try his chocolate torte."

"I'll bet." She took a sip of wine before getting back to the real conversation, the one Jess hoped no one around them could hear. "He actually tied you up and put a knife to your throat?"

"Scarf. He was strangling me. Besides, he wasn't himself. He was possessed."

Chandra raised both eyebrows while tilting and jutting her head in a way she had of declaring your statement ludicrous.

Jess refused to bite.

Chandra shook her head. "Let me see if I have this straight. Your house was haunted by a lady who was murdered by a Vietnam vet who possessed the chef here who tried to strangle you."

"That pretty much sums it up. Except the vet didn't possess Tyler. Bonnie, my ghost, did."

Chandra twisted in her seat to stare at the doorway to the kitchen behind her. She faced Jess again, "Damn! That is the craziest thing I have ever heard. That guy…" She pointed over her shoulder.

"Chandra," Jess urged. "Let's talk about this at home." She raised her glass. "To independent women."

Their waiter, an angsty young man with a safety pin through his ear and pants that barely hung onto his ass, stopped by their table and lit the candle. He took his time sliding it to the precise middle of the tabletop before glancing at each of them in turn and asking if they needed anything else. Jess shook her head. She had hoped Denise would serve them tonight— she thought Chandra would get a kick out of her—but Denise was off and they were stuck with her boyfriend, Bruce.

Chandra raised her glass when Bruce at last moved on. Jess brought hers up and they clinked them together over the newly-lit candle.

The community garden, which buzzed late into the evening, enclosed a spring that bubbled up from an underground stream. The building that now served as the café dated to the 1890s. Its foundation edged the spring and the basement housed a millstone that had been connected to the water wheel on the building's side, turning the community's grain into flour. A wooden footbridge arched over the spring, connecting the garden to the café's entrance. The Water Wheel was, in Jess's opinion, the primest piece of real estate in Skoghall, the turning water wheel being the single most charming feature of anywhere in town.

Beckett arrived at the café as they were finishing their salads. He wore his blond hair in a short ponytail at the nape of his neck and gave Jess a kiss hello before she made introductions. He shook Chandra's hand and took a seat beside Jess. Chandra flirtatiously tucked a spiraling curl behind her ear. Beckett laid his arm across the back of Jess's chair and asked Chandra the typical set of introductory questions. What did she do? How did she meet Jess? Where was she from? Jess listened to their conversation, seeing no need to interject, and instead waved Bruce over to order a bottle of wine and— she checked that Beckett had already had dinner—three slices of flourless chocolate torte. With the order in, she turned her attention back to her friends. She and Chandra played a little game whenever they met someone new, especially someone in a bar where alcohol lowered social inhibitions. She tucked her lower lip between her teeth while Chandra told Beckett she grew up in Minneapolis proper, a city girl her entire life. Beckett had a drink from Jess's water glass, then told Chandra he was glad she'd finally made it to Skoghall. Jess wanted to slap Beckett on the back and congratulate him, but of course he had no idea what he'd done to deserve it, so she settled for casting a knowing look at Chandra, who returned it with an amused grin.

"Am I missing something?" Beckett asked.

"Yes," Jess said, "but it wouldn't be fair to tell you now."

"Fair?"

Bruce arrived with their wine and a third glass for Beckett, diverting him from pressing his curiosity. The cake followed and Jess and Chandra giggled as they ate their first bites, another inside joke Beckett was better off not knowing about.

"You're right, Jess. This torte is amazing."

"I told you."

As tables emptied, Jess found herself speaking in a hushed tone. Dusk settled over the garden. The water wheel groaned audibly with each rotation now that the café was quiet. As Bruce said good night to the last customers, Tyler came out of the kitchen. He slid a bandana that served as chef's hat off his head as he approached, then ran his hand through his dark curls to free them from his damp scalp.

"I'm glad you're still here," he said.

"Tyler, this is Chandra."

"Would you like to join us?" Chandra gestured to the open chair beside her.

Tyler stepped away to get himself a wine glass and told Bruce to comp the bottle from their ticket. When he sat down, Chandra filled his glass with a smile. Beckett raised an eyebrow at Jess. She leaned in to whisper to him, "Yes, Chandra is always this welcoming, especially to men."

"It looked like a good dinner crowd tonight," Jess said.

"It was. I could have used more help, but Denise and Robin, the other chef," he added for Chandra's benefit, "both wanted the night off." He sipped the wine. "Good choice, by the way. This is one of my favorites."

"You can thank Jess for that," Chandra said. "She has much better taste in wine than I do, but…" she leaned slightly into Tyler, "I'm always eager to learn something new."

Tyler sat caught between Chandra and the window. He sidled closer to the wall and glanced over his shoulder as though he'd like to escape.

"What does Bruno do when you're at work?" Jess asked.

"Bruno? I think he sleeps a lot."

"Is he here?"

Tyler glanced at Chandra and then at Beckett.

"You're safe with them."

"I've known for weeks," Beckett said. "It's cool, man."

Tyler slid his chair back and went into the kitchen.

"What's this all about?" Chandra asked.

"Change seats," Jess said. Chandra obliged with a puzzled expression and a shrug.

When Tyler returned, Bruno, a russet-colored Golden Retriever, walked by his side, tail wagging ecstatically. Tyler paused at the café's entrance to bolt the door and flip the sign to closed. Bruce wiped up the tables around them, earbuds piping music into his head and blocking out the world.

Chandra cooed at Bruno and grabbed his head to give him a kiss and scratch his ears as soon as he was within reach. He dropped his rump into an obedient and expectant sit and soaked up the attention. "He's so sweet," she said.

"Chandra," Beckett pointed at the back pack Bruno wore. "Do not pet."

"Oh crap. Sorry." She pulled back, seeing the PTSD Service Dog designation for the first time, and folded her hands in her lap.

Bruno stared at Tyler, his tail paused, anticipating the next command.

"Release," Tyler said.

Bruno's tail beat the floor as he scooted forward and shoved his chin onto Chandra's lap. She happily resumed his ear rub.

Tyler took Chandra's old seat at the aisle with a more relaxed air about him. "He's been shut in the office all evening. This is a treat."

Chandra had plenty of questions about the dog, and Tyler answered her easily. Jess turned to Beckett. "How are the pots?" He told her about a new glaze he was mixing, the test tiles, and how he was drawing closer to the speckled blue he'd imagined. The North Shore Gallery in Duluth would be showing Beckett's pottery in a few weeks, and he had some new art pieces ready to glaze in time for the show. Jess kept one ear tuned to the other conversation, and it wasn't long before Tyler asked the question.

"If you don't mind me asking, what are you?"

Jess thumped Beckett's thigh with her knuckles under the table.

"Ouch."

She thumped him again.

"I am Afro-Norwegian." Chandra had different answers depending on who was doing the asking and how the question was being asked. There was simple curiosity, hitting on her, tinged with racism, and probably more nuances Jess couldn't recall. This was the straight-forward answer, a response to the well-meaning but curious. "My mother is African-American and my father is Norwegian-American." The combination had resulted in a fair-skinned blonde with freckles, tight, spiraling curly hair, brown eyes, and a somewhat broad nose.

"That's cool," Tyler said. "I don't even know what I am. I guess I'm a mutt. But Bruno is pure-bred." He rubbed Bruno's head. "Speaking of, I should take him out back."

"I'll go with you," Chandra offered.

"Does she know?" Beckett asked when they had left the dining room.

"She knows enough to be fairly warned."

He rubbed his goatee. "Maybe you should warn her again."

"She's a big girl, Beckett." Jess tilted the wine bottle over her glass and poured out the last of the wine. "And she's not me."

"I don't want you or your friends getting hurt."

"I can't promise anything. You might have noticed that she has a mind of her own."

"Yeah. I just hope she doesn't drag you into anything."

Jess laughed. "Like what? Beckett, this is Skoghall, population sixty-six. What kind of trouble is there to get into around here?"

Chapter Two

SKOGHALL'S MAIN STREET sloped downhill toward the Mississippi, intersecting the River Road before ending at a small park with a boat launch on the shore of the river. Beckett's pottery studio sat between the River Road and the park with a set of train tracks marking the divide between them. His studio had been a diner in the 1980s, and before that a motor garage, and before that the livery. Skoghall had grown up in the time of the horse and carriage, was saved by the railway, then nearly lost to time after World War II. The spring at the center of town and beauty of the surrounding bluffs saved it when artists recognized the charm and made it a tourist spot along the Wisconsin River Road.

Jess explained as much of Skoghall's history to Chandra as she could while they walked Main Street. They stopped at Miss Grundi's ice cream parlor and ate their oversized cones in the garden next to the spring. The water wheel creaked, its old wood paddles dipping endlessly into the cool water below. When they left the garden, the logical next stop would have been the antique store, sitting as it did next door to the café, but Jess said she wasn't in the mood for browsing and would rather walk. The truth being that she wasn't in the mood to see Lora Zabrowski, the proprietor, or Isabella, the little girl who died there in 1918. Jess had been avoiding them for over a month, since she cleared up the Bonnie thing, and she'd almost convinced herself that she was entirely normal again, that her seeing ghosts had been an aberration, a side effect of her house being haunted and really nothing to do with her. If she went into the antique store and saw Isabella, it would ruin her plans to be normal—and just when she was having so much fun. They did stop in the hardware store to say hello to Dave, Beckett's employee and friend, then went into the Amish furniture shop on their way to the studio. To browse. Jess finished Chandra's nickel tour of Skoghall at Beckett's pottery studio. The weekend traffic along the Great River Road made it impossible for him to stop and chat. Normally, Jess and Shakti would be there to help when he needed it, but Chandra's visit trumped selling pots—for Jess anyway.

"What's that way?" They stood outside the studio, facing north, and Chandra pointed at the buildings that seemed to spill off of Main Street onto the River Road.

"That one's vacant," Jess pointed at the remains of a 1950s gas station on the corner. "House. House. And there's a turn off to an old cemetery up the road."

"And that way?" Chandra faced south.

Jess looked across the street at a gift shop, another vacant storefront, a house. On their side of the street, a short hike uphill on the other side of a stand of trees and shrub, sat three more buildings, a line of Harleys and a couple of sport bikes parked in front of the middle one.

"That," Jess pointed at the first building, "is a creamery, in case you have a hankering for cheese curds. And that," she gestured at the next building, "is obviously the biker bar." Beyond that, perched on the peak of the slope before the River Road curved away from the village, sat a weathered duplex without any signage to indicate a business. "I have no idea what that is. It might be a private residence. It might be vacant. I've never really given it a thought."

"Well, I'm ready for a beer." Chandra stepped away from Jess, cheerfully heading toward the line of hogs.

Jess caught her arm. "Let's go up the hill to the Water Wheel."

"Let's try something new. It'll be fun."

Chandra's encouraging tone made Jess feel ridiculous, but it didn't make her feel comfortable with the thought of drinking in The Two Wheeler. "But, we don't go there."

"*We* don't go there?" Chandra repeated. "What does that even mean?"

Jess cringed. Her easy-going friend only had one or two buttons, and Jess had just pushed the big one. A car rolled past them on the River Road and turned up Main Street. The heads of children were visible through the back seat windows, excitedly bouncing, most likely over the promise of Miss Grundi's homemade ice cream. A couple came out of the bar. They wore black leather chaps with silver-colored studs lining the outside leg seams. Her chaps were lined with fringe that swished with her every step. He wore a leather vest with a large logo on the back and she a tank top that showed off skinny arms caramelized by the sun. Jess hoped the contrast between these two sets of passersby would make her case for her, but Chandra pressed her with raised eyebrows and pursed lips.

Jess sighed. "Skoghall is an arts community. The people who live here and make up the community are Beckett, Tyler, me, Dave…and a bunch of others you haven't met. These guys, they're transients. Not community. They just pass through. And their bikes are noisy. Sometimes they get drunk. Sometimes they brawl. So, we just give them their space and do our drinking *not* at the biker bar."

"Listen to you, Jessica Vernon. *Us* and *them*."

"I know. I totally hear it."

"You are such a snob!"

"Jesus, Chandra. Say it louder." Jess knew she had touched Chandra's nerve and the only way of getting out of it now was to have a drink in The Two Wheeler. "Fine, but if it's weird, I'm leaving."

"It'll be fun." Chandra smiled, having won again. "Just get your biker mojo on."

"I don't have any biker mojo, Chandra. Not unless you mean bicycle mojo."

Chandra snickered as she linked her arm through Jess's and led her along the row of parked motorcycles to the bar's entrance.

They walked up the two steps to a wooden porch that ran across the front of the building. It slanted toward Beckett's property and newer boards had been inserted as time required, though plenty of the older boards showed signs of rot. Jess wondered if it took somebody's foot going through a board to move the owner to replace it. Patrons sat tightly packed around small plastic tables littered with beer bottles and ashtrays.

Hanging lights covered in red glass shades provided the only light indoors, but for one window that overlooked the front porch. Nearest the window were the pool tables, one then the other. A row of booths lined the long wall across from the door and a few open tables sat between the pool tables and bar. To the side of the window stood a dart machine, flashing its readiness. *Maybe the dim lighting enhances the effects of beer goggles,* Jess thought. Then, *Chandra's right. I am a snob.* She let Chandra lead her back to the bar, forcing herself not to notice the eyes tracking their movements—evidence that Jess wasn't the only person in Skoghall who thought of an "us and them." Chandra might fit in anywhere, but Jess was feeling more and more like one of *them.*

"What can I get you ladies?" the bartender asked as he dried a glass with a rather gray bar rag. Jess hoped it was just the lighting that made the rag look dirty. His shaved head lent his waxed handlebar mustache a special prominence. His biceps, thick as phone books, bulged from a souvenir t-shirt from the Sturgis Motorcycle Rally.

Jess ordered a vodka tonic. Chandra asked for a Summit. "I like your mustache," she said as she slid a ten across the bar.

"Who don't you flirt with?" Jess whispered as Chandra led them through the back of the bar toward a rear exit.

"I do like his mustache. They're making a come back, you know."

"I saw my share of hipsters with facial hair before I left Minneapolis," Jess reminded her.

The back door opened on a deck that overlooked the Mississippi River floodplain. Jess hadn't thought about it before, but the River Road rose as one headed south away from Main Street. That meant from the bar's deck, she could look across the creamery's short yard, over the treetops between the lots, and down on the gravelly yard behind Beckett's studio. Though trees offered some screening, she had a clear view of the outdoor brick kiln. A sudden surge of longing swept over Jess as she wished Beckett would emerge from his studio, hair in a ponytail, sweat-marked t-shirt, biceps flexing as he lifted pots from the cart and placed them in the kiln. Jess shook her head to clear the vision. They had just seen Beckett and he was wearing new cargo shorts and a decidedly fresh t-shirt so he could work with customers.

"Come on," Chandra said with a tilt of her head. She led the way through the plastic tables and down a long staircase to a strip of grass bordering the rocky bed of the train tracks. Tucked under the deck, a cinderblock wall that had once been painted orange faced the train tracks and wild land beyond. It had two small, curtained windows and a door that opened on a brick patio. Weeds pushed up between the bricks and a good number of them had been dislodged, sitting at odd angles to each other. Despite this, the patio appeared in use with another plastic table and chair. A towel had been draped over the back of the chair to dry. Tacked to the trunk of a nearby white oak, a squirrel feeder full of corn sat too low to be for the benefit of the bar's customers on the deck above. "Think this is where your mustachioed friend lives?" Jess said.

"Mustachioed. Nice word." Chandra stood on one of the train rails and gazed down the length of the tracks. "Who said he's my friend, just because I complimented him."

Beyond the tracks, a footpath led through an unkempt patch of vegetation that included milkweed, big bluestem, cord grass, and sedges. Red-wing blackbirds swooped in and out of the marsh, landing on grasses without bending the reedy stalks. The ground squelched and they carefully chose each place they set their feet. The appearance of a stand of cattails, their rich brown fur already molted, with creamy bald patches and tufts of feathery seeds ready to take flight at the next breeze, announced the wet meadow's transition to marsh. A few old willow trees draped their bows to the ground and a frog's long, low ratcheting call sounded from the water's edge. Across the pond, a white egret stood gracefully on one leg, its other bent at the knee at an impossible forward angle. It moved slowly, then in a smooth dart stretched its neck, plunged its head under water, and snatched a fish from within. Behind it, garlic mustard, reed canary grass, and buckthorn staked a claim on the land before a stand of silver maple rose some sixty to seventy feet tall. The trees stood close together, crowding out other species like elm and ash, creating a dense canopy and dark pockets within the woods.

"This isn't working for me," Chandra said.

Jess put her foot down with a loud squelch and mud filled her shoe, squishing between the sandal's webbing. "Yeah. Now we know why no one else leaves the deck." She looked around them. To the south, the marsh and forest became denser. To the north, they could skirt the floodplain and find their way to the grassy park behind Beckett's studio. She pointed in that direction and they changed course.

They picked their way along the marsh's edge until the ground dried and the trees turned to upland species that probably would not survive a flood, like oak and hickory. Jess and Chandra turned west into the grassy park and walked down to the river's edge. Seashells covered the pebbled shore several inches deep. Lake Pepin, a widening of the Mississippi behind the confluence with the Chippewa River, had been known for its freshwater mussels, which provided the nation with mother of pearl buttons in the nineteenth century. Jess walked far enough into the river to clean the mud out of her shoe, while Chandra picked through some seashells at her feet. They shared the quiet, thick atmosphere of an August afternoon and sipped their drinks.

"It's wild, isn't it?" Chandra asked. "We could get on this water and be carried all the way to the Gulf of Mexico."

"Yeah, I love the..." A wave of terror passed through Jess's body, a hot flash that gripped her stomach and twisted. The moon reflected on the rolling waters of the Mississippi. Jess stared at a spot some fifteen yards off the shore, her breath halted with anticipation. A dark shape bobbed to the surface. A log? It rolled onto its back before starting to drift along the current. Not a log. Jess was next to it now, over the water or in the water, she couldn't tell. A piece of milfoil curled over the man's forehead and traced a branching green line across one eye and down his cheek before trailing back into the water. Deep black cuts in his left side showed through the tears in his clothing, thoroughly bloated, the wounds had ragged edges, as though partially eaten. He opened his eyes as a hand shot up from his side to clench Jess's wrist.

Jess jumped back and spilled her drink. She looked out over the river, then left and right, her chest heaving as she took in the sunlight, and then Chandra who was holding her by the wrist. The drink had splashed down her clothes. An approaching freight train overpowered the sound of the waves lapping at her feet.

"What just happened?" Chandra asked.

"I. *Shit!*"

"Jess?"

The freight train blasted its warning horn as it approached the village. Jess stood there with Chandra's hand on her wrist and the river at her back, watching the train as it sped past, the ground shaking, the solid rumble-click of the wheels on the rails. She counted the cars, long open beds carrying pyramids of shorn trees and closed cars tagged with graffiti. She was on sixty-two when Chandra shook her by the wrist.

"What the hell happened? You went all white and I think you stopped breathing."

Jess finished her drink, what little hadn't spilled, then sighed. "I need to change. We can talk about it when I don't smell like a bottle of vodka."

They walked up the Main Street extension, a gravel road that led to the boat launch, to Beckett's apartment across from his studio. He lived in the tiny upper half-story of a house owned by an old resident of Skoghall, Mr. Tansley. A staircase of unstained, splintered cedar boards led to Beckett's front door, which was never locked.

Chandra waited while Jess splashed water on her face and neck, leaning over the old wall-mounted sink. Her vodka soaked shorts and top lay in the rust-stained tub. "Won't Beckett be surprised to find your clothes in his tub?"

Called out of her thoughts, Jess looked at Chandra, uncertain what her friend had just asked.

"Hello? Where are you?"

"Oh. We'll stop by the studio after I've changed." She wrung out a washcloth and wiped her abdomen and hip where the drink had soaked through her clothing. Jess squeezed by Chandra and went into the bedroom. The closet, like the bathroom, sat tucked under a gable, its ceiling slanting sharply toward the floor. Near its peak hung one of Jess's sundresses. Beckett didn't have much worth hanging—a single suit, a pair of khakis, a couple of button-down shirts, and two ties. The closet primarily served as laundry basket with a mound of dirty clothes on its floor.

Jess clipped her hair up off her neck and faced Chandra.

"So are you going to tell me what happened back there?"

"I could really use that drink now. I'll tell you in the bar, all right? Five minutes and we'll be settled in with drinks in our hands."

They swung through the pottery studio on their way to the bar. Beckett said he'd meet them for a drink when he closed up. If the bartender noticed that Jess had changed her clothes, it didn't show, probably because he fixed his attention on Chandra's big brown eyes. They slid into one of the high-backed booths lining the wall.

Jess covered her face with her hands and groaned. "I don't know how to explain this. I don't get it myself. It's weird. Really weird."

"Now that you've built it up, spit it out."

"I see dead people."

Chandra laughed like Jess had just delivered the world's best punchline ever. Her laughter seemed to fill the bar and a couple of guys at the pool table turned to look at them, pausing their game like they might be invited to join in the joke. "That's great, Jess. Really." Chandra leaned over the table. "What do you mean you see dead people?"

"I told you my house was haunted."

"Yeah. That woman, Bonnie, who was murdered there. But you fixed that and it's over."

"It's not over. I thought it was. I wanted it to be. But I think…" Jess glanced toward the pool tables, checking that Chandra's audience had returned to their game. "I think the haunting opened up a psychic ability or something."

"Or something? Is there another name for seeing dead people?"

"Curse. Burden. Weird. Freaky. Scary."

"Hey," Chandra soothed. She reached across the table to lay her hand on Jess's. "I got you."

Jess looked up from her drink and met Chandra's gaze. "I haven't told anyone. Not even Beckett."

"Why not?" Chandra shifted on the vinyl bench seat, unsticking her thighs.

"Because I didn't have to. As long as I wasn't seeing any…*thing,* there was nothing to tell. I kind of knew. I suspected it might not be over. I don't know why, but I figured no news is good news, right?" Jess looked at Chandra, her expression grim, "Besides, we got off to a pretty rocky start between the Tyler thing and the Bonnie thing. I was afraid to spoil our fun, like 'Oh, by the way honey, I'm still haunted.'"

"And now?"

"Now what?"

"Now you have to tell him. He'll either get it or he won't, and if he doesn't…"

Chandra was of the if-he-doesn't-get-me-fuck-him school of thought. It was easier to belong to that school in a metropolitan area than in a village. Jess was about to explain that fact, as well as the fact that she really liked Beckett and wanted it to work.

"Tequila. For courage." Chandra slid out of the booth and left Jess to visit the bar. Jess watched the pool players, young men in tight jeans and tight black t-shirts—the crotch rockets out front must belong to them—watch her friend. Chandra's ass was perfect. Firm, round, significant, but not "big." And Chandra knew it, accentuating her asset with figure hugging short skirts. The pool players knew it, too. No wonder she didn't worry about losing a man, there were always three more in the wings. Jess, however, hoped to build something with one man in particular.

Chandra slid into the booth and set down two shot glasses. The bartender arrived behind her and set a plate of lime wedges and a salt shaker on the table. He nodded to Jess, but he lingered over Chandra. She graced him with her smile, and he left a satisfied man.

They rubbed the lime wedges over the fleshy pads at the base of their thumbs, then liberally poured on the salt. "Courage." Chandra raised her shot glass. Jess raised hers. Their eyes met before they tossed back the tequila. Jess shook her head as the vapors rose from the back of her throat into her sinuses. She sucked the lime and salt off her hand. "Damn! I can't remember the last time I did shots."

"I can," Chandra said. "When you told me you were filing for divorce, I got us shots."

Jess cocked her head. "Do I sense a pattern here?" Chandra shrugged. "By the way, you have some admirers." Jess gestured toward the men at the pool tables.

"Don't change the subject. Besides, I knew that already."

"Of course you did." Jess admired Chandra's social radar. Her own was certainly not so finely tuned. "Courage, huh?"

"Need another?" Chandra looked ready to make another bar run.

"Better not." Jess sighed and got down to the business of telling Chandra about her troubles. Besides the body in the river that had so recently startled her—scared the crap out of her was more like it—there was Isabella, the antique store ghost. She considered Isabella more of a little friend than a haunting, and suddenly felt guilty for not visiting the house-bound specter.

"Hey, if the whole writing thing doesn't work out, you can become a medium," Chandra offered cheerfully.

"Chandra, this is serious."

"I am serious. That shit's big again. Everyone wants to get in touch with the mystical."

"Not me."

"Not me what?" Beckett stood beside their table.

Jess had been sunk back into the dark corner of the booth, hardly aware of her surroundings since she began talking about the floater. "Hey," she said. "I didn't see you come in." She moved her feet off the bench and made room for him to scoot in. They kissed hello.

"I just saw a psychic," Chandra said.

Beckett raised an eyebrow quizzically. "Any good?"

"It was…interesting."

Jess wanted to kick Chandra under the table, but figured Beckett would notice the scuffle and then she'd have more explaining to do. Chandra sat there grinning, proud keeper of a secret.

"Tequila?" Chandra said as she slid out of the booth. She didn't wait for a response.

"Is she trying to get us drunk?"

"Probably, but someone has to drive us home."

"Is she always like this?" Beckett's hand found Jess's between them and they linked comfortably together.

"I think her motto is 'work hard, play hard.' How were sales today?"

Beckett told her about his day. Chandra seemed a long time returning. When she did, she carried three shot glasses before her and bent to lower them to the table without spilling. "I think I just got propositioned."

"You aren't sure?" Beckett asked.

"I definitely got propositioned. But the details aren't real clear. I don't think he wants me to come back to his place and I don't have a place to take him—"

"No you do not," Jess confirmed.

"I think he was suggesting we do it here in the bar."

"Oh, that's gross," Jess said.

"Or hot," Chandra corrected.

"Will you?" Beckett asked.

Chandra looked outside the booth to survey the bar, her gaze roaming over the furnishings and patrons alike. "No. I'm not opposed to slumming it once in a while, but I'm here to see Jess."

"Here, here." Jess raised her glass and Chandra and Beckett joined her.

They downed their shots then cut the taste of the liquor with lime and salt.

They decided to play darts. Jess won the first game and Chandra the second. Jess stood at the throwing line, dart in hand, midway through the third game. Somewhat tipsy, she figured they'd be walking to Beckett's place to sober up. Beckett and Chandra chatted behind her, getting along well. And she was winning. Jess raised her dart, felt the weight and balance of it, took aim, and threw.

It joined her first two darts in the small round of the bullseye. "Hat trick!" she yelled. Jess spun around to proclaim her superiority to their faces. Her glee disappeared as she watched Beckett stride out of the bar. Jess looked at Chandra, who held a beer bottle in front of her, rubbing the glass with her thumb. "What did you say?"

Chandra looked at Jess through mascara'd lashes without raising her chin. "I *just* asked him if he knows he's dating a bona fide psychic."

Jess cursed under her breath and left the bar at a run. She caught up to Beckett on the River Road and grabbed his arm to stop him walking away. "Beckett. What the hell?"

He shook free as he spun to face her. His face had flushed with anger or tequila or both. "Jess." He said her name in an exasperated snarl. He looked her over before throwing his hands up and turning to walk away again.

Jess glanced over her shoulder to see if Chandra was coming out to help or keeping her distance. As much as Jess wanted some kind of reinforcement, Chandra might not be the best ally right now. She was nowhere to be seen, but the people on the front porch of The Two Wheeler and those standing amongst the hogs, talking wheels and chrome over their beer bottles, watched Jess without a single polite pretense among them. She hurried down the hill after Beckett.

"Aren't we going to talk about this?"

"No."

"No?"

Beckett stood in front of his studio door and dug in his pocket for his keys. "Not tonight, Jess." He faced her and his expression softened when he took in the panic in her eyes. "Look, I'm angry and I had a few shots of tequila, which is fine if everything is fun and games. But right now I might say something mean. So if we're going to talk this through, it had better not be tonight."

"Why are you so upset? I thought you could handle my…ability."

"It's not that. You *lied* to me, Jess."

"What? I—"

"Not tonight," he cut her off and turned to go into the studio.

Jess turned to head back up the street. Lied? The accusation perplexed her, but Beckett made it clear she wouldn't get anywhere with him tonight. Some of the bar's patrons muttered as she passed. One woman with shorn hair, a tank top and a full-sleeve tattoo of koi and lily pads reached for Jess's hands. "Men are jerks, honey," she said. Jess responded with a small nod and went inside. The men drinking with the koi lady laughed and cajoled her, claiming she was on Jess's side only because of some *us and them* logic. *Sisterhood*, Jess thought, *is what got me in this trouble.*

Chandra stood at the bar with her purse, talking to the bartender. He seemed to be listening to her while smoothing and curling the tip of his waxed mustache between finger and thumb. "Let's go," Jess said and turned to leave without a word.

"You okay to drive?" the bartender asked.

"I am now."

Chapter Three

DAN THREW HIS garment bag and dock kit into his trunk and slammed it closed. Another week. Another road trip. Another dollar. Samantha came out in her robe and slippers to see him off. Their Boston Terrier, Minnie, ran out with her and circled their feet before dropping in between them. Samantha handed Dan his travel mug and gave him a kiss while he hugged her close. "God, I wish I could work from home like you do," Dan said.

"No, you don't. You need people."

"You're right. I just don't feel like hitting the road today."

"It's a perfect day for driving." Samantha moved her arm, showroom model style, in a sweeping gesture that took in the quiet of their street. A nice mid-century subdivision near an elementary school and—admittedly less desirable—the Iowa City municipal airport. Ramblers with pink-tiled bathrooms and single-stall attached garages packed their neighborhood. Some still had the bar and smoker's fan in the semi-finished basements. Their house did—a noisy little exhaust fan in the ceiling with a beige and gold control knob in the wall below it. They used it once when Dan lit a fire with the flue closed and smoke filled their rec room. He liked the bar for all its kitsch. Though not quite the same era, it set off his Wurlitzer jukebox, which was the centerpiece of the house as far as he was concerned.

"That's the problem," Dan said. "It is a perfect day. Perfect for taking my wife and daughter to the zoo or on a picnic. Perfect for swinging in a hammock or going down to Sand Lake." He clutched Samantha around the waist and drew her in. "You know how I feel about the Terry Trueblood Recreation Center."

"Oh, Dan," Samantha panted, "say it again." They had been joking about the unusual name since they bought their house three years ago.

"Terry Trueblood," he mouthed next to her ear. He adored his wife's green eyes and freckled nose.

"What must the neighbor's think?" Samantha put a hand to his chest and pushed him away, though not enough to escape his grasp. "If it makes you feel any better, I'll be inside most of the day, sitting at my computer while the babysitter plays with Annie."

"Yep. I feel a little better."

Samantha socked him playfully in the arm. "Now off with you. Go sell some drinks machines and deep fryers and catsup bottles."

"Yes, ma'am." He kissed her again without the mock passion, a warm, familiar kiss, a kiss of sincere devotion. "And you'd better get inside before Annie wakes up."

Samantha put her hand in the pocket of her robe and withdrew a baby monitor.

"Aren't you the clever one."

"Yes, I am. Now go collect some new stories for me."

Dan backed out of the driveway and stopped to wave to his wife. She stood before their home, wearing a bathrobe, Minnie tucked under her arm, and waved back. It was like looking at an ad for the American Dream. Dan reluctantly drove away.

While sitting at a stoplight, he pulled up an audiobook, his companion for the drive up into his Wisconsin territory. When he first got the job with Food Service Suppliers Plus, Samantha liked to come with him. They'd talk while on the road, sometimes discussing things in the news, sometimes planning their future, whether a concert next weekend or a trip abroad someday. She'd work when he worked, using any wifi hotspot she could find to log in with her company, and they'd spend the evenings together, always ending the day somewhere Dan did not have business. He was forbidden shop talk and schmoozing when they were out for dinner. Sometimes they'd find a movie theater or bar to round out the evening, then back to the motel. Samantha always said they should have a trophy for the most sex in motels, or sex in the most motels—one of the two.

Annie changed all of that.

Maybe he didn't want to work from home, but he was going to look for a new job as soon he got back from this trip.

Chapter Four

SHAKTI AND BRUNO tore around the yard like four-legged maniacs, kicking up dust and clots of dead grass. Jess and Tyler sat on the porch steps with their morning coffee, ignoring the sticky heat, tolerable in the eighties but heading for the mid-nineties this afternoon.

"Is your friend still sleeping?" Tyler had Bruno's Helping Paws pack and leash across his knee. Jess wondered if just having the pack where he could touch it gave him comfort.

"No. She's out there somewhere…" Jess motioned toward the road, "training for a half-marathon."

"You don't run?"

Jess snorted. "No. I jog. I'm good for a 5k and that's about it. Chandra went all hardcore on me."

Tyler sipped his coffee, his eyes on the dogs. "You seem…I don't know, like you're mad at Chandra or something."

"Is it that obvious?"

He nodded.

"She said something stupid to Beckett last night after too much tequila and now I'm in trouble with him, so that makes her in trouble with me." She smiled, trying to pass it all off as no big deal, but Jess didn't know if it was a big deal or not.

"What's he steamed about?"

Jess sighed and watched the dogs loop around the sugar maple. It was due for a good watering. She let the grass dry up, not particularly caring what happened to it, but the sugar maple and the stand of birches near the garage were special to her. To let them suffer a dry spell when she had a hose available would have been to dishonor the people who lived here before. *Bonnie and John Sykes,* she told herself. She wanted to be able to think of them without being scared or sad.

"Jess?"

"You're sworn to secrecy," she said. "After Bonnie left, or was put to rest, or whatever, I thought that would be that."

Tyler raised an eyebrow, questioning.

"That I'd be done with ghosts. No more Bonnie, no more ghosts for Jess."

"And you aren't?"

"I saw a body in the river yesterday. I don't know who or when it happened, but I saw it…him." Jess had placed her hand on the porch boards beside her and Tyler laid his hand on top of hers. She studied it, the clean nails, chapped knuckles, raised veins under the skin. She considered removing her hand, but didn't.

"Why does that upset Beckett?"

"I don't know. He said I lied to him, but I haven't. Not that I'm aware of, anyway." She chuckled dryly. "It's all weird and overwhelming again. Would you want to date someone who has ghosts demanding her time?" Jess looked at Tyler, her eyes asking for reassurance that she wasn't a freak, that her newly acquired set of baggage wasn't more than any sane person would endure.

"Yes." Tyler leaned toward her and his lips found hers.

It was only a second or two, but it seemed longer, long enough to jeopardize everything. Jess pulled back.

Tyler raised his hand to her temple and brushed some hair back from her face, gently tucking it behind her ear.

"You should go."

"I should go," he repeated, "but I mean it. If Beckett's willing to let you go, he's a fool." Tyler stood and called Bruno as he strode across the yard to his truck. He looked back at Jess before getting in the cab.

Jess wanted to find Tyler and talk about what had happened the previous morning, just in case he was going to let his imagination invent possibilities that didn't exist. The café wasn't open yet, so she went around the back, climbed the steps to the stoop, and pulled the screen door open. "Hello," she called into the kitchen.

Robin wore a fine dusting of pastry flour on his hands; the white powder contrasted nicely against his brown skin. The dough on the counter before him had been rolled flat. He set his pin aside and took up a stainless steel mixing bowl.

"Am I allowed to come in when you've got food out?"

"Sure, Jess. Just don't bring those long dark hairs of yours near my work surface."

"Deal." She entered the kitchen and put her hands in her pockets like a kid in a museum, making it easier to resist the urge to touch things. She had been the first person Robin met in Skoghall, and not under the best circumstances. Tyler disappeared, leaving the café in the lurch at the beginning of the tourist season. Then Robin turned up, and Jess practically accosted him trying to find out what happened to Tyler and why he had keys to the café. Robin used the back of a wooden spoon to spread a layer of creamy custard over the dough. "That looks good. What is it?"

"Pain aux raisins." He smiled at Jess over his creation, a man in his element.

"How was your trip?"

"Good. I'm trying to convince Clarissa to move here."

"Your fiancée? Would she do that?"

Robin switched bowls and sprinkled raisins over the surface of the custard. "We have to live somewhere, might as well be here." Robin had an easy smile, quick to light up his face and spread warmth. Jess wondered how much of that had to do with loving his work. Her gaze fell on his hands, the long, slender fingers dancing above the surface of the dough, sprinkling raisins like mana. "Tyler lets me do what I want—for the most part, and I like Skoghall. It's quiet and pretty out here."

"It is that." *For some of us more than others,* Jess added to herself.

"Tyler's in the dining room." Jess headed for the swinging door between the kitchen and dining area. "But he's meeting with our rep now."

Jess peered through the round window in the swinging door. Tyler sat at the farthest table, studying a glossy brochure. A man in a white dress shirt sat with him, his back to Jess. He filled out paperwork while Tyler browsed.

"Anything seem off with him lately?" Robin asked.

"No. Why?" Jess turned away from the window and pulled her hands out of her pockets. They had begun to feel moist trapped against her thighs like that. She made her way to the back door.

Robin wiped his hands on a linen towel. "I just thought, since you know Tyler as well as anyone around here, maybe you'd noticed something."

"What's going on, Robin?"

Robin glanced past Jess toward the dining room before meeting her gaze. "I know he's back and he's got Bruno and everything's better..." he trailed off, "but I got the sense something is going on. Maybe something new. Should I be worried about him? About the café?"

"As far as I know, he's fine."

"Really?" Robin looked Jess in the eyes. "If he's under some kind of duress, I'd sure like to know about it. I am his business partner."

"Have you asked him about this?"

"I always try the direct approach first." He lifted the edge of the dough and began rolling it. "He says he's fine, fine, fine."

"Maybe he is fine."

"Nobody's that fine."

Chandra wanted to revisit The Two Wheeler, though Jess wasn't sure she should ever go back there again. "Come on," Chandra urged. "Get your darts and let's go." Jess's dart set hadn't been unpacked yet, so getting it took more effort than Chandra had patience for, but Jess liked the idea of their weight in her hands and the crisp, new flights flashing toward the dart board. Bar darts were always crap, bent and abused. "Go play with Shakti," Jess instructed and dragged a box out of the back of the closet.

It was worth it. Her dart felt so much better in her hand than the cheap plastic ones she'd played with the night before. Jess took some practice throws while Chandra bought their drinks. She had texted Beckett to let him know where they were. The question of whether he'd show up or not hung in the back of her mind. If he didn't come, would that be the end of them?

"I don't think this guy is known for his wine selection," Chandra said as she handed Jess a glass of Chardonnay.

"That's all right. I'm going slow tonight. No tequila?"

Chandra raised her beer bottle. "Nope. I'm going slow, too."

"Good." Jess turned back to the dart board and threw. Her dart hit the inner band in the 20 wedge of the board and the machine flashed its lights.

"Damn, girl. Triple score. Have you ever thought about competing?"

Jess grinned at Chandra over her shoulder.

"Jess," Chandra's tone went serious. "I'm sorry I opened my big mouth. I had no business…"

Jess let another dart fly. "No, you didn't. You broke the code."

"I know."

"I'm over it." She waved her hand, brushing the subject aside. "It had to come out some time, right?" Jess retrieved her darts and handed them off to Chandra. She didn't know what she was going to do about Tyler, but if she shared the incident with Chandra, it would be after she was safely back in Minneapolis.

Chandra pushed her long curls over her shoulder and squinted one eye while taking aim. Jess grimaced as Chandra moved her hand forward and back in front of her shoulder in an exaggerated motion. The dart hit hard outside of the board, bounced off the machine, and landed under a table.

Jess went to retrieve it. "Oh, sorry," she said to the people sitting in the booth. She hadn't seen them before, cozily tucked back against the wall. A man with dark brown hair, black-framed glasses, and a tie that had been loosened enough to open the top two buttons of his shirt leaned into the red vinyl bench like he was at the end of a very long day. He glanced at Jess, a look of boredom evident behind the lenses of his glasses. His companion sat up against the table, her elbows on its top and her chin in her hands. The effect being that her breasts were squeezed between her forearms and her cleavage amplified. The drink before her looked untouched. Next to it lay a shiny lipstick tube. When Jess glanced at her, she slid her hand over the tabletop and placed it over the lipstick. The young woman then turned her head toward the back of the booth, avoiding Jess's gaze. Jess bent down to grab her dart. The young woman's red glittered platform pumps caught Jess's eye, and so did the pink edge of a cut above her ankle.

"Got it." Jess held up her dart for the couple to see. The man turned up the corners of his mouth in a polite smile.

Jess turned back to Chandra, stifling a laugh. She grabbed Chandra's wrist and pulled her away from the booth. "I think the girl in there is a prostitute," she whispered.

"Skoghall has a hooker? I didn't think you had the population to support that kind of trade."

"Neither did I." Jess straightened the tip of her dart and handed it back to Chandra. She decided to hold off on giving friendly advice since she had a pack of new tips in her purse.

Chandra went back to the throwing line and peeked around the side of the booth in question. They must have looked at her, because she smiled and waved. The art of subtlety had been lost on Chandra, though if she even knew the meaning of the word, Jess couldn't be sure.

The place felt empty compared to the night before. Whenever the door opened, Jess couldn't help looking to see if it was Beckett coming in, but it only brought people from outside, coming through to use the bathroom or buy fresh drinks. The bartender, who'd decided to introduce himself as Jake tonight, put on a Rolling Stones album. After Jess beat Chandra at their third game of Cricket, she was ready to go home, sit on her porch, and watch Shakti run around the yard. Then Beckett came through the door.

"Oh," Chandra said. "I think I'll sit at the bar a while."

Jess and Beckett slid into one of the booths across from each other. Jess laid her darts before her and lined up the tips. She wanted Beckett to go first.

"What's going on?" he asked. Not exactly what Jess had in mind as a conversation starter, but she decided to play along. Jess told him about the body in the river. She kept her eyes on her darts while she talked, her fingers lining them up, turning them around, standing them on end, until Beckett put his hands on hers to still their motion. When she finished, he asked why she hadn't told him before now.

"Before now? I just saw the body yesterday."

"What about the girl?"

"The girl? Isabella?" Jess shrugged. "I haven't been inside the antique store in over a month. I guess she was out of sight and out of mind."

Beckett rubbed his goatee, looking thoughtfully across the table at Jess.

"I didn't want to think about her, never mind see her, Beckett. I wanted to be done with ghosts after Bonnie, you know?"

"I know." He nodded. "I thought... When Chandra told me you had this

35

little friend in the antique store, I thought you'd been keeping her a secret from me."

"More like I was keeping her a secret from myself. I mentioned her to Chandra after I saw the river body, because she seemed, well, *undeniable* after that."

With dusk's arrival and the bar's only window facing east, it had grown dark in their booth. An old candle in a blue glass sat between them unlit. Jess looked out of the booth, wondering if a book of matches or lighter sat nearby, maybe abandoned by one of the smokers outside. Anything to make it easier to see Beckett's eyes.

He reached across the table and put a hand on Jess's. "I'm sorry."

"You are?" Jess didn't think Mitch had ever apologized to her during their marriage. The fact that Beckett was able to speak those two little words sent a surge of appreciation through her body.

Beckett nodded his head. "I was mad at you for not telling me. I thought after everything I did to help you with Bonnie, you'd trust me. And I thought you'd lied or lied by omission. I see now that you didn't really lie." Despite the dark, Jess could see his lips curl into a gentle smile and the corners of his eyes crinkle. "You were just scared."

Jess reached for her darts and slid them closer. As she began to fiddle again, Beckett put his hand over hers, then slid the darts out of her reach. "If I'd told you about Isabella right after John's funeral, would you have stuck around?"

Beckett paused to consider. "Maybe not, but I would have missed you and come back." He looked her in the eyes. "There is something I need if we're going to work."

"What?"

"Total honesty. I can't stand being lied to, Jess. Not after what my parents did."

Jess nodded. Beckett's parents had lied to him most of his life about his being adopted and the wound had barely healed after more than a decade of knowing the truth about himself. Jess drew in a breath and straightened up. Her lower lip found its way between her teeth.

"What is it?"

"Promise you won't freak out."

"What? Do you have another ghost?" His smile faded even before Jess answered.

"Tyler and Bruno came over yesterday." Jess felt Beckett tense up. "It was no big deal. He just…" Even without the candle lit, she could see the scowl deepening on his face. "Okay, you have to relax. I won't tell you anything if you go all caveman on me."

"If I go *caveman* on you?"

"Beckett."

He sighed deeply. "There. I'm relaxed."

"He kissed me."

Beckett clenched his hand into a fist before sliding it into his lap.

"It was nothing. I didn't invite it and I didn't reciprocate."

"Okay."

"Okay?"

"No, it's not okay. It pisses me off, in fact. But I believe you and I trust you and I'm glad you're telling me this."

"Good. Because it was nothing."

Beckett spoke in a measured tone. "I'd rather you not see him again, of course."

"Beckett, I don't know if I can agree to that. Shakti and Bruno…"

"And Tyler. You have some kind of weird soft spot for that guy, Jess."

"Maybe I do, but I think he's a decent person and I trust him. He tested the waters and I asked him to leave. I don't think he'll try anything like that again." Jess put a hand on Beckett's arm and looked across the table into his eyes. "I think he's lonely. I think he's got Bruno, Robin, and us, and that's it. He needs support."

Beckett brought his hands above the table and laced his fingers through Jess's. "You're a good person, Jess. I hope you don't bring home *too* many strays, but I like how much you care."

Even in the dim light of the booth, Jess could see the sparkle had returned to Beckett's eyes. She began to rise, to meet him over the table in a kiss, when Chandra appeared beside their booth, pulling Tyler into view with her.

"Hey, look who's here," Chandra said.

Beckett propelled himself across the length of the vinyl bench seat and lunged into Tyler, knocking him back onto a nearby table. With one hand at Tyler's throat, he drew the other back in a fist. Jess yelled at him to stop, but not before he struck Tyler a blow to the jaw.

Chapter Five

DAN'S HEAD DIDN'T feel right, like a balloon was inflating where his brain should be, creating pressure and a sense of not belonging. He didn't belong. His hands didn't belong. His gut didn't belong. Nothing fit together anymore.

Who was this? April? May? August? This girl named for a month. Damn if he could remember anything with that balloon in his head. She had him by the hand, the not-belonging hand, and led him, giggling, down the stairs from the deck. The long staircase had been bleached gray by years of afternoon sun, the boards bowed by the weight of so many travelers, each footfall a burden. A flood light on the corner of the building illuminated the tall grasses behind the bar and steel glinted where the train tracks crossed the circle of light. Beyond the tracks, marsh and forest and the dark waters of the Mississippi and settling night. Dan headed toward the water, but a tug on his hand redirected him.

April pulled him under the deck into its shadow and pressed a finger to her smiling lips. Such pretty lips. Mischievous lips. Another pair of pretty lips came to mind. They seemed so important to him, those lips, but he couldn't be certain of anything that wasn't in front of him. April and her lips. And her tits showing through that flimsy top. Dan grabbed her, his hand pressed to the small of her back, and drew her into him. He put his lips to hers and kissed her forcefully. She gasped, resisted. He kissed harder.

Gripped her tighter. He knew she wanted him. *She* had approached him in the bar, looking for a drinking companion. And why not? He was bored. It would make a good story to tell Samantha when he got home—some poor hick kid looking for... *Samantha?* April pulled back, their lips separating with a wet noise.

"What do you want?" he insisted.

"I..." She looked over both of her shoulders, a nervous little rabbit. "I know a place we can go."

Dan loosened his grip on her and she led him along the back of the building, up a rise covered by dark, untended flora to the neighboring property, a double barrel shotgun house. The curve of the land rose to meet it. Lattice work had once been fixed around a crawlspace, but unrepaired breaks and tracks in the dirt showed evidence of squatters. April pulled Dan up a single set of wooden stairs to a back porch. Dan sat on the steps to catch his breath. His heart thrummed in his chest, another balloon, this one fixing to bust. He pulled his glasses off his face and rubbed his eyes with his fist. "What are you doing to me?" Two doors with peeling paint opened onto the deck. The girl put her hand on the one with a strip of duct tape holding its cracked pane of glass together.

"Almost there," she chirped. She turned back to Dan and wrapped her small hands around his arm and pulled at him.

As Dan got to his feet, his glasses slipped from his fingers. He tripped over the top step. "Wait."

April opened the door and pulled him inside. She shut the door behind them and announced, "Okay, we're here."

She was too loud. Too loud. It hurt his head. For a moment, Dan couldn't remember why he had come here. May spun to face him, a nervous smile playing on her pretty lips.

And then he remembered.

Chapter Six

JESS GRABBED BECKETT'S arm as he readied to swing again. She'd never felt a muscle so taut, so dangerous. He stepped away, first shaking loose of Jess and then shaking out his hand and examining his knuckles. She looked at Tyler, bent backwards over the table, his hand on his jaw, worrying the area where Beckett had made contact. Chandra stood back from them holding her beer bottle up and out of the fray, eyes wide, mouth open.

Jake arrived with a baseball bat in hand, a staple of his trade. He reached for Tyler and pulled him to standing by the shirt collar. "What the hell is going on here?" He looked Tyler up and down before letting go of him. "Beckett?"

"Nothing," they replied at the same time. Neither man seemed interested in looking anybody in the face, let alone the eyes.

"Yeah?" Jake lowered the wooden bat to his side. "One or both of you has to go."

"No problem." Beckett squeezed past Jess and walked out of the bar without so much as a glance over his shoulder.

Jess looked at Chandra, speechless and desperate for help.

"You go take care of Beckett," Chandra said. "I'll stay here with Tyler."

Jess grabbed her darts and purse out of the booth and ran after Beckett. She was aware as she made her escape that some of the customers on the front porch seemed familiar, that she was chasing after Beckett for the second night in a row. And the whole thing seemed so ridiculous and cliché that she almost turned around. And then she realized something. She wasn't chasing after Beckett to take care of him. She was going to chew him out.

Jess followed him into the studio and traced his path past the work tables and potters' wheels, past the booths and into the kitchen from the old livery's days as a Western-themed diner. Beckett stood at the counter, scooping ice from a bucket into a towel.

Jess stopped several feet away and put her hands on her hips. "What the hell was that?"

He wrapped the ends of the towel together and held it on his punching hand. "I'm sorry, Jess." He turned to face her and leaned against the counter. "I saw him and I just lost it."

"I'll say. Where do you get off punching him out?"

"Okay. First, I didn't punch him out. He remained fully conscious. Second—"

"How could you?"

"Don't defend him," Beckett yelled. "Tyler is not defendable. Not after he…"

"Kissed me? Beckett, it was nothing. It was…"

"No. Not after he hurt you." Beckett dropped the ice in the sink and crossed the space between them. "Jess, I've wanted to do that since the party." He put his hands on Jess's head, one on each side, holding her gently, and brought his lips to kiss the scar under her eye, the one made by Tyler's ring.

Tears welled in Jess's eyes. She had no idea it would feel so good to be defended.

Jess walked back into The Two Wheeler and slid onto a barstool beside Chandra.

"Want anything?" Jake asked. He had a bar towel over one shoulder that he could have used to wipe the sheen of sweat off his bald head. His mustache fared better in the humidity, its ends curled to fine points. He popped the top off a bottle of Leinenkugel and set it at the empty space beside Chandra.

"No thanks." Jess plunked her keys onto the bar in front of Chandra. "I'm going to stay at Beckett's tonight. Can you go home soon and feed Shakti?"

"Why?" Chandra tilted her head. The bar area was better lit than the booths and Jess saw that Chandra had applied a fresh coat of pink paint to her full lips.

"Because she'll be hungry."

"Smart ass." Chandra lifted a paper coaster from the bar and scraped at its edge with her nail.

"Because Beckett wants me to." Jess sighed, tired of explaining herself to people. "He comes to my place all the time, because it's...let's be honest, it's a lot nicer. And I have the dog. I think he wants me to come to him for a change."

"I get it. He wants to make wild monkey jungle love with you, but he's shy." Chandra's lips spread into a mischievous grin, and Jess caught a smirk cross Jake's face.

"Just feed the dog." Jess picked up her keys and dangled them in front of Chandra, who swiped them out of her hand.

Tyler rounded the corner, coming from the hallway to the bathrooms. He took the seat next to Chandra. "Jess." He raised the bottle of beer to take a swig and winced as the glass met his cut and swollen lip.

Jess stepped around Chandra to face Tyler. "I'm sorry about that."

"Yeah, well, I probably had it coming."

"Are you all right?"

"Fine." His face said otherwise. There was a sort of hollow desperation to his eyes that bothered Jess, but she wasn't in a position to help him, not with Beckett waiting for her at the studio. At least she knew he was going home to Bruno.

Chapter Seven

WEDNESDAYS WERE THE week's end in a summer tourist town, and local businesses closed for the day. Jess had gotten used to it and expected Wednesdays to be quiet, lazy even, while Sundays felt more like midweek. This reinforced a sensation of being outside the flow of normal life in American society, a life ruled by office hours and the global clock. Some days Jess felt like she was in one of those commercials for Country Time Lemonade that she had grown up with. She would look out her office window at the sugar maple, sunlight filtering through its leaves, and half expect to see a picnic table spread with a red checked cloth under its branches, children swinging on a rope from the old barn's loft.

She woke before Beckett, momentarily disoriented by the unfamiliar bed, the sloped ceiling that cut the room into halves—one in which she could stand fully and one in which she couldn't. Beckett turned over and kicked at the sheet. His blond hair swept forward over his eye and brow. Jess got up to dress. She missed Shakti.

The bed sat pushed into the corner, so there was only one way to reasonably get on or off of it, and Beckett chivalrously took the inside against the slope of the wall so that Jess wouldn't have to feel trapped. She crawled across the mattress and brushed the hair back from Beckett's face. "Beckett," she whispered, then kissed his shoulder. "Wake up, Beckett."

"It's my weekend," he grumbled.

"I know, but I want to go home." Jess kissed his brow.

Beckett grabbed the sheet and jerked it up over his head. "Is there coffee?"

"Yes. At my house."

Once on his feet, Beckett was ready to leave in about two minutes. "Why can't I sleep in?" he asked as they turned off of Main Street at the end of the village.

"Because I miss Shakti."

Beckett shook his head. "I want more than coffee for this."

Jess opened the front door and stepped into the vestibule, blocking Beckett's entrance. Shakti rushed her like a furred torpedo. Jess laughed and threw her arms around Shakti's neck while the puppy licked her face. Beckett shook his head again and picked his way around them to head for the kitchen.

Shakti wouldn't let him escape her verve. She dashed down the hallway and leapt against his legs, slamming him into the kitchen counter. Beckett turned, but Shakti was already off, racing laps around the main floor of the house, circling through the rooms, paws scrambling on the wood floor as she cornered at a full run. Jess joined Beckett in the kitchen and, a moment later, they heard Chandra yelp as Shakti tore past her at the base of the stairs.

"Morning," Chandra said through a yawn. She wore a skimpy t-shirt and underwear, her blonde spirals a wild mass of hair bobbing around her head as she walked into the kitchen. "I didn't expect you so early." She nudged Beckett away from the sink to fill a glass with water.

Beckett scowled, the coffee carafe in his hand.

"Careful, Chandra," Jess said. "Beckett's a little grumpy today. I wouldn't get between him and his French press."

Shakti skidded to a stop in front of Jess, bowed her forelegs to the floor, butt in the air, tail wagging, and barked a single sharp *woof*. Beckett's scowl deepened at the sound, but he ignored it and focused on getting the water on the stove.

"Drop," Jess said. Shakti lowered her rump to the floor and panted happily while Jess got her food. The dog's muscles rippled under her thick coat as she fought the temptation to spring for her bowl. When Jess said, "Release," Shakti uncoiled, launching for her kibble in a single, smooth movement.

Beckett had been watching from his spot by the stove. He raised an eyebrow and nodded. "Impressive."

"Yeah, Ty… Bruno taught us that. Watch this." Jess knelt next to Shakti's bowl, put a hand on her shoulders, and with her other hand moved her food around under her snout while she ate. "See?" She beamed up at Beckett. "No resource guarding."

"When did *Bruno* become a dog trainer?"

"Tyler has taught me some of Bruno's commands—"

"It looks like I'm making you coffee," Beckett cut her off, apparently done talking about anything to do with Tyler. "What're you making me for breakfast?"

Chandra fried some diced potatoes and scrambled eggs, while Jess threw together scones, this time adding cinnamon and chopped chocolate. Once brushed with milk, the large round went into the oven and they sat down to their eggs and hash in the dining room.

The dark wainscoting below the chair rail and poppy-covered vintage wallpaper above it gave the room a luxurious feel, while the windows on both exterior walls ensured plenty of light. Jess had taken to sitting with her back to the built-in buffet where her antique glass dishes sparkled in the morning light so she could see out the windows. Chandra sat across from her, the window light creating a halo of her curls. Beckett sat at the head of a contemporary table her ex-husband had chosen, then given up in the divorce. One day she'd find the right dining set for her 1921 farmhouse. With each bite of breakfast, Beckett's mood improved. He and Chandra were discussing visual aesthetics when Jess's phone signaled a new text message. She excused herself to check it.

"Tyler's coming over so the dogs can have their playtime," she said, standing in the doorway between the kitchen and dining room.

"And…" Beckett said.

"And…" she mimicked his tone, "nothing. I'm just letting everyone know."

"Jesus, Jess. I wish he'd just get out of our lives."

"You mean out of mine, don't you?"

"Fine. Out of yours. How many times are you going to forgive him for what he did?"

"Let's see…" She feigned deep calculations. "Seven times seventy."

Chandra rose from the table and swooped over to Jess, throwing an arm around her shoulder and planting a kiss on her cheek. She pointed to Jess's chest while looking at Beckett. "She's got a big heart, this girl." She looked at Jess. "What are *we* up to?"

Jess smiled. "I'll have to check the log, but I think it's around seven times forty."

"See?" Chandra grabbed her plate and pranced into the kitchen.

"I'm not the one who has to forgive him," she said in a lowered voice. "Besides, Bruno is Shakti's only playmate. She needs this."

Beckett rose and cleared his dishes. "Fine. I'm not happy about it, but obviously it's out of my hands."

"Just be nice."

"I'm always nice."

Chandra guffawed. "That's not what I saw last night. You're lucky Jake didn't use that bat on you." Jess shot Chandra a look. "All right," she held her hands up in surrender. "I'm going upstairs to get dressed." She pointed a finger in their direction, wagging it between Jess and Beckett. "You two kiss and make up now." She bounded out of the kitchen and they heard her springing up the old stairs, probably taking them two at a time.

"What was in *her* eggs?" Beckett said.

The oven timer went off and there was a knock at the front door. "Scones or Tyler?" Jess asked.

Beckett made some sort of grunt, indecipherable on its own, but he started for the front door.

Jess grabbed her oven mitts and slid the scones out of the oven. She listened, but if the men exchanged a single word, she couldn't hear it. Beckett led Tyler and Bruno into the kitchen. Shakti danced around Bruno, making play bows, then yipping when he ignored her invitations. Jess greeted Tyler cheerfully in an obvious effort to cover Beckett's irritation. He sported a purple bruise along his jaw to complement the fat lip Beckett had given him. Jess had the urge to apologize again, but stopped herself. If the men were going to pretend it had never happened, so was she.

"Want some coffee?" Beckett said, his tone devoid of warmth or welcome.

Tyler accepted and knelt to rub Bruno's chest before removing his service dog pack and releasing him to play.

Chandra bounced into the kitchen wearing a yellow sundress and flip flops. She and Tyler exchanged a look, flirtatious on Chandra's part, cautious on his. Jess wondered about it briefly, but didn't have time to give it real consideration before the dogs tore down the hallway toward the kitchen. She stepped to the back door and yanked it open. "Out!" she commanded. The Goldens raced through the doorway into the great outdoors like it had been their objective all along. Jess sighed, "Peace at last."

"You made scones," Tyler observed.

"I hope you aren't tired of them. They're so easy and quick to make."

"I love scones," he said.

From the corner of her eye, Jess caught Beckett muttering *I love scones* under his breath "Would you get out the plates?" she directed Tyler away from Beckett with a smile.

"How long are you staying?" Tyler asked Chandra.

"Another day or two. Have laptop, will travel." Chandra went on to tell Tyler and Beckett about her graphic design work as she plated the scones.

Someone passed by the kitchen window and knocked on the back door. Beckett opened it to find John, Bonnie's son, standing on the stoop.

"Good morning," he said. "I followed the dogs around the yard." Shakti raced by, her tongue hanging out the side of her mouth, Bruno giving chase.

Jess introduced him to Chandra and Tyler as he came inside.

"John Ecklund Sykes," he said, shaking Tyler's hand.

"You're changing your name?" Beckett asked, putting the first cup of fresh coffee in John's hands.

He nodded. "As part of the divorce filing, I can make the change without any extra fuss or expense, so it seemed the thing to do."

"Your parents would appreciate that," Jess said.

John, the son of the woman who had haunted Jess's house, had been only two years old when his mother died and his father was incarcerated for her murder. His grandparents raised him with his mother's maiden name, Ecklund. The grandparents, however well meaning, had denied John the opportunity to know anything about his father, John Sykes, Sr. Through Bonnie's insistence, Jess and Beckett had reunited father and son, and gotten to know John in the process.

"I hope you don't mind an uninvited visit," he said. "I was in La Crosse for my grandfather's funeral..."

Jess and the others murmured their sympathy.

"Thank you. It seemed a shame to just drive by and not say hello."

Chandra put a plate with a scone in his hand. "Guests are always welcome *chez* Vernon."

They called the dogs inside and sat at the table. Chandra tossed her curly blonde hair and smiled at John. And Tyler. It was difficult to say whether she favored one of them. John and Tyler both expressed interest in her work and she in theirs. Jess had to lift her coffee cup to hide the smile spreading across her face—here at her table sat a potter, chef, graphic artist, scholar, and herself, the writer. Could it be? The life she had envisioned for herself throughout the most painful year of her life—her divorce—was actually coming true? Beckett seemed to sense her pleasure. His hand found her knee under the table and gave it a squeeze. She looked at him and found the spark in his eyes deeply satisfying.

"Say, Jess," John said. "I talked to my editor at the U's press about our project. She's interested. We have to get a book proposal to her as soon as possible."

"A book deal?" Tyler asked.

"I've been meaning to talk to you about this, Tyler."

He tensed, a subtle motion, but Jess knew the reflex. Tyler exhaled and pushed his hand through his hair, moving some dark curls off his forehead and revealing the scar she'd never been able to ask about. "Me?"

"John and I are co-writing a memoir about his family. My part is about the haunting and everything that happened…" There was no need to finish the sentence. Tyler knew exactly what had happened and his role in it all. "I'll protect everyone's identity, of course. It's just that I need to tell my story and you're one of the key players."

Tyler swiveled on his seat, turning away from the table. For a moment, Jess worried he was leaving, but he patted his thigh and Bruno trotted into the room with Shakti on his heels. Beckett grabbed Shakti's collar and redirected her attention to him. Tyler whispered, "My lap," and Bruno rose, his front paws on Tyler's thighs. Tyler wrapped his arms around Bruno and rubbed his neck ruff while Bruno looked happily across the table at everyone seated there.

They waited for Tyler to respond, their attention fixed on him. Jess tried to think of something to say. She looked at Beckett, seeking his help.

Chandra stood up. "More scones? John, would you help me in the kitchen?" They left and, with their going, the tension eased.

"I'm sorry, Tyler. I need to write this book. I can't do it without your part."

"My part?" he snorted. "Jess, I won't tell you not to write the book. I won't even tell you how uncomfortable that makes me. I'm going to trust you." He lifted his gaze from Bruno's head to meet hers. "I think I owe you that much."

"Thank you."

Chandra's laughter floated out of the kitchen.

Chapter Eight

JESS AND CHANDRA made margaritas and stayed up all night drinking them. It was Chandra's send-off. It was also her idea, not that Jess was an unwilling participant. She regretted it now as she lay in the booth, her feet up on the wall and an arm draped over her eyes. Her jaw slackened with sleep and she snored softly.

Some kind of light catcher hung over a counter. Sunlight filtered through a dirty pane of glass, illuminating the golden coil so it glowed translucent. It was beautiful.

A fly buzzed toward it, erratic in its flight, finally alighting on the amber-colored strip. It tried to raise one leg and then another. It buzzed its wings without taking flight. The coil twirled slowly in the mote-filled sunlight.

Another fly came from the same direction as the first. It too landed on the coil, only to meet the same fate. Then another. And another.

Jess opened her eyes to see Beckett standing above her, holding a potter's bat with his latest creation right over her head. She waved and grunted at the bottom of the wooden plate. Beckett set it on the table. Jess scooted herself upright in the booth and looked at a white vase still glistening with moisture. She blinked at it. "Porcelain?"

"Geez. Hung over much?"

"No. A little, I suppose. Mostly I'm tired. Chandra doesn't slow down." Jess folded her arms on the table and flopped her head into their cradle, dangerously close to the vase. Beckett slid it away from her. "Sorry. Did I get it?"

"No."

"Good. What if I had?"

"You'd be making me a new one."

Jess laughed. "I'd like to see that. It would never sell, unless there's a market for surrealist pottery."

"Yeah, I'd like to see it, too." Beckett nudged her over and sat beside her. "So? Are you glad she's gone?"

Jess shrugged. "I'll miss her, but yes. It'll be nice to get back to my life."

A fly landed on the table and Jess startled. Beckett slid a magazine slowly off the table while it rubbed its legs together, performing a balancing act as each pair lifted in turn. Beckett rolled up the magazine and smacked the table with it. The fly buzzed away.

"What's with the flies today?" Jess said.

"I don't know. They must be blowing in off the river."

The front door swung open and Dave burst inside, skirting the display area of pots for sale, narrowly avoiding knocking over a large urn, and hurried to the booth. His face had flushed as red as his hair and his large hands clenched in front of him, though for want of something to hold or something to strike Jess couldn't be sure. "Beckett!" he blurted and then stalled.

"What? Is the shop on fire?"

Dave, Beckett's employee at the hardware store on Main Street, was a beer-drinking, pickup-driving, deer-shooting redneck. He was also obsessive-compulsive, generous, responsible, and in love with Shakti. Jess had grown quite fond of him over her months in Skoghall. "No, it's my cousin." Dave looked over his beefy shoulder at the door as though expecting someone to charge in after him.

"Why don't you sit down, Dave," Jess said.

He nodded and sat across from them.

They waited for him to gather his thoughts.

"Skipper. My cousin. He owns the junk shop on the other side of The Two Wheeler."

Jess and Beckett nodded together as though things made sense now. She had never heard of Skipper and she thought the place next to The Two Wheeler was vacant or possibly condemned.

"He's being arrested. They found a body in his shop or something. Anyway, I wanted you to know I closed up the hardware store. I have to get over there and see what they're doing to Skipper."

"Okay. Go."

Dave stood up from the booth, then turned to face Beckett, his hand swinging out from his hip in some kind of loose gesture. He backhanded the porcelain vase, crushing its side. "Um…" He looked from the vase to Beckett to the vase. "Thanks," he said and rushed away.

Jess and Beckett walked up the River Road hand in hand. She used her free hand to shield her eyes and still she squinted into the glare. Jake stood on the front porch of The Two Wheeler.

"Hey," Beckett called. "Do you know anything about this?"

"Just saw the cops arrive about twenty minutes ago," Jake responded.

Two cruisers lined the shoulder in front of the ramshackle building. Cars on the River Road slowed, and Jess watched as the people inside turned their heads to stare at the vehicles and speculate. They were curious, but they didn't really care, their interest vanishing with the scene in their rearview mirrors. It seemed callous. Jess had made a practice of sending up a little prayer for whoever needed it whenever she saw an ambulance or firetruck with sirens on. She turned her head from the road and gazed at the cruisers parked on the shoulder. Jess hesitated. She already knew they were there to collect a body and it seemed too late for a prayer.

A deputy sheriff unrolled a band of yellow tape, cordoning off the entrance to the junk shop. She looked hot in her chocolate brown shirt, a wide belt circling her hips with heavy gear. It was no wonder Jess has assumed the building was vacant. Now in disrepair, it had been built, like the bar next door, to minimize frontage along the road. A duplex, two staircases led up to the narrow front porch, one at each end of the building. Matching doors flanked a pair of matching windows. The left window had a dingy curtain pulled shut, while the right window displayed a shelf of miscellany, including an old toaster, a rag doll, and an unopened blue and orange Maxwell House coffee can. An open sign hung on the outside of the right screen door, marking it as the entrance to Skipper's junk shop, but no other signage called attention to the business within. Pillars supported the roof over the porch, wooden columns with faded yellow paint peeling off in large flakes. The house had once been a gay blue, now faded and peeling like the yellow. Gingerbread corner brackets framed the porch's ceiling with Victorian charm. Jess imagined it had been home to loving caretakers in another era.

"I can't let you come any closer," the Deputy said, her hand held up before Beckett and Jess. Jess had been so busy taking in the scene, she'd hardly realized they had moved to the inside of the patrol cars.

Dave sat on the left-hand set of steps with a man, his cousin presumably. They'd been tucked behind a half-dead bush planted between the staircases. Dave rose and came over. The Deputy stepped aside, but remained watchful.

"Are you all right?" Beckett asked Dave.

"A lot better than him," Dave glanced over his shoulder at his cousin.

The cousin, Skipper, hunched over his knees, head in his hands. He had Dave's fair skin, but darker hair, a dirty auburn color, and unkempt. He lifted his head to stare out at the road, and Jess saw that he had several days of stubble on a face that melted into a neck like a turkey's wattle.

"He found a body in the junk shop, way at the back," Dave continued. "He didn't stick around to get to know it, so I don't know much else." Dave pressed his hands together and cracked his knuckles.

"So you don't know if it's a man or a woman?" Beckett asked.

"Man," Jess said before Dave could respond.

Jess felt Beckett staring at her, but kept her eyes on the porch in front of the junk shop. A man stood outside the door wearing neat blue jeans, a white button-down shirt with the sleeves rolled up, and a tie that had been loosened enough to open the neck of the shirt. He looked at her like he couldn't decide what to do about the fact that she could see him. He put a hand to the back of his neck and rubbed at his hairline, then turned and walked back inside the shop.

"How do you know that?" Dave asked.

Jess shrugged. "It just makes sense." She glanced down and saw that Beckett had let go of her hand. Funny, she hadn't noticed when he let go. She wiped her palms up and down her shorts. "Can we do anything?"

Skipper rose from the steps and walked unsteadily toward them. Beckett greeted him and introduced Jess. She was about to extend a hand when he shoved both of his into his front pockets. "They're going to arrest me," he said.

"No, Skipper." Dave put a hand on his cousin's shoulder. "They're going to interview you. That's all. They have to find out what happened."

"But they're going to take me in." Skipper glanced at each of them in turn, his gaze merely skimming their faces.

"That's all right, Skip. They've got to do their jobs, that's all." Dave let his hand drop away from Skipper's shoulder. "I'll find out where they're taking you and see what I can do."

A new-looking, black Ford Taurus pulled over onto the shoulder behind the others. Two men got out. The younger of the two wore wrinkle-free khakis with cargo pockets and a blue polo shirt with the Sheriff's Office logo on it. The older of the pair wore a button down shirt with a tie, though, likely a concession to the heat, he did not wear a jacket. The Deputy who'd been watching the front of the building, standing within hearing range of Jess and the others at all times, nodded to them as they approached. She grabbed a clipboard off the porch and handed it to one of the men. They moved onto the porch—away from Jess and the others—and she briefed them on what was inside. The newly arrived men signed something on the clipboard and handed it back to her. The younger man turned to look at them. He had black hair clipped short on th graying sides, but curled at the top where it was longer. He pushed a pair of sunglasses up onto his head and returned Jess's look with scrutiny. He put his hands on his hips before turning away from her, the gold badge attached to his belt flashing in the sun. His partner, older, taller, and less athletic looking, jerked a thumb in their direction. The Deputy nodded and came down to the road while they went inside.

"The Investigators will need to speak with you when they finish inside." She collected their contact information and resumed her post at the door.

It hadn't occurred to Jess that by wandering up the road to see if Dave and Skipper needed help, she would become part of an investigation. The thought created a knot in her stomach.

"What did you see back there?"

Jess looked at Beckett, trying to read his face. Suspicion? Concern? She sighed and turned her head to gaze at the brick kiln. They sat on an old picnic table bench in the yard behind the studio. "A man. In his early thirties. He had a tie on." She shrugged as if to say, *and that's all.*

"A tie?"

A light breeze made the aspen leaves dance over their heads, rustling like the softest of wind chimes. Jess listened to the chatter of sparrows in the shrubs and tree branches lining the livery yard on the south side, grateful for the shade of the trees. In another half hour, the sun would be far enough west to beat down on the clearing. She plucked her shirt away from her skin and fanned the moisture there. "Would you blow on the back of my neck?" She lifted her hair up onto her head and Beckett obliged, his breath a cool relief on her skin.

"Not many people wear ties around here," Jess said, "so I thought it remarkable."

"Are you going to tell them?" Beckett asked.

"The cops?" She looked at him, his ice-blue eyes showed concern, but was it for her? "What do you think?"

"No." His gaze shifted from her face, past her toward the studio. He had both of the old wooden doors opened wide. Built to admit horses and wagons, they slid on steel tracks along the side of the building, creating a throughway with Skoghall on one side and the park on the other. "At best, they'll think you're crazy. At worst, they'll think you have something to do with it."

Jess shivered as a quick electric tingle pulsed through her spine. "I hadn't thought of that."

"Here they come."

She looked toward the livery. The two men entered the studio through the wide doorway and went around the sales display. They passed Beckett's work table, electric kiln, and potter's wheels before exiting through the other carriage door. Jess and Beckett stood to greet them.

"I'm Investigator Martinez with the Rice County Sheriff's Office, and this is Investigator Johnson with Pierce County," Martinez said, gesturing to himself and his partner. Beckett and Jess introduced themselves. Investigator Johnson opened a small notebook and wrote down their names. "How do you know Mr. Matheson?" Martinez asked.

"Who?" Jess asked.

"Skipper. Dave's cousin," Beckett said to Jess. He addressed the investigators, "I own the hardware store and Dave's my employee there. Skipper comes into the hardware store from time to time."

"I just met him today," Jess said.

"Other than his cousin, do you know if Mr. Matheson has any friends?" Investigator Johnson asked. Jess could see a sheen of sweat on his scalp through the spiked strands of his short hair.

Not so with Martinez. The investigator kept his hands lightly clasped in front of his navel and watched Jess and Beckett closely, making the kind of eye contact so rare in the culture that it made Jess take a step back and cross her arms over her chest.

"I think he's practically a shut-in," Beckett said. "In fact, I think he tries to go to the hardware store when I'm not there so he only has to see Dave."

"Really?" Martinez said, raising a thick eyebrow over the rim of his sunglasses. "A shut in with no idea how a body wound up on the floor of his business."

Jess drew her lower lip between her teeth. In the minutes she'd spent with Dave and Skipper outside the junk shop, Skipper had seemed like a frightened child, looking to Dave for direction.

"We may have questions for you later," Johnson said. "And if you think of anything…" He handed them a business card.

Martinez passed them his card as well. "Can we get to the junk shop this way?" he asked, pointing up the slope toward the bar, its deck barely visible through the aspens.

"Sure," Jess said.

"There's not really a path," Beckett added. "If you follow the tracks it'll be easier."

The investigators thanked them for their time and left.

Jess and Beckett watched them walk out toward the train tracks, stop and discuss something, pointing toward the river with sweeping motions before starting uphill toward the junk shop.

"That was easy," Beckett said.

"Only because we don't know anything." Jess stared toward the river with her brow furrowed.

Beckett took Jess's hand and turned her toward him. "What's going on in there?"

"I *do* know something," Jess said, "something I'm not supposed to know."

And the man I saw saw me.

Chapter Nine

JESS STARED UP at the junk shop, a bucket hanging from her hand. Beckett and Dave flanked her, their apprehension mounting along with her own. Jess had no idea what to expect. She'd never entered a crime scene before and she wouldn't be doing it now, except that Dave had asked. Dave—who had helped Beckett install her wood-burning stove, who watched Shakti anytime she needed a dog sitter—called in a favor and there was no way she would turn him down. Skipper came out of his house and joined them in the road. Dave picked up an extra bucket sitting at his feet and handed it to his cousin. The yellow crime scene tape had been removed, as had everything else… presumably.

"They said I could go in." Skipper took a cap off his head and scratched at his scalp through thinning hair. He and Dave were both flushing red under the hot morning sun.

"Let's get this over with," Beckett said. The longer this took, the more business he stood to lose with both him and Dave away from his shops. In a couple of hours, Friday traffic would begin flowing. He pulled a facemask out of his bucket, stretched the elastic bands over his head, and set it in place over his mouth and nose. The others did the same.

They stood in their line, mops and brooms shouldered like rifles, soldiers nervously waiting for the cry of "Charge!" No one moved. Jess felt the heat on the back of her neck. Beads of sweat formed at her temples and trickled past her brows and down the sides of her face, while the mask made it too stuffy to breathe. She wiped at her neck, then resolutely picked up her bucket and marched forward.

Jess opened the door onto the scene of the murder.

The hot stench of iron and spoiled hamburger sent her reeling. She stepped backwards and knocked into Beckett who had come up onto the porch behind her. "Jesus," she gasped. Jess stepped to the side of the door and leaned over the porch railing, hoping to catch a breeze coming off the river and up between the buildings. She yanked her mask down around her neck and sucked in the fresh air.

"You all right?" Beckett asked. Jess nodded. He called over his shoulder, "Skipper, you have any fans so we can air this place out?"

The men organized a search for fans, Skipper retreating into his home while Beckett and Dave went to the studio to grab all of Beckett's fans, leaving Jess alone on the porch.

The hair on the back of her neck stood up. She turned around slowly and went back through the door of the junk shop.

Her eyes had to adjust from the glare of the sun to the dark interior. To the left of the door sat the sales counter with an outer surface of cheap paneling, the cracked and peeling veneer had warped with time. Above an old electric cash register hung an amber coil, twisting lazily this way, then that way, as though swayed by some subtle current Jess couldn't feel. Sunlight peeking through the dirty front window caused it to glow faintly, making the small black corpses that littered the list all the more gruesome.

The front room, a square with another window in the side wall and a thin, two-paneled door that opened against the outer wall, had been lined with ugly metal shelves, the kind sold for organizing garages and tool sheds. The shelves had been erected across the window and the stuff on them blocked any hope of natural light. They also prevented opening the window without first excavating the sash. Jess could discern no order to the things jumbled on the shelves, or the furniture crammed into the middle of the room, all of it stacked with piles of junk. She felt her breath hot and moist on her face behind the dome of the paper mask. Jess pulled it down around her neck and inhaled a shallow breath, testing the air. It was completely rank.

She stepped through the doorway cut into an impossibly thin wall. The second room was a copy of the first. If anything, the walkways were narrower, the junk piled higher, crammed deeper into corners, stacks threatening to topple off of shelves and bury the casual browser. This was the second hoarder Jess had encountered since moving to Skoghall, but unlike the old man with the outbuilding full of treasures, Jess found little if anything redeeming about this place. No wonder the junk shop hadn't made the list of tourist attractions in Skoghall.

Before her stood the open door to the third and back-most room. Through the doorway she could see the rear exit of the house. Once she got that door open, it would create a breezeway, and when the fans were in place, they could really move some air. Jess fixed her eyes on her goal and stepped into the third room.

The sight and stench of blood stopped her. Her stomach curdled and Jess fought the urge to retch where she stood. It wouldn't do to vomit all over a crime scene.

It made no sense—Skipper said they'd released the scene. She and Beckett had watched, along with a small crowd, from the front deck of The Two Wheeler, as first the Peaceful River Funeral Home hearse left, followed by a Rice County Sheriff squad car. Then the big cube van from the Department of Criminal Investigations packed up, even taking the yellow crime scene tape with them. That had been around 11:00, well past closing time for local businesses, all but the bar. Yet the body remained laying on the floor of the back room. "Floor" was to be used loosely, since the body actually lay on top of a slew of junk that until recently someone might have considered merchandise. The man lay prone, head pointing into the corner of the room, his face turned so that one glazed eye stared at the ceiling. A fly perched on a raised, sticky, blood-black lock of hair, rubbing its front legs together obsessively, miniature Lady Macbeth. The blood had pooled and congealed around the head in a haloed circle, and for the briefest instant, Jess had the impression of a Christian icon, the martyr just before his Heavenly ascent.

The man's left hand lay near the head, his arm angling out at both shoulder and elbow. He wore a watch with a silver band and a gold wedding ring.

"Jess? Jess, what are you looking at?"

Jess pointed at the body as she looked over her shoulder at Beckett. "The bo..." She realized mid-word that there was no body and that Skipper stood behind Beckett, holding a large box fan with the cord draped over his shoulder. "Um. The…" Jess had to look back at the floor to see what was real, "…blood." Much of the junk had been shifted, either carted away as evidence or moved to allow removal of the body, but the blood remained. It no longer reminded Jess of a halo. Now it looked like a stain, large and sad, marking some unknown tragedy.

Beckett took the fan from Skipper and went around Jess, stepping carefully. He opened the back door and set it up. The moving air brought instantaneous relief, though it would take time to clear the stench of decay from the room.

Jess shook off the sight of the body, unable to talk to Beckett about it with Skipper around. Dave entered, his presence filling the crammed space. "All right," he rubbed his hands together as though eager for the task ahead. "Who wants what?"

"Dave…" Skipper looked lost, standing in his own shop, shoulders slouched and head hanging like an overgrown child. "I don't like this."

"And we do?" Dave clapped his cousin on the shoulder. "It's your place, so you get to scrub the floorboards." He looked around the room, not just at the area where the body had lain, and his mouth curled down with disapproval. "Shit, Skip, if we're going to do this, let's do it right. We'll haul most of this crap to the dump and organize anything worth selling so you can work an *actual* business."

Jess pulled on a pair of gloves that came up to her elbows. The insides of the gloves felt chalky and already the heavy purple rubber with the decorative floral cuffs made her hot. She shook open a large garbage bag and looked around for a place to start. A small steel table with casters that had been painted institutional green—built to hold a typewriter, it could be wheeled out of a corner and stationed next to the boss's desk for his secretary to take dictation, her soft, manicured hands poised over the keys—had been upended and a wire record wrack toppled to the floor, spilling its contents. Jess knelt next to the pile of 45s and picked up the two pieces of "Great Balls of Fire." She flipped them over and lined up the edges—the B side, "You Win Again," a song she'd never heard, went in the garbage along with the hit title. She put the salvageable records back on the table in a neat pile. Beckett worked nearby, heaping things into his garbage bag with far less discrimination than Jess. Dave had taken Skipper to the front room, where pieces of their conversation were audible throughout the shop. Mostly it consisted of Skipper saying, "What about this?" and Dave replying, "Toss it," followed by the sound of something being dumped into a heavy-duty bag.

"Why are we doing this room while they're up front?" Beckett asked from behind his mask.

"Did you see Skipper's face? He looked ready to have a melt down."

Beckett threw a pair of women's heels with a once-shiny gold lamé finish into his bag with a violent aim.

"What's his story, anyway?"

"Skipper? I don't know." Beckett threw a cigar box into the bag without looking to see if something interesting was inside. "He's a recluse. He's always been considered an odd ball, but harmless. Kind of sweet."

"Yeah? How'd he get this place?"

"Ask Dave. Or Skipper."

"Okay, grump."

"Okay, grump? Yeah, I'm grumpy. I'm spending my day cleaning up after a bloodbath, for fuck's sake!"

Jess sat back on her heels, a stack of brochures, circa 1948, for a sanitarium on the Superior shore in her hand. "I know that, Beckett. I'm here, too, but I'm not taking it out on you." She dumped the brochures into her garbage bag, hesitated a moment, then pulled one back out. It could come in handy for one of her stories some day.

Beckett threw some kind of knickknack into his bag, the sound of breaking glass accenting his irritation. "What did you see?"

"I saw the body, but you already knew that, didn't you?"

"Yeah, I already knew that." He pulled his mask off his face and stared at Jess. "Is it starting over again?"

Jess shrugged. "This one isn't in my house." She waited for Beckett to say something.

He looked toward the front of the building where Dave and Skipper were working. "Let's take a break."

They left through the back door without telling the others. The old shotgun house didn't have anything resembling a yard. Just off the back steps, which showed signs of rot, a seldom-used, overgrown path angled down the slope toward the bar, creamery, and Beckett's studio. Beckett led Jess across the train tracks instead, holding her hand as they walked single-file onto a trail that led into the floodplain.

Purple spiderwort and milkweed decorated the trail's edge. Jess picked her way carefully while prickling thistles and burs snagged at her legs. The green fruit of a walnut tree littered the path, many whole, many only the casings discarded by resident squirrels. The trail came to the edge of a marsh fringed by cattails and blue-green triangular sedges. It appeared they had arrived at a pond in the middle of a forest, a single willow tree surrounded by silver maples stood tall across the water from them. Jess pointed at the sleek, chestnut-colored head of a muskrat gliding across the surface of the water, its body hidden from view. She enjoyed being out of the junk shop, the small stuffy room and stink of spilled blood had gotten to her, too, though she hadn't realized how tense she felt until coming outside. Jess gave Beckett's hand a squeeze and leaned into his shoulder, happy for the first time that day. "Thanks for bringing me out here," she said.

"You're welcome." He turned his head to kiss Jess's cheek.

"Beckett," Jess clutched his arm, "I see another body."

"Where?" He looked out over the water.

"Don't you see it?" She stared at it to direct his gaze toward the bluegill resting atop a bed of bent marsh grasses at the water's edge, its empty eye socket and mossy scales drawing nature's housekeepers.

"What? Oh…ha ha."

"At least this one died of natural causes." Jess couldn't help giggling.

"Jess."

"I'm sorry. I had to." She took his hands and looked to him for understanding. "To break the tension."

Beckett shook his head and sighed. "Will it always be like this?"

"How should I know? And what if it is?"

Beckett shrugged. "Fair enough." He fixed his gaze on the marsh pond. "What did you see?"

Jess joined Beckett in watching the water. She told him about her vision. She thought the smell had been fresh while she stared at the body, stronger, riper, and the great relief that came when Beckett and Skipper turned up with the fans hadn't been so much from the movement of air, but from the end of the vision. It hadn't occurred to her before that her smell could be affected during these moments, but why not? Jess took an inventory: she had seen things, heard things, felt things, and now probably smelled things.

Isabella was the only spirit she'd encountered who wasn't cryptic, perhaps because she didn't seem to realize she was dead, or because she'd had so many years of practice already.

They stood quietly watching the water long enough that Jess's thoughts turned away from ghosts and settled on what was before her. The marsh's murky surface glimmered where the sun shone on it through the surrounding trees. Water striders, with their obscenely long legs, hunted its still surface. And the movement of fish could occasionally be seen between the aquatic plants at the edges of the pond.

Beckett reached out and put his hands around her waist. He drew her to him and held her. "What are you thinking?"

"Just watching the pond. You?"

"I was thinking we should tell the cops what you saw."

"Hello, Investigator Martinez." Beckett showed him into the studio and led him to the booth where Jess sat waiting. She nodded hello. Martinez slid onto the bench opposite her and Beckett beside her, trapping her between him and the wall.

After spending half the day helping Skipper and Dave clean the junk shop, Beckett opened his studio and caught the afternoon traffic. Now, nearly 7:00 on a Friday, Jess wondered if Martinez had a girlfriend at home, holding dinner, or a cat waiting to be fed. She was relieved, perhaps unfairly, that he had left his partner behind.

"You thought of something that could help with my investigation?" Martinez asked. He wore the same pants and polo shirt as the other day, a uniform. His badge and Smith and Wesson were worn on his hip, and there was no mistaking the casual attire for a lack of authority.

The way Martinez looked at her made Jess shift and pull her hands into her lap. It was ridiculous, this childish notion that she had something embarrassing to hide, but she couldn't help feeling precisely that. And Martinez knew it already.

"Go ahead, Jess."

Jess looked at Beckett and he nodded, his blue eyes offering the encouragement she needed. "This is going to sound crazy, but I seem to be able to see…things."

"Things?" Martinez said.

Sweat trickled down Jess's brow and she resisted the urge to wipe it away, certain it was an indication of guilt and not simply the fact that it was a humid ninety degrees outside. Jess looked at Martinez and marveled that he wasn't sweating.

"I have some iced tea in the fridge," Beckett said and stood up, pausing to confirm they were wanted before going back to the kitchen.

"I don't know why this is so hard," Jess said.

"It's the badge," Martinez said. "It makes people think I'm out to get them."

Jess met his eyes for the first time. They were deep brown and kind. She offered a reserved smile. "I don't want to get involved in a murder investigation. I didn't ask to see…things. It just started happening when I moved here about four months ago."

"I had an aunt who was gifted. She had conversations with angels. People talked like she was crazy behind her back, but when they wanted something, they ran to her and asked her to pray for them."

"I think I'd rather see angels."

"Here you go." Beckett set three bottles on the table, their sides already slick with condensation.

"Why don't you just tell me what you saw, and we'll go from there."

"Okay." Jess told Martinez about the spirit watching the investigation at the crime scene. He had looked dismayed by everything going on, and though she thought he'd seen her and known that she could see him, he did not try to communicate. She felt like he wanted to remain close to his body. Then she told Martinez about the body, the blood around the head like a halo, the fly, and his hand. She was certain it was the left hand, because his silver watch and gold wedding ring were so clear in her mind.

"Thank you, Ms. Vernon." Investigator Martinez raised his bottle of iced tea to drink, and Jess noted the dark circle of a sweat mark under his arm. It reassured her to see that he did not have some superhuman tolerance for the heat.

"Is that helpful?" Beckett asked.

"I don't know yet. It might be, but right now we don't have a lot to go on. I was hoping you could help us ID the victim."

"Great Balls of Fire." Jess tucked her lower lip between her teeth as her cheeks reddened.

"Excuse me?" Martinez and Beckett both stared at her.

"I have no idea why I said that." Jess wiped at the back of her neck with her palm.

"All right then," Martinez said. "If you think of…or see…anything else, give me a call."

Chapter Ten

THE DOORBELL RANG. Juney came bleary eyed from her bedroom wearing pajamas, her mousy-brown hair a tangled mess. She rubbed her eyes sleepily as she tripped down the short staircase and leaned against the doorway from the split-level's landing to the entryway, suddenly afraid to see who it was.

Her mother tsk'd, "Put some clothes on *before* you come out of your room, young lady."

Juney folded her arms across her chest, but did not leave her position at the edge of the entryway. Glancing down, she noticed a purple bruise on her upper arm and laid her hand over the mark, lining up her fingers over the finger-shaped lines of the bruise. Her mother opened the door and Juney stared at her mother's back, at the flabby arm that ended in the chapped hand on the doorknob. Her mother, ever the lady, only wore pants for gardening and boating, because her father preferred skirts. Her father was a leg man; he liked to see his wife's calves and slender ankles. Her mother also wore her hair long, but so did most of the women in Sunders Grove. Juney's sister, Rachel, wore her hair shorn, but she was a sophomore at UW. Rachel came home for Christmas in love with her new hairstyle and laughed when their father complained and called her manly. "Just because all the stylists in Sunders Grove are allergic to their scissors doesn't mean I look like a man." Their father fumed, even threatening to pull her out of school. "Try it," Rachel had said, "and you'll never see me again." Juney knew who was at the door, even though from where she stood she couldn't see them, and she hoped she was wrong. She hoped it was only the milk man.

"Good morning, Mrs. Roberts."

Fuck, she thought.

"Good morning, boys. It's a little early to call on Juney, isn't it?"

"We're not here to see Juney, Mrs. Roberts. We'd like to speak with Mr. Roberts."

Juney's stomach lurched and she tasted the spot of vomit at the back of her mouth. She grimaced, but her toothbrush would have to wait. If they were here for her father, it meant they'd gone through with it, and as bad as that had been, this morning was already worse. She shifted from the doorway to the landing at the bottom of the stairs, a movement of a few inches, and flattened herself against the wall, while her mother called her father out of the kitchen.

"What is it?" he said, his footfalls heavy on the vinyl flooring. Juney could hear her father's breathing, a familiar low *huu...huu,* which meant he was mouth breathing, which meant he was already pissed off, and it was only 7:30 in the morning.

Juney waited for the explosion.

"I'll have eggs and toast," her father said.

"Yes, dear." Juney didn't have to look to know her mother retreated obediently into the kitchen, the only room of the house that was truly hers.

"What is it?" If the boys at the door didn't produce something to impress him, the explosion would come now.

"Sir, we've heard that you're the man to see if we seek to serve as the hand of our Lord." That was Ethan. Erick would be too scared to address her father. Juney imagined him a step behind Ethan, staring at his shoes in a posture of fear and reverence. Her father would like that. If Ethan didn't watch himself, he'd blow it. Even a whiff of cockiness made her father irate.

"What makes you think I know what you're talking about?"

Juney's breath caught in her chest. One wrong word...

"It's what we heard, sir." Ethan paused and Juney counted to three, filling the requisite space in their conversation. "If we heard wrong, we'll be on our way for we mean only to serve in whatever capacity we are able. If we heard right, we brought this offering to prove our worth."

He got that part right. Juney peeked around the corner and saw her father holding an insulated plastic bag with Super America on it, a kind of temporary cooler good for getting your frozen peas or cold beer home from the store on a hot day. Her father pulled apart the snapped-together handle and looked inside the bag. "What in Hades..?"

Juney pressed herself to the wall, her fingers spread against its whitewashed surface. She heard the sound of a smack, not the sharp clap of skin to skin, but the dull thud of a hand to the skull, and the immediate response of "Ow! What the fuck?"

"Get away from my house," her father roared. "If I ever see you again, you will suffer mightily by my hand," he shouted after them.

Juney fled up the stairs and down the hallway to her room. She dove into her bed and pulled the covers over her head, praying her father would not connect his visitors to her. At the bottom of the stairs, her sweaty palm prints dried on the surface of the unimaginative white wall.

Chapter Eleven

JESS HAD TO see Isabella.

The string of bells chimed musically when she pushed the door open and entered the antique store. Lora stood behind her counter looking as fresh as ever in a green paisley dress with a ruffle that ran from one shoulder along the neckline and down the skirt, crossing her body diagonally. A part of Jess admired Lora's commitment to looking stylish no matter the day, but only a very small part. "Haven't seen you for a while," Lora said in an indeterminate manner. She wore her hair up with spiraling tendrils falling to her shoulders.

"I've been writing a lot, and I had a friend visit last week."

"That's nice. Can I help you find something specific?" She really was damn near perfect, with her fair skin and heart-shaped face, her large breasts and petite-yet-curvy body. Lora had been cool with Jess from the very beginning. Eventually, Jess learned that she and Beckett had dated for a while, though she couldn't imagine why, unless she factored in proximity; Skoghall's dating pool was more of a puddle. If there was anything else behind Lora's demeanor toward Jess, she hadn't identified it yet.

"No thanks. I'm in the mood to browse." Lora smiled the way one does when dismissing somebody from one's company, and Jess gladly went upstairs.

She entered the smaller of the bedrooms and whispered her name. Isabella giggled, drawing Jess to the closet. Her boots with the scuffed toes and cloth-covered buttons showed below the hems of the carefully hung vintage clothing. Jess couldn't help smiling. She slid her hands between a long blue-gray dress of summer-weight wool and a cotton chemise with a drawstring neckline, and parted the garments. Isabella stood with her hands covering a broad smile. Jess reached out to stroke Isabella's hair and smooth her hand down one of the girl's long braids. Where her hand touched Isabella, the air shimmered and a crawling sensation moved across her palm. Jess's smile faltered and she wiped her palm on her shorts.

"Isabella, I have a question for you." The girl nodded and stepped out of the closet. Jess looked for somewhere to sit, but the only chair in the room had a ribbon strung from its scrolled back over the edge of the embroidered seat and an impressive price of $650 attached to it. Jess sat on the floor next to a traveling trunk and patted the floor in front of her. Isabella sat, holding out the edge of her skirt and laying it over her knees. "Do you know what you are?"

"Well…" she looked thoughtful, lifting her gaze as though to search the contents of her head. "Papa says we are Swedish, but my teacher says we must consider ourselves American first, since we are citizens of this nation." Isabella looked to Jess for confirmation.

"Yes, I suppose that's true," Jess smiled at the girl. She'd had the urge to pat her knee reassuringly, but remembered not to before extending her hand. "When you sleep in the dark place, is there anyone there with you?"

"What a funny question," Isabella exclaimed. "Why would there be anyone with me when I sleep?"

"Well, if you go away to school, you might sleep in a big room with lots of other girls. Or in hospitals, they put lots of people into one big room. I thought it might be like that."

Isabella's expression darkened and she picked at the hem of her dress. "It's dark there. That's all I know. It's very dark."

"Do you talk to other people or only me?"

"There was one girl a long time ago. I think it was a long time ago. It's hard to tell. Her name was Grace and she said this was her bedroom."

"Isn't this your bedroom?" The string of brass bells clattered as someone let the screen door slam against its frame downstairs. She heard Lora greet her customer, her welcome seeming clipped by irritation. Jess lowered her voice, "Someone could come in here now, so I'll have to be going soon."

"I want to show you something," Isabella whispered. She turned and crawled to the closet, then looked over her shoulder, beckoning Jess closer. "Back in that corner," she instructed.

Jess crawled under the hems of Lora's old clothing, hoping nobody walked in right then—especially Lora.

"See that short board?"

Jess couldn't see much in the corner of a closet full of long clothing, but yes, there was a floorboard only about eight inches long with a gap between it and the wall. The gap had filled in with the blackened dust of decades.

"Pry it up," Isabella insisted.

Jess reached into her pocket and pulled out her keys. Using the tip of her house key, she pried at the board. It lifted easily, revealing a space between the floor and the ceiling below it.

"Do you see it?"

"What am I looking for?" The dust that had been disturbed by lifting the board itched Jess's nostrils.

"The book."

Jess shifted around so she could reach into her other pocket and took out her phone. She turned it on and directed the light into the hole.

A small book stood on end, tilted to rest against the wall. The top edge had a coating of dust to rival that in the crack between the board and the wall. Jess reached into the narrow gap. If she tipped the book over, she'd never reach it without taking up more of Lora's floorboards. Using her index and middle fingers like pincers, she held her breath as she lifted the treasure from its resting place. *Steady...steady.* A flash of memory came to her of playing Operation with her brother and cousins when she was a kid.

She lifted the book above the lip of the floorboards and safely away from the hole. She wanted to laugh at her success, but a creak on the staircase outside warned her of someone's approach. Jess put the board back hastily and it banged into place. "Now what?" she whispered.

"It's for *you*."

Without time to think, Jess tucked the book between the waistband of her shorts and the small of her back, then pulled her shirt over it. She got out of the closet just in time to see Lora round the corner at the top of the stairs.

She crossed the landing and entered the room. "I thought maybe you got lost up here."

Jess tried to laugh and hoped it didn't sound as false to Lora as it did to herself. "No, but I could. I love the old books and linotype." She realized her phone was still in her hand. "Mostly I've been texting."

"Oh." Lora eyed her phone like it could reveal something else. "I thought I heard you talking."

"Yeah. I, um, sometimes I say what I'm typing. Thinking out loud." Jess looked at her phone in her hand. "Weird, huh?"

"Not that weird, I guess." Lora poked a finger into her bun and scratched. Maybe she did sweat after all.

"Do you have any clothing from the late 1920s?" Jess hated herself for engaging Lora further, but needed to do something if she ever wanted to come back to the antique store.

"Sure." Lora stood beside Jess in front of the closet. She slid hangers across the bar, opening the garments to a lovely dusty rose-colored slip dress covered in ivory lace. It had the straight cut and dropped waist of the flapper era with just enough gathering where the skirt attached to the bodice to give it some movement. The intricate lacework took Jess's breath away. She lifted a hand to touch the edge of a cap sleeve. "I have a long string of vintage fresh water pearls, harvested from Lake Pepin no less, that would be the perfect accompaniment to this dress."

"It's gorgeous." Jess dared to look at the price tag and almost gasped. Beside the price, Lora had dated it 1924. "Wait…" Jess pointed at the garments collectively, "are these hung in chronological order?"

"Yes, and the tags all include a date or date range."

"That's impressive."

"Thank you for noticing." Lora's pink lips turned up in a smile. "Are you interested in the dress?"

"Not today." *Not if I want to eat this month.* "But now I know what one of my character's will wear to a dance. Thanks."

Jess left Lora to adjust the clothing across the hanging bar. As she walked out of the room and down the stairs, the smooth surface of the book caused a rectangular patch of sweat on her lower back and Jess prayed it wouldn't drop down through the leg of her shorts. She had shoplifted once when she was thirteen because a short-term best friend was doing it. She felt so guilty, she couldn't bring herself to break the seal on the compact of eye shadow. She fantasized about returning it to the drugstore, but every time she ran the scenario, she imagined being caught, arrested, shamed. After sitting unopened in her bathroom drawer for two months, she threw it away. *This,* she told herself, *is not stealing.*

By the time Jess reached her car, the book had slid down several inches. She held it in place while pretending to scratch her back and got behind the wheel before pulling the book from her clothes. Jess pressed her hand to the small of her back and it came away covered in a paste of dirty sweat. "This is what you get for not carrying a purse," she told herself and turned up the air conditioning.

Shakti bolted outside as soon as Jess opened the door. She startled, her first instinct fear after months of living with an angry ghost. Jess swiveled on her heels, still propping the screen door open, to watch Shakti take gleeful laps around the sugar maple, a dish towel waving triumphantly from her grinning mouth, ears flapping in the wind, tail held out like the team pennant. Her relief caused her to laugh, that and the dog's clear and abundant joy in playing with a piece of fabric. "We should all be so happy," Jess said and went inside to put down her things.

She returned to the porch with a glass of iced tea and Isabella's book. Shakti lay under the sugar maple, the towel between her paws, happily chewing on an end. Jess decided it would make a better dog toy than dishtowel and let it be. She sat in her rocking chair and held the book. It had taken two passes with a damp cloth to clean all the grime off its cover. She didn't dare use the damp cloth on the head, so she dusted it best she could, sneezing twice. A swash resembling lily of the valley decorated the first page of Isabella's diary. The words "This is the diary of" had been printed on the page, followed by two neat lines. In ink faded with age, Jess found the signature of the young Isabella Osterlund and the beginning date, December 25, 1917. The end date remained blank; Isabella had died less than a year after receiving her first diary. Her signature belied her age, showing the careful penmanship of a young student, each letter formed meticulously by one trying to perfect a skill, as opposed to the script of one who'd had time to develop a personalized style, who was more concerned with the act of communicating than the act of writing itself. Jess traced the loops of the capital I with her finger before turning the page.

Today is Christmas. Mother prepared a glazed ham and Karna and I made mashed potatoes. We had a jelly for dessert that came out of the mold just so. It looked like a palace of green glass. Mother allowed me to decorate the top of it with juniper sprigs with the pretty little blue berries.

Isabella's recounting of the Christmas holiday touched Jess more than she had expected. The simple pleasure of family time seemed lacking from her own life. She had expected when she married that she would have a family and develop holiday traditions of her own. She and Mitch never got around to having children, probably because even while she was trying to make the marriage work, deep down she knew it wouldn't and bringing a child into the mix would only make it harder to escape the doomed relationship. Jess flipped through the diary. Toward the middle, the handwriting changed, signaling the start of a new chronicle.

October 12, 1948
My name is Grace. This is the diary of the most special and strange friends Isabella and Grace. We are the same age and we live in the same house in Skoghall, Wisconsin very near the Mississippi River.

Jess liked how Isabella seemed to write for herself, perhaps her future self who might one day read the diary to remember what had happened, while Grace seemed to write for an unknown reader. Did Grace imagine someone discovering the hidden diary one day far into the future? Did she think that after she moved on, Isabella would find a new playmate and this girl would continue the account? Jess flipped to the last entry.

May 22, 1950
My family has decided to move to Chicago, because Father's brother has offered him a job that will pay better than anything around here. We will have to live in an apartment, at least at first. The school I go to will be large, and I won't know a soul besides my cousins who are older than I am and are boys, so that

won't do much good for me. Isabella said she could come with me and keep me company, but Mother says it is time I give up imaginary friends. She says I will make lots of friends in Chicago, so I will not need Isabella anymore. Mother indulges my talk of Isabella, because she thinks I am lonely, but of course, she doesn't know Isabella.

All the same, I have decided Mother is right.

Chapter Twelve

INVESTIGATOR MARTINEZ LEANED against his car in Jess's driveway, his cellphone in his hand like he'd been catching up on email while waiting for her. He continued to look at his phone, but Jess had no doubt he was completely aware of his surroundings. He wore another polo shirt today with the Sheriff's Office star logo on one breast and his name embroidered on the other. The short sleeves were hemmed with bands that hugged the fine tan muscle of his arms.

Jess had taken Shakti for a walk, trying to get out early before the heat made it impossible for the dog to do much other than lie around panting. She glanced at her watch, 7:20. Shakti pranced forward then halted every few steps, equal parts excited and unsure of the stranger on her property.

"Ms. Vernon," Martinez called when she had closed enough of the distance between them.

Shakti halted, looked up at Jess for a read on the situation, then coiled into a play bow and sprang into the air, launching toward Martinez. Jess choked up on the leash and tried to contain her dog.

"How old?"

Jess was relieved to see him smiling. "Eight months."

He stepped closer to them with a hand, palm out, near his hips. When Shakti jumped at him, his palm found her chest and deflected her. Jess got Shakti into a sit while Martinez patted her head and she tried to lick his hand.

"You're out early," she said when Shakti had calmed down.

Martinez bent and rubbed Shakti's face and ears. "I'm glad to see you're not a late sleeper."

Jess led the way inside and dumped some ice cubes in Shakti's bowl, then offered Investigator Martinez a cup of coffee.

"No, thank you. This won't take that long, Ms. Vernon, but please do whatever you need to. I don't mean to interrupt your morning."

"All right." Jess poured herself a glass of water and invited him to sit in the living room.

"We've identified the man from the junk shop."

"That's good." Jess felt the intensity of his gaze upon her, or was it just the presence of the gold badge clipped to his belt?

"Do you know who he was?"

"Why would I?"

Martinez leaned forward and rested his elbows on his knees. "Because you mentioned "Great Balls of Fire.""

"Great Balls of Fire?" Jess had forgotten about the 45, about blurting out the song title when she last saw Martinez. "What does that have to do with anything?"

"We matched the victim to a missing persons report, then confirmed identity through the description of identifying marks."

Jess nodded, though she wasn't sure why.

He expounded, "The report includes a description of scars and tattoos."

Jess nodded again, though if there was something she was supposed to understand, some subtext, it was lost on her.

"The John Doe had a wife." Martinez paused like he was waiting for the significance of all this to soak into Jess's head. "You mentioned the silver watch and the gold wedding band. The watch was her wedding present to her husband, and she'd had it engraved, so it was described in the report."

"Oh...he wanted us to know he has a wife," Jess said it softly, more to herself than Martinez. "I don't really know what stuff means when I see it." She paused. "Did you come out here just to tell me he has a wife?"

"I asked his wife if 'Great Balls of Fire' meant anything to her."

Jess sat up straighter and once again became aware of Martinez studying her.

"He had a juke box. His prized possession, apparently. He restored it himself, and the first record he put in it was 'Great Balls of Fire.' They danced to it ten times that night."

"Oh, wow…" Jess fell back against the cushions on her couch. "God, that's so sad."

"Sad?"

"It seems to me the most tragic death is one that parts true love." Bonnie and John Sykes came to mind, and Jess made a mental note to write that down and use it in the book.

"Hmm. You might be right, Ms. Vernon." He stood up from his chair. "I won't take up any more of your morning." He walked to the door and Jess followed to see him out. Martinez turned around before entering the vestibule. "I'd like you to come with me to the junk shop, see if you can pick up anything else."

"Now?"

His phone rang. Martinez held up a finger to pause their conversation. "Excuse me." He stepped away from Jess while he answered the call. "Investigator Martinez." The call was brief. "I have to go translate for a domestic disturbance call. Can I phone you later to set up a time?"

Jess stood inside the screen door with Shakti wedged between her legs and watched Investigator Martinez leave. Shakti's wagging tail swatted Jess's calves until Martinez disappeared on Haug Drive.

"Oh, crap." Jess realized what she'd just agreed to do.

Jess's chest felt tight with anxiety. She'd never tried to see before. The things she saw just came to her, usually when she wasn't expecting them. If she failed, then what? Would Martinez think she's a fraud? Would that be a bad thing? She wasn't interested in police work or notoriety. Only a select few people even knew about her ability. "Does Dave know?" she whispered to Beckett. They walked up the River Road from the studio to the junk shop. Jess wanted to hold Beckett's hand, but thought it inappropriate in front of Martinez.

"Know what?"

"About this. About me."

"I haven't told him, if that's what you're asking, but I think he's going to find out now."

"Nervous, Ms. Vernon?"

Jess looked across Beckett at Martinez. His eyes were hidden by his sunglasses, which was just as well right now. His expression seemed friendly, maybe even supportive, but Jess couldn't help feeling like something was riding on this show, *her* show, but nobody would tell her what. "What do you want me to do exactly?"

Martinez shrugged. "Whatever it is you do. Just let me know if you see or sense anything else. Even if you don't think it's important, I want to hear about it."

Jess climbed the steps onto the porch of the junk shop. Martinez knocked on Skipper's door on the other side of the porch. It took a couple of long minutes for Skipper to open it, minutes in which Jess began wishing she'd never told Martinez what she saw. Beckett's hand found hers and gave it a squeeze. She looked to him and found reassurance. She wanted to kiss him and push her fingers into his hair, tuck it back behind his ears, but the presence of Martinez stopped her. Every action fell under his subtle scrutiny, and maybe because she was an observer of people herself, Jess was keenly aware of being watched.

Skipper tripped on his own doorsill coming onto the porch in bare feet. He wore a pair of baggy shorts with some kind of sauce staining the thigh and a t-shirt that had likewise seen better days. He fumbled with his keys at the door to the junk shop, then swung it open with unnecessary force. "There," he said. "There." He looked at Jess, meeting her eyes for only a millisecond, then shifting his gaze to her chin, her chest, her hands. "What are you doing in there?"

"Looking."

"Skipper, you all right?" Beckett asked.

Skipper rubbed at the red and gray hairs on his cheeks, enough growth to suggest he hadn't shaved since finding the body. "Sure. Sure I am."

"Give Dave a call. Tell him I said he can close up the hardware store early and come over here. Or you can go sit with him there."

"Yeah, yeah. Thanks, Beckett." Skipper turned and retreated to his home, shoulders sloping forward, one hand gripping his keys, the other opening and closing like some kind of hyper-nervous tick. They waited for Skipper's door to shut before entering the junk shop.

"Ugh," Jess put her hand to her nose.

"What is it?" Detective Martinez asked.

"Just the smell in here." After they spent the day cleaning up the shop, Skipper had brought in a bunch of air fresheners and set them out, each tub of gel fully open, then closed the doors again. Chemical perfumes hung thick in the air and scratched the back of Jess's throat. "Let's get the doors open. This stuff is going to choke me."

"Agreed." Beckett propped open the front door, then went through to the back door.

"Wow. You really went to work in here." Martinez stood with his hands on his hips, surveying the front room. Much of the junk had been hauled to the dump and what remained had been organized on recently washed shelves. With so much clutter gone, Jess could see that most of the wares were common household items, including decor from the 1950s, 60s, and 70s. The kitschy retro stuff could actually earn Skipper some cash if he put out a sign and got tourists to come inside.

Jess walked through the middle room, which had been equally transformed thanks to Dave's industrious organization, and into the back room, followed closely by Martinez. Beckett sat waiting on a barstool he'd used to prop the back door open. What Jess saw in that back room made her stop and reverse in her tracks, bumping into Investigator Martinez.

He put his hands on her shoulders to steady her. "What is it?"

Jess looked at Beckett, sitting across the room framed by a square of blue sky. He looked back at her with an expression of concern and curiosity, and she wished she could be normal like him, could be unaware of the man sitting in the corner. "He's here," she whispered.

"Okay." Martinez loosened his hold on her shoulders and patted them before removing his hands completely. "That's fine. What's he doing? Does he see us?"

The man sat on a small chair in the corner, his forearms resting across his legs, shoulders slumped forward, head hung down. His hands, which should have hung limply inside his knees, were missing. The man lifted his face slowly to look Jess in the eyes. His eyes were red-rimmed, the left one bloodshot and glazed over, his right one clouded as though by a cataract. His head had a large dent in it over the right eye, the hair matted with blood. As he stared at Jess, a trickle of blood emerged from his hairline. She watched it run down his forehead, then follow the slope of the brow around the eye and continue its path over the cheekbone downward to the jaw.

The man sprang off his chair, launching himself at Jess, waving his arms. His face stretched into a roar of agony. Jess ducked and covered her head with her arms. Blood from his severed wrists sprayed her. And then he was gone.

The room was now still, sticky hot, and sickly sweet with the smell of too many air fresheners. Someone touched Jess and she jumped. Beckett stood in front of her, his hand on her arm. Martinez had remained right behind her. They both looked perplexed and concerned. Small droplets of blood marked the Investigator's brow and cheek. Jess rubbed at her own forehead and cheeks, wiping anywhere she might have felt the splat of liquid against her skin.

"Ms. Vernon?"

"Um…" She wanted to tell him to wipe off his face or reach up and do it for him. "Let's go to the studio." Jess brushed past Beckett and out the back door. She paused to close her eyes, lift her face to the heat of the sun, and breathe deeply.

"What are you doing?" Skipper stood at the other end of the back porch.

Beckett and Martinez joined Jess. "Oh, there you are," Martinez said to Skipper. "Thank you, you can lock up again." Martinez went around Jess and off the porch. She hurried after him to spare herself the need to answer Skipper's question.

Beckett checked his watch as they entered the studio and flipped his sign from "Back soon" to "Closed." There was no point in staying open on a Sunday evening for a straggler or two. "Want a beer?"

"Just water for me," Martinez said.

"Jess?"

"Glass of wine, please."

Martinez followed Beckett into the kitchen and helped by carrying his water to the table. Beckett handed Jess her wine glass and they sat in the booth across from Martinez.

"Tell me what happened in there."

"He was crazed. Full of rage. It was like…" She paused to sip her wine and look at Martinez' face just to make sure the blood spatter wasn't really there. "I don't know. There was so much hostility."

"The man was just murdered," Beckett said.

"But it wasn't that. This was out of control and directionless. Or not directionless, but *pointless*. It felt like he wanted to kill me, but for no reason other than I was there in front of him."

"Do you think the guy has issues with anger?" Martinez asked.

Jess considered, shook her head. "No. More like the rage was something that was done to him." She looked at Martinez. "But that doesn't make any sense."

"You know who this man is," Beckett said, "did he have anger management issues?"

"As far as we know, he was a great guy. I've talked to my share of bereaved spouses, and his wife sure seems like the real deal."

Jess looked out the window at the dirt yard behind the livery. She wished she had a view of the river from here.

"There's something else," she said, looking back at Martinez. "When I saw the body before, I saw his hands. One of them anyway, the left one that was up by his head. The right was tucked beside his body where I couldn't see it. But today...it doesn't make any sense...his hands were gone."

"Gone?" Beckett said.

"Chopped off, I suppose. He just didn't have hands."

"Well, I'll be damned." Martinez took a deep breath and leaned back against the booth. "You're for real, aren't you, Ms. Vernon?"

Jess sat on the edge of the bed rubbing lotion into her calves and feet. Her long hair fell wet against her bare back and, for the first time all day, she felt comfortably cool. Beckett lay in the bed beside her, while Shakti snored on the floor under the open window, stretched out and belly up. "What do you think he meant by I'm the real deal?" Jess said as she slid into position at Beckett's side and rested her head on his chest.

"I suppose..." Beckett moved her wet hair back from his shoulder while he talked, "he meant that today was a test. He wanted to know if you're a fraud. Some kind of thrill-seeker trying to get in the middle of his investigation."

"Would people really do that?"

"And then some."

Jess moved her fingertips through Beckett's chest hair. With her head resting in the nook of his shoulder the hairs were at eye-level, magnified, with each hair an individual strand to be inspected. As blond as the hair on his head, he hardly looked like he had chest hair at a distance or in certain light. Jess liked the process of learning his body these last few months. Bodies were their own language, communicating secrets to those privileged enough to be intimate, exposed to another's vulnerability.

Jess and Beckett pressed their bodies together, arms wrapped around each other. Beckett's hand moved down Jess's back to hold her, draw her closer. She put a hand in his hair and smoothed it back on his head. She loved feeling the smooth strands lift and flow between her fingers. She nestled her nose against his neck and found his scent comforting, like oatmeal sweetened with brown sugar...

"Oh my God." She lifted her head off his chest.

"What?" Beckett looked at Jess, his brow, at first pinched with concern, opened in surprised disbelief. "Don't tell me that guy is here."

"No, he's not here." Jess reached for the sheet and quickly drew it up over their bodies.

"Then what's going on?"

"Hello, Jess," Isabella said while keeping her delighted eyes on Beckett's backside.

"Shit." Jess covered her face in her hands. "You can't be here."

"Jess?"

"Not you," Jess put a hand on Beckett's arm, "but cover your butt, would you?"

"Jess."

"We have a visitor. She's only eight years old."

Beckett searched the room, looking over both shoulders. "I don't see any girls in here."

"She's..." Jess mouthed the words, "a spirit. I don't think she knows it though."

"For fuck's sake."

Isabella gasped and clapped both hands over her mouth, then giggled delightedly. Her smooth braids hung in front of her shoulders with the blue ribbons dancing like butterflies when she laughed.

"Beckett, please," Jess groaned. "She's a child. Watch your mouth."

Beckett threw the sheet completely back and stepped out of the bed, leaving Jess scrambling to re-cover herself with the linens.

"Okay. I know you're upset, but could you please just cover up so we can talk about this."

"No. I will not cover up for some kid I can't even see." He walked around the bed, his arms held out to better display his nakedness. Isabella's smile grew so big her hands couldn't conceal it. Jess rolled her eyes.

Shakti woke and jumped up to see what the fun was about. She wagged her tail and was about to jump at Beckett when she noticed Isabella across the room. Her tail straightened and the hairs between her shoulder blades stood up. Shakti growled at their guest from deep in her throat.

Isabella's mirth disappeared and then so did she.

Beckett spun around to look where Shakti pointed. He'd no more than turned and Shakti was already wagging her tail and licking his knee. Beckett patted her head and moved her away from his leg. "What just happened?"

"She disappeared when Shakti growled at her."

"Great. The dog can see her, too." Beckett walked back around the bed, picked up his shorts and pulled them on.

"Beckett, can we talk about this?"

"I just want to relax and sleep and make love with you without an audience. Is that asking too much?"

"No, but…" Jess wasn't sure of her objection and trailed off.

"But what?"

"I don't know. I don't really know what's possible. It's all so new."

He yanked his t-shirt down over his chest and patted the pockets of his shorts, checking for his keys and wallet. Beckett stopped at the door to the bedroom and threw up his hands. "Jess. It's the bedroom. The bedroom." He pushed his hands through his hair, shook his head, and sighed. "I don't want to sleep here with that…her… Look, do you want to come back to my place?"

Chapter Thirteen

JESS AND BECKETT agreed that a night apart wouldn't hurt them. They could sleep and wake to a new day in their own beds. Before Jess could sleep, however, she had to slow the wheels in her head. To help the process, she poured a Bailey's on the rocks and went onto the porch. For company, she brought Isabella's diary. She settled into a rocker and sipped her drink. Bright stars and a nearly-full moon lit the yard. A large raccoon lumbered out of the barn's shadow and crossed her driveway, one of her lodgers. A bat swooped, its dark wings beating the night air. She watched another bat sweep her sky for insects, pleased to have such neighbors. She hadn't read much of the diary, and now she wondered if Isabella knew that she'd be able to come with the book when she gave it to Jess. Had Grace known? Is that why she left the diary behind when her family moved to Chicago? Shakti whined inside the house; Jess had crated her so that she could have a moment of peace.

It is at last warm enough to shed our coats and hats, though a shawl is still recommended in the mornings and evenings. The sun, my glorious friend, remains far enough to the south that it takes most of the day to warm our little village, and then the heat quickly disperses. Mother complains bitterly of the damp. The snow has all melted finally, but it rains plenty. The ground is soaked. All that damp, she says, settles in her bones and makes her ache. She had a terrible fever when she was a girl and contracted the roomatik. Some mornings she cannot even remove a lid from a jar, her hands are so stiff. Poor Mama. Karna and I always try to be the first to please Mother on those days by opening the jars for her. She says, Oh my, what would I ever do without my big strong girls? I do not mind the weather one bit. As long as there is some sunshine and I am able to get out into it, I am happy. Father has begun calling me Duckling because of it.

Karna said I have a bow, because I shared my slate with Tomas during arithmetic, and then Papa saw fit to tease me throughout supper. He was not being mean hearted, but I did not enjoy the teasing anyway. To give Karna what was hers, I went out across the railroad tracks and into the marsh. I took a jar with me and collected some pretty little frogs. They are only as big as the tip of my thumb, and they are so plentiful you can hardly walk without stepping on them. The ground is very soft from all the rain and I do not believe stepping on them kills them, but only pats them down into the mud. With so many frogs about, it was an easy task to collect a few.

They are green with spotted backs. Those in my jar hardly make any noise at all, but the rest of them together in the marsh constantly sing to each other. My teacher, Miss Frederickson, calls them a chorus of peepers, but I thought a chorus made music. The frogs I heard only make noise. Still, it must be a song to them, for Papa says beauty is in the eye of the beholden.

I slipped one of my little frogs into Karna's porridge. I believe at first she thought it was only another raisin or lump of sugar. Then it moved its tiny arms and legs, swimming to the top of her mush. I swear it looked up at her. Karna screamed!

It was so funny I fell out of my chair for laughing.

Father did not think it so funny. Nor did Mother.

Father made me collect my frogs and take them back to the marsh where they might rejoin their friends. When I came home again, he was waiting for me with his pipe between his teeth even though it was before noon. He paddled me for what I had done, as much for the sake of the frogs as for Karna, I believe, because Father is awfully fond of all of God's creatures. He only used his hand and not the belt, which is why I can still laugh about it when I think of Karna screaming at the breakfast table over a tiny little frog in her porridge!

"Beckett," Jess called out to him as she entered the studio. They hadn't spoken all day, not even a text, which was unusual. But their night had been unusual, and Jess figured she would give him some down time to process the latest event in their life together—a ghost child in the bedroom. She would find it disturbing herself if she didn't know and like Isabella. "Beckett?" She found him behind the studio loading his brick kiln. Jess stood next to the wheeled cart full of bisqued and glazed pots, waiting for him to acknowledge her. He glanced at her, flashing a quick smile and a hello, before lifting a large urn off his cart and positioning it carefully inside the brick structure. A bandana tied over his head kept his hair away from his face, and he reached up to rub sweat from the back of his neck.

"You look a little red back there." The late afternoon sun hung high beyond the river and Beckett had full exposure out here. Jess put a hand on his neck and gently touched the pink. Something felt wrong—not wrong, changed—but she didn't know what, then Beckett leaned in to her and they kissed hello. She forgot all about the sense she had of something changed. "Are these for the show?" She looked at the pots, mostly large works, some with odd shapes or cut-outs, not your average serving dish.

"About last night. Jess…"

Jess held her breath. She'd been hoping they could move past last night without an actual discussion, not the mature way about it, she knew, but easy.

"I've thought about it all day. I'm not comfortable with ghosts in the bedroom," he paused to sigh heavily, "but if my choice is you plus your friends or not you, I'll just have to learn to live with them, too."

Jess threw her arms around Beckett's neck. "Oh, thank God. I wasn't sure which way that was going."

"Really?" His smile broadened, his eyes brightened.

Jess lifted her chin and kissed him. "That makes me happy," she said softly, "very happy." She put a hand to his temple and slid the bandana off his head so she could slide her fingers through his hair.

"What..?" Jess stared at him. "Where's your hair?"

Beckett's new hairstyle, if there was one, had been flattened under his bandana and plastered to his sweaty scalp. Jess grabbed his shoulders and turned him away from her to get a look at it. The back of his neck was clean, the sideburns short. She pushed her fingers through the hair on the top of his head and lifted, raising no more than an inch and a half of length.

"What brought this on?" she asked.

"I needed a change." He shrugged. "It was impulsive, I know."

"But why?" Jess stared at him, her expression belying her dismay.

"I get restless and mix things up sometimes. I guess it's because sudden changes to my appearance annoyed my mother."

"Oh. Were you trying to annoy me?"

"No, Jess." He chuckled. "It's a thing I do and I'm not used to anyone caring, not since I was a kid. That's all."

"Where'd you go?"

"Lora cuts my hair."

"Lora Zabrowski?"

"She used to be a stylist. She's cut my hair for ages."

Jess reached up to touch his hair again, but hesitated and then withdrew her hand.

"Hey…it's just a haircut."

"I know," she said, "but I liked your hair long."

Beckett looked at Jess like he didn't know what to say. "I just wanted a change, Jess."

"Yeah, okay. I'm going to Red Wing for groceries. Want me to bring you anything?"

Jess called Chandra from her car as she wound northward along the river. "It's just a haircut," she said, echoing Beckett.

"Then why does it bother you, Jess?"

"His ex cut his hair."

"That's an ouch."

"So it's not just me?" Jess had to shout to be heard through the microphone in the roof of her car. "This is foreign territory. I got *married* at twenty-three, you know? What do I know about dating?"

Almost nothing. She married the first guy she fell for at what now seemed an impossibly young age, which meant her entire adulthood had been spent learning to read one set of reactions, developing one set of coping skills. She wasn't sure how to tell Beckett the haircut thing bothered her, let alone why, because she *really* liked him. She knew things with Mitch had been terminally screwed up, and Jess couldn't imagine a worse mistake than judging Beckett's actions by her knowledge of Mitch's myriad motivations, most of which were manipulative, if not malicious. If Mitch had suddenly chopped off his hair, knowing Jess liked it long, it would only have been to hurt her. Of course, he would have claimed, like Beckett, that it was *only* a haircut.

"What should I do?" she asked Chandra.

"Sleep on it. If you're still bothered in a few days, figure out why."

Jess nodded as she signaled her turn toward the Mississippi.

"And Jess," Chandra said, "you were wise to not react now. Acting like he's Mitch would only get you in trouble."

Jess let her screen door slam and bounce against its frame behind her as she hauled groceries through to the kitchen. She let Shakti out of her crate, then stood in her entryway and called, "Isabella! Isabella, show yourself."

A breeze brushed Jess's cheek and she heard the lilt of Isabella's giggle.

"I'm not playing, Isabella. I need to talk to you." Isabella stepped out of the corner of her living room, as though emerging from a shadow, except there were no shadows this time of day with windows drawing light from every side of the house. Shakti pressed into Jess's leg, a growl not quite emerging. "There you are." Jess sighed and approached the little spirit. "Isabella…"

"Are you angry with me?" She lowered her eyelids as though the thought of Jess's disapproval were too much for her to bear.

"Not really, but we need to have some rules. You can't just turn up when I have guests. I'm sure your mother and father had rules, like knocking before you entered their room."

Isabella nodded. She laced her fingers together and let her hands rest before her hips. Her head hung. She sniffed.

"What's wrong?" Jess wanted to put an arm around her shoulder, but of course it would be futile, awkward, and creepy.

"I miss my parents. And my sister. But mostly my parents."

Jess sat on her couch and patted the cushion beside her. Shakti jumped up and curled into a ball against Jess, but kept her head lifted, her eyes on Isabella. "Have you considered that they might not be coming back? Maybe they're waiting for you somewhere."

Isabella tilted her head the same way Shakti did when puzzled by something. "What do you mean?" Her green eyes seemed piercingly bright.

"Only that they've been gone an awfully long time, haven't they?"

"They…"

The door bell cut Isabella's reply short and she vanished. Shakti jumped off the couch and trotted to the spot where the girl had been to sniff the area thoroughly, her ears lifted. "Let me know what you figure out, Bear," Jess said as she got up from the couch.

Investigator Martinez and his partner, Investigator Johnson, stood on the other side of Jess's screen door. "I wasn't expecting you, was I?" She opened the door to admit the men, and Shakti rushed forward to crowd the vestibule. Jess grabbed her collar and backed them both inside the house so the men could come forward.

Martinez knelt to greet Shakti while Johnson held back. "She's harmless," Jess said. "All tongue."

"I have allergies." Johnson had a stiffness to him—stiff collar, stiff upper lip, stiff handshake. Jess figured if they ever played good cop-bad cop, he was the bad cop. Shakti rubbed happily on Martinez' pant leg while he scratched her ears. "Martinez, you're going to bring all that dog hair into the car with you," Johnson complained.

"I'm sorry. We can talk outside," Jess offered.

"He's allergic to outside, too," Martinez said with a smirk in his voice.

"Well, can I get you something?"

Jess poured them all a glass of iced tea while Shakti whined in her crate. She couldn't decide if Johnson was watching her or if she was imagining it.

He hardly seemed the type to be pro-psychic, and she wasn't all that eager to let more people in on her secret. If he didn't know about her visit to the crime scene with his partner, she didn't want to be the one to inform him of Martinez' extracurricular activities. "What can I do for you?" she asked as they sat around her dining room table.

"We have some questions for you about Tyler Cross," Johnson said.

"What does Tyler have to do with this?"

"Probably nothing," Martinez said, "but we have to be certain one way or the other."

Good cop, Jess thought. "Why would he be connected to the man in the junk shop?"

"The man is Daniel Grunner. His car was found in Winona."

"Winona?" Jess said. Winona was about fifty miles south and across the river in Minnesota.

"Yeah," Martinez said, "that's what we thought."

Johnson all but rolled his eyes. "Dan sells restaurant supplies. He had papers in his trunk showing that he'd met with Mr. Cross the day he was killed."

Recognition set in.

"Do you know something about this, Ms. Vernon?"

She looked across the table at Investigator Johnson. Her gaze moved up the length of his striped tie to the razor burn above his shirt collar. "I went by the café earlier that day. I saw Tyler and another man sitting at a table with brochures and stuff between them."

"Did he seem agitated in any way?" Martinez asked.

Jess shook her head. "He was just looking at brochures. I didn't want to bother them, so I didn't stick around." She looked from Johnson to Martinez. "You don't think he's got something to do with the murder?"

"It's too early to say that," Martinez said.

"But you *might* think it."

"You think he doesn't?" Johnson asked.

"There's no way Tyler killed that man." She felt Martinez reading her.

"Your boyfriend," Johnson pulled a slim notebook out of his breast pocket and flipped the cover open, "Beckett Hanley, stated that Mr. Cross struck you at a party in front of the entire village." He lifted his eyes from his notebook to stare at Jess over his untouched glass of tea.

Jess waited to see what direction he would take this. When Johnson seemed unlikely to say more, she prompted him, "And?"

"That's true?" Martinez asked.

"You just said the whole village witnessed it."

"Do you still maintain Mr. Cross could not have murdered Mr. Grunner?"

"Yes." Jess took a drink of her tea then wiped the moisture from the outside of her glass onto the leg of her shorts. "Tyler is a veteran with PTSD. Did Beckett tell you that? I startled him and he swung before he realized it was me. That's all it was."

"Is that how you got that scar under your eye?" Johnson asked.

Jess kept her hands in her lap. Had he really spotted that on his own, or did Beckett tell him about it? "Have you met Tyler and Bruno?"

"Bruno?"

"I guess not." She reminded herself not to be snarky or defensive, though it may have already been too late. "Bruno is his service dog. Tyler's got Bruno now and his issue is under control."

"Really?" Johnson wrote something in his notebook.

"Really." Jess looked at Martinez. His face was an impasse and his glass was sweating all over her tabletop. Jess stood up and turned to the buffet in the wall behind her. She grabbed a couple of placemats and put them down, then moved their glasses on top of them. It felt good to move out from under their critical gazes, even for a few seconds.

Martinez had a drink of his tea while Jess settled back into her chair. "Ms. Vernon," he said, "the bartender at The Two Wheeler said Mr. Cross and Mr. Hanley got into a fist fight that same evening."

"Beckett threw the first punch," Jess said, "so that hardly makes Tyler guilty of murder."

"Do you know what this fight was about?" Johnson asked.

"Yeah." Jess decided to look at Martinez instead of Johnson. "It was about me."

Chapter Fourteen

JESS PULLED OPEN the screen door and hesitated. A sort of last all-systems-check before crossing the threshold. She tested the air coming from inside the junk shop, and while it didn't exactly smell fresh, the stench of rotting corpse—she'd had no idea how bad that stink was, or how it would lodge in her memory like some olfactory nightmare—had at least cleared out and the sickly sweet stink of air fresheners had mostly dissipated. When she focused her attention, she heard her heart thrumming in her chest like some binaural beat. She reminded herself to breathe before commanding her feet to take the next step.

"Jess." Skipper sounded surprised to see her. He sat on a folding chair at his counter, a tabletop fan in industrial silver with a wire cage you could stick a fist through hummed behind him. His cheeks were characteristically red and sweat trickled down his brow.

"Hi, Skipper. I thought I'd check out your wares." She forced herself to smile, though she wasn't sure it would affect her reception one way or another.

"Go ahead." Jess stepped away from the counter. "Wait," Skipper said. "Do you want a Mountain Dew? I got cold ones." He held up his open can with one hand and pointed at a mini fridge on the floor in the corner with the other.

"No thanks." Jess's smile was genuine this time, figuring it took real effort for Skipper to be hospitable. She went into the middle room and browsed the shelves for a minute, recognizing Dave's handiwork. He must have spent hours in here, organizing everything into categories. A display of pink glass dishes, a full luncheon set from the looks of it, had a place of prominence in front of the window, which had been cleaned. Sunlight caused the glassware to shine becomingly. Jess lifted a coffee cup to find a price tag on the bottom. Five dollars for the single cup. That would make the set...a lot. Apparently Dave had also spent some time online to figure out the value of Skipper's stock.

The back of Jess's neck prickled and a chill ran the length of her spine. She set the coffee cup back on its saucer with a soft clink and turned to face the third room. The light on the other side of the doorway had an orange hue. Jess's mind told her it was the sunlight coming in from the west, then reminded her that was only wishful thinking: dusk was hours away. Her feet moved her forward before she meant them to and she stood in the murder room, waiting for something to happen.

The back door opened and night flooded the room. Jess felt suddenly claustrophobic, as though the shadows bound her where she stood. A young woman stumbled through the doorway and looked around, an anxious expression pinned atop layers of mascara and red lipstick, the shade Chandra liked to call fuck-me-red. "We're here," she called. Jess glanced over her shoulder, expecting—as did the girl—someone to step out of the darkness and greet her.

Dan Grunner came inside, holding his head in his hands. He said something, but his words sounded garbled. *What are we doing here?* Jess thought. The room spun around and she was behind Dan, seeing it over his shoulder, seeing the girl's back, her tight ass in the tiny skirt, her bra closure through the flimsy top she wore... No. Jess wasn't seeing over his shoulder. She was seeing through him. Her heart beat in her ears like it had been bottled, each thump echoing against the glass chamber.

The echo wasn't an echo. It was another heartbeat.

Jess's head throbbed painfully and she gripped her temples. Her vision blurred, edges became fuzzy, features less distinguishable, but she could still get around. *The girl did this. That little bitch.* Jess took a step forward and the girl backed away, teasing now like she'd been teasing all night. It didn't matter before, because she wasn't interested. But now. Now it made her angry and…something else. "We're here," the girl said again. Jess moved closer, followed the girl around a center island of crap. She put her hand out to stabilize herself and the mound she touched shifted, sliding away from her fingers and clattering to the floor around her feet. Jess looked down and saw a bunch of 45s, some out of their paper sleeves. It always amazed her, the ability to record sound and play it back. She took another step and heard the crack of a record under her heel. She stooped to pick it up and held it inches from her nose. "Great Balls of Fire," she liked that one.

"Just wait," the girl pleaded. She had backed herself into a corner.

"Wait for what?" her words sounded under water. "You brought me here, April. Why did you bring me here?"

The girl was crying now, her mascara staining her face with black tears. She didn't think the girl was pretty, but that didn't preclude a little fun. Jess grabbed her by both arms and pulled her in. She seemed slight. A little piece of nothing. Like a tissue to be used and discarded. May stared up at Jess, her mouth a lopsided O of shock. Her eyes wide with terror, made even wider by the rings of black. Jess pulled her up onto her tiptoes and mashed her mouth against April's. The stupid little girl didn't even know how to kiss. She kept her mouth open and their teeth clattered against each other unpleasantly. Jess kept one hand on the girl and put the other one over her brow and pressed, smoothing her hand back over the girl's head the way one would pet a dog. "You're so…" She looked at the girl's face and had never been confronted by such fear before. It was amusing really. "…stupid. You're just a stupid, mousy, little girl playing grown-up people's games, aren't you?" April sobbed and pulled against Jess's grasp, but she held tight. "Want to grow up? I can show you a grown-up game." Jess reached for her fly and tried to slip the metal button at the top of her jeans through its hole. April jerked herself away from Jess's grasp before even that small task had been carried out. But no matter, it only prolonged the game.

The girl faced the wall of shelving and scrambled upwards. *Where does she think she's going?* Jess reached out a hand, mischievous glee rising so fast it was all she could do to suppress her laughter. She noticed the watch and the ring, or some part of her did, but the noticing wasn't enough to stop her teasing this girl, this…month. Jess stroked the inside of her thigh, moving her finger upward along that soft flesh until it tucked under the hem of that itty-bitty skirt.

"No!"

"Jessica?"

Jess spun around. Skipper stood in the doorway between rooms, his eyes perhaps as wide as hers. He gripped the doorframe so tightly the tips of his fingers were white. Jess stared at his chewed up fingernails while she collected herself.

"I'm sorry," she said. "Did I scare you?"

Skipper nodded. "You sounded scared."

"Oh." Jess pushed her hair back from her face. "I was thinking about that man. I guess I scared myself." She faked a chuckle.

Skipper continued to stare at her as though nothing she said would affect his determination of the situation, which made pretense seem suddenly foolish. The silence grew uncomfortable, and Jess was about to excuse herself, however awkwardly, when Skipper said, "I feel him, too."

Jess left the junk shop and turned toward town. She strode downhill past The Two Wheeler and the creamery. Her first impulse was to head to the studio, but she changed her mind. She wasn't ready to talk about what had happened. She needed to think somewhere she could be alone. When she reached the intersection, she looked toward the park and saw it was busy with people picnicking and fishing, so she crossed the River Road and headed up Main Street. She knew one place she was likely to be undisturbed. The one-room building with the Village Hall placard above the door seldom drew visitors.

It served as the local museum and hadn't changed much since Jess's first childhood trip along the Great River Road. The displays included faded photographs, newspaper clippings, and the discards of various long-gone residents. A steel plow with wooden handles and an ox harness hung over a sawhorse filled one corner. A dais with a sturdy oak lectern, probably original, held an old family Bible open to the frontispiece where a large branching tree had been printed with lines over each limb. Faded brown script labeled most of the branches. The oldest entry, positioned on the trunk of the tree like the Adam and Eve of this particular family, read Fredrick og Ase Adolvsson, Kalmar, 1848. Jess had always been drawn to pieces of the past. She stood next to the wicker doll carriage and wax-head lady doll that had belonged to Isabella. She picked up Isabella's doll, ignoring the DO

NOT TOUCH placards all over the one-room museum, and smoothed the skirt front, which had developed a crease across the lap from sitting up in the carriage for so many years, looked at but unloved.

Jess sat on the edge of the dais, holding the doll, stroking its dress and examining the tiny fingers and painted nails. She thought about what she'd seen in the junk shop. Dan Grunner and that girl. The way he touched her while she tried to climb the shelves.

Jess took out her phone.

While it rang, Jess turned her head to search the corners of the room, realizing that if Isabella could visit her house via the diary, what would prevent her from coming to this place via the doll? As if summoned, Jess felt a cool breath of air across her cheek and heard Isabella's soft giggle.

The girl stood beside the doll carriage, her green eyes shining. She appeared more solid, if that was possible.

"Hello?"

"Investigator Martinez? It's Jessica Vernon." She kept her eyes on Isabella. "I have information that I believe proves Tyler Cross had nothing to do with Dan Grunner's murder."

A couple of Harleys, a Goldwing, and Martinez' black Taurus were parked in front of The Two Wheeler when Jess arrived. The hogs, she assumed, belonged to the men lounging on the front porch. Half helmets rested next to beer bottles on the table and a couple of denim jackets lay over the back of a chair. These guys at least had a modicum of self-preservation. The bigger of the two winked at Jess, a playful grin on his lips. Caught scrutinizing and judging, she hoped her blush hadn't fully bloomed before getting inside.

Martinez stood at the bar, talking to Jake, whose mustache had been waxed out and then up, forming right angles at the bend, à la Salvador Dali. Jess greeted them and asked for water.

Martinez carried a can of Sprite away from the bar. "Now tell me exactly what you saw."

"Here or in the junk shop?"

"Start with here."

They sat at a table and Jess walked Martinez through the events of the evening. She and Chandra playing darts. Chandra's sucky throws and her dart bouncing off the board and landing under the table. Jess stooping down to retrieve the dart and seeing those ridiculous high heels, the shaving cut on the ankle, the pale legs and miniskirt.

"Ms. Vernon," Martinez stopped her, "that's a great description of her legs, but did you see her face by any chance?"

"Yes, and call me Jess."

"Jess, what did her face look like?"

Jess picked up a paper coaster with the bar's logo on it, a drawing of a chopper, the rider holding out a beer glass, his ZZ Top-style beard flowing behind him to suggest motion. Not exactly a campaign for responsible drinking, but it suited the place. Jess turned it over in her fingers while she considered how honest to be.

"Problem?" Martinez asked.

Jess looked at him. He sat with his forearms resting on the table so his upper arms had just enough flexion to look firm against the ribbed cuff of his shirt. He wasn't a big man, but Jess doubted he carried more than an ounce of fat. His expression said he had all day, though she knew that wasn't true. *Good cop.* She decided to be totally honest, even if it meant she wasn't as much of a help as she wanted to be with Tyler's freedom—or worse, his sanity—on the line. "I did see her face here in the bar, but that was a week ago and I wasn't paying that much attention to her." Martinez nodded for her to continue. "Chandra and I joked that we didn't know Skoghall was big enough to support a prostitute, because she was dressed..." Jess stopped short of saying the word she was thinking.

"Slutty. You can just say what you mean, Jess."

She nodded, thankful Investigator Johnson wasn't here to take her statement as well. Was that what she was doing? Giving a statement? Or just talking? "She was young. Mousy hair, pulled back. Too much make-up. Skinny."

"Okay, and the girl you saw in the junk shop?"

Jess flipped the coaster against the table top, sliding its edge between her fingers, until she noticed Martinez watching her hands. She laid the coaster flat and pulled her hands into her lap. "I don't know if I can describe her any better, but I think I'd recognize her if I saw her again."

"That's a good start. We can place Dan and the young lady at the bar here, so maybe someone else noticed them, too." Martinez stood and headed back to the bar. Jess followed him. "Jake," he called.

Jake came out of the back carrying two cases of beer stacked on top of each other and set them down with a grunt.

"Do you remember seeing a young lady here that night, maybe looking for someone to pick up? Or drinking with a guy who's not one of your usual types?"

"Yep." He nodded at Jess.

Jess was about to object.

"Oh," Jake said with a wink, "you mean besides her and her friend?" Jess leaned onto the bar, directing a scowl at Jake. "Well…" he said, "you and your friend might not have been looking for trouble, but I remember a punch being thrown in your direction."

Jess's cheeks flushed with heat. "Sorry about that," she mumbled.

Jake reached under the bar and set a small digital camera in front of Martinez. "Old barman's trick," he said. "Not too old, I guess, since these things haven't been around all that long, but…" he trailed off as he flipped the camera over and powered on the view screen. "Whenever I get a funny feeling about someone, or if trouble breaks out, I'm ready for it." He flipped to an image and turned the screen toward Jess and Martinez, a grin lifting the sides of his mustache. Jess looked in horror at an image of Beckett and Tyler. Tyler was laid across the table, and Beckett gripped his sore knuckles in his non-punching hand. Despite being a grainy low-light image, it left no doubt who threw the first punch. "I snapped that right before I grabbed my bat and jumped the bar," Jake explained.

Jess hadn't noticed a flash going off or Jake jumping over the bar—also not surprising. She leaned closer to the camera and squinted until she found herself in the image, tucked behind Beckett with her hands over her mouth.

"Now this," Jake scrolled back a picture or two and held the camera up again, "is a legitimate ID, but the girl carrying it gave me a funny feeling." A photo of a Wisconsin driver's license filled the screen. It belonged to the twenty-one-year-old Carla Stanley.

Chapter Fifteen

THERE WAS SOMETHING Jess didn't understand. Why, if Dan Grunner was such a nice guy, such a loving husband and father, was he attacking the girl from the bar? She wanted to believe the version of him that showed her the wedding ring on his finger and somehow planted "Great Balls of Fire" in her head. But she'd seen him, felt him, *been* him pursuing that girl, reveling in her fear and vulnerability.

The River Road stretched out on a quiet morning. Jess climbed the rise from Main Street, past the old livery and creamery. A car she knew to be Jake's sat on the shoulder in front of The Two Wheeler and another car she didn't recognize was parked just beyond the junk shop. She paused to look up at the shotgun duplex and wondered why someone had built there instead of across the road in town. To be near the river, perhaps, though the trees behind the house blocked the view of the water. Wedged between the road and the train tracks, there was no yard at all. Maybe this was the outer edge of Skoghall's expansion in its heyday, and the lot would surely have been cheap with every freight rattling the walls as it passed. Jess would have to ask Dave how his aunt wound up living in it.

She climbed the steps to the porch and put a hand on the turned wood column supporting the roof. It had the delicate, fussy look of the Victorian decorative aesthetic. Wood bric-a-brac trimmed the corners. Above the porch, protruding from the roof, sat a small dormer with a window big enough for a child's face to peek through. Dormers that served no purpose other than creating the appearance of space that did not actually exist inside the home amused Jess. Decoration was one thing, but adding miniature walls, a window, and extra roofing just to pretend there was a spare room tucked under the roof seemed a waste of building supplies. She pulled the screen door open and entered the junk shop, expecting to find Skipper perched on his stool behind the front counter.

He wasn't there.

She listened for signs of life. Someone in the back room set something down on one of the metal shelves with a thunk, then turned and came toward Jess, the floor shifting under his weight. Jess watched the door from the second room to the first, anticipating that it was not Skipper; this movement seemed hard, while everything about Skipper felt soft.

A young man with a ball cap and aviator-style sunglasses obscuring his face came into the front room. Jess held her breath, the muscles in her neck and shoulders tensing. When he came within a couple feet of her, his face converted from an impassive mask to a contemptuous grin. One of his front teeth had broken, the inside corner chipped away, creating a noticeable triangular-shaped gap when he parted his lips. The young man brushed so close to Jess that she leaned back to avoid contact. He pushed the screen door open and went down the steps, then turned up the road and out of sight as the screen door slammed and bounced against its frame.

Jess remembered to breathe again. She shivered, the same reaction she had to seeing a large spider in her house. Jess stared at the screen door, then forced herself to turn away.

She went through to the back room, once again astounded by Dave's handiwork. She circled a small drop leaf table covered in board games from the 1960s and a set of luncheon dishes with a different song bird on each plate. She let her fingers trail objects on the shelves. She expected nothing, but hoped something there would spark some knowing in her and make sense of her riddle.

The screen door opened and closed. Skipper shuffled into the shop and around the counter to sit down with a huff. Jess didn't want to startle him, so she called out as she came forward through the rooms. "Skipper, it's Jessica Vernon."

"Hello, Jessica." He looked at the counter between them. "When did you get here?"

"Just a minute ago." She smiled, but he didn't lift his gaze. "You and Dave did a great job organizing everything. In fact, I think I'd like to buy something."

He looked up, his surprise evident. "What?"

"I saw some cute dishes in back." She excused herself to get them. The kidney shaped plates had circular rims on them for keeping the matching coffee cup from sliding around when a lady carried her plate from the buffet line to the hostess's sofa, a remnant of the era of the happy housewife. Jess could display them in her dining room's glass cabinets. They had the kind of retro charm that would work with her poppy-covered wallpaper.

"I...I don't know how much these are," Skipper said, holding one of the plates up before him and turning it over several times.

"How about twenty for the set?" Jess winced when he put the plate down on the counter with a loud clink. "Do you have some newspaper to wrap them in?"

Skipper bent down behind the counter and when he rose, he held a large plastic bag stuffed with wads of old newspaper. Jess uncrumpled a sheet and sought out the date at the top of the page: 1999.

"You know, Skipper, with this place all cleaned up, you could really do some business. Maybe you should put a sign along the road so people know to stop here."

"Oh." Skipper stopped wrapping the blue jay plate to stare out the window at the road. "I don't know about that."

Jess had wrapped all the cups before he finished the single plate. She picked up the plate with the wren and another crumpled piece of newsprint. "There was a young man here when I arrived," Jess said.

Skipper nodded his head and set the wrapped plate on the counter. He bent down, disappearing behind his shelves. Jess stood on tip toe and leaned over to see, afraid she had scared him into hiding. But he straightened up, a tape dispenser in his hands. He set it next to the cash register and pulled out a strip of tape at least six inches long. He held the strip with an end in each hand and laid it carefully over the plate he'd wrapped.

"Do you know him? The young man I saw?"

Skipper looked up at Jess with an almost startled expression. She wondered if he'd lost track of the fact that she was there. "That's my little cousin, Erick."

"Erick?"

"Yeah. Oaky thinks I should go stay with them a while, because I don't like it here anymore." Skipper rubbed the gray and red stubble on his chin, so that his jowly cheek pushed up his face before falling back into place. "I'll probably do that."

Chapter Sixteen

THE HANDS OF the evil-doer shall be given up unto thy master. The least of the punishments He shall mete out to make right your sins. Better for ye if ye sacrifice thy own self on the alter of the Lord.

Juney thought the Lord was her father for the longest time. Everyone always prayed to the Lord Our Father. She thought her father was everyone's father, or at least everyone in the Family. She learned first and foremost that there was the Family and then there was everyone else. *Us and them.* That much even a toddler could understand. They made sure of that with their parables and coloring books—poor drawings one of the Family wives made and photocopied for the Sunday School. Sometimes the kids in the drawings were colored before the image was copied. That was how the children recognized them as *them*. Not Family.

Juney used to hold her mother's hand in the grocery store and when her mother got tired of that because she needed two hands to select a watermelon or lift a bucket of vanilla ice cream out of the freezer case, Juney held her skirt. She was always on the lookout for *them*, the gray people on her Sunday School coloring sheets.

One day, as they were leaving the grocery store, she saw a family getting out of a rusty 4Runner. The dark-haired man had brown skin and a tattoo on his forearm. His short, curvaceous wife wore a tight green dress and high heels. She had a large white purse with a gold tassel swinging from it over one shoulder and held the hand of a girl about Juney's age. The girl wore a sundress and rubber sandals. She had pretty black pigtails long enough to touch her shoulders. "Mommy," Juney said, "are they Family?" Her mother clucked her tongue and leaned into the shopping cart and pushed on toward their minivan. Juney had to run to keep up.

For her birthday that same year, Rachel received a book of fairy tales by Hans Christian Andersen. She was not very much interested in it, believing fairy tales were for babies, so she handed it to Juney when their parents weren't looking. The beautiful watercolor illustrations stunned Juney, and none captivated her so much as the one of Karen dancing across the heath in a pair of red shoes, her blonde braids flying, her eyes wide, and her mouth a round O of shock. Behind her sat a soldier with a long beard, indifferent to her suffering. Juney made Rachel read "The Red Shoes" to her three nights in a row until she knew the story by heart. For her sin, Karen sought out the executioner and begged him to chop off her feet.

All she had done, as far as Juney could tell, was admire a pair of red shoes enough to wear them to church. Such a natural thing to do. For much of Juney's childhood, she suffered a recurring dream in which her father chopped off her feet because she had somehow stepped wrong.

Chapter Seventeen

JESS STUDIED A map before leaving home. Skoghall and Durin, the county seat, sat on opposite sides of a shape somewhere between a square and a circle, equidistant no matter which side of the loop she took. As the crow flies was not an option, unless she wanted to risk getting lost on a series of county roads that wound through farm country. Jess decided to make the entire loop, taking the northern route into Durin and the southern route out of it.

Rice County's interior consisted of farmland that rose and dropped as it blanketed rolling hills edged by forested bluffs. Jess crossed over several creeks along the way, tributaries to either the Mississippi on the east edge of the county or the Chippewa on its western edge. The drive soothed her nerves as she focused on the scenery, instead of her destination.

A city person, Jess always left home early, allowing for the unexpected traffic jam en route. She rolled across the Chippewa River bridge sooner than expected and hooked south along the river into Durin's old downtown. She had time enough to explore before finding the government center and jail.

Durin's main street ran parallel to the river, lined by shops and cafés interchangeable with those in any midwestern small town. Perched on a hill above the main street with a view of the river, the old county courthouse kept watch over its domain. Though only two stories tall, the ridged columns and large triangular portico of the Greek Revival style, along with a once fashionable though empty bell tower, created the impression of grandeur as the courthouse rose above and watched over its citizens. On the lawn below the courthouse, a sculpture of a man on horseback greeted visitors as they approached. He sat tall in the saddle, his duster open on one side to reveal the holster and six-shooter at his hip. Jess stopped to stare up at the face under the brim of his hat. He squinted into the distance, scanning the horizon for the next threat to his people, a shotgun held in both hands across his body. The plaque at the base of the statue read, "Sheriff Charles Coleman. Killed protecting the people of Rice County from the outlaw Williams Bros. July 10, 1881." A large oak with two trunks and a great many gnarled branches spread above the statue, creating a canopy that shaded a good portion of the lawn. Something about the place unnerved Jess and she stepped away, eager to leave the shadow cast by that old oak. She walked across the lawn toward a large brick house that shared the lot. A historical places marker informed her that this had been, until the mid-1980s, the Rice County Sheriff's home, and that attached to the home at the back was the county jail, which was unlocked.

Jess found the small attachment to be nothing more than a room with a couple of windows, one on each side. Two side-by-side cells, made of iron sheets riveted together like holding tanks in a cargo ship, filled much of the room. The cells were barely bigger than the iron cots attached to the interior walls. They shared a small rectangular cage constructed of flat bars of iron that had been riveted together at each cross point. This latticework provided all the light and air the prisoners could hope for, which was not much since the cage sat inside a stuffy little room at the back of a house. A back door to the house opened into the jail. Instead of the usual screen door found outside of a solid door, this one had a door of iron bars. A cage of bars at head height bumped-out into the jail, like a bayed window. This allowed the Sheriff to get his head into the room and turn it to see every corner of the jail without actually needing to unlock his door or risk his head.

Jess wondered at the ingenuity of people, the solutions to problems as diverse as life itself. She could not imagine being imprisoned here, and could hardly believe that the jail, like the house, had been in use until the mid-1980s. She walked around the iron cell and examined the graffiti. N.B. + C. B. had been scratched into the light blue paint inside a heart with an arrow through it, while Neil Berger had written his name in pencil with the date "1/11/83" and "71 days" below that. *Seventy-one days*, Jess shook her head. She was already feeling claustrophobic after about ten minutes.

Somebody coughed. Jess turned to see who it was, expecting someone to enter the jail behind her.

A soft snoring emanated from one of the cells.

Jess stepped sideways and peered through the iron bars. The cells were quite dark. She felt her heart accelerate and her muscles pull her toward the door to the outside, yet she resisted the panic and leaned closer, searching the shadows. At the end of the iron cot, a pair of spurred cowboy boots lay crossed at the ankles. The wearer of those boots coughed again, then stirred. He sat up and swung his legs off the cot, leaning forward to rest his elbows on his knees, then he turned his head to look through the outer set of bars at Jess.

The man looked to be in his early twenties, fair-haired, and he wore a sort of goatee that widened over his chin, wrapping under his jaw. His hair had been cut close to the scalp on the sides, while the longer hair on top, which was perfectly straight, had been parted over his right ear. He wore a white shirt buttoned up to the narrow banded collar and a close-fitting gray jacket over striped woolen trousers. He had the unkempt look of one who'd been away from civilization for a while; the sleeve of his jacket had torn and his boots' toes were caked in mud. He turned his face to stare at Jess.

She looked back at him, wondering if this was some kind of reenactor, placed here for the tourists, or something else, something only she could see. He parted his lips in a malicious grin. His eyes looked cold and dead without so much as a glimmer of light. Jess ran from the room.

She stood in the gravel parking lot behind the courthouse and jail, catching her breath. She began to wonder about the man in the jail and an image came to her, only a flash, but a fully formed tableau. She saw the man leading a string of horses away from a corral. He rode a horse of his own; a rope tied to his saddle horn connected the stolen horses to his. The horses tossed their heads, their nostrils flaring, eyes wide, but they were unable to whinny. He had done something to them, put something in their nostrils. Wool soaked with whiskey. Jess put a hand to her chest and felt her heart beating. She willed it to calm, took a deep breath, felt the sunshine on her face and a slight breeze from the west.

She'd had enough sight seeing, and it was time to find the government building. Jess walked around the old courthouse toward her car on the street below.

From the branches of the large oak, now devoid of leaves, swung the man, a noose about his neck. His hands were cuffed and leg irons dangled off his left foot. As she passed the tree, her arms suddenly cold and hairs standing up, she heard faintly the jeers of a crowd calling for him to go to hell.

When Jess looked back up the hill at the oak and the courthouse, it all looked as before, the sun shining off the white boards of the stately building, the oak full of leaves, shading the statue of Charles Coleman.

The government building had been a hospital on the edge of town closest to the highway, a single-story of concrete blocks with two wings off a central one, it offered an entrance to each wing labeled accordingly. Jess chose the door on the south wing labeled "Jail & Sheriff's Office."

Once inside, she found the doors off the entrance locked and no sign of a buzzer. She called Martinez.

"Hey," Martinez said, leaning into the hallway. "How was your drive?"

"Fine. Got here early, in fact." Jess felt her smile falter. "Do you know if someone was ever hung outside the old courthouse?"

"Sure. A mob lynched a horse thief there. Durin was known as 'Hanging Town' after that." Martinez paused. "Oh…you didn't…"

"Yeah. I think I just met the horse thief." She went through the security door Martinez held open for her.

A short way down the central corridor, a deputy stood beside an open door, his hands on his hips above his belt. Martinez stopped to introduce them. "Ms. Vernon, Deputy Wicklund here will take you through the identification process."

Wicklund showed her into a room with a table with four chairs, the telltale dome hiding a security camera in the corner, and a mirrored window in one wall that faced into an adjacent room. "There are recording devices in this room, so any statements you make concerning the identity of the suspect will be recorded. Do you understand?"

Jess nodded.

"Please speak your answers."

"Yes, I understand," she said.

"Now, Ms. Vernon," he began, "I am going to show you a series of individuals. The person involved in this crime may or may not be included." Deputy Wicklund continued with a set of directions, then asked Jess if she understood. She signed a document stating she did understand, and a young woman was directed into the room on the other side of the window.

The young woman resembled Carla Stanley with longish, mouse-brown hair, a slender build, somewhat unremarkable features, and looked too young to be in a bar. Her hair had been pulled back to resemble the description Jess had given Martinez. The first subject looked bored, shifted her weight over one hip, and lifted her eyes to the ceiling. "Is this the person you saw in The Two Wheeler the night Dan Grunner was killed?" Deputy Wicklund asked.

"No."

She exited the room, and another subject entered. Jess studied her, certain even before she'd faced fully forward that she was not the girl from the bar, but equally certain that it would be important she appear to practice due diligence, giving each subject ample consideration so as to avoid rushing a judgment. It was nothing Jess had been told, but common sense that with such high stakes prudence was essential.

The fourth subject immediately drew Jess toward her. She stepped closer to the glass and peered at the girl. She was scared. While the others had seemed to stare at the glass or at nothing, her eyes kept moving, unable to rest on anything, even her own reflection. Jess studied her and leaned in until her forehead bumped the glass. She jerked away from it and found Deputy Wicklund suppressing a smile.

"Happens all the time," he said.

He pressed an intercom button on the wall. "Face left." The girl obliged. She wore jeans and a tank top, but when she turned, Jess saw a flash of bare leg. "Face right." Jess saw the girl with her hair falling untidily around her face, mascara running under her eyes. The look in those eyes was not that of a killer, but that of a victim. The panic she felt, the vulnerability, overwhelmed Jess.

"Ms. Vernon?" Wicklund had stepped forward and taken hold of her elbow to steady her.

She looked at him and, though she found nothing comforting in his sharp features, the surge of terror subsided. "I'm fine, thank you." Jess glanced back through the window. "That's her," she said.

"Is this the person you saw in The Two Wheeler the night Dan Grunner was killed?"

"Yes."

"In your own words, can you describe how certain you are?"

"I'm totally certain."

Wicklund took her through the rest of the line up, per procedure. Jess pretended to care about the remaining girls, to give them equal time, but only because she couldn't explain her certainty to the Deputy. Were she relying solely on her eyes and memory, she wouldn't have been certain at all.

When they'd finished, Martinez came into the room and excused Wicklund. "Since you're here, we'd like to get an official statement from you." Johnson joined them with a notepad and pen in hand and three bottles of water. He passed around the water and uncapped his pen as he got situated. A metal bar looped up from the table, bolted near where Jess sat. She told them everything that had happened in the bar that night, including her drinking with Chandra and Beckett punching Tyler. She was aware that if she became a witness in court, she might not appear credible thanks to their partying.

Johnson honed in on that and asked Jess how many drinks she'd had, how much food she'd eaten, and over how long a period.

Jess answered, hoping she sounded immanently reasonable. As she talked, Martinez watched her and Johnson took notes. All the attention made her fidgety. Her hands found the metal bar and she absentmindedly ran her fingers back and forth along its surface.

"We cuff people to that," Martinez said.

Jess jerked her hands away from the bar and tucked them in her lap. "Busy hands. They're usually typing. Occupational hazard. Or something." She looked at Johnson. Was he marking her a fool? A ditz? An unreliable witness? All because she happened to be tactile? He made notes on his legal pad with his head bent low enough to hide his expression. *Screw it*, Jess thought. *What do I care what he thinks?* "Can I ask you a question?" she said. Martinez and Johnson glanced at each other, but didn't refuse. "How did you find the girl from the bar? She's not the girl on the license."

Johnson raised an eyebrow at Jess.

"I saw the bartender's photo of the ID. She could pass, but she's not the same person."

The detectives exchanged another look, then Johnson threw his hands up. "Go ahead," he said, and sat back in his chair, crossing his arms over his chest.

"We tracked down the woman whose license it was. She's a college student, and that license was stolen from her last May. She's got a new license and an alibi for the night of the murder."

"Oh."

"Yeah, her entire rowing—"

"Crew," Johnson corrected.

"*Crew* team was together. Some kind of pre-season, team-building slumber party. So we tracked down the girl who stole her license."

Johnson snorted. "Maybe we should have a slumber party. Pajamas in lockdown." He put his broad hands on the table and pushed himself up from his chair, ending their time together.

Martinez escorted Jess back down the hallway to the security door. She began to say goodbye, and he offered her a lunch recommendation. Jess nodded and left the building.

She climbed into her car and started it quickly so she could get the windows down and release the stuffy hot air. She pulled out her phone and looked at a map. She had to meet Martinez for lunch somewhere on the east side of town, Broadway and 12th. At least she assumed that was what Martinez meant when he gave her a recommendation in response to a question she didn't ask. She set the phone down on the passenger seat and signaled to pull away from the curb.

Two spaces behind her, a small, green pickup pulled away and followed.

The map on Jess's phone took her away from the heart of town and into a neighborhood of small houses built during the post-war boom. Once a slice of the American pie, most of these houses now had peeling paint, sagging porches, and satellite dishes mounted on their sides. Jess saw more than one pit bull chained to a porch railing or behind a chainlink fence, the strength of which she doubted. She was about to call Martinez when she came to an intersection with the sort of commercial buildings built when a shop was a family business and storefronts were attached to the family home.

A hairdresser specializing in braids sat on one corner, a convenience store on another, a nail salon on the third, and on the fourth, La Tacqueria. The diner had a yellow awning with a spurred cockerel painted on it. Martinez sat at a picnic table out front with a can of Coke and a paper tray of food before him.

"Sorry," Jess said as she approached the table. "I had trouble finding it."

"Don't worry," Martinez waved away her apology. "The chicken tacos are the best, but the fish isn't bad."

"I'm a vegetarian."

A woman came out of the restaurant wearing a hairnet over tight black curls and stood facing the sun, her feet planted on the concrete sidewalk. She breathed in deeply.

"Jaunita," Martinez called to her. She came to his side and they spoke in Spanish. Jaunita looked at Jess more than Martinez during their exchange. She had small dark eyes and acne scarring on her cheeks. If Jess characterized her in one word, it would be proud. She picked out the words *pollo* and *si,* and gathered from Martinez' inflection that something was too bad. She knew before he told her that it was too bad for her. Juanita went back inside. "I'm sorry," he said to Jess. "She uses chicken broth in the rice and beans. In pretty much everything. I didn't know."

"Don't worry about it." Jess's stomach growled, despite the food in Martinez' paper basket having no appeal to her vegetarian palate. "Something happened back there. I got a flash of panic."

"You were panicked?"

"No, that girl was. The night of the murder, she was scared out of her wits. I think," Jess dropped her voice, "Dan was trying to rape her."

Martinez placed a piece of shredded chicken in his mouth and licked his fingers before reaching for his napkin. "What makes you say that?"

"When I saw them in the bar, he looked bored and she looked like a prostitute. But in the junk shop, I see him going after her. She's terrified and he's…I don't know. Teasing her or something. And now, during the line up, I felt her fear when I looked at her, like she was scared for her life. I think she might have killed Dan in self-defense."

"Okay, but we don't know she killed him. What if Cross went next door? Maybe he heard a scuffle, went over to check it out. Maybe he killed Grunner to protect the girl. Maybe it was all an accident."

Jess started shaking her head before Martinez got to the word scuffle.

There was no way. "No way," she said. "Tyler has nothing to do with this."

"Why are you so certain?"

"Because…" Jess had trouble finishing that sentence. *Because I believe in Bruno.* Martinez might believe she sees ghosts and can help solve a murder, but he wouldn't believe Tyler's innocence just because he had a service dog. She shrugged, "I know him."

"And you realize that's not enough to stop me digging into Cross's whereabouts at the time of the murder. But the information about the potential attack is interesting."

Jess stood up to leave. "Enjoy your chicken."

She didn't think anything of the green pickup parked in front of the convenience store across the street. She had to look at her map again to get herself out of town. She would head south along the Chippewa River, then northwest along the Mississippi to Skoghall. Jess thought about the time she'd lost today to driving, time she could have spent writing—John had given her a deadline for an outline they had to submit to his editor— but she stopped herself before resentment could set in. She'd spent many an hour traversing the Twin Cities, covering half the distance in a fog of exhaust without anything resembling nature outside her windows. With that perspective, she found her way out of the neighborhood and onto the highway with something like gratitude for her new life.

The pickup was still with her when she turned onto the River Road.

Jess stopped in town on her way home, hoping to find Tyler. She wasn't disappointed. He and Bruno stood on the arching bridge over the spring that connected the community garden to the café's entrance. He leaned on the railing, watching the old water wheel make its slow turn, lapping at the spring below. Jess approached quickly at first, eager to talk to him, but slowed as she came near. She watched him for signs of tension and said his name while she was still well out of arm's reach.

"Hi, Jess." He turned to face her now, his smile strained. "I was just thinking about you."

"Something good, I hope." She meant it as more than a platitude.

"I knew it was you just now. Well, I figured it must be." He pointed down at Bruno, who sat at his feet, tail thumping the boards of the bridge, even as he faced Tyler with his chin lifted, eyes glued on his friend, master, and charge. "Bruno's happy to see you."

Jess longed to greet him, but he had his service dog pack on and she knew better than to create a distraction.

"You can say hello," Tyler said to Jess, then to Bruno, "Release." Bruno swiveled to face Jess and sat before her, his excitement contained but for the tail, which swept side to side with a force that could knock you over. He had been trained that affection is given when he's in a sit, which was motivation enough not to jump. Jess knelt and thoroughly rubbed his face and neck, then kissed the top of his auburn head.

She stood and faced the spring, leaning over the railing next to Tyler. The silvered boards of the water wheel carried on, the motion both ceaseless and pointless. The small mill, a community treasure when it had been built, was long defunct, the grinding stones removed, the wheel kept over the spring as decoration. "You've heard about Dan Grunner?"

"Yep." Tyler sighed heavily. "Am I suspect number one?"

"No." Jess sounded too emphatic to her own ears. "I don't know, actually. But there's this girl who had a drink with him at The Two Wheeler. I think she's the last person to see him alive."

"Yeah? Does that get me off the hook?" He reached down and put a hand on Bruno's head, then stroked one of his silky ears.

Jess shrugged. "I would think so, Tyler. You had nothing to do with it, so there's nothing to worry about."

"Isn't there?" He brought his hand to his brow and pushed his fingers through the curls on his head. "That cop—Johnson, I think—sat there telling me statistics about veterans and PTSD." His voice became strained. "Like how many of them snapped and killed people for no apparent reason."

Everything about him felt explosive. Jess said his name, and he looked at her. Something in his eyes opened, like a realization of who he was and whom he was with. Tyler knelt and wrapped his arms around Bruno's neck. "He was trying to get to you, but that doesn't mean he thinks you did it," Jess said.

Tyler pressed his cheek against Bruno's head. The dog shot his tongue out the side of his mouth and gave him a kiss. Tyler smiled. It was brief, but it was there. He patted Bruno's shoulder and stood up, wiping dog saliva off his face. "You know, when I first saw that this place was for sale, I got so excited. I thought this was *home*."

Jess turned to face out into the garden, resting her elbows on the bridge railing and leaning against it. A hummingbird hovered at the feeder, its emerald head shimmering. "Skoghall is a great place."

"Now it just feels toxic to me." Tyler faced Jess. "I don't know what I'd do if I didn't have you here."

Chapter Eighteen

ETHAN SAT IN a green pickup truck in front of the Skoghall Village Hall. In the passenger seat, Erick, whom he considered of limited intelligence and ambition, stared at his phone, overly interested in the moronic texts of his slut girlfriend. Ethan didn't enjoy keeping the company of fools, but he found it useful. Being…well, being *him* required a certain degree of solitariness. He knew he was still young, which was partly why he was being so ambitious now, but he'd lived long enough to know that most people didn't think the way he did. Most people would be appalled by his actions, but that was only because they were limited in the scope of their…scope.

Sometimes he felt like he was drifting on high, above it all, but also beyond it all. He saw the pointlessness of everything. He also saw the incredible sad beauty of it. He remembered a particularly windy day when he was a child—one of those days when trees shake and wind chimes are clanged about in a way that is anything but melodic and beneath all the other sounds is the sound of leaves dry as paper skittering down the pavement. He sat on his front stoop breaking a fresh stick of sidewalk chalk into little nubs, and he saw a plastic bag blow by. A short while later, a piece of newspaper. And after that, a crunched up beer can skidded past. He realized then that if there was a God in Heaven who had created this place called Eden, He had since abandoned it to His low-rent tenants. And those tenants, they were trashing the place.

And if there was no God in Heaven to look down upon him, to witness his every thought (which was what his mother told him every single night), then there was only himself to know what he was up to, only himself to hold him accountable. The thrill of it surged through his body with such sudden force that his bladder emptied, right there on the concrete steps of his stoop. Since nobody was there to witness it, not even God, it did not count against him. Instead of flushing with shame, the way he'd been taught, he flushed with a secret pride and his first inkling of power. He remained on those steps, crumbling his red stick of chalk into powder, sitting in his wet shorts. He wanted to see if someone would come and notice, if there would be any punishment. Finally, he stood up, wiped the chalk dust from his hands onto the front of his shorts, and went inside for a snack.

His mother noticed the chalk, for which he was lightly scolded. She did not notice the urine that had dried in his shorts. If she had, she would have paddled him.

That was the start of his great experiment. And this...how to characterize this? He stared across the street, through the haze of heat that glazed the pavement, at the community garden, watching the woman talk to a man with a dog. This marked the end of his apprenticeship. In six weeks he'd turn eighteen and, with this project successfully completed, he'd declare himself a master.

Chapter Nineteen

SHAKTI PRACTICALLY DRAGGED Jess out onto the road. She'd been in the house all morning and the chance to take an actual walk outside of her own yard was about too much fun to bear. Jess reined her in so they could practice walking nicely together and headed away from town, down the corn-lined county road where she and Chandra had gone jogging. With a water bottle and treat bag belted to her hips, sunscreen topping her freckled shoulders, and her phone strapped to her arm, she felt ready for anything a summer walk could throw at her.

Sweat beaded on her skin. She enjoyed the smoothness of motion that came with warmed muscles and working joints. Shakti trotted happily beside her, tongue panting rhythmically. Jess had surprised herself by falling into a relationship so soon after moving to Skoghall. The thing with Tyler had been a given, really. She needed attention after the long starvation period of a dying marriage. As much as she liked Tyler, Jess could now see that he was a transition person. She was serious about Beckett, which was something she had not intended. Jess had been looking forward to living along, to being independent, to having space outside a relationship. And here she was smack dab in the middle of another one. It got good after Bonnie went to the light, or whatever spirits really do when they move on. July had been fantastic with river kayaking, a weekend on the shore of Lake Superior, and Wednesdays— their Sundays—always in each other's company for at least part of the day.

No wonder she felt jealous of Lora giving him a haircut, but was it too soon for that? Jess filled her lungs with country air and sighed it away. Had they been moving too fast?

A car sped toward Jess and Shakti. She glanced behind her before moving from the blacktop to the gravel shoulder, shortening Shakti's leash. The engine revved behind them, then the vehicle dipped onto the shoulder. The tires spit gravel, and rocks clattered against the undercarriage of the green pickup. Jess launched herself toward the cornfield, yanking Skakti's leash. Her ankle twisted all wrong as she fell into the ditch between the shoulder and field, Shakti landing on her chest and knocking the wind out of her.

Jess's sunglasses sat cockeyed on her face, with one eye behind its lens and the other exposed. It took her a moment to realize why the blue overhead seemed painfully bright to only one eye. She squirmed her shoulders and shoved at Shakti, who took that as her cue to get on her feet and bark madly at the now-empty road. Each time Shakti tugged at the leash, Jess's arm jerked painfully away from her body. She sat up and straightened her sunglasses. She smacked her lips together and spit out some of the dirt she'd managed to eat when she landed in the ditch. A large scrape on her shoulder stung and her hip ached. "Shakti!" The dog continued her barking, straining at her leash. "Shakti, come!"

No good. The dog had to see for herself that the threat was gone. Jess tried to get to her feet. She put weight on her left ankle and cried out in pain. Shakti stopped barking mid-bark to look back at Jess, her head cocked to one side. "Shit," Jess said. She tried to hobble forward, but there was no way she could get up the steep embankment on a sprained ankle, especially with the Dingo pulling on her leash.

Jess turned her back to the road and sat on the embankment. Shakti bounded to her and licked her face, comforting both of them. "Okay, Bear." Burs prickled Jess's hands when she touched Shakti's shoulders. *Great,* she thought and brought her hands up to her own ponytail. Her hair had twisted into clumps around at least a dozen of the prickly seeds. Jess yelled, a sort of primal groan, to make herself feel better. Then she yelled a few curse words at the top of her lungs, because she knew no one could hear her, just like no one could see her sitting in the ditch.

Shakti looked at Jess uncertainly and wagged her tail a few times.

Jess pulled her phone off her armband and checked the workout data.

They'd walked over a mile—no way she'd make it home on her own.

"Down here," Jess yelled. She'd been sitting in the ditch for half an hour, the sun broiling her shoulders. She'd given Shakti all the water, at least as much as she could lap up while the rest poured onto the ground. Poor Shakti didn't even rouse herself at the sound of Beckett's voice. She lay in the weeds, panting heavily.

"There you are," Beckett said, finally appearing over the lip of the road. Jess had given him the distance walked from her front door, which landed him close enough that she could hear him calling her from the road. He scrambled down the embankment and Shakti jumped up, finally excited. Jess let go of the leash, relieved she no longer had to keep her dog out of the road while unable to stand. "Woah!" Beckett deflected Shakti's jump at his chest and grabbed her by the scruff of the neck. "Yeah, I'm glad to see you, too, girl." He looked at Jess, his smile bright. She hadn't had a chance to get used to his short hair and it surprised her to see him so clean cut. "You, too." Beckett leaned down and kissed her, then scooped her up in his arms.

Jess put her arm around his neck while he carried her out of the ditch and wondered whatever had she been thinking about moving too fast. He helped her into the passenger seat of his cargo van and handed her a bottle of cold water. He pulled a dog bowl out of the back seat and poured Shakti her own drink. "You thought of everything," Jess smiled at him appreciatively. "Where'd you get the dog bowl?"

"I pulled it out of stock at the hardware store."

"I missed you," she said, and though she hadn't been missing him before this moment, she meant it.

"You did?" He smiled at her and his eyes lit up with that spark that Jess adored. Beckett helped Shakti into the van and came around to his door. "I think we should head straight to urgent care and have that ankle X-rayed."

"No way. X-rays are a few hundred at least. My insurance deductible is ridiculous and cash is tight right now."

"So you want to live with a screwed up ankle the rest of your life?" He pulled the van onto the road and made a U-turn.

"Beckett."

"Jess."

She sighed. "Let's not start, okay? Take me home, and if it's not better after some R.I.C.E. I'll let you drive me to urgent care."

Beckett didn't agree, but he turned into Jess's driveway. Once he got her laid out on the couch with a bag of ice under her ankle, he started the inquisition. "How exactly did you fall into the ditch?"

"I didn't fall. We were…" Jess had been so concerned with being in the ditch and getting out of the ditch that she hadn't thought through how she wound up in the ditch. "We were run off the road." She slapped the couch cushion with her fist. "Damn it! He could have killed my dog."

"Jess." Beckett sat on the edge of the couch and put a hand on her thigh. "Who ran you off the road? Does this have to do with that man? That ghost?"

Jess reached around the back of her head and yanked the hairband off her ponytail, pulling out several hairs tangled around a bur. "Crap!" She held up her hairband. "Look at this. It's going to take me hours to get these things out." She tugged at one of the spiky seeds and it separated in her fingers, the seed pod becoming half a dozen clumps of seeds, all equally sticky. She stared at Beckett, one hand held in front of her with the lost hairs and sticky seeds on her palm. "I don't know if this has to with Dan Grunner. Why would it?"

Beckett closed his eyes and shook his head. "Christ, Jess. You sure do attract trouble."

"I'm sorry, Beckett. I don't know…" She started to scoot upright on the couch, knocking the bag of ice to the floor.

Beckett held up his hand to stop her. "Lie back down." He retrieved the bag of ice and set it atop her ankle once she'd settled. "You're a mess. You know that, right?"

Jess didn't know whether to protest or agree with him wholeheartedly.

"Your hair…" Beckett gestured toward his own head. Jess hadn't seen a mirror yet, but he gave her the impression "rat's nest" would actually be an appropriate descriptor. "And," he pointed to the back of his shoulder, "I wasn't going to tell you this, but you missed a spot with the sunscreen. You have a big red handprint back here where you burned." He joined her on the couch and looked into her eyes. "You can't walk. Not very well anyway." He took her hands in his. "Oh, and I think I'm falling in love with you."

Chapter Twenty

"EVERYONE HAS A story," Dan said.

"Oh, is that a fact?" Samantha grinned at him, pushed the ice around in her glass with a cocktail straw and took a sip. Even while she tilted the glass to her mouth, her eyes smiled up at Dan.

"Sure. You see that couple over there?" Dan pointed to a heavyset man and woman seated at a corner table. They bent toward their plates of spaghetti, minimizing the distance their forks traveled from plate to mouth. He wore his napkin tucked into the neckline of his shirt, a Hawaiian print in yellow and green. Despite this apparent concern for tidy eating, a glob of tomato sauce stuck in his beard near the corner of his mouth. She wore a pink frilled blouse, napkinless, and used an oversized spoon to assist with the twirling of noodles, making a production of spooling them before raising them to her mouth. "She works in a garment factory," Dan said. "Her job is to load big spools of thread onto the machines and then run the threads through the guides."

"It's a giant machine," Samantha said, "like a labyrinth."

"And her boss, the fabric factory foreman, is a cruel man."

"He only cares about efficiency."

"When he was a boy," Dan continued, "he had a nanny who was as ugly as she was terrifying. She read him Greek mythology every night to put him to sleep with dreams of chimera and boys falling out of the sky, so he installed his own Minotaur in the weaving machine."

"No employee has ever seen it and lived to tell the tale." Samantha's eyes gleamed over the candle flickering on their table.

Dan reached across the table to touch his wife's hand. "Some say it's a six-headed guinea pig. Some say it's a rabid gorilla. Others say it's the foreman's own bastard child." Dan paused to have a sip of his drink and gazed at his wife. He adored the way she looked at him, the simple pleasures they shared. Samantha kept telling him to write these things down, but for Dan they were just an amusing way to pass the time. Still, he supposed he could never have married a woman who didn't enjoy these fabrications of his.

"She needs a name." Samantha dipped a hunk of bread in the olive oil plate. "Gertrude? Gerty?"

"Gerty."

"Gerty it is." Samantha gave Dan's hand a squeeze.

"Gerty loads the spool at the beginning of the labyrinth and ties the thread around her waist, so that she can keep her hands free."

"So she won't drop it."

"That too. She takes a deep breath, counts down from three, and she's off!"

Samantha looked over at the corner table, at Gerty, and laughed softly. "Poor Gerty. She runs so hard. What she doesn't know is..." Samantha looked at Dan, passing the story back to him with a slight nod of her head.

"Is that it's only a little dog. He was retired from the circus after he developed an irrational fear of tutus."

Samantha giggled. "He rides a tricycle through the labyrinth, trying to catch Gerty, but..."

"He only wants a belly rub."

They laughed, raised their glasses and clinked them over the candle. "To the Minotaur."

Shortly after this trip, Samantha discovered she was pregnant. By the fifth month, sitting in the car for long hours had lost its appeal and there was much to prepare at home. Samantha said she was fine with the time alone, even admitted to enjoying it since it was about to become an impossibility. Besides, she said, laying her hands on her belly, she wasn't really alone.

All the same, Dan didn't like the thought of leaving Samantha behind when he had to travel. He brought home a rescue dog to keep her company, a black and white Boston Terrier. They named him The Minotaur. Minnie for short.

Chapter Twenty-One

JESS AND BECKETT each sat at potter's wheels, U2's *Joshua Tree* on the stereo. He leaned forward, shaping a mug with a flexible rib—his second, while Jess was still trying to center her first ball of clay. The open back carriage door invited a westerly breeze. The sky had turned a dark blue over the past hour and the last of the day's orange glow settled onto the bluff tops across the Mississippi. Soon they'd have to shut the door against mosquitoes, but for now it couldn't be better.

"Honey," Beckett said loud enough to be heard over the music, "untuck your lip."

"Huh?" Jess looked up from her ball of clay.

Beckett climbed off his wheel and wiped his hands on his canvas apron as he came over to Jess's wheel. "You tuck your lip between your teeth when you concentrate."

"Bad habit."

"It's cute." He kissed her forehead, then turned and reached for a small potter's bat on the work table.

"You're done with another one?"

Beckett smiled at her as he wet the bat with his sponge. "You'll get there." He grabbed a stiff wire with small wooden dowels on each end and cut the mug away from the wheel head. "Maybe not here. But somewhere. Give it more time."

"Okay. But tonight I want you to center for me or I won't make anything." Jess climbed off the wheel and limped for the kitchen, trusting that when she returned she'd find a beautiful ball of clay waiting for her. And from it she would make...probably another thick-walled, lopsided...vessel. She hadn't even been able to make a decent mug yet. Her mugs held about two ounces and weighed about two pounds.

She came out of the kitchen with a bottle of wine and two glasses just as Investigator Martinez came in the back door carrying a manila folder. "Hello. I tried calling," he shouted over the music.

Beckett grabbed a clay-smudged remote control and turned down the music. "Sorry. We weren't expecting company."

"I know. I decided to take my chances. Good album." He nodded toward the stereo.

"Should I get another glass?" Jess asked.

Martinez considered a moment. "Sure. I'm off-duty and this is an unofficial visit."

Jess returned from the kitchen with the third glass and found Beckett turning her ball of just-centered clay into another mug, explaining to Martinez about pulling up the sides. She wanted to say *hey, that's mine,* but her grown-up self reminded her inner child that there were more balls of clay. "Here we are," she said with a smile instead, and poured the wine. She handed Martinez a glass. He turned it, inspecting the smudge of clay on its stem. "Welcome to the studio," Jess said with a smile. Beckett finished his demonstration, a mug in about five minutes, and they settled into the booth.

"To what do we owe the pleasure?"

"I'm afraid that while my visit's not official, it's not for pleasure," Martinez said. "Beckett called me about your little trip to the ditch."

Jess looked at Beckett. "But it was nothing. Some jerk on his phone or something. He probably never even saw us."

"It's possible it's more than that. What kind of car ran you off the road?"

"It was green, a sport pickup," she said, "but that's all I can tell you. That and I feel lucky to be alive."

"How's your ankle?"

"Fine. More or less." She extended her leg to show off the elastic bandage Beckett had carefully wrapped around her ankle.

"I wish she'd get it X-rayed," he said.

Jess flashed him a look to leave it alone, and he put his arm over the back of the booth behind her. She would have snuggled against him if they didn't have company, even *unofficial* company.

"Investigator…"

"I'm drinking your wine, you'd better call me Victor." He held up his glass to his hosts, then added, "But only when I'm off-duty."

"Victor," Jess said, "you don't think the guy who ran me off the road has something to do with Dan Grunner's murder, do you?"

"We have cameras around the office where you came for the line up." He opened the folder and passed some papers to Jess and Beckett. Three images from surveillance cameras had captured Jess leaving the building, crossing the street, and pulling away in her car. The third picture had been taken from a different camera, one that faced the road instead of the building's entrance. It clearly showed a sport pickup truck pulling away from the curb right behind Jess.

"I have to get home."

"What?" Beckett turned his gaze from the paper to Jess. "Why?"

"He followed me from Durin." Jess slid out of the booth. "He had to wait for me while I talked to Tyler at the café. He knows where I live, and Shakti's there right now."

"Jess!" Beckett tried to grab her as she turned to leave, but she was already running for the door, her ankle's protests ignored.

Jess fumbled to get her cell phone out of her pocket before it went to voicemail.

"Jess," Beckett barked into the phone. "You couldn't have waited two minutes for me to come with you?"

"Shakti." She turned from Main Street onto Haug Drive with one hand.

"Okay, what's your plan?"

"Pack a bag, grab the dog, and come stay with you, I guess."

"Martinez is following you. If anything looks weird, just wait for him."

"I know, Beckett. He's right behind me. Or the bad guy has got new wheels, one of the two."

"That's not funny, Jess."

"It wasn't meant to be." She said goodbye and put on her signal, figuring Martinez wouldn't be able to spot the turn to her house. She hardly knew where it was some days.

Jess slowed way down to minimize the damage her rutted drive could do to her hatchback's suspension in the dark, but also because she wanted to scope out her property. The barn suddenly seemed too big and too dark, a good place for someone to hide until she thought she was safe. *Shit.* At least with Bonnie, Jess knew what she was dealing with.

Martinez got out of his car quicker than Jess did hers and they reached the front door at the same time. Still locked—a good sign. And there was a man wearing a gun right behind her. She would never have thought to find that comforting before moving to Skoghall.

Shakti stood at the door to her crate, tail thumping the sides in welcome. Jess released the latch and opened her arms. Shakti rushed to lick her face, wiggling in Jess's embrace.

"How long have you been gone?" Martinez whispered.

"Couple hours."

He stepped around the happy reunion and turned on the hallway light before removing his gun from its holster. Jess took hold of Shakti's collar and wrapped an arm around her chest to still her. She watched Martinez disappear into the kitchen. The dining room light came on and he emerged on that side of the house before completing the loop through the living room. "This floor is okay," he said. "I'll check downstairs first, then upstairs." Jess nodded and tightened her grip on Shakti.

Once Martinez had checked the house, Jess went upstairs to pack a bag. He lugged the bag of dog food to her car. Jess locked the door on her home, vacating it *not for the first time*, she thought ruefully.

They found the studio as they'd left it, three wine glasses sitting half-emptied on the table, only Beckett had returned to the wheel and made three more mugs in the time they'd been gone.

"How do you make those so fast?" Martinez asked, looking at the mugs on the work table.

"Lots of practice." He pulled some pieces of plastic from a box and handed one to Martinez. "Wrap that over the pot. Gently. If you pull on it you'll dent the mug."

Martinez obliged, carefully tucking the edges of plastic under the bat, then he helped Beckett carry the new pots to the wet closet. Jess had heard the explanations before and knew that tomorrow Beckett would unwrap them, trim them, score the clay, attach the handles, blah blah blah. It was this whole amazing process that actually fascinated her, but at the moment, all she wanted was a good sulk over the fact that her home was not safe. Again.

She limped heavily after her careless dash and decided to take care of it before Beckett noticed. She went to the kitchen for ice, then climbed into the booth. Jess leaned against the wall, put her leg up, and hid her throbbing ankle under the bag of ice. Shakti jumped up to join her and curled into a ball. Beckett grabbed a stool, slid it up to the end of the table, and straddled it. Martinez resumed his seat across from Jess. And they were back where they'd begun, plus one. She rubbed Shakti's ears thoughtfully.

"Hey, you all right?"

Jess shook her head. "I'm mad. I'm mad as hell. That creep could have killed Shakti and now I'm out of my house again."

"Victor," Beckett said, "I thought you were interested in Tyler Cross. Then Jess went to identify that girl from the bar. So what does this pickup have to do with Dan Grunner?"

"That's what I'm trying to put together. My guess is whoever was driving is connected to the girl from the bar. She could have told someone she was going in for the line up. Jess, I'd like you to visit the junk shop with me again. If this is about Dan Grunner, maybe he can show you something that'll help us."

"Sure thing." Jess took up the bottle and refilled her wineglass. Something occurred to her as she poured. "How did you find the girl from the bar? She's not Carla Whatever-Her-Name-Is, so how on earth did you track her down?"

She passed the bottle to Beckett. He tilted it toward Martinez' glass, but he put his hand over the rim.

"Johnson called Carla, found her at some small college in Appleton, rowing on the Fox River."

"Right. Crew. Slumber party," Jess said.

"Last year she had a roommate who was all right, but her creepy little sister came to visit a few times. People kept commenting that Carla and the little sister looked more alike than the two sisters. Then a few weeks after her twenty-first, little sister comes to visit for the weekend, and Carla's license disappears."

"Why didn't she report the sister?" Jess asked.

"No proof. She said she confronted her roommate, but the roommate stuck up for her sister for a while, then pleaded mercy. Claimed if her sister got busted their father would beat the crap out of her or something. Carla believed her and let it go."

"Why did she believe the story?" Beckett asked.

Shakti stretched along the bench and pushed her claws into Jess's thigh. She grabbed a paw and repositioned it.

"Carla said the parents had come to visit once and they seemed weird to her, super religious or something. And during the visit, her roommate was changing and Carla saw some bruises around her waist like she'd been pinched really hard."

"That's so messed up," Beckett mused. "Look," he tapped the tabletop as he enumerated his points, "the girl Jess identified is a minor, who stole an ID to get into a bar, then seduced a man almost twice her age, so that some guy with a green pickup could…I don't know what…" he stopped tapping the table, "and then Jess and Shakti get run off the road."

"That pretty much sums up my case," Martinez said. He raised his wineglass and took a final sip. "Jess, 8:00 a.m., junk shop."

"Eight?"

"I'm telling you now so you can cork the wine and get some sleep."

"I thought you were off duty, Victor," she joked.

He slid from the booth. "Yeah, but I'll be on duty at 8:00 a.m. at the junk shop."

"You heard Victor. Get some sleep." Beckett curled his body around Jess's. Shakti snored somewhere on the floor nearby. Jess grabbed his arm and snugged his embrace even tighter around her.

"I know, but I have too many thoughts."

He brought his hand up to smooth the hair away from her brow. "Let them go. They'll come back tomorrow. I'm sure of it."

"That's the trouble." She spoke softly in the dark of his room, the slope of the gabled ceiling making it feel close and stuffy, even with the window open and the cicadas chirring in the trees behind the house. Stuffy or not, the weight of his arm around her brought a comfort that far outweighed the slippery feel of sweat forming behind her knees.

"Remember telling me that you think you're falling in love with me?"

"You mean, remember telling you that this afternoon?"

Jess nodded. "I'm sorry I'm so much trouble."

"Thing is, Jess, you're a package deal, same as me. I mean we all have our baggage right? Yours is just unusual. *Really* unusual." His finger traced the outside edge of her ear. "You might not have a choice to take it or leave it, but you've got me. I'm here and I'll help you."

Jess squirmed around to face him. She placed her hand against his cheek, felt the stubble under her palm, then stroked his goatee. Even in the dark, he had the bluest eyes she'd ever seen. "What about Isabella? I mean, stuff like that could happen again."

"I know. I'm sorry I left like that. I just thought that as long as Bonnie was gone, the house would be a safe zone or something. A place we could be alone, rest, make love." He pressed his lips to her neck and she felt his breath on her skin, his hand on her hip…

Beckett pulled his face away from her, suddenly moved by another urge. "Hey, I've got that van right?"

"Right."

"I'll paint some big green and purple paisleys on it." He opened his eyes wide in faux excitement, waiting for Jess to catch on.

"And we'll call it the Mystery Machine?" she ventured.

Beckett laughed. "You got it. And you can say things like jinkies."

"Oh no. There's no way I'm Velma to your Fred."

"Okay. Daphne then."

"I'm more of a Buffy kind of girl."

"I've got it." Beckett wore a goofy, gleeful expression that matched the degree of his fun. "Your name is Jessica. You're a writer. You live in a small town."

"Don't say it." She climbed on top of Beckett and put her hands over his mouth. "Don't you say it."

"You're Jessica Fletcher!" he cried through her fingers.

"You said it!" Jess yelled. She snatched a pillow and batted his shoulders on one side and then the other. "How could you say it?"

Shakti scrambled onto the bed and dove into the middle of the shenanigans. They laughed and yelped and barked in a jumble on the creaky mattress until Beckett's downstairs neighbor yelled up through the floor.

"We're really sorry," Beckett hollered back down. Jess bunched a pillow over her own face to stifle the end of her laughter, and Shakti pawed at her leg, trying to get her to re-engage in the best playtime ever.

Jess and Beckett settled back into a cuddle, this time with Shakti between them. "Feel better?" he whispered.

"Yes," Jess said, and she really did.

Jess woke to the sound of Beckett's breathing, a rumbling too soft to be considered a snore. She leaned toward him and kissed the round of his shoulder, the body part closest to her head. She stretched her legs and her feet bumped Shakti, curled into a ball at the foot of the bed. As Jess came more fully awake, she took in the room. The way Beckett lay with his torso uncovered and one arm bent up over his head. The slight stirring of air coming through the window across from the bed. The sound of night insects outside, singing their own songs to each other. Beckett's chest of drawers hulked against the wall beside the window. The window, softly illuminated by millions of stars, undimmed by the rural landscape, outlined the silhouette of a man. Jess sat up and stared across the room, willing her eyes to refocus and prove her impression wrong. There could not be a man in the room with them, without Beckett or Shakti so much as stirring.

The figure moved to the end of the bed and lifted his arms, showing Jess the absence of his hands, confirming what she already knew but was trying hard not to believe.

Dan Grunner stood over her in Beckett's bedroom.

"Damn it," she muttered. So much for their sanctuary, their safe space for cuddling and sleeping and lovemaking. "What do you want?" It was more of a complaint than a question. Beckett stirred and rolled onto his side.

Samantha.

With that, Dan disappeared.

Jess flopped back onto the bed, shaking it enough to wake Beckett. He rolled over with a grunt, slid a hand toward Jess and rested it on her arm.

"Dan was just here," she said.

"What?" That woke him up.

"Sorry." Beckett sat up and looked around the room. "Don't bother," Jess said. "He's gone."

"What did he want?"

"I don't know. He said, 'Samanatha,' and disappeared. "But he was calm. Sad. He's a lot easier to handle without the rage."

"Great." Beckett reached for his side table and picked up his watch. "It's 4:00." He groaned and lay back against his pillow.

"Since we're both awake, I know something we can do."

"Yeah?"

Beckett rolled over onto Jess, kicking the sheet down and landing a foot against Shakti's back. She slid and dropped to the floor with a yip. They laughed softly and coiled their bodies against each other, reclaiming their sanctuary.

Chapter Twenty-Two

JESS HAD A knot in her stomach before she even entered the junk shop. Martinez held the door open for her and she let him wait a moment while she collected herself, though what she was collecting she wasn't entirely sure. "What's wrong?" Martinez asked.

"I don't know. This place makes me feel sick. Not just nervous, but actually ill."

"Can you go in?"

Jess nodded and stepped through the doorway. Skipper had given Martinez the key, so at least Jess didn't have to see him. She wondered what Martinez had told him, but decided not to ask. A strange green light cast a sickly glow over the interior of the shop and the air felt thicker than before, like if they stayed too long they'd suffocate. Jess passed through the first two rooms and into the back one with Martinez following.

A pain stabbed at Jess's temple and she pressed a hand to her head as she stumbled backwards. Martinez caught her elbow and steadied her. Even after Dave had been through the place, organizing it with his OCD running on high, there wasn't much margin of error. One wrong step and Jess could topple a table or trip over an elephant-shaped plant stand. She thanked him and found a chrome-legged barstool with a brown and white spotted cowhide top. The seat had worn thin from years of people sliding their own seats on and off of it. It might've looked nice beside Dan's Wurlitzer jukebox. She sat and closed her eyes to wait while Martinez watched her from the doorway.

A wave of nausea came over her and she put a hand to her stomach. She felt sick-drunk. Her vision blurred and her head hurt. Jess gripped the sides of the barstool to keep from falling off.

"Dan, I need you to show me what happened after the girl left."

Screaming filled her head, low in pitch, angry, a man's scream of frustration and rage.

Jess closed her eyes tight and put her hands over her ears. "Help me catch your killer," she insisted.

The screaming stopped. She shook her head and rubbed her ears as though it would help clear the sound of Dan's scream from the inside of her head. She opened her eyes to find Dan's face only inches from hers. Jess jerked backwards. The barstool swayed onto two legs. She caught her balance by getting a foot on the floor and bracing the stool. Her heart raced from the shock. Dan remained, his pale face steadily in hers. The blow above his eye had ruptured skin and broken bone. Dan's right eye appeared cloudy behind the veil of blood that ran from the gash. He'd been struck on top of the head as well, also on the right side, hard enough to dent his skull. That must have been the killing blow. All sorts of things could go wrong with a blow to the head; death could be sudden or take days.

Jess allowed her eyes to travel down his blood-soaked shirtfront to his missing hands.

"Dan, I want to help you."

How? It wasn't a voice. It wasn't even a word exactly. It was more a feeling Jess had that Dan was demanding to know how she would help him, how she *could* help him. And why.

"I'm helping one of the investigators with your case." Jess worked herself off the back end of the stool, putting some space between her and Dan. He didn't look impressed with her answer. "You can show me things and I'll tell him." Dan's appearance didn't change, but the room softened, felt less hot and stuffy, the light more yellow. The subtle shift came as a relief. Jess didn't know how to answer the why. Why was complicated. It had to do with her sense of right and wrong, of duty. It also had to do with Beckett and Tyler, and even Martinez. And Shakti and her house, her home—that had to do with Bonnie and could be traced back to her divorce and that one fight of many when Mitch made it clear that he wouldn't leave the house, and Jess realized she no longer had a home, a place where she felt safety and comfort. "The man who did this to you is trying to take my home away."

She studied Dan, his dress shirt, his jeans. She'd seen him at the Water Wheel that day, only his back while he was writing up Tyler's order. If she'd met him, she probably would have thought him a really nice guy. "Dan, who's Samantha?"

Jess felt a blow to her head, the pain intense, sharp. It knocked her over, but she stayed on her feet, staggering, crying out, clutching her head. When Jess regained her equilibrium, she looked around the junk shop, at the body on the floor and the crap piled everywhere. A set of dusty glassware with McDonald's characters lined the front of a shelf at about chest-height. The Hamburgler was mostly obscured by a teardrop-shaped spray of blood, while Grimace had only been peppered by tiny droplets, as though he'd been walking in a red rain. The girl stood beside the glassware, holding something round and slick with blood. Jess looked at her across a half wall, like...like... Understanding dawned. She was seeing the right side of the room by looking across the bridge of her nose and by turning her head; she had lost vision in her right eye.

The girl started trembling and backed up until she was against the shelves. She dropped the bloody glass object with a heavy thud that Jess felt through her feet. Startled by the solidity of the shelves, the girl turned and took a step away from the corner of the room, a step that shrunk her by a good three inches. Jess looked at her feet and saw one of her sparkly red shoes laying on its side. The girl kept her back to the shelves and her arms out like she was restraining a crowd. She stared at Dan lying prostrate, his head twisted to the side, the clouded eye staring up at her.

Dan made a guttural sound. A death moan.

The girl startled, jumped forward and her bare foot landed in the blood seeping from Dan's head wound. She turned and ran, putting her foot down on a scattered pile of yellowed brochures.

Jess stared at the bloody footprint. The perfect bloody footprint.

A tsunami of rage hit Jess so hard it knocked her over.

She spun around to face Martinez. "What did that little cunt tell you?" she snarled, her voice uncharacteristically deep.

"Jess, you all right?" Martinez looked fuzzy around the edges and the room seemed to disappear on one side.

"April. Or June. You talked to her, didn't you? What did she tell you? Did she tell you what they did with my hands?"

"*Dios mio.*" Martinez took a step away from Jess and crossed himself, then came closer and peered at her face, getting right up in it. "Mr. Grunner?"

Jess felt herself sucked through a straw. She wobbled and extended a hand, grabbed onto the edge of a shelf to keep from falling. When her head cleared, she found Martinez staring at her intently, his nose inches from hers so even his pores were in focus. She blinked herself back to reality, then dodged Martinez and rushed out the back door to vomit over the rail of the deck.

Martinez came out as she was wiping the corners of her mouth with the back of her hand. "Gum?" He pulled a pack from the leg pocket of his 5.11 pants and held it out to her.

"Thanks." She put the gum in her mouth and chewed, letting the mint wash over her taste buds and fresh saliva envelop her teeth. She sank to the floor of the deck and put her head in her hands.

Martinez leaned against the building. "Has that ever happened before?"

"What? A ghost talking through me?" She guffawed. "I hope it never happens again."

"Tell me about it?"

Jess sat on the steps facing the trees behind the building. With the sun still in the east, they had shade. A light breeze ruffled the leaves in the canopy. She lifted her face to it and closed her eyes. When she opened them, a hawk circled overhead with several small birds, too small to identify, circling it in flight, driving it away from their nests.

"He's raging," she said. "I've never felt anger like that, it's like…" she shook her head while the right word eluded her. "Pow."

"Pow?" Martinez had a pocket notebook in hand and he flipped the cover closed.

"Pow's not note-worthy?" Jess teased. "It's explosive. Is that better?"

"Yes, but it doesn't sync up with what we've learned about Dan Grunner. The story his wife tells is that he's a loving husband and father, doesn't have a single mean bone or enemy."

"Something is wrong with him, but I don't know what. A transformation or something." Jess looked back at the hawk and wondered how it could soar so gracefully with the small birds attacking it. "How'd you identify him so fast? That was fast, right?"

Martinez nodded. "Because of you, actually. You said you saw his hands and a wedding ring and a watch."

"Yeah."

"You were right about the watch, so I decided to start with missing persons reports filed by wives in the last forty-eight hours. Grunner's from Iowa, but since his wife knew he was traveling in Wisconsin, we got the bulletin on him and I made the match."

Jess reached to the side of the steps and picked a tall stalk of grass that had gone to seed. "You ever do this as a kid?" She pinched the stalk right below the seed head. "It's a tree." She ran her fingers up the stalk, stripping the seeds from the stem and bunching them together, their bases between her fingertips. "It's a bush."

"You must've been really bored as a kid."

Jess chuckled and released the seeds to the breeze. "Victor, who's Samantha?"

"His wife. Did you see her?"

"No. I saw Dan. Last night at Beckett's place." Victor cocked his head, one eyebrow raised high. "I guess he followed me home."

"Will the weirdness never cease?"

"That's what I say. Every frickin' day." Jess smiled at the remark, though the truth of it concerned her more than she let on. "So…I need to find his wife."

"No way." Martinez stepped toward Jess, full of assumed authority. "We've already been in touch with her, and we've convinced her to stay put while the investigation is ongoing. If this were a normal death, I'd say come on up —"

"Normal death?"

"Hit and run, bar fight, hunting accident… With some nut job hanging onto her husband's hands, the last thing I need is the bereaved widow wandering through town, asking questions."

"Okay then. I'll scratch *find Samantha* off today's to do list."

"Good."

"Victor, I'm on your team," she reminded him.

"Right. I know, Jess. Just remember who's the detective here, all right?"

Jess didn't answer. She plucked another stalk of grass from beside the deck and began twisting the stem around her finger. "What about the girl? If Dan's such a good man, why did he follow her out of the bar? What was he after if he's not the type to cheat on his wife?"

"Maybe he is the type, and his wife just doesn't know it."

"He showed me something new this time. Um…" Jess didn't quite have herself back to herself yet. She took a deep breath and let it out slowly. "There were McDonald's glasses with blood on them. And on the floor there was a bloody footprint on some papers, and…" Jess closed her eyes to bring the vision back to her mental screen, "…a shoe. A tacky one. The girl lost a shoe during the scuffle."

"We got the spatter, but no shoe. You say he showed you a footprint?"

She nodded. "It was on a pile of brochures that were…" she gestured with her hand, "fanned out on the floor. The print would have been across several of them."

"Well, I'll be damned." Martinez folded his arms across his chest and leaned on the doorframe. "If I didn't believe in your ability, I'd have to conclude the only way you could know so much about this crime is if you had committed it."

Jess stared at Martinez. She guessed cops were better at hiding their emotions than poker players. "Good thing you do believe me."

"*That* is why I'm keeping you all to myself. At least for now. If my task force partner knew what we were doing, he'd…"

"What?"

"Let's just say it would suck to be both of us."

"That's not very comforting." Jess put her hands on her head and smoothed her hair away from her face.

"He needs convincing is all."

She studied Martinez, his high brow and hooked nose. *Aquiline,* she thought, then wondered if the word was overused. "And you're going to convince him?"

He faced her and leaned against the deck railing. It sagged under his weight. "Your talent could prove useful in my line of work."

"Your talent could prove useful in my line of work? He actually said that?" Beckett tore a hunk of bread off the baguette and dipped it in the olive oil between them.

"Yep."

After Martinez had finished with her talents, Jess spent the day writing at home, one of her most productive days yet. It seemed having a deadline was good for her. In the evening, she made a gazpacho and brought it over to the studio. Beckett spent the day there, working toward his own deadline, creating custom dinnerware for one of his wealthy clients, in addition to preparing for the gallery show in Duluth.

"What does that even mean?" Beckett asked.

"I don't know. He wants a psychic in his back pocket?" Jess caught a glimpse of a bat swooping past the window beside their booth.

"That sounds dirty."

"I'm not willing to be on call for Investigator Martinez. I'm not a crime fighter."

"You kind of are. Good gazpacho, by the way." He splashed some hot sauce into his bowl.

"I only want to write books. That's why I moved out here. Speaking of which, I have to go the Cities tomorrow to see a woman about a book."

"Should I know what that means?"

"John and I have an appointment with his editor. I know it's short notice, but after that stuff at the junk shop, I thought I'd spend a night or two with Chandra."

"Since you *shouldn't* be at home anyway." Emphasis on *shouldn't*, a reminder that he hadn't wanted her writing there today.

"Something like that."

"Is my place not good enough for you?" he said with a wry smile.

"I've been meaning to say something about that…" Jess teased.

Shakti had chosen to curl up under the worktable and chew on her bone, leaving them to eat their supper in peace.

"Why do you think Dan showed me the shoe and the footprint?"

"I don't know. Because," Beckett waved his spoon like it could conduct his thoughts, "they're important. They hold the key to solving the case." He put his spoon back in his bowl. "Okay, I know that was lame."

"Actually, I think you're onto something."

"Really?"

Jess got up and grabbed her phone from the worktable. She tapped the screen a couple of times and put the phone to her ear.

"Oh, you aren't in Martinez' pocket, but you've got him on speed dial."

Jess winked at Beckett. "Hello, Victor?" Martinez greeted her informally, which Jess took to mean he was free to speak about her talent. "I was thinking about the shoe and the footprint. They must be important or Dan wouldn't have shown them to me. Can I put you on speaker phone?"

"I looked into those today," he said as Jess set the phone on the table between her and Beckett. "We got impressions coming up the hill from the bar to that back door. One set for Dan Grunner, and another that matches a lady's pump. I double-checked with forensics. There was no footprint at the scene. We did get a partial off one of the lower shelves. It could be a toe print, but it's smeared, so it's a long shot."

"What does that mean?" Beckett asked.

"Well, even if the partial is a match to our girl's toe, it only puts her at the scene before Grunner was killed. A bloody footprint, a good match, would prove she was there at the time Grunner sustained his injuries."

"What about the shoe?" Beckett asked. "Can you match that to the girl, like Cinderella?"

"We already checked that. The shoe's a size nine. Our girl's a seven and a half."

"Another riddle," Jess said as she hung up the phone.

"Now what?"

"Find the footprint and we'll find the killer."

Jess ran home in the morning to pack a bag for her trip to the Cities, her first since moving to Skoghall. Shakti wandered around the bedroom, sniffing the floor like maybe something had changed. Jess stood in her closet, pulling out clothing, holding it up to herself in front of the full-length mirror. "What do you wear to a meeting with an editor?" Shakti plunked her rump down and looked at Jess, head tilted. "I don't know either, Bear."

"I'm an artist." She held up a floral top with a deep V-neckline, something she'd bought on a whim, then almost never wore. She tossed the top onto the bed. "But this is a nonfiction editor."

She held up a pencil skirt and jacket, a suit from her days of eight-to-five. "Nope. Can't do it." She threw it on the bed, making a mental note to get rid of it.

At the back of the closet hung a pair of slacks she'd almost forgotten about. Light gray in color with a neat crease down the leg. She had a sleeveless top with a scooped neckline and a tiny frilled edge that paired with a soft knit cardigan. "Perfect." Jess pushed garments aside to dig into the recesses of her closet. For a book contract, she was willing to wear heels.

Jess set her bag on the porch and locked the front door, making sure to latch the screen door. As the humidity rose over the summer, the wood framing had warped enough that it wouldn't close without a good tug. She took a moment to sit on her front steps and watch Shakti meander around the yard. Tyler and Bruno hadn't been by for a playdate since Martinez and Johnson considered him a suspect. She hoped he and Bruno were doing all right. Shakti sniffed the sugar maple, circling it with her nose, snuffling the bark. When she found something interesting, she licked the tree. "Shakti, come on girl." Shakti might as well have been deaf. Jess stood up and went to see what was suddenly so interesting about the old tree. Shakti licked the trunk again.

Several large cicada exuviae clung to the bark, defying gravity, wind, and sun. But not Shakti. Her snout appeared between Jess and the remains she was studying and with an adroit motion of the lips, the alien-looking shell disappeared. Jess watched Shakti crunch the remains between her teeth. "Good snack?" Shakti looked up at Jess and swished her tail happily. "Let's go, Bear." Jess grabbed her bag and led Shakti to the car, shaking her head.

She pulled out onto Haug Drive and headed for town. A green sport pickup parked off the shoulder between some trees edged onto the road and followed her. When Jess slowed to turn onto Main Street, she checked her mirrors and her heart jumped.

Jess made the turn and dug in her bag for her phone with one hand. She hoped Beckett had the big sliding door open on the front of the studio and that he was looking up. At the stop sign where Main Street met the River Road, Jess decided to call Martinez. If she called Beckett and he came to the door, whoever was in the truck might see him, might connect him to her. She took a right and headed toward Bay City.

"Okay," Martinez said, "that's good. Can you read a license plate?"

Jess stared in her rearview mirror. "No. He doesn't have one on the front of the truck."

"Damn. Just one guy in the truck?"

The road curved between the river and bluffs, and it took some time before she was able to get a fix on the driver in her rearview mirror. "Just one." Jess felt calmer and less vulnerable with Martinez on the other end of the phone. She slowed down in the village of Maiden Rock, named for the legendary Indian princess who hurled herself from the bluff in the name of true love. She let the truck get right behind her and looked up in her rearview again. "He's wearing a ball cap and mirrored sunglasses, aviator style frames."

"Don't get too clever, Jess. If he figures out what you're doing, it might prompt him to attack."

"Attack?" She glanced at Shakti curled in the footwell of the passenger seat.

"He ran you off the road before. He's playing with you now. Maybe he's trying to figure out what you know, or maybe he's just trying to scare you."

"It's working, Victor. I'm scared." The driver kept a reasonable distance behind her, not calling attention to himself. "Here's Bay City," Jess said. "What do I do?"

Another river road town, though larger it lacked the attractions of Skoghall. Jess slowed down and scanned the roadside. An ice cream shop. A gas station. A single cross street could lead her toward the river or away. A string of several cars came toward Jess along the River Road. She stepped on the gas and swung left into town without signaling, cutting off the first of the cars and forcing the guy in the pickup to yield if he wanted to come after her.

She bumped over the railroad tracks, dropping her phone and jolting Shakti so that her head smacked into the glove box. On the nearest corner, people sat at umbrella-covered tables outside a diner advertising homemade donuts. Jess pulled over next to them and craned her neck around to see if the pickup had followed.

Martinez' voice called her name from the phone on the passenger's seat and Shakti sat up to stare at Jess. "I'm fine," she called toward her phone as she picked it up. "Victor?" She continued to scan the road. "I think he went north. He didn't follow me into town."

She heard Martinez relay the message to someone else, probably Johnson. "We're on it," he said to Jess. "We'll try to cut him off before he hits the state line." The nearest state line being the bridge across the Mississippi into Red Wing.

"I hope you catch him," she said, more to the ether than Martinez.

She returned to the River Road and headed back to Skoghall. She still had a puppy to drop off and a meeting with an editor to get to.

"If they don't catch him now, they'll put someone on my house in case he turns up there again," she relayed to Beckett what Martinez had said. "He seems to be after me." Jess shrugged. "Aren't I lucky?"

"Yeah, lucky."

Chapter Twenty-Three

JUNEY DIDN'T UNDERSTAND why she was wearing these shoes. Okay, so they weren't hers. The guys had picked them up from the Salvation Army store and they got them about two sizes too big. Stupid boys. She couldn't decide if they were kind of cute or just trashy. She supposed guys liked trashy. Her father would kill her if he saw her now, wearing a mini skirt that barely covered her ass—also provided by the guys—and platform pumps covered in red glitter. Dorothy's ruby slippers all grown up. And slutty. Heels were hard enough to walk in, especially since she'd never had the opportunity to practice, never mind adding a couple inches to the ball of her foot so she teetered like the squirrels that swayed across her mother's clothesline.

There was that one time, when she went to visit her sister at college. Rachel let her try on her heels and promenade the hallway outside her dorm room for about two minutes. After her short walk, which mostly consisted of figuring out how not to twist her ankle and fall on her face, Juney stood in front of Rachel's full length mirror and admired her legs. Before that moment, she'd had no idea her calves could swell at the top and her ankles could look so thin. "What will you do with them over the summer?" Juney had asked. "Father doesn't own us," was Rachel's terse reply. Juney dropped it, but she didn't know how Rachel would keep them while living under their father's roof. There was no privacy, no secrecy, and no good hiding place when you abided by the Family's code.

Juney slid into the booth across from the man, relieved to be off her feet. "Hi, I'm Ju—ly." She'd begun to say her own name, changed midstream, and what came out was July like the month, not Julie like the girl's name. Her neck prickled with embarrassment. She'd been at the game two seconds and almost blew her cover.

The man looked surprised to see her, but not altogether unwelcoming. "Hi," he said back. "I'm Dan." Was he laughing at her?

"Want to buy me a drink, Dan?"

"Um…no. You look kind of young and I'm married." He was laughing at her, she was certain of it. But the bar was practically empty, so she'd have to stick it out.

Juney stared at him across the table and her heart began to pound. She didn't want to do this anymore. She tried to look Dan in the eye. "Eye contact," Ethan had insisted, "is how you'll get his trust." He wore glasses and the dim lighting in the booth made it hard to get a connection. Juney was grateful for that, whatever Ethan thought about eyes and trust. "I'm meeting some friends here," she said. "We can kill some time together is all." They had rehearsed this part in Ethan's garage. Ethan called it being coy. She thought coy was a type of goldfish, but she didn't correct him. Just like she never corrected her father. Dan lifted his glass a couple inches off the table and nodded his head toward her in a gesture of assent, like one of those men in the black and white movies her mother watched on late night television.

She slid to the end of the booth and carefully set both feet on the floor before standing on those ridiculous shoes. *Damn Ethan*, she should have insisted on going to the Salvation Army with them. She made her way carefully to the bar, a clutch on a string slung over her shoulder so she couldn't drop it. That had been Ethan's idea, too. He had dressed her like a doll. She snorted at the thought. Erick was so different than Ethan— quiet and nice. He worked at his dad's lawn service and liked planting trees. "Every single tree makes the world a better place," he told her. Juney was almost smiling when the bartender stood in front of her, his big hands spread on the counter between them.

"I'll need to see some ID," he said before she'd even ordered a drink. He spent his time with her license, tilting it this way and that in the light, then holding it down where she couldn't see it behind the bar. He probably had one of those violet lights. *Go ahead,* she thought, *it's real.*

She made her way back to Dan's booth, practically breaking a sweat trying to stay upright and not spill her drink.

Juney smiled at Dan and raised her glass to him. "See? I'm not too young." She'd ordered a rum and Coke and hoped the bartender made it weak. Any other time, she'd have wanted it strong just because, but not tonight. She took a sip, grateful she'd also practiced drinking, otherwise the prickling warmth of the rum would have shocked her.

"July," he said, doubting her already. "What do you do?"

"I'm a college student. UW La Crosse."

"So what are you doing in Skoghall?"

"I'm visiting my boyfriend. He lives at home and goes to a technical college, so I come home for the weekend whenever I can." The more story she told, the more she liked it. She could be a college student. She could have a boyfriend at a technical college. *Father doesn't own me.*

"I hope your boyfriend isn't the jealous type." Dan was teasing her, his eyes suddenly bright, even behind the lenses of his glasses.

"He's got nothing to be jealous of. What about you?"

"I'm the Fuller Brush Man."

"Oh, what kind of brushes?"

He laughed quietly as he straightened up on the bench seat. "I'm a door-to-door salesman. Encyclopedia Britannica, Hoover vacuums, Fuller brushes." He paused to see if she'd catch on.

It made her mad, feeling left behind, but then something occurred to her. "You mean Girl Scout cookies? Band candy? Christmas wreaths to send the basketball team to State?"

"I suppose I do." He continued to smile, but Juney no longer felt he was laughing at her. He took a drink of his amber liquid, and she raised her own glass to her lips. It wouldn't do to let it sit, ice melting away, not if she wanted him to trust her.

She didn't really know what Ethan and Erick had planned for Dan. He seemed like a nice enough man, a family man, though the sense that he was having fun with her kept returning. Not at her expense, however, and that lowered Juney's defenses, let her actually enjoy talking to this man. Or was it the pretending that she enjoyed? Being someone entirely different. July. Erick would laugh when she told him that her name was July. Some day, when she was out from under her father's thumb and her mother's watchful eye, she'd come to bars like this one and sit across from men like that one and sip her rum and Coke and she'd be grown up. No, better than grown up, she'd be free.

That's all Rachel wanted, too. Rachel had told her she wasn't going to stop at a bachelor's degree and move home to marry some hick and raise his hick kids in the way of the Family. "Take college seriously," she'd told Juney. "Father's willing to pay for this much, because it's expected today that even a housewife have a decent head on her shoulders, that if the Family gets into tough times she can go out and start bringing in a paycheck. "Shit," she'd said *shit,* "this economy has our country so backwards that men are getting laid off and women are supporting their families. But once you've got your bachelor's, the Family cuts you off and reels you in, might as well hobble you while they're at it. Nobody takes 'ball and chain' and 'barefoot and pregnant in the kitchen' literally anymore…except the Family." Rachel would go to graduate school. She'd get a fellowship and get as far away from Wisconsin as she possibly could. Never look back.

Juney didn't know if she'd follow in her sister's footsteps or not. If she did, their mother would be left to fend for herself and Juney couldn't do that to her, not if she stopped to think about it for a minute. If a moment had led up to this one, to her buying Dan a drink with Rachel's roommate's license, it was that one when Rachel convinced her she either had to get out from under the code or she had to bend the code to her own will. If her father accepted Ethan and Erick into the Family, then she'd be just about safe. She'd have Erick, and her mother would have her.

"You could use another one," Juney said when Dan had just about emptied his glass.

"Oh, I don't think so…"

"I'll buy." Juney colored at her own insistence. "Look," she gestured apologetically at her glass. "I'm not even half done and I think I'm getting stood up. Let me buy you one for the road."

Juney left a dollar on the bar and took her time putting her change into her clutch. She took out a tube of lipstick, leaned forward so she could see into the mirror behind the bar, and applied a fresh coat. The bartender, with his waxed mustache and bulging arms, turned away, slinging a damp towel over his shoulder. Juney looked around the barroom before applying another coat of the red paint. She stuck her pinky finger into the drink and gave it a swish. Since the cocktail napkins were across the bar, she put her finger in her mouth and had her first taste of scotch.

She took her time getting back to the table, wobbling more than once, but managing to keep herself on her feet. She was glad the booths had walls that went all the way up to the ceiling so Dan couldn't watch her walking back to him. A couple of women played darts near the booth, cheering whenever the machine lit up a hit. Juney had to stop and wait for the one with a big head of tight blonde curls to notice her and step out of the way. Rachel would have cleared her throat or said "excuse me" really loud, but not Juney. *The meek shall inherit the earth,* she told herself.

Chapter Twenty-Four

JOHN POURED WINE for Jess and Chandra before tipping the bottle to his own glass. As soon as the libation was poured, they raised their glasses. "To our book," John said.

It had been a tough call: Japanese or Indian. Indian food seemed more celebratory, so Chandra met Jess and John at Ghandi Mahal. They were early enough to beat the dinner rush and got a table near the musicians' dais in the front window. Jess admired the ornate, shiny brass vent covers that had been repurposed to decorate a column dividing sections of the restaurant.

"I could tell she was impressed with you," John said to Jess.

"I want to hear everything," Chandra said as she broke a papadum over her plate.

Jess grabbed a samosa and spooned on some tamarind sauce. She hadn't realized how much she'd missed this kind of food until she saw it sitting in front of her. "We signed contracts. Chandra," Jess turned on her seat to face her friend, "I have a book deal."

"Damn!" Chandra hugged Jess, her long spiraling curls all Jess could see for a moment. "That's a dream come true, isn't it?"

Jess could feel her cheeks stretching to contain the smile on her face.

John's phone rang in his pocket and he pulled it out. "It's my daughter," he said. "Excuse me." He stood and went outside to take his call.

"Jess." Chandra gripped her arm and the glass Jess was about to raise wobbled dangerously. "John and I are seeing each other."

"Really?"

"Say it's great. I think it's great."

"Let go of my arm first."

"Sorry." Chandra released Jess and stared at her like a child watching the arrival of her birthday cake.

"It's great. Are you happy?"

"I think so. It's really new, but yeah. I am happy."

Chandra had that new love look about her, a look Jess knew well. It seemed like Chandra fell in love with a new man every other week, which, if she wasn't actually settling down a bit, meant John was about to hit his expiration date. Should she say something about Chandra's track record or John's recent divorce?

"I mean that thing with Tyler was kind of fun, but..."

"What? What thing with Tyler?" As soon as Jess asked the question, she didn't need an answer. There was only one night she and Chandra weren't together, the night Beckett hit Tyler in The Two Wheeler. "*Chandra!*"

"What?" Chandra stared at her over the rim of her wine glass.

"You were with Tyler the night of the murder."

"The point I'm making, Jess, is that a hook up is all well and good once in a while, but I'm ready for something serious."

"Oh my God, Chandra," Jess spat out the words in exasperation. "Tyler is a suspect and you can alibi him."

Chandra's expression froze as she processed the news. "If that's true," she said, "why didn't he just tell the police about us?"

"Because..." Jess studied Chandra, as though the answer was somewhere on her face. "I don't know. Why wouldn't he?"

"Maybe," Chandra made her pronouncement like she was stating the obvious, "because he's in love with you."

Chapter Twenty-Five

JUNEY THOUGHT THE line up was terrifying, then they'd released her into her parents' custody. She didn't know who she had to thank for that, or if she should even be thankful. In some ways, a jail cell would have been preferable. Her father had practically thrown her down the stairs, but her mother reminded him that they were under scrutiny. And if they were under scrutiny, the Family was under scrutiny. *The Family.* Why couldn't she just have been born into a normal family? Why did she get stuck with these freaks? The fact that Rachel had escaped to college only made things worse for Juney, increased the pressure to be perfect, to *participate.* She had her mother to thank for that. Her mother helped Rachel get away. Maybe she thought it would pave the way for Juney to follow, or maybe she really had always liked Rachel better. Either way, her father wasn't going to let both of his children escape the Family.

And then she met Ethan with his...what? Her mother would call it charm. They got drunk one afternoon in a field and she said too much about the Family. She knew better, but the alcohol got in the way of reason. So much so she was prepared to give it up to Ethan, right there on the edge of a pond behind a screen of cattails. Somewhere she heard the engine of a tractor, but it wasn't close enough to worry about. She tried to kiss him. He said no. He said it gently so she didn't feel rejected. He said tell me more about the Family. Juney blinked at him in wonder. A boy wanted to listen to her talk more than he wanted *it*. He mentioned respect and beauty and waiting for the right time and coaxed her into saying too much. She would never admit she wasn't forced to reveal their secrets, but she knew it hadn't taken much. She was starving, and the attention he offered her was enough to get her to do anything.

Now her parents had delivered her to the Sheriff's Office in Durin for the second time and she'd never been so scared in her life. She sat awkwardly on the edge of a blue vinyl chair with white piping at the seams, holding her sandal, just her left sandal. They didn't need the right. A woman with cold eyes, eyes that sank back inside her head when she looked at Juney, held Juney's foot in one gloved hand while the other pressed an ink roller to the sole. She spread ink up the side of her foot, across the ball of it, and onto all of her toes. Her parents stood behind her chair like overseers. Mother dismayed, teary-eyed. Father fuming, crushing the rim of his hat in his hatefully strong hands. Not a cap, like normal men wore, Juney had noted about him numerous times, but a proper hat like he was Ward-fucking-Cleaver. If Juney was heading for Hell already, it wouldn't be for swearing, so she figured she might as well.

The Deputy knelt and placed Juney's foot down on a piece of white card stock. "Stand up." She then pressed each toe to the card individually, using her thumb to effect a rolling motion from one side to the other. Juney had an ingrown toenail and it hurt, this woman in a chocolate brown shirt, her hair cut short, squeezing Juney's toe between her fingers while she pressed it to the card, then rolled it from one edge to the other, creating a square print with an easily distinguished whorl in its middle.

What were you thinking? She could hear her father's voice in her head. *What were you thinking?*

Juney stared at top of the Deputy's head. She'd been thinking that if Ethan and Erick got in the Family, she could marry one of them. Erick. She could marry Erick. He would need her to show him the way things are done, to help him understand the rituals and secrecy. And if her husband needed her, she would have some kind of power, even if it was only at home, it would be better than having none.

And one day, Erick would help her escape.

Chapter Twenty-Six

KEEPING AN EYE on her place, Jess discovered, meant deputies patrolling the area came onto the premises to check on her house.

"Martinez."

"Hello…" she remembered not to use his first name, "it's Jessica Vernon."

"Ms. Vernon, how are you?" His formality confirmed that he was on duty and Johnson was probably nearby.

"I just got back home from a night in the Twin Cities, and I gave a friend your number. She was with Tyler Cross the night of the murder."

"Yes. She called us earlier today. We're no longer focussing on him, though we didn't consider him much of a suspect once the pickup guy turned up."

"Good. Also, I've met the deputy watching my property." Jess looked at a squirrel dozing sprawled over a tree branch outside her kitchen window. Shakti lapped water from her bowl next to the fridge.

"That's *good*." Martinez put emphasis on good, as though Jess had just complained about something.

"Yeah, thanks. What have you found out about my stalker?"

Martinez paused. "Nothing yet."

"But he's connected to the girl from the bar. Hasn't she..?"

"No. Her story is that Grunner tried to rape her and she ran away before he had the chance to *spoil* her." Jess could practically hear him shaking his head. "That's the euphemism she used."

"But we know she took him there. She teased him and—"

"*You* might know that, Ms. Vernon, but the evidence doesn't prove one story over another. All we know for sure is she and Grunner met in the bar and parted company in the junk shop. You even said it looked like Grunner was going after her, and that's what she says, too."

"But what about the hands?"

"Exactly."

Jess scowled out the window, wondering how her life had become so complicated. "And that's where the green pickup guy comes in."

"That's my guess."

"Now what?"

"Now you go back to your boyfriend's place and wait for us to do our job."

Jess wasn't very good at waiting and she didn't like being told what to do. She took a check from her book deal out of her purse and stuck it to the fridge with a magnet. It was the first third of her advance on the book, and she still couldn't quite believe it. She counted the zeros again, and again came up with three of them left of the decimal point. Six-thousand dollars. That was a beautiful thing. That would see her through three months if she was frugal.

She spent the day at home, writing. It felt good to be at her own desk and she got more done than she ever would have in the studio, with Beckett throwing pots and customers coming off the River Road, browsing, asking questions, buying things. Jess couldn't be there on a Saturday without helping him, which meant she couldn't be there on a Saturday, not when she had a book to write.

She decided to take Shakti for a walk after lunch, a blatant act of defiance. As she walked along her neighbor's soybean field, she wondered what made this guy come after her. She made a list. *First, this guy is crazy. Second, he probably has Dan's hands, which makes him really crazy.* Jess told herself that wasn't helping and tried again. *I identified the girl from the bar.* That was better, concrete, rational. So, her guy in the green pickup didn't want the girl identified. *Because he didn't want her to give him up. Because he has something to hide, like Dan's hands.* Jess couldn't help feeling that there was some bigger purpose behind all of this, that the green pickup guy was crazy and was after her, but he wanted something beyond all of that. She just didn't know what.

Jess stood on the shoulder while Shakti squatted in the grass at the edge of the ditch. About a dozen sparrows perched in the branches of a nearby elderberry shrub, chattering noisily. Jess recalled the hawk and the sparrows she had seen behind the junk shop, the sparrows driving the hawk away from their nests. Green pickup guy thought he was the hawk and she the sparrow. He thought he could have her for lunch. But those little birds had something the hawk didn't: the fierce determination to protect their nests and their young. Shakti tugged at the leash and Jess started moving down the road again.

Jess would not be run out of her nest. Not again.

Chapter Twenty-Seven

HE SHOULD HAVE slapped Erick around for bringing pot to a job. But once the pipe was lit, he figured what the hell. Just enough for a nice buzz. It might help Erick get through it all, and now that they'd come this far, he needed Erick to stick it out. If Erick turned tail, he could turn Ethan in. Then what? A whole lot of shit for Ethan and a slap on the wrist for Erick, the good boy, the weakling who got coerced by the bully.

Ethan smiled to himself. He wasn't a bully. Bullies lacked subtlety and craft. Ethan saw himself as a manipulator. A mastermind. A genius even. It would take genius to craft a terror spree, stump law enforcement, escape undetected, pile up cold cases as the years went on. And his mother thought he was directionless. She had no idea.

Erick was one of those red-headed kids who turned beet-faced at the slightest provocation—insult, embarrassment, intoxication...guilt. His cheeks were already flushed from a single hit. If he was ever brought in to question, Ethan doubted he could tell a lie without turning the color of a baboon's ass. So...he passed the single-hitter back to Erick and looked out at the dark water of the Mississippi...he'd have to make sure Erick was more afraid of him than of the cops, that's all.

Ethan turned his head to stare at Erick's profile. He was tall, slender, a cross-country runner with high cheekbones and deep-set eyes. A regular Viking. You'd think he'd be a natural at the rape and plunder thing, but it seemed to have been bred out of him by generations of civility, the great pretense. Erick tapped the spent weed out of the bowl and put the pipe away in an old Altoids tin. His hand trembled and he glanced at Ethan to see if he was watching. Ethan met his gaze, saw the apprehension there.

"Don't be a pussy."

It was 9:00, plenty dark, and they had work to do before Erick's dad's cousin—or whoever he was to them, another tame Viking as far as Ethan was concerned—got home from the bonfire. *Who has a bonfire on a Tuesday?* Ethan wondered. But this was better, less traffic, fewer people around. He grabbed his backpack and dragged it next to him, unzipped the top and pulled out his gear.

He handed Erick a headlamp with the warning not to turn it on unless he was told to. Erick put it on. Ethan grabbed the lamp and yanked it off, glad when the elastic band snagged some of Erick's firey hair. "Ow," Erick complained. Ethan handed him a plastic shower cap. "Here, since you wouldn't shave your head." Erick grumbled as he stretched the cap over his head and tucked in the ends of his hair. "Now the lamp," Ethan commanded.

He took out two pairs of men's shoes. Both size twelve Oxfords with almost nothing for tread. He had stuffed the shoes with tube socks so they'd stay together in his bag. He and Erick removed their shoes and layered on the socks. Erick's size eleven clodhoppers only required one extra pair of socks. Ethan needed two pairs and maybe could have fit in three. Shoes and socks alike came from the Salvation Army store in Chippewa Falls, where he'd paid $13 cash for everything. He tossed their shoes in the backpack. Next, he removed a box of latex gloves and they each layered on two pairs.

"Dude," Erick said as he snapped on the last of his gloves. Even in the dark, Ethan could see he was sweating. "I don't want to do this anymore."

"Too late, Erick. Juney's already done her part. You want to leave her out to hang? In your cousin's shop or whatever that place is?" Ethan waited for Erick to either dig in or cave. He counted on Erick to think this through with his gonads and not his brain. If he'd used his brain once in all this, he wouldn't be here right now, and Juney wouldn't be in that bar. But Juney was one fucked up kid and Erick was in love with her. "Erick, if we don't go do our part, she's going down."

"Fuck!" Erick made fists and pressed them to his temples. "Fuck me!" He dropped his hands to his lap. "All right. Let's go get Juney and get the fuck out of there and then I never want to talk about this again." Erick jumped up and took a step, tripping over the elongated toes of the dress shoes.

"How much weed did you smoke?"

"I'm fine. Let's get Juney."

Ethan stood up and looked around where they'd been sitting. He checked the area for footprints, cigarette butts, any sign they'd been there. When he was satisfied, he turned on his headlamp and led Erick across the floodplain toward the road. They had to move slowly, their path following one swell of land to another, diverting constantly around marshy areas, and slogging through water when he saw no way around it. Erick kept swatting mosquitoes and cursing under his breath. That was fine, until Ethan saw lights through the trees. He shushed Erick and signaled him to turn off his lamp. They came out of the trees and walked along the back of the shotgun duplex, sticking to the shadows.

Ethan moved slowly, listening to every engine on the road out front for a sign someone was pulling up to the junk shop. Voices carried over from the deck behind the bar along with the smell of cigarette smoke. He and Erick were dressed in black hoodies and sweat pants, $36 cash at K-Mart, also in Chippewa Falls. They crossed the railroad tracks and the short stretch of something too small and unkempt to be considered a yard, and went up the few steps onto the back deck. He put his foot down on a pair of eyeglasses. So far, everything was going according to plan.

Ethan took hold of the doorknob. "This is the moment," he said quietly enough that Erick couldn't hear, and pushed the door open.

Chapter Twenty-Eight

SKIPPER NODDED TO Jess when she walked through his front door. Since Dave cleaned up the shop, Skipper had dutifully sat at his front counter, opening the doors and waiting for customers who never came. "How are you, Skipper?"

"I'm all right," he said. "Are you going to the back room again?"

"Actually, I want to talk to you."

"You do?" He reached under his counter and slid open a drawer, then closed it without retrieving anything.

"Skipper," Jess began her query hesitantly, "you don't leave home often, do you?"

"No. I don't much like going out."

"But the night Dan Grunner was killed, you went out."

Skipper nodded and put a hand up to his ear. He rubbed at its edges and tugged the lobe like a toddler with an ear infection.

"Where'd you go?" Jess tried to make it sound like a friendly question.

"My cousin's bonfire."

"Dave's?"

"My other cousin. He's got a hunk of land about forty-five minutes east of here, sits on a small lake, woods, deer, fox, that sort of thing. He has lots of bonfire parties in the summer, says it takes care of our primal urges, but I don't never feel that primal anyway. I hardly ever go to it."

"Why'd you go this time?"

Skipper rubbed at his ear with thick fingers, and with each pass it burned redder. "Oaky and his boy Erick come by the other week and told me I had to go. Oaky said he had something special planned and nobody had seen me in months. He said the family would forget about me if I didn't show myself once a year at least."

"Thank you, Skipper." Jess reached a hand toward Skipper's arm. He avoided her touch, and she swung her hand up to the back of her neck as though that had been her intention all along. "What was the special thing?"

Skipper seemed to think about it before finally shrugging his shoulders. "Drums, I guess. Oaky made everybody bang a drum and some of the guys howled at the moon. It was full. I guess that was special."

Jess turned toward the door, stepping away from the counter, a fake move to depart intended to calm Skipper. She paused and turned toward him again, but maintained her distance from his counter. "Do you know," she said like it was a casual afterthought, "if you had something in that back room that was big and round? Glass, I think. Something that isn't there anymore."

Skipper touched his earlobe as he nodded. "Ashtray. Like this." He held his hands in front of himself to shape a circle a good nine inches across. "I remember because it was Mom's. Always sat on the TV tray beside her chair. That's where she liked it. Easy reach. I would have kept it, but I never got the hang of smoking. Makes me cough."

Jess walked up Main Street toward Skoghall Hardware. A middle-aged couple sat on the porch of the Skoghall Inn at the wrought iron café set, demitasses before them on demure saucers, a dish of sugar cubes with an antique silver tongs between them. Beside that, a plate of biscotti. Carrie and Mike Cummings did a nice job charming their guests. *Welcome to picturesque Skoghall on the Mississippi! Enjoy the arts, the eagles, the garden and the spring, the water wheel...the murders.* Jess snorted at the thought of how her experience of Skoghall had changed since moving here. The woman watched her pass and Jess waved and called good morning across the street. The woman smiled and waved back. *The friendly locals.* The man raised his demitasse and nodded above it. Jess would have to stop in the Water Wheel and get an espresso now.

She climbed the steps onto the porch of the old Western-style triplex. The Amish furniture store had the large corner shop. The middle was currently vacant, though Jess had heard a rumor—from either Beckett or Tyler because she hardly ever spoke to anyone else in this town—that Carrie and Mike were thinking of opening a gallery shop for her couture clothing and his paintings. The end space housed the hardware store, previously the village grocer. Jess thought Beckett should expand into groceries, a few convenient staples everyone needed on short demand. She had yet to convince him.

"Hey, Jess," Dave said as she entered. "Where's the little one?"

"The little one with four feet and a wagging tail?"

"That's the one. Uncle Dave misses her."

"Uncle Dave, huh?" Jess raised an eyebrow and grinned at him. "All right. You've earned it with all the dog sitting you've done for me. Uncle Dave."

Jess grabbed a bottle of iced tea from the drinks cooler and set it next to the register. She pulled a couple of ones out of her back pocket.

"Not a purse lady, are you?"

"Only when it suits me." She opened the bottle and took a drink while Dave rang her up. "You know those bonfires your cousin hosts?"

Dave's fingers froze over the keys on the cash register. He looked at Jess, suddenly serious. "So this isn't a social call?"

"Not entirely."

Dave rubbed his cheek. His beard, a short, tidy compliment to his face, added definition between his chin and neck that otherwise might be hard to see. Where Skipper had auburn hair, Dave's flamed red. The gray in his beard added a silvery highlight to his ruddy coloring. "Shouldn't you leave the detecting to the detectives?" He tapped the last button on his register and the drawer sprang open. He slid Jess's bills off the counter and replaced them with two dimes.

"This guy ran me and Shakti off the road the other day, then he followed me out of town."

Dave nodded. "Beckett told me about that."

"I figure the detectives could use some help keeping me *and* your four-legged niece safe.

Dave cracked a grin at Jess, "I knew you were tough soon as I laid eyes on you, Jess."

"Who all was at that bonfire?"

"You want a list?"

Jess nodded. "I think someone knew Skipper would be away that night."

Dave shook his head, rubbed his chin again. "Someone wandered over from the bar, found it empty."

"Maybe. But what if someone picked the bar because he knew the shop would be empty?"

"Jess, do you know what you're saying?"

"I think so, Dave."

Dave stepped back from the counter and sat on a stool against the wall. "These people are my family. They might not be the best or the brightest, but they're good people."

"If you tell me who was at that bonfire, then all of those people can be ruled out. They'll have alibis, won't they?"

"I suppose so." Dave folded his meaty, freckled arms across his chest and looked at the ceiling. "These are good people, Jess," he hesitated, "but there's a lot of drinking and smoking going on at those bonfires."

"I don't think the cops care about harmless recreation. They're after a murderer. Dan Grunner has a wife and baby girl."

Jess grabbed a quarter sheet flyer for a river boat charter and flipped it to the backside. Dave handed her a pen with a further shake of his head. She jotted down names as he listed them. When he finished, she had one question. "Was Oaky's son there?"

"Erick?" Dave shook his head while he tried to recall. "I don't remember seeing him, but, Jess…he's a good kid. He was probably playing video games in a friend's basement."

"Yeah, I'm sure you're right," she said. "He was probably playing games."

It wasn't hard to find Erick. Dave had told Jess he worked for his dad's lawn service company spring through fall, saving up for college. He stressed the word college, like maybe Jess should know that. As if her grand scheme was to screw up his chances of getting away, of leading a better life than his parents, than his big cousin Dave. Jess assured Dave she understood his concern, then assured him that if she talked to Erick, it would be better for his future than if Martinez and Johnson talked to him.

A breeze kept it tolerable in her car, parked on a residential street atop a bluff with a private overlook—*private*, she wondered about that. Who declared the land his and how long ago? When was it parceled off into an exclusive community of houses with over 3,000 square feet, great rooms, granite and stainless kitchens, three story entryways with hanging chandeliers visible from outside the house, and garages with room for the boat? Some early settlers had staked their claims on high and farmed the bluff tops. Jess had trouble imagining why anyone would farm up there, back then at least. Getting supplies up and crops down to market by horse or ox-drawn wagon must have been difficult. The isolation in winter must have been maddening. It seemed, as lifestyle choices go, kin to being a lighthouse keeper, just you and your family against the elements for a great part of the year. But all that was past and now wealthy people owned the bluff top with their SUVs and ATVs and 4x4s. Jess wondered, if she could afford it, would she live in one of these houses? No, these houses weren't her style. She would, however, buy land on top of a bluff, closer to the sky.

Erick came out from behind the house. Even with a bandana tied over his red hair, he was unmistakeable: tall, chiseled-features, pale, freckled. He looked like a nice kid, the kind of kid you'd ask over to help move furniture for a quick buck. His dirt-smeared cargo shorts hung loosely from his lanky frame. The green company t-shirt stuck to his ribs where he'd sweat through it. Jess picked up her camera and pointed it at him. Her big lens only went up to 150 mm, hardly enough for this kind of work, but hopefully she'd never need it again. The motor drive whirred as she collected images one after another. Erick faced the car and Jess ducked, lowering the camera to her lap, knocking it clumsily against the steering wheel. Magnum P.I. she was not. She tucked the camera into the foot well of the passenger side of her car and slid her sunglasses back down over her eyes.

He didn't appear to have noticed her. Erick stretched toward the sky, his t-shirt coming untucked in the front. When he finished stretching, he pulled a ramp down from the back of the truck and went up it into the bed. He brought down a wheelbarrow, then began loading bags of mulch into it. Jess took a deep breath and swung her car door open. *Now or never.*

"Erick." She stood only a few feet from him as he swung a fifty pound bag of cedar wood chips onto the stack in the wheelbarrow. His shoulders bulged impressively. He seemed taller than he had in the junk shop and what appeared to be a freckle-faced string bean of a kid was actually a powerful young man, all lean muscle and runner's legs. Jess doubted her purpose, but he stared at her now, too late to back away. "I'm a friend of your cousin, Skipper." He wiped the sweat from his face with the back of a gloved hand, placing a smear of loose dirt across his brow. "I think you might know something about the murder that occurred in Skipper's junk shop."

He staggered backwards as though someone had given him a shove, just enough to set him off balance, and quickly recovered. "I don't know what you're talking about," he said.

"I think you do."

He shook his head and reached for the wheelbarrow's handles.

"There's a girl involved," Jess said. "Maybe you go to school with her? Maybe you helped her? We think she might have acted in self-defense."

He kept his hands on the wheelbarrow's red rubber grips, but didn't turn away. "Yeah," he said barely audible, "self-defense."

"So you know Miss..." Jess pretended to search her mind for a name that had momentarily slipped away.

"Juney," he provided. Dave was right, helpful kid.

"You could corroborate Juney's story?"

"Is she in trouble?" His squint deepened from the addition of concern to the general brightness of the sun.

"A man's dead. A man with a wife and baby girl at home. So what do you think?" Erick glanced over his shoulder, then back at Jess. He tightened his grip on the wheelbarrow, lifted its feet off the ground, but made no move to turn. He didn't like hearing about the baby. "His name's Dan," Jess added.

Erick's lips parted, some word on the verge of escape, a word he resisted, possibly the key to everything.

"Erick!" a man barked as he came around the corner of the house. "They're waiting on you." He was an older version of Erick, though shorter and thicker with a strong resemblance to Dave. He smiled at Jess. "Hello. Are you interested in landscaping your property? I could show what we're doing here."

"No, Dad. She's a friend of Skipper's."

His smile dropped from his face. "Get that mulch round back."

Erick obeyed with haste.

"What is a friend of Skipper's doing talking to my son while he's at a job site?" he placed his hands on his hips, broadening his stance. It had the same effect as a lizard puffing out its chest.

"You're Oaky, right?" Jess held out her hand. Oaky looked at it until Jess dropped it to her side. "There's a girl involved in the death at Skipper's shop, a girl Erick knows." Jess looked him in the eye. "Have you ever met a girl called Juney?"

"Juney?" He scratched his head, his nails making tracks through the sweat-dampened military-cut hair. "I don't think Erick's ever mentioned a Juney. I met a Liz once."

"All right. Thanks." Jess slid a finger into her back pocket and pulled out a card with her name and cell phone number on it, something she'd had printed up for her move, expecting she'd be introducing herself to lots of new people. This might have been the first she'd handed out. "If you think of anything, give me a call. And if I ever need landscaping, I'll call you." She smiled her best and-that's-a-promise smile.

Oaky slipped her card into his shirt pocket, grabbed another bag of mulch, and turned. Jess watched him cross the lawn toward the back yard. "Hey," he hollered, "tough guy." When he reached the corner of the house, a young man appeared to meet him. He wore a baseball cap and sunglasses. He took the mulch from Erick's dad, who quickly pulled a phone off his belt and stuck it to his head. The young man stared across the well-watered grass at Jess, unmoving.

She wanted to turn and climb back into the safety of her car and get away from there, but she refused her urge and returned his stare. She couldn't imagine why, but they had just entered the childhood competition. *First one to blink loses.* She refused to be cowed—she had once been the undisputed champion of staring contests in the Vernon household. Oaky had his head bent away from the wind and a finger in the ear opposite the phone. He straightened up, looked at Jess, then turned to see his employee standing across from her with the mulch pinned to his shoulder. He shouted and pointed at the back yard. The tough guy waited for a long moment, testing his boss's limits, then turned slowly, deliberately, and disappeared behind the house.

Jess trembled as though shaking off some unwanted touch.

She had to tell herself to slow down as she passed the last house and began the winding descent. At the base of the bluff, before turning to head north on the River Road, she pulled a small notebook out of her purse and scratched out the words, *Who is the tough guy?*

Shakti loped across the yard, tongue lolling to the side. Cicadas droned their single-note song from the trees that surrounded Jess's property. Officially, she lived with Beckett now and knew she wasn't supposed to be home, but she couldn't help herself and came by every few days to work, to let Shakti run around the yard, and to sooth herself when she got depressed about being dispossessed. She sat in her rocking chair and opened Isabella and Grace's diary.

April 3, 1954

Mother and Father don't believe that I have a friend named Isabella who lives in my closet. They are certain she is imaginary, but won't they be surprised when I prove to them that she is the little girl who lived in my bedroom thirty-six years ago. Mother just turned thirty last week, so Isabella is older than her! Isabella and I tell each other stories. Sometimes we stay up very late whispering our stories while Mother and Father sleep. Then Mother wonders why I am so tired the next day.

Jess's phone rang. She checked the caller ID before answering, "Hello, Investigator Martinez. Thanks for returning my call."

"Is everything all right?"

"So far. I talked to Skipper and his cousin, Dave, yesterday—"

"What for, Jess?" Martinez cut her off. "Playing detective isn't your job. It's mine."

"Gee, where have I heard that before?"

Jess heard Martinez breathing on the other end of the line. Maybe he was weighing his comeback options. Maybe he was just waiting her out.

"Do you want the information I got?" she said finally.

"Yes, go ahead."

"Dave and Skipper have a cousin who throws bonfire parties."

"I already know that."

"Do you know that Skipper was talked into going this month by his cousin, Oaky, and that his cousin's son, Erick, was there when it happened?"

"No, I didn't know that. So, you're thinking Erick chose the junk shop because he knew it would be vacant that night?"

"We've been thinking the junk shop was convenient to the bar and Skipper's absence was just a coincidence, but what if it's the other way around?"

"I'll follow it up."

"Good." Jess took a deep breath and let it out. "Victor? There's one more thing. I talked to Erick—"

"You did what?" his voice was stern, bordering on angry.

"He told me the girl's name is Juney. That's the name of the girl you've been investigating isn't it? The one who stole Carla's license."

Jess took Martinez' silence for agreement, though it could have been contained anger.

"This proves Erick is connected to the girl and therefore to Dan's death. I'll bet he's also connected to a certain green pickup truck."

"Do you know what happens when civilians get in the middle of investigations? They screw them up. They ruin evidence, tip off criminals, damage witness reliability, and get themselves killed."

"Wow. All that?"

"It's no joke, Jess."

"You wanted my help, remember?"

"Not like this. Stick to the spirits and leave the investigation to us." He paused. "All right?"

"All right." Jess felt like a scolded child. "Victor, Erick's behind Dan's death."

"Maybe so, but we can't do anything about that without evidence."

"I'm just saying, if he comes at me again…"

"You'll do what exactly?"

"I don't know *exactly*."

Chapter Twenty-Nine

JUNEY RESTED HER head on Erick's shoulder. His scent—dried sweat trapped in the synthetic material of his shirt mixed with his Axe body spray and Old Spice deodorant, borrowed from his father's glove box where it was kept in case of emergency pit stink—comforted her. She equated the rank odor of sweat trapped in clothing with a long day of honest work, something she'd been raised to value, whether anyone in her family actually suffered long days of honest work or not. Axe belonged to her generation, pervaded the hallways of her school where it rose off the heated skin of adolescents constantly parading in search of validation, and wafted from the locker rooms, where students ritualistically applied it after each phy ed class, through the ventilation system and into the biology lab next door. There it was not altogether unappreciated, especially on dissection days when the pungent smell of formaldehyde overtook the room. The Old Spice deodorant added a more nuanced note to Erick's bouquet, one that seemed to Juney particularly masculine. She snuggled down against him. If Ethan wasn't there, she would be bold enough to ask Erick to remove his shirt and she would place her cheek against his bare chest.

"Now, Juney," Ethan said her name like he was talking to a moron.

She had her eyes closed, pretending, and now that he'd intruded, he wasn't going to just out with it. He was waiting for her to look at him like a good little girl. Like she was his pupil or something. His groupie or something. Who the hell did he think he was? Manson? She raised her eyelids slowly like she didn't care one bit and gave him her best *fuck you* look.

"Your father didn't like our present. Why do you think that is?"

She scooted upright on the sofa and looked at Erick. Was he a part of this *our present* business, or was Ethan just being Ethan? Erick tilted his head down to meet her eyes. At this proximity, she could see that his freckles had layered themselves one on top of another, some lighter, some darker, some smaller, some bigger. She couldn't help smiling at this amazing fact that had escaped her notice before now. She wanted to put her fingertip to his nose and touch those amber spots, but not with Ethan watching. "How should I know?"

"Because you're his daughter."

Juney pulled a hairband off of her ponytail and let her hair swing freely around her shoulders. Her sister called it dirty blonde just to make her mad. Juney preferred medium blonde or light brown and was going to dye it one day soon. Maybe orange. Maybe black. Maybe green. She'd recently decided dramatic was her new thing. She ran her fingers through her hair, separating the strands, and pulled it all over her left shoulder. She began to braid it. Ethan and Erick watched her. It took at least a minute. Their eyes on her made her feel like a prize, like her hair was the source of her power. When she got to the end of her locks, she wrapped the hairband on and rested the braid over her shoulder.

She'd no more than dropped her hands away from her hair and Ethan was pulling it. Juney's head whipped around to accommodate the strain on her roots. He'd been sitting across the room, his mother's ugly family room, in a glider with plaid upholstery and a matching ottoman. Now he knelt in front of her with her hair in his hands. She stared over her shoulder at Erick and he stared at Ethan. His lips thinned and his face turned crimson, but he did not rise to her defense.

"His daughter should know," Ethan said through clenched teeth. "All of this was because of you. Erick there wants in your pants, but in a good-boy way. He'd even marry you tomorrow if he could." Ethan pushed his fist into Juney's face, then opened his hand so he could mash her braid into her mouth and nose.

Juney pulled back, but the couch and Erick sitting beside her blocked her retreat. She spluttered against her own hair, her eyes scrunched tight against the loose end of her braid. It was like being jabbed with a paint brush. "Damn it, Ethan!" she yelled and put up her hands to push his away. He dropped her braid. She opened her eyes, but kept her hands up before her. Ethan perched on the edge of the coffee table with the feet rotted from sitting in a flooded basement, grinning at her like the kind of kid always trying to get away with something. Juney had had enough. She jumped up off the couch and shoved him, her hands square on both of his shoulders. Ethan fell backwards, landing with a thud on the thin rug with the burn mark.

She stood over him, triumphant for the first time in her life. "You prick, Ethan. I should go straight to the cops right now and tell them you killed somebody. You're a murderer. A freak. And a loser." Erick stood beside her and she felt even stronger. Ethan took his time righting himself, like he was waking up from a nap on some kind of cushion too plush to get out of. His slowness disconcerted and angered her. "Right, Erick?" She looked at Erick and couldn't read his face. The look there did not say *confident* or *righteous*.

Ethan situated his feet beneath himself and stood with a surprisingly graceful maneuver. "Now, Juney. Let's don't be foolish."

"Let's don't? Who the fuck says let's don't?" She looked at Erick again, but he didn't scoff. He stared at Ethan dead serious.

"You will not go to the police," Ethan said, "and here's why." He stepped around the coffee table and pushed his fingertips into her shoulder right below the collar bone, which forced her back onto the couch where she'd been to begin with. Erick joined her without being shoved. "First, I have the ashtray you used to kill that man. It's covered in your fingerprints and his blood. The only reason you haven't been charged with murder yet is because I'm holding the evidence."

"You..." she stammered, "you killed him. I didn't kill anyone."

"He was dead when we arrived. Wasn't he Erick?" Ethan looked at Erick. Erick dropped his head and looked at his lap. "So you killed him all by yourself, June. Second, I have your footprint in that guy's blood. It's a thing of beauty. I'd like to have it framed, actually." He turned away from them to muse. "I suppose I'll have to frame it myself. It's not exactly the kind of thing I can send out." He spun around to face them again. This time, he stared at Erick. "And I have the prescription bottle with your mother's name on it, Erick. You two have no way out. So play nice, or we'll see who's turning in whom."

Juney grabbed her purse off the floor and ran out the door, making sure to slam it behind her. She walked away as fast as she could, willing the tears behind her eyes to roll back into her head. Suddenly she couldn't get any air in her lungs. She looked up at the sky and thought she was going to die right there on the sidewalk and that it wouldn't matter to anyone if she did.

"Juney, wait up." Erick jogged after her. He put a hand on her elbow. "Are you all right?"

She faced him, gasping for breath, her cheeks wet with tears. She shook her hands in a gesture of helpless panic.

"Jesus..." he breathed out the word. "Juney, you're hyperventilating."

She gasped again, a croaking sound caught in her throat.

"Hey, hey, hey," he soothed. "It's all right. Just breathe."

She tried to suck in air and couldn't.

Erick cradled her head in his hands. "Breathe, Juney. Breathe, Juney."

She listened to his instructions—breathe, Juney—and tried her best. Breathe. The panic subsided just enough for her to catch some air. And then some more.

"There." Erick stroked her head. "That's it."

When she was breathing again, almost normally, she wiped the tears from her face and looked at Erick. "Is it true? What he said about you wanting..."

"Yeah, but I wouldn't put it the way he did."

Juney stared at the long freckled nose, the high cheekbones and forehead, the red hair. "How would you put it?"

"I'd say that I'm probably...um...in love with you." He finished the sentence in a whisper.

Juney stretched up onto her toes and put her hands on Erick's shoulders, drawing him to her. He bowed his head and placed his big strong hands on her waist. Juney had never kissed like this before, with lips pressed fully to lips, eyes squeezed shut against the world, his hands holding her. Their lips parted and her tooth knocked against his. When he tilted his head, his nose brushed hers. *Juney and Erick.* She felt reckless, didn't care who knew, and then they stopped kissing and opened their eyes. They smiled at each other before grasping hands and turning back toward Erick's car.

Ethan stood outside his house, watching them with a nasty little smirk she could read from across the street. Juney gave him her best dirty look.

Erick kept hold of her hand and when they reached his car, he opened the passenger door for her. She slid in, only then breaking eye contact with Ethan. *I'm not afraid of you, you bald freak,* she thought. The words were intended to create courage where none existed, because, in truth, he scared the crap out of her.

Chapter Thirty

SHAKTI JUMPED OFF the bed at a run, her paws scrabbling on the hardwood floor as she cornered to get through the door and tear downstairs. Jess and Beckett were shook awake first by the dog's sudden movements and then by the sound of Shakti's frantic barking, and finally by an engine outside gunning and spitting gravel on the road, though they couldn't say how many precious seconds had passed before they realized what it all meant.

"Jess, wait!" Beckett called after her, but she was already out of bed and racing down the stairs after Shakti.

When Shakti saw Jess, she gave her tail a couple of swishes, but remained standing inside the vestibule, nose to the door, eager to encounter something outside. "Wait, Bear." Jess put one hand on Shakti's collar and the other on the doorknob.

Beckett pounded down the stairs and arrived behind her, buttoning his shorts. "Wait!" He looked around, twisting his head over his shoulders, seeking something he hadn't identified yet. Beckett stepped out of the vestibule and ran into the library. He grabbed a fire poker from the stand next to Jess's parlor stove and came back to the hallway with the poker raised over his shoulder. "Crate the dog."

Jess tried directing Shakti toward her crate, but the puppy planted her butt and refused to move, keeping her nose on the crack between the door and its frame. Jess wrapped her arms around Shakti's chest and hauled her off her spot, then grabbed a fistful of fur and skin between the shoulder blades and part guided, part dragged her into her crate. "Sorry, girl." Shakti flopped onto her side and huffed out her disappointment. "Beckett, whoever it was is gone. Shakti would be going nuts if someone was out there." Jess pulled her messy hair away from her face and twisted it up behind her head, then realized she didn't have a clip within reach and let it go. She knelt on the couch and leaned over its back to get a look outside.

"Jess," Beckett snapped. "That guy could be hiding in the trees or behind the barn. He could have a gun or arrows…"

"Arrows?"

Beckett shrugged his shoulders while keeping the poker raised above his head. "He cut off Grunner's hands, so he's not exactly conventional, is he?"

Jess pulled back from the window and joined Beckett in the hallway. "I didn't see anything outside. I think we should open the door and…you know."

Beckett stepped into the vestibule before Jess and unlocked the deadbolt, then turned the latch to release the door. He pulled it open a few inches and paused. He leaned around the edge of the door to get a look outside before pushing open the screen door. He raised the poker higher and then let the door swing wide enough to step through.

Jess saw it first. She gasped and covered her mouth with both of her hands.

Beckett looked down. "Oh Jesus." He stepped backwards, his heel landing on Jess's toe, slammed the door, and bolted it. He laid the poker on a narrow shelf above a row of coat hooks.

Jess grabbed him around the ribs and pressed her face against his chest. His arms circled her and held her tightly. She felt their hearts pounding against each other.

An uncomfortable hour passed before Martinez and Johnson arrived. Shakti dozed in her crate, uncomplaining. For that, Jess was grateful. She felt the need to spare Shakti from the ghastly thing left on her doorstep, and to spare herself from her puppy's likely reaction: curiosity, sniffing, and possible other things, *animal* things she couldn't let herself consider. Jess had dressed, then busied herself with making coffee and blueberry muffins, anything to keep herself busy.

Martinez called her from outside the house to let her know they would deal with the remains before coming inside, and that there was nothing for Jess and Beckett to do in the meantime. Just sit tight, he told her. The muffins were already out of the oven and she and Beckett had hardly spoken since calling Martinez. Sitting tight was all that remained.

They watched through the living room window. Martinez and Johnson stood near the front door, studying *it*. Jess kept her gaze focused on the crime scene techs who'd driven a mobile unit from Wausau. A man and a woman searched the property for signs of trespass. They found a trail through the yard leading back to the trees. They marked each shoe print with a numbered yellow tag in the shape of a miniature easel and photographed them. The woman, a slim but broad-shouldered figure with short dark hair, carried a soft-sided case to one of the prints and set a frame in the dirt around it, then filled it with modeling material. Johnson called the man over to the porch to photograph the remains. Jess refused to look, but she'd already seen it and couldn't help imagining little yellow easels set up around the head with the eye dangling outside its socket, the open gut, the intestines spilled out and scorched, the patches of fur black and bloody.

Jess shivered and turned away from the window. She stood in the middle of her living room, head bent, and wiped tears from her cheeks. Beckett placed his hands on her shoulders. "I know," he said. "I know."

There came a knock on the back door. Beckett kissed Jess's head before leaving her to answer it. She sniffled and wiped her cheeks before following him into the kitchen. Martinez and Johnson stood on the other side of the glass panes, looking grim. Beckett let them in and Jess got out the coffee cups.

They sat around her dining room table, coffee and a muffin in front of each of them. It wasn't that Jess felt obliged to feed them or play the hostess. It was that she needed to make herself busy, even in the most inane manner. Anything to keep her from imagining the work of the technicians outside. She picked at the crumbs around her muffin, unable to actually lift a bite to her mouth.

Investigator Johnson spoke first, "The technicians will take the—"

"Remains," Jess blurted.

"*Remains* back to the forensics lab and we'll see what it can tell us about who we're dealing with." Johnson had foregone the tie today, opting instead for a short sleeved woven shirt. The collar stood perfectly despite a few creases in the front and sweat marks at the pits. It would figure if he had collar stays tucked away to keep it rigidly vertical, like his carefully gelled hair. "It would be best if Ms. Vernon vacated the premises until we catch this man."

"I thought you already had," Martinez said. "Weren't you supposed to be staying at Mr. Hanson's place?"

"She was," Beckett said, "but we wanted to stay here last night. Jess missed her home. That's reasonable, isn't it? And I was with her the whole time."

"No, Mr. Hanson. Based on what's on your front steps, I'd say it's unreasonable for either of you to be on the premises until this investigation is closed."

Jess began to tremble. She shoved her fists between her thighs, drawing her elbows tight against her ribs.

"What my partner means," Johnson said, "is that we can't make you vacate your home, but it is highly advisable. It may be a coincidence that you were home when the..." he faltered, "remains were deposited here, but it's likely this person is watching your comings and goings."

"This is personal. A warning. The fact that it's a...a..." Jess couldn't bring herself to say the words. Beckett reached over and took her hand, drawing it out of her lap, and held it securely.

"We realize that," Martinez said. He looked at Jess across the table, his jaw set in a stern expression of disapproval. "I know this is little consolation, but this could reveal a great deal about the man we're after, what kind of suspect we're dealing with."

"Homicidal maniac," Beckett said under his breath. "Look, Investigators, I know you're doing your job and all, but this guy came right up to the front door, and I want to know how you're going to stop him."

"We're doing everything we can right now," Johnson said.

Jess wondered how many times in his career he'd said that. Martinez at least spared her the pat reply, though she was certain he'd used it plenty himself.

Shakti began to whine in her crate. The sound made Jess's heart ache. She began to rise, but Beckett stopped her with a hand to her arm. "I'll take her out back," he said. He rose and left the table.

Shakti ran to Jess and put her paws on her lap, eagerly giving affection as though she realized it was needed. Jess kissed her head and she licked at Jess's face. Beckett brought over her leash.

When he and the dog were outside, Jess asked, "Have you looked into Erick yet?"

"He doesn't seem like the type for this," Martinez said.

"But he knew the junk shop would be empty," Jess protested. Johnson's face became an impasse. If she hoped to have a conversation about this, she'd have to get Martinez alone. She tried another question anyway, "And the girl? Do you know yet if she's a victim or a killer?"

Johnson looked sideways at Martinez and tapped his fingers on the tabletop.

Martinez acted as though he hadn't noticed. "We know she's scared and is probably hiding something, but we don't know what just yet." He smiled at Jess, a half-smile, one she doubted was for her benefit. He picked up his muffin. "If you don't mind," he said, "I'm not going to let this go to waste."

Someone rapped on the front door before opening it. The crime scene tech called out hello. "Investigators," she said, "we're almost done, but thought you'd like to see a few things."

"Be right there," Johnson called back to her.

"Go ahead," Martinez told Johnson. "I'll just finish my muffin."

Johnson scowled at Martinez, but left the table all the same.

Jess and Martinez were alone.

"Has it occurred to you," Martinez began, "that this might be the result of your digging into the case? The detective work you did the other day could have precipitated this."

"You said Erick's not the kind to do this."

"Well somebody is," he snapped. "Somebody who knows where you live and that you have a dog and who probably knew you were home."

"And when to drop off the..." she choked on the word. "When to come between your patrols, your area watch, or whatever it's called."

Martinez stood up and shook his head at Jess. He raised a hand to point at her. "Jess, you're going to get yourself hurt if you don't back off."

Jess stood up at the table to face off with Martinez. "What do you want? Do you want me to go hide or talk to the ghost? Because if I'd backed off, you wouldn't know about the ring and the footprint."

"We'd have gotten there."

"You brought me onto the case." She stared at Martinez across the table, daring him to deny it.

"I don't want to live to regret that, Jess." He put his hands on his hips before delivering his final directive, "Just cool it so you don't get hurt."

Martinez turned away from the table and left her there to consider the risk she'd supposedly brought on herself. The screen door slammed and bounced against its frame as he stepped out onto the porch.

Chapter Thirty-One

JESS STOOD AT the worktable while Shakti gnawed noisily on an elk antler underneath it. Jess hadn't let her out of her sight since that morning. She wedged her sixth ball of clay, shoving it against the tabletop, transferring force from her shoulders, through her stiff arms, into the ball of clay. Press and turn. Press and turn. Like bread dough, but she didn't have to worry about it getting tough and chewy. She could exert herself as much as she liked, and right now all she wanted to do was wedge the shit out of some clay.

Beckett placed his hand on the small of her back, then lifted it to show her his palm. "You're sweating," he said. "You can slow down, you know."

"No." Jess huffed as she pressed the clay into the table again. "This is his head." She flipped the clay and pressed with the heels of her hands. "I'm squishing it." She picked up the cone of clay and smacked it into a ball with her palms, then threw it against the table, adding it to a growing mound of wedged clay. Jess grabbed the plastic-wrapped block of fresh clay and a wire cutter.

Beckett slid it away from her and folded the plastic back over the block. "I can't use that much clay tonight." He reached for one of her balls of clay. It didn't budge. He grabbed it with both hands and tugged until it released the table with a slurp. "Here," he handed it to Jess. "Do this one again."

She hated this, feeling helpless, hunted, waiting for someone to save her. Jess drew her arm back and hurled the clay across the studio. Beckett shouted, "Not that way!" his hands jerking up as though he might catch the ball mid-launch. The clay hurtled toward the front door and cleared his sales display. The front door opened and the clay splatted against the frame, inches to the right of Martinez' head.

Martinez stood with his hand on the Smith and Wesson strapped to his hip. Beckett's hands were up, shoulder's raised, bracing for the worst. Jess stood beside him, glowering across the worktable, wishing the ball of clay really was somebody's head. The clay released from the wall and fell to the floor with a heavy thud.

Martinez moved his hand away from his gun. "Is this a bad time?"

Shakti trotted out from under the table and approached Martinez, tail wagging. Just as he was about to pat her, the clay caught her attention and she bent her head to give it a good sniffing.

Somebody moaned nearby. Jess tilted her head. Beckett began to say something and she shushed him, turned toward the back door and listened. A sorrowful moan of despair came from outside. Jess hurried to the carriage door and slid it open to reveal the yard behind the livery.

"What's going on?" Beckett asked.

"I don't know." Jess stepped outside and looked south, toward the junk shop.

Dan approached, ambling along the train tracks. He looked lost and hurt and very real. If Jess didn't already know he was dead, she would have dialed 911. She rushed toward him. He stopped when she stood before him and raised his face to look at hers.

Jess stared at him, the short brown hair, the white dress shirt with the tie loosened enough to open the top two buttons, the neat blue jeans and leather belt. He squinted, one eye clouded over, and blood trickled down his brow. He lifted his arms to show Jess the absence of his hands. The drone of the cicadas encircled them in a buzzing, vibrating ring of sound that drowned out everything else.

Beckett and Martinez had followed Jess out of the studio and stood nearby, watching without interfering. They didn't matter, and they couldn't help her.

The cicadas raised their volume again, so loud it hurt her ears, and Jess had the impression they also raised a wall.

She lifted her hand to the side of Dan's head. Her fingertips touched the dent in his skull. It felt like the inside of a bowl coated with molasses. Her body convulsed as she was swept through a tunnel. Beckett called her name, and Martinez did, too, but it was already too late.

Jess sat in The Two Wheeler, leaning into the corner of one of the booths, and sipped her scotch, a creamy eight-year blend, smooth. She lifted the glass and swirled the contents then stuck her nose over the rim and inhaled. A note of lemon. She sipped. Buttery finish. She'd have to see the bottle again and track one down when she got back home. It was enough to give her nice little buzz before heading back to the motel in Durin, where she'd phone Samantha before calling it an early night. She had several clients in Eau Claire and Chippewa Falls lined up for tomorrow. She watched a couple of loud women with darts moving in and out of her view as they played a game of Cricket, occasionally cheering and high fiving each other. It seemed they were all the entertainment she was going to get this evening, which was just as well: early night, bigger clients in the morning. The Water Wheel certainly didn't give her anything worth reporting. Some days in these hick towns, she swore she was being nickeled and dimed to death. Other days all that change added up to a pretty penny. She snorted, amusing herself again, and tilted her glass to peer into the amber liquid. *The day's almost over*, she thought.

A girl slid into the booth across from her. *Uninvited. Well,* she blinked at her guest in surprise, *at least that's not boring.* She introduced herself as July, like the month. *Here,* she thought, *is a story to tell Samantha.*

The air around Jess shimmered and the cicadas' collectively hiccuped.

Now Jess stood at the bar, herself again. Jake came out of the back carrying a giant bag of mini pretzels and stack of paper baskets. He dropped the baskets onto the bar and lined up a half dozen of them before opening the top of the bag. July slid out of the booth and approached the bar, wobbling once or twice on red, glittered platform pumps she obviously couldn't fill. It was like watching a little girl play dress up in her mother's high heels. July finally made it to the bar and stood beside Jess, leaned forward, showing off her cleavage, and flashed an unpracticed smile at Jake. He stared at her, unimpressed.

July took a tube of lipstick out of her purse. She turned up the stick of make-up and puckered at her reflection in the mirror behind the bar before smoothing on a fresh coat of red.

Jake placed a glass of scotch in front of her. She paid. She applied more lipstick. She stirred the scotch with her pinky finger before dropping the tube of lipstick back into her purse.

Jess began to wonder about July and her tube of lipstick, the unnecessary second application to her lips. The air shimmered again, like a gust of wind moving a bank of fog without dispersing it.

The cicadas' song stuttered, then resumed louder than ever.

She lay in the back room of the junk shop, unconscious. Or...no...dead. She couldn't be sure.

Two men dressed all in black moved about the cramped space. The shorter of the two placed things inside a heavy-duty garbage bag, then slid the bag inside a backpack. He instructed the tall one to wipe off the doorknob, the edges of shelves, with wet wipes containing bleach. Jess wanted to stand up and shout at them, but she couldn't move, couldn't speak. From another pack, the shorter man removed a new garbage bag. He opened it and arranged it beside Jess. The tall man obediently stepped over her body and took hold of her arm, lifted it off the floor and held it. Jess's watch and ring. The happiest day of her life. The short man pulled a pruning shears out of the bag. He opened the blades and placed them on either side of Jess's wrist. The tall man holding her arm squeezed his eyes shut and turned his head away. Jess couldn't feel the sharp edge of the blade against her skin; she wondered why. It was so interesting, what was happening. The short man pushed the handles together and the top blade caught on her watch, scratched the glass face and nicked the gold casing as it slid off its edge and cut into Jess's flesh. The blades couldn't go through her bone all at once. They slid back, slicing but not severing. Jess had the same experience when the doctor let her cut the cord at Annie's birth. It took her three tries with the scissors to work her way through the slippery, rubbery twist of tissue. The man with the shears opened the blade again, repositioned it. "Wrist," he said, and slammed the blades together. Jess's hand dropped into the garbage bag with a small spray of blood.

Chapter Thirty-Two

JESS'S COLLAPSED ONTO the gravel bed beside the train tracks. The cicadas surrounded her with their deafening drone. She wanted to press her hands to her ears, but her body didn't respond to her will. She saw Beckett looking down at her through the shimmering wall of sound, then nothing.

Sweet nothing.

She woke slowly, her tongue stuck to the roof of her mouth. She tried to swallow and made some kind of smacking noise. She mumbled something incoherent even to herself. Her eyes opened enough to see light. She felt the soft curves of Beckett's mattress beneath her, the dents made by his habitual sleeping position. Beckett...

He knelt beside her and stroked her forehead. "Hey there. Welcome back. You had me scared."

"Scared?"

He offered her a glass of water. Jess pushed herself upright and reached for the glass. She jerked her hand back into herself and grabbed her wrist with her other hand.

"Jess? Honey?"

She rubbed her wrist, looked up at Beckett, his concerned face, then down at her hands. She spread them over her lap, admiring the presence of each finger. She was dressed, but in bed, wearing the same shorts and tank top she'd had on the night before. "I..."

Beckett put his hand on her chin and lifted her face until his gaze held hers. "You're all right, Jess. You're safe. Martinez is still here."

She glanced up, past Beckett. Martinez stood in the doorway with his arms folded across his chest. He stepped into the room, his concern obvious in his expression. "You blacked out," he said. "You'll be fine, but you're disoriented now. Just relax and give yourself time to come back around."

Jess nodded, took the glass of water from Beckett, and drank. Thankful to wash some of the stickiness out of her mouth. She handed the glass back to Beckett. "Shakti?"

"I guess you're ready for visitors." Martinez turned from the room and a moment later, Shakti barreled in, her leash trailing her. She leapt onto the bed and Jess embraced her.

"Victor," she touched her fingertips to her lips. "The girl, Juney. Get her lipstick."

"Why would he want her lipstick?" Beckett asked.

"The girl bought Dan a drink." Jess paused to consider her words. "She put on lipstick, then she stirred his drink with her finger." Skakti leaned into Jess and pressed her head against Jess's hand. She resumed petting. "I know all the dots aren't connected, but that's what he showed me. I think if you get her lipstick, you'll get the drug she used on him."

"Don't you guys run a tox screen no matter what?" Beckett asked.

"Yes." Martinez leaned against the wall and refolded his arms over his chest. "We haven't gotten those results yet. It helps if we have a drug category to search for, otherwise there are so many possibilities, it takes a long time to narrow them down to something productive."

"Can you get a search warrant for a lipstick?" Beckett asked.

"I can get a search warrant for anything I want. The question is, how do I explain why I'm after her lipstick to a judge?"

Beckett reached a hand over to scratch behind Shakti's ears. "Tell him you called the Psychic Friends Network," he chuckled, the sound forced, almost artificial.

"What else can you tell me?" Martinez asked Jess, ignoring Beckett's comment.

She looked at her hands again, rubbed her wrists. "I'd like to get up," she said.

They relocated to Beckett's kitchen table. Beckett offered Martinez a beer, then advised Jess against drinking. She accepted his offer of toast and water, then asked for a cider as well. "I don't know what just happened to me, but it's not the stomach flu," she said. "Besides, a cider sounds appealing." Beckett made her toast, then served the cider with a slight scowl of concern. Jess thanked him anyway.

"The girl bought Dan a drink," Jess began. "She went up to the bar and she had a little purse, like a clutch or pocketbook, but it was on a string. She gave Jake her ID and took out her lipstick. She put on lipstick. Paid for the drink with cash. Jake walked away from the bar. She put on lipstick again." Jess looked at Martinez and Beckett. "That was weird. Women don't put on lipstick twice like that. It was a nervous thing, or she did it to cover up something else. Then Juney put the lipstick in her purse and stirred the drink. But the drink was straight liquor. There was nothing to stir."

Martinez turned sideways in his chair and crossed his legs, putting an ankle over a knee. His pant leg hiked up, revealing a snakeskin cowboy boot with a square toe. "I can get a warrant for her purse and its contents due to the likelihood that she poisoned him."

"What else happened, Jess?" Beckett stared at her across the table, his blue eyes intent upon her.

She picked up her glass of cider and took a sip. Then another. "I was right. This does taste good." Now Martinez was staring at her, too. Apparently, stalling would do her no good. "Dan showed me his hands being cut off. There were two men. The shorter one did the actual cutting." She ran her fingers up and down her glass, making trails in the condensation. "With a pruning shears."

"That's consistent with the ME's report," Martinez said.

"Two of them? So Erick's not the only killer."

Jess shook her head. "The shorter of the two did the cutting."

"And since we know Erick's a tall kid…" Martinez said.

"The short one is the ring leader," Jess finished for him.

"What do we know about this guy?" Beckett asked.

Martinez scratched at the label on his beer bottle with a thumbnail. "You sure?"

"Go ahead." Jess picked up her toast and pulled the crust off, breaking it into pieces. Martinez stared at her for a second, probably deciding for himself if she could handle the news. "Really."

"What this guy did to the…" he waved his hand in a circular motion, "left on your porch wasn't done just to scare you." Martinez stopped to take a swig of his beer. "He wanted us to know what kind of person he is…"

The small kitchen window looked toward the village. Jess couldn't see anything from where she was sitting, but she heard a car go by on the River Road. The Mississippi flowed by on her other side, too far to hear it and no window from which to see it, but she knew it was there and that was something. The Mississippi had a permanence and magnificence she appreciated, a swath of water cutting across the entire country. Minnesota, Jess's home state, was about as Midwestern as a state could get, yet it wasn't landlocked thanks to the Mississippi and the Great Lakes. Jess's ancestors some five generations before had crossed the Atlantic and put in at Louisiana, where they boarded a steamer and traveled up-river, into the wilds of the north, looking for a place that felt like home. The river felt like home to Jess. She'd lived near it in Minneapolis and had the superstitious hunch that if she ever lived far from it, it would create a hole in her life, though what size or shape she could not define. She stared into the graying sky and pictured the river flowing by them, gathering strength from a current that could carry her all the way to the ocean.

"…an organized killer," Martinez continued. "Thoughtful. Careful. The coroner believes he inflicted wounds in such a manner so as to keep it alive as long as possible."

Jess stood up and carried her cider to the couch. She sat down cross-legged and pulled Shakti up onto her lap.

"I'm sorry, Jess," Martinez said.

"That's all right." She didn't bother to look over her shoulder at him. "You aren't telling me anything I hadn't figured out for myself."

The gloaming spread through the apartment as the sun sank behind the bluffs across the river. The atmosphere changed from the warm amber glow of late evening to the cool blues of dusk. Still August, and sunset had backed up a full hour since the solstice.

She stood at the door to the junk shop, her heart pounding, blood racing through her veins. The cicadas droned on all around her, their song obliterating the rest of the town, the River Road, the forest, as though the shotgun duplex floated unmoored in a sea of nothing. She lifted her hand to the handle and pulled the screen door open.

The darkness inside swallowed her up. She told herself to go back, get out, but she couldn't turn her body. There was only going into the darkness. The back door had to be straight ahead. She could push through to it. Her foot moved, took a step. *That's it. One foot...* She placed her other foot. *...in front of...* Again. *...the other.*

When Jess stood in the back room, a spotlight came on, illuminating a small table across from her. Lying atop it, the Golden Retriever.

Run! Run!

Jess kicked at the covers and twisted to one side then the other. The sheet wound around her ankle. Her foot thumped Shakti in the shoulder. The dog stretched her legs and snorted without waking. Beckett lay unmoving beside Jess, curled on his side.

On a smaller table—no, the typewriter stand she had admired—someone had set out a number of instruments, cruel and gleaming in the spotlight.

I don't need to see this, Jess insisted. *I know what he did. I know what he did. WAKE UP!*

Jess's body jerked upright, suddenly freed from the chemical restraints of sleep. She stared around the room, wide-eyed, breathing heavily. A slight breeze from the window cooled the sweat on her skin. She was safe and she wasn't alone. Jess looked at Beckett, sleeping soundly beside her, and there was Shakti, curled in a ball at the foot of her bed. Goosebumps rose up and down her arms and the back of her neck tingled. Jess lifted her gaze.

Dan stood before the window, backlit by the ambient light of the stars, a handless shadow. He stared at Jess, his brown eyes sad.

"You did that," Jess said. "You sent me that dream."

The specter did not respond, only continued to stare at her as blood began to trickle down his brow.

Jess swung her legs beneath herself and knelt on the mattress, facing Dan. She lifted her arm to point an accusing finger at him. "That was pretty shitty. You know that? You think I needed that? I *saw* what he did. I *know* all about it. It was left on my fucking doorstep!"

Shakti rolled up to a sitting position and faced Dan, hackles raised.

"Jess?"

Beckett sat up beside her as she grabbed her pillow and hurled it at Dan.

The pillow struck the window and fell harmlessly to the floor. Dan turned around and evaporated through the wall.

Beckett looked at Jess, then at the window across from the bed. "What's going on?"

Shakti hopped off the bed to sniff near the window.

Jess looked at Beckett, "I don't know how much more of this I can take."

He took her hands in his. "You're okay. We're all okay. Can you tell me what happened?"

"I'm going to make some coffee first."

"You're kidding." Beckett grabbed his watch from the bedside table. "It's 4:00, Jess."

"I'm not going back to sleep. No way."

Chapter Thirty-Three

A SIGN OVER the door warned Jess, "You are on camera." Above the printed words, a pair of eyes bulged cartoonishly at her. She stepped into the store and scanned the corners of the room for domes of smoky glass concealing the spies. She quickly found four of them. She supposed that, in a gun shop, keeping them in plain sight to remind visitors of their presence was a good thing. Jess certainly didn't think anyone should be too comfortable around all these weapons—especially the big ones. The shop, set off a county road away from the regular tourist traffic of the River Road, boasted to hold all your weapons needs under one roof, from ammo to targets. They housed an indoor shooting range, simulation room, and outdoor ranges behind the building for both guns and bows. Jess found the place disquieting. Uncertain what to do with herself, she turned to leave the way she'd come in.

"Can I help you?" a young man with a beard and earring asked her from behind a counter full of handguns. He wore an olive-green t-shirt with a machine gun across the top of the chest. Beneath the gun, it read, in all caps, "Keep calm and carry one." His coworker, or maybe his boss, a large man helping a customer at the other counter, wore a shirt with a gun-toting skeleton on it that said something about being a beer-drinking, meat-eating, liberal-destroying something or other. The text disappeared beneath the edge of the counter he stood behind, but being a vegetarian, liberal, wine-drinking, something or other, Jess was glad the "Keep calm and carry one" guy had approached her.

"Um, yes." She peeled her eyes away from the other man, his t-shirt, and the shotgun he was handing to the customer. "I have an appointment for a lesson. Jessica Vernon."

"Sure." He glanced at a date book on the counter, asked for her license, then said, "You'll be with Fern."

"Fern?"

As though on cue, a woman entered the storefront through a doorway behind the counters over which hung the mounted head of a moose, its massive rack spreading a good five feet between points. She reached up to pat the underside of the animal's neck as she passed beneath it. "Hi," she said, coming outside the counters to stand in front of Jess. "I'm Fern." Fern had a husky voice that suited her large frame and robust build. She stood at least five-ten, wore Timberland work boots, and a t-shirt tucked into her belted jeans that thankfully had nothing to do with guns. It instead displayed the silhouette of a pit bull wearing a silver-studded collar. Her square face had a scrubbed-clean, slightly chapped look to it, and was topped by a mass of curls, worn short, away from her ears and off her neck. Fern looked like she'd just stepped out of the woods with an axe slung over her shoulder, or perhaps in this case, a semi-automatic rifle. She looked Jess over. "Ever fired a gun before?" Without waiting for Jess's answer, as though asking was only a formality she had little use for, Fern collected a gun from behind the counter and put it in a tray along with a box of bullets. She handed Jess her eyes and ears, a pair of plastic safety glasses and noise protection earmuffs, then led her across the store and through a doorway.

They stood in a small, dimly lit room with a wall of small lockers, the sort that released the key if you fed them a quarter. Fern instructed Jess to stow her bag and put on her eyes and ears. Jess obeyed. She then opened another door and they went onto the shooting range.

Just as Jess stepped into the range, a cannon boomed beside her and she jumped, her hands flailing helplessly near her heart. Fern appeared unaffected as she proceeded past the man with the semi-automatic machine gun to the far end of the range. The reality of where she was and what she was doing came home and Jess wondered if getting up at 4:00 a.m. after multiple...*visitations*...with Dan would possibly lead to a lapse in judgment. More likely, Jess reasoned, her decisions would tend toward the impulsive, not the unsound. And experience had shown her that most impulses, if not all, could be undone.

"This is a Glock 19," Fern said. She demonstrated to Jess that the magazine was unloaded and the chamber empty, then put it in Jess's hands.

It weighed less than Jess had expected, looked surprisingly uncomplicated, and scared her, but she wasn't going to admit that to Lumberjack Fern.

"Now," Fern continued, "let's teach you how to use this thing." She took the gun from Jess and demonstrated how to handle it, naming all its parts while discussing gun safety. "The first rule is to always treat it like it's loaded and only point it in a safe direction." She showed Jess how to load the magazine. "These are nine mil Parabellum bullets," she said. "The mag will hold fifteen bullets, which means the gun can take sixteen. The mag plus one in the chamber." She slid bullets into the magazine like she was loading candy into a PEZ dispenser. When she'd inserted five bullets, she handed it to Jess.

Getting the bullets in the magazine took some getting used to. She had to press down while angling the bullet just right. Sometimes the lip of the bullet she was loading stuck on the line where the brass case met the copper head of the bullet beneath it. When the "cannon" at the other end of the range boomed, Jess's fingers slipped and she dropped a bullet. She stared at it laying between the toes of Fern's work boots. Fern bent and swept it up. "Don't worry," she said, handing the bullet back to Jess. "It takes a lot more than that to make one of these go off."

Fern showed Jess how to slide the magazine into the grip. "The bullets always point uphill. If they point downhill, you'll jam the gun. That's bad." *That's bad* seemed like an understatement to Jess. She didn't want to find out what would happen if she inserted a bullet backwards in the chamber. Fern removed the magazine and continued the lesson with the gun unloaded. "This is the slide. It'll tear your knuckle off if you don't hold the gun properly." Fern put the gun in Jess's hands and made sure she had her thumbs down. Then Fern looked at Jess's feet. "That's an isosceles stance," she tapped Jess's feet with one of her own while using her hands to rotate Jess's elbows. "You want to absorb the recoil into your chest, instead of up into your face."

"That's a lot to keep straight."

"It's easier than you think. Remember driver's ed? Remember being told about gears and mirrors and signals and pedals? And then it all became so easy you could drive without hardly paying attention to the car?" Fern handed Jess the magazine. "Load your gun."

Jess looked at the top bullet, inspecting its angle and making certain it pointed uphill before sliding it into the Glock's grip. She looked at Fern, uncertain what came next. Again the machine gun shook the range.

Fern grabbed the Glock's slide and pulled it back, exposing the barrel, then released it so it snapped forward. "Now the gun is loaded and this is a live weapon." Fern laid it on the counter in front of them, barrel pointing down range, and stepped back.

Jess picked up the gun, took her stance, rotated her elbows, all the things Fern had taught her, and looked down the barrel at her target. "Curve your back slightly forward, like you're going off a diving board," Fern said, her voice surprisingly easy to hear through the ear muffs. "Dot the i in your sights." Jess stared, trying not to squint one eye shut, and lined up the sights with the bulls eye. She squeezed the trigger with the pad of her finger, as instructed, taking up the slack, then felt the resistance when the trigger engaged. It took forever to pull the trigger, holding her breath, her concentration so focused that she registered the sound of the machine gun being fired nearby without startling. She drew the trigger the rest of the way and the gun fired with a loud crack and jerked upwards in Jess's hands. She glimpsed the muzzle flash as the brass case ejected, arcing up and back past her head.

Jess looked down range at her target. Her bullet had pierced the paper in the outer ring of the bulls eye near the bottom. "That's good," Fern said. Jess continued to practice under Fern's guidance until Fern deemed her safe enough to be left alone on the range. Fern returned to the store where she could keep an eye on Jess through a window of smoky glass. Jess carefully worked her way through the box of bullets that came with her lesson, fifty of them. By the time she'd finished, her arms ached and her aim, which had moved steadily toward the center of the bulls eye, had slipped outside of it again with her fatigue.

She brought the gun out to the front counter in its carrying tray. Fern received it with a smile. "How'd it go?" Jess showed her the targets she'd shot up. "Pretty good. This is a nice cluster here." Fern took Jess's license out of her drawer and set it on the counter. "Anything else I can do you for today?"

"Um…" Jess felt like she'd just stepped outside the realm of possibilities. "If I wanted to buy a gun…?"

Fern's smile broadened. "You betcha, honey. You'll want a handgun like the one you just fired." Jess nodded. "I have a beauty just came in. I haven't even put it out yet." Fern turned away from the counter. She patted the moose's neck on her way into the back room. When she returned, she carried a gun case and, perhaps because she held something in her hands, did not touch the moose.

"Can I ask about the moose?" Jess said.

"That's Buddy. I bagged him myself in Alaska. Went up there for my honeymoon. Buddy outlasted the marriage, which oughta tell you something." Fern laughed a throaty *huh huh huh*. "I should have known it wouldn't last when my husband got mad that I scored a moose and he didn't. Some men are such babies." She snapped the latches open on the gun case. "Your home is your bunker, you know? It's a safe place to retreat to at the end of the day—or the end of the world when it comes. If you're gonna marry somebody, you better make damn sure he's somebody you want sharing your bunker."

Jess had no idea what to say. She was busy digesting the information that Fern had shot a moose on her honeymoon and that her philosophy of what makes a good marriage was somehow tied to Armageddon.

"I did a lot better for myself when I bagged Lou." Fern glanced over her shoulder at the liberal hater and winked. He returned her wink before going into the back room. Fern watched him pass underneath Buddy, then returned her gaze to Jess. "Got your license on you?"

Jess set her driver's license back on the counter between them.

Fern closed the latches on the gun case and locked it inside the display counter. "It's not like a credit check, honey. Don't worry. I'll get you set up. First you'll need to take our safety course, then file the application with the DOJ."

"How long will that take?"

"Our next safety course is…" She looked at the guy in the Keep Calm t-shirt and called across the counter to him. "Tom, when's the safety?"

"Tuesday."

"Tuesday," Fern repeated to Jess. "You can file with the DOJ on Wednesday and they'll get back to you within twenty-one days."

"Oh." Jess looked down at her hands. "I might not need a gun in twenty-one days."

Fern cocked her head over her shoulder and gave Jess a quizzical look. "Guy trouble?"

"You could say that. Yeah." Jess shifted away from the counter and looked toward the door then back at Fern. She hoped the tears she felt welling behind her eyes weren't visible. "I don't know why I came here. I mean, what did I think I was going to do? Learn how to protect myself in an hour?"

"This guy's that bad?"

Jess nodded, unable to speak for fear she'd burst into tears, never mind the impossibility of explaining Dan, Erick, and her stalker to this woman.

"Look, honey," Fern slid a business card out of a holder and wrote something on the back while she talked, "I can't help you today, but once you have that license we'll be happy to sell you something." She slid the card across the counter to Jess, tapped it with her finger and turned away briskly. She stood in the doorway under Buddy, one hand over her head on the moose's neck. "Lou," she hollered into the back room. "Get your fat ass out here again so I can take my lunch."

Jess slid the business card off the glass counter and left the store, not sure what had just transpired between them. When she got into her car, she turned the card over and found an address hastily scratched onto the cheap card stock. Below the address, Fern had written "300 cash." Jess left the shooting range and found a gas station with an ATM machine. Five minutes after that, she parked on Meadow Lane in Nelson across from a shoebox of a house on a corner lot. A gravel driveway led to a garage as big as the house and a plastic aboveground pool filled most of the back yard. Jess put her windows down and cut the engine. She double checked the card and wondered if it was all a mistake.

Fern honked her horn as she landed a vintage Dodge Charger in the driveway. The blue car had the straight lines and sharp corners of the early '80s, a sporty little subcompact with a wide silver racing stripe down its middle. She swung the door open and planted a foot on the rocks before gripping the frame of the car and pushing herself out of it. Jess had the impression of a giantess emerging from a clown car and would have laughed if she wasn't still caught in the realm of the surreal. Jess got out of her car and followed Fern up the driveway.

Fern pushed open a side door without the use of her keys. Just as Jess began to wonder that she didn't lock her doors, even in a town the size of Nelson—it was a River Road community with plenty of strangers flowing through—she heard the sound of nails clicking across linoleum flooring. "Baby!" Fern greeted the tan and white pit bull who rushed the length of the house to leap into Fern's open arms. Baby wore a leather-studded collar, just like the dog on Fern's t-shirt.

Jess reached a hand toward him, only to pull it back when Baby growled with full fangs.

"Now, Baby," Fern knelt and grabbed the skin at the base of the dog's neck while pressing her forehead to the dog's, "you know if Mama brings somebody home with her, she's a friend." She looked up at Jess. "Baby'll tear anyone apart who enters this place without me."

Jess stepped back from the happy reunion until she stood against the kitchen cabinets, not making any sudden moves.

"Come on, Baby." Fern pushed herself to her feet and crossed the kitchen into an informal dining room with brown carpeting. She pulled open a sliding glass door and shooed her dog outside. Jess leaned forward to peek after the dog, relieved to see he had been released into an enclosed dog run. Fern slid the door shut and waved a large hand dismissively. "Ah, Baby's a pussycat. He knows to guard his home and his mama. That's all." Jess didn't know what to say. Fortunately, Fern didn't wait for her to come up with a response. She rounded her nicked and battered dining table and elbowed Jess in a comradely way. "Have a seat. Be right back."

An advertising poster for the car in the driveway hung on the wall across from Jess. She hadn't noticed it, or much of anything, with Baby in the house. Instead of sitting, she crossed the room to examine it. A 1983 Dodge Charger just like the one in the driveway sat on a road with a choppy Lake Superior behind it. A tall, buxom blonde with a tight perm sat on the hood of the car, one knee bent, the other leg extended. She wore a red skirt of layered ruffles and a short jacket with a large black and white hounds tooth print. Jess leaned in closer to get a good look at the model. Completing the ensemble, black stirrup tights, white Keds, and black driving gloves. All that was missing was a large bow on top of her Poodle perm. Fern came back into the room, saw Jess staring at the print and laughed that *huh huh huh* of hers.

"Oh!" Jess pointed at Fern. "That's you." She spun to point toward the driveway. "And that's *that* car?"

"Sure is. My daddy had a dealership and I modeled for his ads. There was a time I thought I would make my fortune on the catwalks of New York City. You ever see *Flashdance?* You're probably too young, but I wanted to be Jennifer Beals—hence the perm, like I needed it. Only instead of a welder and dancer, I was going to be a mechanic and model." She set a gun case on the dining table. "That Shelby in the driveway was my payment for all the modeling I did. My daddy never did give me an actual paycheck. The fucker said since we were family no money need exchange hands. But then he gave me that car, so I guess I did all right. That car retailed at $8,290." She shrugged happily like it was the fondest memory of her life.

"It looks so good," Jess marveled.

"Yep. I swore I'd always have that car, and I've taken good care of my Shelby."

"Did you ever drive it out to New York City?"

"Naw. Guess I figured out I'd rather be a grease monkey than a super model." Fern put a hand on the gun case and her expression turned serious. "Listen, honey, I know you aren't ATF—"

"What?"

She smiled. "That's what I thought. There's nothing wrong with a private gun sale, but I'm only doing this so you can keep yourself safe. You get your ass back to the range on Tuesday for the safety and then you get that license. This is just for the meantime."

Jess nodded gravely like she understood. "Why?"

Fern sighed, her large shoulders sagging into her frame. "Let's just say that if you went home empty handed today and then I found out you got beat up or killed or something because you didn't have a way to protect yourself, I would have a hell of a time living with myself after that." Jess wanted to protest, to explain that her boyfriend was really wonderful, but Fern lifted her hand and shook her head. "You came to the shop because you're scared. I can smell that shit a mile away." Her gaze receded, turning inward to the land of memory. "Takes one to know one, I guess."

She was right. Jess was scared.

"Now," Fern spoke the word like an affirmation that could chase away her past. "This sweet little number is the same as what you just fired at the range, a Glock 19." She flipped open the lid, showing Jess the weapon on its eggshell foam padding with two magazines beside it. In a corner of the case, where the foam had been cut out to accommodate it, sat a box of bullets. Fern picked it up, opened the chamber to show it was unloaded, and set it back down.

Jess reached tentatively toward the gun, then withdrew her hand.

"Go ahead," Fern encouraged, "If you're going to own a piece, make friends with it."

Jess picked up the gun, wondering how on earth she would make friends with it. As she removed it from the case, it pointed across the table.

Fern put her hand on the Glock and swung it away from herself. "The first rule of handling firearms is…"

"Never point it at another person," Jess replied with a slight question mark, aware that she was paraphrasing Fern's lesson rather loosely.

"Sure." Fern smiled and added with a hint of sweetness, "Unless you intend to shoot him."

"You did what?" Beckett said.

Jess assumed the question was rhetorical, since she'd just shown him her new Glock 19. "Look. I'm not a fan of guns, but I think it might be necessary until…" They perched side by side on the picnic table behind the studio, enjoying a quiet afternoon break while Shakti ambled about the yard. Jess kept an eye on her, listening for cars on their way to or from the boat launch.

"Jess, I'm not actually opposed to you having a gun. As long as you know how to use it," he added. "I'm just surprised. I guess I…" He fumbled for words. "I would have thought, or liked to think, that you'd talk to me first."

"Because?"

"Because I don't know. It just feels like something I'd like us to do. You know? Like we're a real couple."

"A real couple?"

"Yeah." Beckett took Jess's hands in his and swung their arms between them. "Let's take this to the next level."

"Why Beckett Hanson," Jess said, smiling, "is this the commitment talk?"

"Sure sounds like it." He returned her smile.

"Aren't we already committed?"

"We are, but it was unstated. Now it's stated."

"All right." Jess leaned forward and kissed his lips, then pulled back. She met Beckett's gaze, her look serious. "But none of this goose and gander crap. You would have liked a heads up on the gun, and I would have liked one on the haircut."

"The haircut?" He pushed his hands through his hair as though needing to confirm that his hair had in fact been cut.

Jess hopped off the picnic table and positioned herself behind Beckett, kneeling on the table so she could reach his head from above. She slid her fingers into his hair, gliding them up the back of his head and forward around his ears. She massaged his scalp with the pads of her fingers. "Lora's your ex," Jess whispered in her best sultry voice. "She washed your hair, stood behind you in her low-cut ruffled blouse…" Jess moved around Beckett and slid off the table to stand facing him. She leaned forward, sticking out her chest, "maybe she leaned over you to show you the mirror."

Beckett laughed, a faint blush rising in his tanned cheeks. "All right, Jess."

"Oh, Beckett." Jess tugged her t-shirt's neckline into a V. "You should leave that Jessica-person and come back to me."

"She said nothing of the sort," he protested.

"She thought it. I've seen the way she looks at you, and she calls you whenever she's got furniture to move."

Beckett laughed again. "I didn't realize you're the jealous type, Jessica Vernon."

"Who says I'm jealous?"

"Besides," he said, "her breasts aren't that great."

"She thinks they are."

"You're right. She does." Beckett got off the table and slid a hand around Jess's waist, resting it comfortably on the small of her back. He pressed her into him and kissed her. "I much prefer your breasts."

"Good. I still don't want her massaging your scalp."

"And Tyler?"

"He doesn't cut hair."

"Look, Jess," Beckett's face turned serious, "these veterans are six times as likely as the rest of us to be violent."

"Six times. How do you know that?"

"I figured if this guy is going to live in our community and hang out with my girlfriend, I should know something about it."

"Oh, come on, Beckett. That's so unfair."

"Unfair? Jess, he hit you. I know he didn't mean to hit you, but that doesn't make him less dangerous."

"He is less dangerous. I believe in Bruno. And Tyler. He's made progress."

Beckett rubbed his goatee, considering. "I'll grandfather in the doggie play dates, but outside of that, I'd prefer you not hang out with him unless I'm around. I just—"

"I can do that." Jess gazed into his eyes and gave him a squeeze around the ribs.

Beckett called Shakti away from the road, then looked back at Jess. He touched her brow and swept a wave of hair away from her eyes. "When I get back from Duluth, we can go to the shooting range," he said. "If you're going to have a gun, you need to get comfortable with it."

"I'd like that." Jess nodded at the gun case on the picnic table. "So would Little Fern."

Chapter Thirty-Four

ETHAN STOOD BEFORE the mirror with a razor in his hand. He took care of his appearance. By seventh grade, he'd realized that if you looked good, people didn't have to find out where you came from. What's more, they generally assumed the best if you looked good and the worst if you didn't. He'd run more than one experiment during junior high to test his theories. He started a rumor that Donny Vasquez was illegal, then sat back and watched to see how far it would go. He picked Donny because he always sat in the back—of the classroom, the lunch room, the bus—trying to be invisible. There were Mexican kids in Ethan's school who were tough and there were others who were smart, or good runners, or hard workers, but Donny was a nobody. He was wedged so deep in the crack, he'd need a fireman's ladder to climb out. Even Mrs. Donahoe, who liked charity cases, ignored Donny. Plenty of families did their back-to-school shopping at Wal-Mart, but even those kids had a kind of style, a sense of what was acceptable. But Donny, there was something *unclean* about him. Maybe in his case, the best thing anyone could do was ignore him, just let him be and give him a place to come every day that was warm and dry. What would happen if somebody paid attention to Donny? Would he remain invisible? Or would people get vicious given half a chance? Ethan decided to give them that half a chance, and within two weeks, Donny had disappeared from school.

Ethan used a fresh blade every time he shaved, lathering his head with shave cream, then scraping it away. It was like being made new every week. He shaved his head the first time right before school let out for the summer, then paraded around the hallways hatless and hairless, letting anyone who wanted to rub the top of his head. Nobody would be able to say that shaving his head had anything to do with what he was up to now…if anyone ever caught on.

He enjoyed the tingle of the menthol shave cream on his bare skin and the slight tug as the blade slid across his scalp. He turned his back to the vanity and held up a hand mirror in his right hand while his left hand guided the razor, carefully removing stubble from his occipital bun. Ethan appreciated obscure facts, especially obscure anatomical facts.

He tilted the hand mirror slightly so the reflection shifted from his head and shoulders to his lower back and buttocks. He impressed himself with his own gluteal fold. He had decided more than a year ago that in his line of work, with so little margin of error, it was critical to be strong and fit. He took up running to increase his cardiovascular stamina. He took gym as an elective so he could use the weight room at school. And he got a job for a landscaping company, because he wanted to be outside, pushing wheel barrows, digging holes, laying paving stones in a herringbone pattern for some rich guy's patio. Sometimes, when he was pruning, he would look at the size of the branch he was about to clip and say, quietly so no one else could hear, "Finger," then trim it away. The pruning shears made a nice clean *snick* when the branch fell away and the blades closed against each other. Sometimes he said, "Wrist." *Snick.* "Neck." *Snick.* Anything thicker than a wrist really required the limb saw, which had its own sound to accompany the marvelous back and forth motion, but sometimes when he was pruning, he liked to say neck all the same. It would be difficult to choose which body part made him feel the most satisfaction.

Ethan adjusted the hand mirror to show him the tops of his thighs, his buttocks, his back, his shoulders. His favorite would have to be his shoulders. They had become broad, well defined, strong enough to heft a hundred pounds of mulch like it was a ten-pound sack of flour.

That woman who was after Juney couldn't weigh much more than a hundred pounds. One-twenty tops. There were things he'd like to try with her, more experiments he could run. Running her and the dog off the road had been an impulse, a foolish maneuver that called attention to himself.

He'd tried to correct it, but she caught on, and now his truck was no good to him. The loss of his truck angered him, though less than he would have thought, because it made him appreciate his opponent. Still, if Erick hadn't been with him that day, he would have run her over then and there.

Erick was already scared. Juney was petrified. He didn't dare give them any more reason to fear him. No, the only way they'd get out of this was by sticking to the plan: if they got caught, then it was all on Juney's father. He was the big man in town. He ordered the kill. The fact that he didn't turn in him and Erick meant he didn't want the attention on himself. That was good. He'd either welcome them into the fold, or go down with them.

Ethan toweled off his head, cleaning errant shave cream from behind his ears. He dropped the towel on the floor, adding it to a growing mound in the corner—his mother could deal with those when she returned from her honeymoon—and walked across the two-bedroom rambler to the kitchen.

He opened the freezer door and withdrew an insulated cooler bag with Super America printed on it in bold red, white, and blue. He carried it tenderly to the front room and sat on the sofa made passable by a beige slipcover. He lowered the bag between his knees and let it rest on the floor inside his feet. Ethan leaned over his erection and opened the top of the bag to look at the spoils inside.

Chapter Thirty-Five

"I'LL MAKE SOME breakfast, then I have to get to the studio." Beckett left the bed and travelled the twenty or so steps to his kitchen. "What are you doing today?" he asked from across his apartment.

"Writing."

"How's it going?" he asked as he pulled eggs, milk, and butter from his fridge.

"Really well. I need to get some papers from the house—"

"I don't want you going there alone." Beckett looked at her across his kitchen table, an egg in one hand, bowl in the other.

"They'll keep until tomorrow," she said. Jess shoved Shakti off her leg and stretched before climbing out of bed. She went to the kitchen, scratching her butt cheek on the way, and gave Beckett a kiss. "What's this I see? Eggs before coffee?"

"My God. Have I gone insane?"

Jess grinned at him and grabbed the bag of beans and grinder from his counter. Shakti trotted over to join them, planted herself in the middle of the kitchen, and added a single *woof* to the conversation. "Sorry, Bear. Beans before kibble." Jess held up the coffee to show her. Shakti tilted her head, ears out in a display of alert curiosity, and gave her tail a hopeful swish. "Tell me your plans again," she said to Beckett.

He whisked the eggs into a froth and poured them over the sizzling butter in the pan. "I've got to unload the kiln, pack up my pots, load my van, and drive to Duluth."

"Sounds like a full day. How far is it to Duluth?"

"About three and a half hours, maybe a little less. After we unload the van, I'll help my buddy set up the show, have dinner and a couple of beers with him, then drive home. But don't wait up, honey."

"Okay, honey." She smiled at him over their domestic play. "And we're going up Friday?" Jess plucked a postcard off the fridge announcing the show. It pictured a gorgeous raku tea set. She read, "Join us for a reception with the artist at the North Shore Gallery." She stepped behind Beckett and wrapped her arms around his chest, hugging him from behind while he stirred their eggs around the pan. "Wine and cheese?"

"I think he's even got crackers."

"You've made the big time." She kissed the back of his neck before stepping away.

Shakti lay on the floor with her chin between her paws. Jess put the scoop into her bag of dog food and she sprang to her feet. When Jess straightened up, she caught Beckett staring at her.

"You're pretty cute in the mornings."

"Just in the mornings?"

Jess and Tyler sat on the steps of her front porch watching Shakti and Bruno race around the yard like a couple of maniacs. Bruno paused to lift his leg and Shakti hip slammed him into the brush at the edge of the yard. He resumed the chase. Jess imagined Shakti yelling over her shoulder, "Catch me if you can!" Bruno could and did. He leapt at her, taking her down with his front paws over her shoulders, his jaw over her neck. She fell and rolled belly up in the dirt. Jess and Tyler responded to the takedown with a collective, "Oooh!" as though they were spectators at a hockey match. Shakti pawed at Bruno, looking a bit like a beetle on its back, while he chewed on her neck ruff. Then, as though a ref had called time, Bruno stepped aside and she popped back onto her feet, shook herself and trotted away, only to turn a moment later and reinitiate.

"I'm glad you called," Jess said. This was the most normal she'd felt in days. She had suggested they meet at Tyler's rented house, but it was set up against the hill with a vertical lot line somewhere above his roof in back

and the street about three feet off his front stoop in front, hardly a yard that could accommodate Golden wrestling matches. She texted Beckett her plans, assuring him she would not be alone at the house and would not stay there long. She'd been nervous pulling into her drive, afraid the front porch would be ruined for her, but Tyler pulled in behind her with Bruno, and she was able to push away her hesitation and take pleasure in their play time after all.

"I needed to talk to you, Jess," Tyler said, drawing her back from her thoughts. He looked at Bruno's pack laid across his knee, ran his finger around the Helping Paws patch with a Retriever in that attentive sit that seemed to say, "I'm here for you."

Jess looked at Tyler, the dark curls that framed his face, the unshaven cheeks that gave him that "rugged good looks" effect, and the brown eyes that looked so kind one moment, so troubled the next.

He glanced up from the pack and met her gaze. "I've made a decision, unless..."

"Unless what?"

"Unless you change my mind." He looked out at the dogs now as though their eye contact had unnerved him. "Skoghall hasn't been very good to me. For me. Well, this place hasn't been very good *to* me either. I thought I was going to make a home here, become a successful ruh-restaurateur..."

Jess smiled at the reference to their first encounter, to her stammered declaration that she was a writer. Tyler fell quiet. "And you don't think you're successful here?" she prompted.

"No, but it's not just that. I'm not happy here, Jess." He looked at her again. "I don't fit in. I don't have friends. Not really."

Jess set her hand on his knee. "I'm your friend."

"I know that, Jess. And I appreciate it." He placed his hand on top of hers and gave her fingers a slight squeeze. He met her gaze again and held it. Jess saw something unexpected in his eyes, a vulnerability approaching a deep human need. He lifted her hand and placed her palm against his cheek. "I want us to be more than friends," he hurried to finish his sentence before she could object, "but I know you don't want that. At least I think you don't."

Jess withdrew her hand, and he let her slip it easily from within his grasp.

"I love you." He faced the yard again and watched the dogs lope past, panting as they recovered from their last sprint. "I said it. I know you don't love me, but I thought I should say it anyway. Before I leave."

"Leave?"

"I've decided that since I'm not happy here and since I'm in love with someone who's in love with someone else," he chortled and pushed his hand over his brow, exposing his pink scar, "I would be better off somewhere else." Tyler glanced at Jess. "I just thought you should know. Because if I didn't tell you and I left without saying it, I might wonder if there was ever any chance for us. But I know there isn't and now I've said it, so it's done. I can leave without wondering. And I can move on with peace of mind. That's what this is about, Jess. My peace of mind. I don't expect you to respond. I—"

"Tyler, I'm so sorry."

"For what?" He rubbed the edge of Bruno's pack, a surrogate for the dog himself.

Jess remembered how his hand used to find the bulge of his knife inside his pocket. Same habit, different object of focus. He was better with Bruno. So much better. "I don't know," she said. "For what happened with Bonnie. For how things have turned out."

"Robin is buying the Water Wheel," he said abruptly. "So that's good. I don't have to worry about the café."

"Where are you going?"

"Lake City, just across the river from here. I have a buddy from high school there, the one with River City Roasters who does my coffee. We're opening a coffee house and bakery together. I'll run the bakery. It'll be good for me, mostly behind the scenes in the kitchen. And he's cool about Bruno. No secrets this time."

"That's good," Jess said, still working to comprehend the fact that Tyler was leaving Skoghall, that she and Shakti were losing good friends. "We'll miss you and Bruno."

"Yeah. We'll miss you, too."

"How soon do you go?"

"I'm heading over there now. I'm staying with my friend while I find a place. He's got a wife and little boy."

"*Now?*"

"Yeah. It seemed best to just go."

"Oh."

And there was nothing left to say between them.

Tyler stood up, stretched, and called Bruno over. Shakti followed, happy to go wherever Bruno went. The dogs lapped water from a bowl on the ground, then Shakti flopped onto her side and lay there panting.

When Bruno had finished drinking, Tyler gave him a command, "Bruno, find Jess."

Bruno tilted his head thoughtfully, looked at Tyler, then at Jess. He turned to face Jess and put his chin on her thigh. "I'm going to miss you," she said, rubbing his ears.

"Bruno, lap," Tyler said.

Bruno rose to place his front paws on Jess's legs.

"Snuggle."

Bruno leaned toward her to rest his head on her shoulder, his soft cheek against hers. Jess wrapped her arms around Bruno and hugged him. She buried her fingers in his thick auburn fur and scratched his neck and shoulders. His mouth opened and he panted happily.

"Tyler," Jess looked up from Bruno to see him smiling sadly at the two of them, "I'm really going to miss you."

"Thanks, Jess. It helps knowing that." He called to Bruno and held out his pack. "Get dressed," he said. The dog walked into his pack, slipping his head through the chest loop.

"Don't be a stranger, okay?" Jess stood and moved to hug Tyler farewell. He took a step backwards.

"I'm just going across the river. I'll expect you to come have coffee with me once the shop is open."

"It's a deal."

Jess watched Tyler and Bruno drive away, her hand on Shakti. She sighed, feeling the closing of a door. They'd only known each other about five months, but Tyler was the first person she'd met in Skoghall, the first man she'd dated after her divorce, and a major part of her experiences with Bonnie.

Her stomach growled and she checked the time on her phone: 6:30. No wonder she was hungry. Realizing she was alone and she had a promise to keep, Jess had to get back to town. She called Shakti and they went inside, letting the screen door bang against its frame behind them. Shakti trotted into the kitchen, scouting for the food bowls that waited at Beckett's place. Jess had to grab a few fresh clothes and her copies of articles about Bonnie's death. *Five minutes,* she thought, *and I'm out of here.*

She entered her library at the front of the house. Originally a music room, it had the high, small windows designed to sit above the family's upright piano, these with diamond-shaped panes of leaded glass that Jess loved. Beckett, Dave, and Tyler had built a hearth and moved the old parlor stove in here from the smokehouse when Jess first moved in. Beckett and Tyler got into it over Tyler's brick-laying skills and he left in a huff. That had been the first sign of a developing rivalry between the men. Jess smiled at the memory. It seemed so near and so distant at the same time. She scanned her bookshelves for something she hadn't read yet, planning to relax with a book and glass of wine while she waited up for Beckett. In the end, she chose a collection of stories by F. Scott Fitzgerald.

She left Shakti panting on the floor of the hallway, still recovering from her playtime with Bruno, and went upstairs. She stopped in her office to grab the papers she needed. She heard a car out on the road. Jess paused to listen for its passing, but her phone rang. She fished it out of her back pocket and checked the screen. John Ecklund-Sykes, her writing partner. She had a bar or two of coverage, probably enough for a brief conversation.

"Hi, John." She went to her bedroom with the phone to her ear.

"How's your writing coming, Jess?"

"Funny you should ask that." She entered her walk-in closet and the phone dropped a bar. She raised her voice, "Hang on. I'm losing reception." Jess grabbed a couple of t-shirts and backed out of the closet. "I'm making slow progress. Things have been really crazy here."

"I'm not doing so hot myself," John said. "That's why I called. I was wondering if I could come visit you for a few days. Maybe staying in the house will shake loose a memory or two. I could use some inspiration."

"Sure. No problem." She wandered into the bathroom and tucked a jar of eye cream and dental floss into the t-shirts in her arms.

Shakti barked at something—a squirrel, the vibration of a passing car, some scent so subtle Jess could never detect it—but the odd thing, Jess thought, was that Shakti's bark sounded like it was coming through the walls of the house and not like it was resounding within them. She hurried downstairs, the phone pressed to her ear by one hand, her clothes and papers held in the other. Shakti no longer lay on the hallway floor.

"John," she said, "I'll have to call you back." She hung up without waiting for a response. Jess tossed her things on the floor before entering the vestibule. The screen door rested against its frame, closed but not latched. She burst through it, panic rising in her chest.

"Shakti!" she yelled as she scanned the front yard, searching everywhere. She cupped her hands around her mouth and called again. "Shakti!" She listened for the jangle of dog tags approaching, but heard only the woodpecker tapping at a nearby tree. Jess looked down her drive, then over her shoulders. Road or woods?

"Shakti!" Still no answer.

Jess ran forward, down her driveway and out into Haug Drive. She stood in its middle looking one way, then turning and looking the other. There was no sign of Shakti.

Jess still clutched her phone in her hand. She looked down at it like she knew it could help, if she could only figure out how. She tapped the screen and brought up Beckett's number. Her reception was better out here in the road. His phone rang several times before going to voicemail. He'd be in Duluth, maybe carrying pots in and out of the gallery, maybe sitting on his phone while having a beer with his friend. "Shakti's gone," she said and stopped. "Beckett, I don't know what to do." She looked at the phone before hanging up. There was too much to say for voicemail and nothing he could do from Duluth.

She called Martinez.

"You've reached Investigator Martinez with the Rice County Sheriff's Office."

"Shit." She hung up.

Jess heard a car approaching from town. She turned toward the sound and waited. She didn't know what she expected or what she was doing, only that she needed help. A sheriff's cruiser rounded the bend and approached Jess. She ran toward it waving her arms. The cruiser slowed and stopped. Jess went to the driver's side window and blurted out, "My dog is missing."

A deputy Jess hadn't met before stared at her from the cabin of the patrol car. She opened her mouth slowly and enunciated, "You lost your dog?"

"Yes. My dog, Shakti, has gone missing. The door must not have latched and then the phone rang and she slipped out." Jess waved her arm toward her house on the other side of the trees lining the road.

"You live here?"

Jess nodded.

"All right. I was doing a check on your place anyway, so I might as well help you look."

Jess stepped back from the car as the deputy pulled into her driveway and parked. When she got out of the car, she was talking into the radio attached to her uniform.

"I called Investigator Martinez," Jess told her, "but I got voicemail. Can you tell him Shakti's missing?"

"Sure. Let's look around here a bit. I bet your dog just wandered off after a rabbit or squirrel. My dogs do that sorta thing all the time." The Deputy wore the classic sheriff's Stetson, a thin blonde braid hanging out the back. "What's your dog's name?"

"Shakti. Could you get Martinez on that radio?"

"Shakti," the Deputy called through cupped hands. "I radioed in what's going on. And I'm sure Martinez will check his messages soon." She moved away from Jess toward the trees behind the barn. "We miss calls a lot, you know. All the bluffs really mess with reception." She hollered back to Jess over her shoulder, "And the office is inside a concrete building." She moved around the corner of the barn. "Shakti!"

Jess ran into the trees on the opposite side of her property, following the trail Shakti had taken when she wandered into the woods after a rabbit. It was possible her disappearance had nothing to do with Dan's killer. It was possible she had her nose in a hole, or pointed up the trunk of a tree, just like the Deputy said.

It was possible, but Jess didn't believe it.

"Look, I'll let Martinez know about your dog when I get back to the office, but I'm sure it's nothing. You got some chicken or something? Dogs can smell their favorite food a mile away. Just bring out the good stuff," she said helpfully, "and I bet Shakti will come running out of these woods, tail wagging like crazy."

"I'll give that a try," Jess said. "But please make sure you tell Martinez right away. He needs to know this."

"Don't worry, Ms. Vernon. I will." She all but tipped her hat as she ducked back into her car.

Jess hit redial before the Deputy was out of her driveway. "You've reached Investigator Martinez with the Rice County Sheriff's Office." This time Jess left a message. "Please, please, please," she said to the phone in her hand, willing Martinez to get her message right away, for Beckett to get his, and then, at a loss for what to do next, she went inside and got a jar of peanut butter.

Chapter Thirty-Six

ETHAN OPENED THE back door of the junk shop and slipped inside. He wheeled in a large duffel bag and slipped a backpack off his shoulders. He looked around. Even with all the cleaning that had occurred, the windows let in very little light, which was just as well. Less light in, less light out. Ethan would stay in the back room, away from the road, even though he had waited for Wednesday—the day the bar and everything else in Skoghall closed—so that he could avoid any curious motorheads getting in his business. It was handy having lackeys who feared him. He'd managed to get information, a key, and a phone number. He couldn't expect that kind of help in the future, but now Ethan saw what was possible. A partner, perhaps, one day. He aspired to greatness in his own right and a partner was unlikely, but oh how he enjoyed manipulating his *friends.*

He tugged at the cuffs of his rubber gloves, two pairs to better ensure against prints, and began. First, he pulled a pair of plastic tarps and a roll of duct tape out of the backpack. He taped one of the tarps to the doorframe so it made a curtain between the back and middle rooms. It took some doing to get around the merchandise and behind the shelving, but he managed to hang the other tarp over the window. With the room sealed off, he turned on the overhead light and arranged the dishes and old magazines and a set of electric hair curlers in a proper display before the window, because he wanted everything to be just so.

A small kitchen table with drop leaves sat in the middle of the room next to a rolling typewriter stand. Ethan set to work clearing their surfaces. He put the board games, records, and a metronome in a cracked wooden case on the shelves around the room. He worked quickly, but took care to keep things orderly.

Ethan was not a hack.

And besides, he wanted his date to enjoy herself.

Well, no. That wasn't really possible. He wanted her to appreciate his effort. She would realize how much care he had put into making their time together special, even if he had to point it out to her.

The table had one leaf out, one down. There wasn't room to have both leaves out and still move around. It would suffice. He wheeled the typewriter stand to the head of the dining table, stood beside it imagining how everything would work. Ethan shoved the table against the shelves along the inside wall, with the rounded leaf extending outward into the room. He placed the typewriter stand alongside the table where it would be easily visible, even to someone seated in a chair.

He hummed a wordless song he'd made up as a child, something that spilled forth whenever he was pleased with himself. He tossed the plastic wrap and cardboard from six-packs of pillar candles into his backpack and lined the shelves with them. He'd spent more on candles than on anything else—buying the Dollar Store's entire stock—but the mood had to be set.

The Salvation Army store had supplied Ethan with a portable CD player and a Chopin CD for the reasonable price of $6. He searched the walls for an outlet, finding one after moving a Playskool record player on a bottom shelf. He pressed play and put the CD on repeat.

Ethan carefully unwrapped a bottle of wine and two glasses brought from home in a paper grocery sack. Knowing his mother, the wine was cheap, but at least it was red. He set these out, making room on the shelf above the CD player, then bringing a half dozen candles together near the wine so that his offering would be surrounded by softly flickering light.

Ethan folded the paper sack and tucked it away before kneeling at the backpack. He pushed its nylon sides open like a mouth to better extract the remaining contents. First, a hand saw, the teeth tinged with rust. It had come with a miter box that disappeared long ago. It must be as old as Ethan, just another thing his father left behind. He set it on the typewriter stand. He withdrew a needle nose pliers and tinsnips from the bag and laid them beside the saw. Then came a scalpel from the first aid kit under the bathroom sink. Ethan slid his hands into the bag like a doctor reaching into a body cavity. Gently cradling it, he extracted a small blowtorch.

Lining up everything on the typewriter stand, Ethan considered his instruments, the wonders he could perform with each one. He picked up the scalpel and removed it from the plastic wrap. There was no need for sterility here. He held it before him, turning it carefully so the blade caught the candlelight. A thing of beauty. He laid it down next to the pliers and straightened them, aligning their handles with the care of a surgeon. Only one thing remained, and it was sleeping in the duffel bag.

Chapter Thirty-Seven

JESS PACED THE front porch, watching the eastern sky turn steely as the sun lowered itself behind the river bluffs to the west. She had walked the woods, calling Shakti's name. She had driven up and down Haug Drive and out County QQ with her windows down, yelling for Shakti until she was hoarse. She still hadn't heard from Martinez. Beckett had called as soon as he got her message and was on his way home. He had urged her to go back to his place, but she couldn't leave with Shakti out there somewhere, just in case she was only wandering through the woods. Jess wished she could believe it, but her gut told her there was something going on. Something bad.

And now the sun was setting. The knot in her stomach tightened.

Her phone chimed. Jess pulled it from her pocket and saw the time flash across the screen, 7:40. It would be dark by 8:00. She swiped it to bring up the text message, hoping it was finally Martinez.

She found a picture of Shakti, lying on her side with her eyes closed.

Jess slammed through her front door and ran into the kitchen. She threw her phone on the counter and turned on the faucet. She splashed cold water on her face and stared out the window until her head cleared.

Her hands trembled as she picked up her phone and looked again. There was no way to tell if Shakti was dead or alive. But she was on a table; the edge of it showed beside her head. Beneath the table, rising precariously through the table's shadow toward Shakti, a stack of magazines. Jess zoomed in on the photo, expanding it until the image pixelated. Visible all the same, one word in white caps, boxed in red: LIFE.

She tapped Beckett's contact.

Even if he did have reception, that van of his was the opposite of a Skinner box, and he liked to crank his music so he wouldn't have to hear the road and engine noise. "You've reached Beckett Hanson," his voicemail answered.

"He has Shakti." She felt her chest heaving with her panicked breath. "Erick, or whoever, texted me a picture of Shakti." She looked out at the darkening yard through the forest's elongated shadow. "Fuck. Beckett. I'm going to the junk shop. I'm going to get her back." She hung up. "Hurry home," she said to the phone in her hand.

She dialed Martinez and got his voicemail again. She left a message. "Victor. He's got Shakti at the junk shop. I'm going after her." She hung up and stared at her phone. *That's it*, she thought. She'd called her back up. The rest was in the hands of God or the Universe or Fate or whatever kept an eye on people like her. *And Shakti,* which was a prayer in itself.

She laid the gun case on the kitchen table and snapped open the latches. "Hello, Little Fern." She lifted the Glock from the foam cushion, felt its cool weight in her hand. Jess pointed it across the room, took aim at the teakettle sitting on her stove, dotted the i, and reminded herself to rotate her elbows outward. She set it down and took a magazine from the case, checked it, slid it into the gun, then chambered a round. She grabbed a small shoulder bag that she sometimes used as a purse and dumped the contents of the bag onto her table. She slipped her license in her back pocket, then muted her phone and zippered it and her keys inside the bag, but nothing else. She didn't want anything getting in the way of her grabbing the gun when she needed it. She slung the bag across her chest and adjusted the shoulder strap's length, then practiced drawing the gun.

It wasn't graceful, especially with the industrial-strength Velcro sounding every time she lifted the flap over the mouth of the bag, but she didn't have time to find a better solution. Jess hoped she was prepared enough for luck to favor her.

Getting to Shakti felt like the need for getting more air.

As Jess parked her car in front of the junk shop, her panic lifted. The clarity of a singular purpose brought her an intensely alert calm. She rushed to the door, then paused at the threshold to listen. Behind the junk shop, frogs, crickets, an owl, and surely other voices she couldn't identify joined the night chorus. They would serve as her companions and witnesses. Them and the stars in the sky. Behind her and all along the River Road it was quiet. She reached a hand along the wall inside the door and found the switch. Nothing happened when she flipped it.

She looked at the wall fixture mounted next to the door and saw that he had taken the trouble of removing the globe and the bulb. Jess stepped into the room and waited for her eyes to adjust, then made her way to the next door.

Jess paused at the doorway to the second room. She heard music. Classical piano. She searched the corners of the room, barely able to make out the shapes of things lining the walls. She could not discern anything large or alive or threatening, so she stepped forward and crossed the room quickly.

She walked into something smooth and cool to the touch. Jess jumped back and gasped as the piano music crescendoed, like walking into a silent movie. She reached a hand out before herself and found the smooth surface of a plastic curtain. If he waited on the other side, he already knew she was here. She opened the shoulder bag, letting the Velcro rip noisily. She put her hand under the flap and wrapped it around the Glock's grip, but didn't withdraw it. Her heart thudded noisily in her ears as she shouldered the curtain and slipped into the back room.

Candles lit the room with soft wavering light. Though not bright, Jess's eyes took a moment to adjust.

Shakti lay on a small table at the back of the room. Jess let go of the gun inside the bag as she rushed to her dog. She put her face next to Shakti's with one hand on the top of her head and the other on her ribs. She felt Shakti's chest rise and sighed with relief. She kissed Shakti's soft brow and ran a hand over her side and down each leg, checking for any obvious injuries, and then her senses, relieved of the greatest concern, opened to take in her surroundings.

Candles lined the shelves, hundreds of them, making some of the merchandise, like a floral teacup, look more appealing and other merchandise, like the baby doll with the lopsided haircut, look ghastly. Jess's gaze circled the edges of the room. A chair had been set across from the table where Shakti lay, a single chair for a single spectator. To the left of the door with the black curtain sat a portable CD player, the source of the music. Next to it, well lit by a cluster of candles, stood a bottle of wine and two glasses. Jess's stomach lurched at the gesture. Her scan of the room brought her attention back to Shakti and the typewriter stand beside her. It held an assortment of tools that caused Jess to freeze. The pianist pounded out several chords, a sudden jolt, before playing quietly again.

Jess shoved her hands underneath Shakti's limp body.

The candlelight flickered.

"Ah-ah-aaah." A young man stepped into the room from the back porch and stood wagging a gloved finger at Jess. "You wouldn't want to leave now and spoil our date."

"You're not Erick." She stared at him, still bent over Shakti.

"No." He stepped fully into the room, shut the door, and locked it. "Erick could never pull this off." The young man sat in the chair. "Erick has his uses…" He paused to consider. "He's been keeping the cops busy. That has been handy. Really. Without Erick I doubt I would have had the time to set this up."

She stood facing him, keeping one of her hands atop Shakti. Jess felt relief every time Shakti's ribs moved against her hand. Her breathing seemed slow to Jess, but she *was* breathing. "What exactly is this?"

"This…Jessica," he said her name with a sharp emphasis on the first syllable, "is a very special night for us. In fact," he took the bottle of wine from the shelf, "we should make a toast." He put his hand over the top of the bottle, but stopped. "You don't trust me. You think it might be drugged, but look." He held the bottle out to her. "It's a screw top. I hope you don't think that's tacky. I understand wines in all price ranges come with screw tops now. It's better for the cork trees or something. Recyclable." He waved the bottle in front of her. "You can see that the top is still attached to the band around the bottle's neck. It's sealed. It's safe." He pushed the bottle toward her, but did not move his feet. "Go on. You can do the honors."

Jess reached into the shoulder bag, the Velcro sounding loudly, and withdrew the gun. She held it with both hands, the way she'd been taught. Her arms trembled, but that shouldn't matter at such close range.

The man laughed. He set the wine bottle on a shelf and held up his hands.

"Get back." She took a step toward him.

He took a step toward her.

Jess faltered, rocked back on her heels and staggered accidentally away from the man. She hadn't meant to give up ground, but she hadn't expected him to step into the gun. He grabbed it, his hands on hers, squeezing them hard around the Glock's textured grip. He raised the gun and pressed the barrel to his forehead. Jess pulled against him, trying to bring the gun away from his head or at least to free her hands, to have nothing to do with this. He wouldn't let her.

"Go on then. Your finger's on the trigger, isn't it? All you have to do is pull."

Jess whimpered.

"What will you tell them? Will you say it was self-defense?" He affected a mocking tone, "I had to kill him. You see, he offered me a glass of wine." He leaned into the gun, holding Jess's hands under his own. Each time she managed to step backwards, he came with her. "Are you a killer, Jessica? Can you do this?"

He lifted his face. His forehead bore the round indentation of the barrel. "Go on," he urged. "Become a killer, just like me."

She pulled her finger against the trigger, felt the slack, then the tension. One more tiny exertion. That was all that stood between her killing and not killing somebody.

He laughed at her. He pulled one of her hands away from the gun and took it from her other hand. He kept hold of her hand while he set the gun on the closest shelf and then, with a movement so swift Jess was unable to track it, he yanked her forward and locked a handcuff around her wrist.

Jess stumbled as he pulled her across the room. He swung her by the arm so she turned and landed almost on the chair set up across from Shakti. She had to right herself while her captor attached the free end of the cuff to the crossbar between the chair's legs.

"Well," he said, and ran a gloved hand over the smooth crown of his head, "I did not expect that from you." He smirked down at her. "But it was fun."

He took up the bottle of wine and unscrewed the top himself. He poured two glasses and held one out for Jess to accept.

He waited.

"I'm losing my patience," he said, and Jess took the glass in her free, left hand.

He held up his glass. "To my success..."

Jess thought he was saying success*ful*. If he had completed the word, he would have said something else to go along with the adjective, but he was being careful, guarding his secrets. She still did not know his name, but she knew Erick did, and she was certain he would give up his friend once presented with a compelling reason to do so. The music quieted. He raised his glass, and she hers. He drank. She touched her lip to the dark liquid, but did not allow any to pass.

He positioned himself directly in front of Jess and stood over her. He wore running tights and a mock turtleneck with long sleeves that caused him to sweat. Every curve of his bulging, young muscles showed through the skin-tight fabric. Like a lot of young athletes, he'd shaved his head, making his eyebrows the only visible body hair. Jess remembered Martinez' words, "He is an organized killer." She looked from his head to the gloved hand holding the wine glass and shivered as she realized this was the event he'd been training for.

The young man set his wine glass down and pushed a bead of sweat away from his brow. "We're going to play a little game."

"Tell me your name." Her voice sounded tense, desperate.

He turned on his heels and walked to the other end of the room, all of ten steps, then faced her again. "Oh, all right." He shrugged like it really was a children's game. "My name is Ethan."

"Ethan?" He smiled when she said his name, the drawing up of his cheeks, the narrowing of his chin, and the sparkle of white teeth with a small triangular gap in the middle came together in a flash of recognition—he had been in the junk shop that day before Skipper went to stay with his cousin. And he'd been there the day she met Oaky and Erick. How had she not realized?

"How did you figure it out?"

"Figure what out, Ethan?"

"You're clever, you know that? You almost cost me the entire operation. How did you know the drug was in the lipstick tube?"

"What do you mean?"

"Juney told me the cops came for all the lipstick in her house. I knew you, the witness from the bar, had to be the one to put it together. Did you see her spike the drink?"

"Oh, that." Jess pretended to drink again.

He looked at her approvingly. "You should drink up. You're going to need something tonight. Now. About that lipstick tube?"

She smiled and shrugged carelessly. "I'm a woman, aren't I? I have experience with lipstick."

Dan appeared, standing where his body had lain. Ethan caught her glance in that direction and followed her gaze, saw nothing there, and stepped closer to the typewriter stand. He traded his wine glass for the pliers.

What drug did you give him?

Jess repeated the words as though they were her own. "What drug did you give him?" Her voice had a girlish quality she didn't like, the sort of flirtatious affectation she might have tried on in high school.

The smug satisfaction of the mastermind returned and Ethan studied Jess, weighing her worth to him. "Diazepam. We have Erick's mother's anxiety to thank for that." Ethan paused to consider. "He was supposed to go to sleep. Instead the crazy bastard tried to rape Juney." He chuckled. "You should have seen how worked up Erick got over that, like I'd planned it that way, like I'd raped her myself."

You wouldn't...

"You wouldn't do that, would you?" His face soured. "You're too smart for that. You don't shit where you sleep."

He grinned, the chip in his tooth the most distinctive feature of his face. "Yeah, that's right."

If she could keep him talking, it would delay him. Beckett and Martinez would get their messages. They would come for her. She just had to keep him talking. "So, Juney drugged him in the bar," she said. "Then what?"

"You've barely touched your wine. Drink up."

Jess took a sip of the wine, a cheap blend, young and heavy with tannins. "I don't know how you got that girl to follow through. What was in it for her?"

Ethan shouted, "Enough!" Jess startled, spilling wine over her lap. "I don't play your game. You play mine." He held the bottle out to her. "Raise your glass."

"I...I haven't finished this glass."

He began pouring wine over her lap, moving from one thigh to the other, until Jess held her glass up to catch the stream. He filled it to the rim and stepped back, set the bottle down, and glared at her. "Drink up."

Jess obeyed, putting her lip to the glass and sucking wine off the top of the bowl. She kept her eyes on Ethan, sensing the depth of rage beneath the surface calm.

"I'm told," he said, recovering his persona, "that alcohol has the amazing property of numbing pain."

Chapter Thirty-Eight

JUNEY SAT AT the interview table, chewing on the ragged cuticle of her middle finger. Since all this started she couldn't help herself. Over the past spring, her mother had bribed her out of the disgusting habit, inspecting her nails at the end of each week and giving her fifty cents for each nail that was in good condition. When her mother first proposed the idea, Juney couldn't handle it. It took her weeks to build up the self-control to leave a single nail unchewed. Her reward, fifty cents, less than a can of pop. But her mother's praise had been worth something, and over several months she set her mind on winning the prize. For two months now, she'd received five bucks a week, twenty a month, and well worth the struggle. When Erick told her she had nice hands, that had felt like the jackpot. And then he and Ethan turned up at her door to speak with her father.

She and Erick sat across from two investigators. Their parents—well, her parents and his dad and an uncle or cousin or something, because his mother had a migraine—lined the wall behind them. Behind the investigators was one of those big windows that reflected your face back to you while letting people on the other side watch what you were doing. She wondered how many people were staring at her right now. She kept looking above the investigators' heads at her parents' faces reflected in the glass. What she saw terrified her.

"June," Investigator Johnson said, "we understand that Mr. Grunner…

came at you…and you were afraid for your safety."

She nodded while getting hold of a hangnail between her incisors and pulling.

"We already know there was someone else involved in all this."

"Just tell them what they need to know, June," her mother pleaded.

"Someone damaged the body. Maybe it was just a prank, meant to be harmless. After all, the man was already dead."

They'd asked her these same questions before, when they had her alone in this room. And they'd already talked to Erick, probably trying the same questions on him. Maybe the cops wanted to see if they'd cave with their parents in the room. What was that called? Turning up the heat. Juney looked in the mirror, seeking Erick's eyes. She couldn't help herself. He kept his head down, hands in his lap, but her father caught her eye. He held his hat before him, the carefully shaped and brushed brown felted wool. His hands crushed and mangled it.

Behind her, a phone vibrated for like the tenth time. She glanced at Erick's cousin in the mirror. He looked caught off guard and a little embarrassed as he fished in his pants pocket. His eyes widened when he saw the screen. He thumbed it, scrolling messages. "I think I have to take this," he mumbled and stepped outside the room.

Investigator Johnson scowled after him, but the other one, the Mexican, looked interested. "June," he said her name like every ten seconds, "we know you hit him on the head. It will help you if you tell us exactly what happened. You're a minor still, and a judge will consider whether or not you've been honest and cooperative."

Juney glanced at her father's face in the mirror. His features were so tight with rage that he had changed color. When she was a child, she liked to pick dandelions and hold a thumbnail to the base of the flower. *Mama had a baby and its head popped…off!* On the final word, she would flick the nail, dislodging the flower from the stem, sending it sailing. Her father's head was about to pop off. She took her finger out of her mouth. Blood oozed from the edge between the nail and the flesh where she had pulled back a long, painful strip of hangnail. She studied the rim of red and decided to tell them what they wanted to know.

The door burst open behind her. Erick's cousin charged Erick, lifting him from his chair by his throat. He slammed Erick into a wall. The adults were all so shocked nobody moved to help him. Not even the investigators.

"Dave! What the hell?" Erick's dad yelled.

Dave looked over his shoulder at the Mexican. "That was Beckett. Their friend's got Jess and Shakti." He looked back at Erick, his face as red as his hair, his eyes scrunched in fury. Not like her father's. Her father had a controlled simmer behind his eyes, something that would become dangerous at a time opportune for *him*. Dave looked like he was going to kill Erick right here, in front his father and the cops and everybody. Juney noticed wetness down at her crotch and realized he had actually scared the piss out of her. Dave's eyes bore into Erick. "If he hurts one hair of that dog…"

Chapter Thirty-Nine

"DRINK UP."

Jess raised the glass to her mouth and drank, sipping, buying every second she could while trying to think of a way out. She could stand up, swing the chair at him. She could throw the wine in his face. But then what?

She didn't know.

How far away was Beckett? Would he walk in too late and find her and Shakti's mutilated bodies? Jess pulled up on the chair with the handcuff as much as she could without being obvious.

Ethan stood over her, holding his glass of wine, a look of enjoyment on his face. "The chair is solid," he said. "I made sure. And I cabled it to the shelves behind you. If you try to pick up the chair, you won't be able to. Or you'll bring the shelves and all that crap down on your head. Maybe the shelves will break your back. Maybe not. But it won't be pleasant."

The little bastard had prepared that speech, probably rehearsed it while he set up the chair. "The cops are on the way, you know."

"Doubtful." He slipped a finger into a pocket sewn into the waistband of his running tights and fished out a small flip phone. "I picked up a few of these at Wal-Mart for five bucks each. Of course, the air time costs me, but they're insanely reasonable. No contracts. No registration. You can add minutes any time you like at a gas station." He stared at the marvel in his hand. "You see," he held the phone toward Jess like maybe she'd never seen one before, "this little baby keeps me informed. I know, for example, that right now your cop friends are wasting their time with my decoys. And why wouldn't they when that's all they've got?"

Jess glanced at Dan. He leaned against the shelves, his arms folded across his chest, one ankle crossed in front of the other. *Help me,* she insisted. He shook his head like she'd hopelessly blundered. And maybe she had. Dan uncrossed his arms. His hands were where they belonged, whether by his will or because of his proximity to the person who kept them, Jess couldn't know. He gestured tipping a glass to his lips. Jess drank her wine. She kept it raised and downed half the glass. When she stopped drinking, she found Ethan grinning at her like the spider who'd just watched a fly stumble into its web. She held up her wine glass for more.

Ethan picked up the bottle and poured, this time with the care of a connoisseur.

"What are we listening to?" Jess said.

"Do you like it?" He picked up a CD case from beside the player. "I found it at the Salvation Army. A bargain. Chopin's piano concertos." He pronounced Chopin like *chop in.*

Jess did not like it. She had studied *Frankenstein* in its various forms, including the 1910 Edison Kinetoscope version. The music reminded her of this earliest horror film, at moments tranquil then suddenly frenetic, jarring the senses as much as the appearance of the monster.

Tell me...

"Tell me something, Ethan. What did you do with the hands?"

He raised an eyebrow. "You know about the hands?" Ethan set the CD on the shelf and went to his table of instruments beside Shakti. He picked up the pliers and stroked the handle. He looked at Jess, his gaze chilling. "They're in my freezer." He came closer, holding the pliers up for her to see. "I'll have to move them soon. My mother is on her honeymoon. Husband number three and a real catch. He has a time-share in Florida and no children. With me about to leave home, they can be as selfish as they want. And the timing couldn't have been better for me, but I'm afraid I won't be able to save you. A little complication of living with my mother." He looked back at the instruments that he'd laid out. "Next one," he said to himself.

Exciting.

"I think what you're doing is...exciting."

He looked back at Jess with new interest. "Oh really?" His brows pinched with skepticism. "How so?"

"It's like you understand." Jess searched her mind for the right words. "The pointlessness. The waste. The joke."

He nodded at her. "Go on."

Jess raised her glass to him. "Why don't you join me and we'll talk about it." Ethan picked up his glass and took a sip. Jess had about a glass of wine in her already, but she hoped that, given his age, he was a lightweight.

"So talk," he said.

Have you seen…

"Have you seen *Natural Born Killers?*"

"It's a classic. One of the best."

"It's a love affair writ in blood. Mickey and Mallory are…are a statement about how pointless society is. How people don't really give a shit about each other. Like the reporter. He did it for ratings." Jess scoured her memory for details from the movie and flashes of gore-filled imagery moved before her mind's eye. "The demon is in all of us. That's the truth of it."

Ethan began to agree with her. His stance relaxed and he took a sip of his wine. "That's right," he said amicably. "That's right."

"We're all killers, but some of us are honest about it. Like Mickey said, the lion kills the elk. The corporation kills the forest." Jess felt herself begin to sweat, her armpits first. As long as he didn't know how hard she was trying—to remember the satirical commentary, to take it seriously, to find those aspects he would relate to without the irony. As long as he couldn't sense her desperation. "The reporter. He deserved to die."

"Why, Jessica?"

"Because he represented everything Mickey and Mallory stood against. The phoniness. The shallowness. The falsity. He was the biggest liar of them all, part of the culture machine that creates killers."

"But Mickey and Mallory weren't created." Ethan stepped toward Jess, loomed over her. His face appeared ghastly in the candlelight, a mask of wavering shadows. "They were *natural* born killers. That is the whole point!"

Jess leaned back against the chair, her right hand in a tight fist straining against the steel loop of the cuff. "Yes. Yes. It is the point. It is. It takes a natural killer to show the hypocrisy of all the phonies."

Ethan's grim mouth stretched into a smile and he narrowed his eyes as he shook a pointed finger at Jess. "You're smart. I took an elective last year in film studies. One of our English teachers wanted to spend a year watching movies, snaked it into the offerings. You should have taught that class. It would have actually been worth my time if you'd taught it."

"Thank—"

Shakti wheezed and Jess jolted against the chair, her desire to spring to Shakti's side destroying her pretense.

Ethan threw his wine glass across the room. It shattered against one of the metal shelves. A nearby candle hissed as the wine extinguished its flame. "Bitch. Think you can toy with me? Think you can manipulate me?" He snatched up the pliers and came at her. He grabbed her wrist. Jess dropped her wineglass as he jerked her hand toward him, pushing his nail into her palm and forcing her fingers to spread. She struggled to free her hand, but he was as strong as he looked. He grabbed her index finger with the pliers and clamped down. Jess cried out. "You or the dog?"

"What?" She could barely get the word out. Fingers, so delicate, so subtle, so sensitive, so easy to damage.

"I can play with you or the dog." His voice held steady while a hasty crescendo accompanied it, lending the moment a requisite melodrama.

Jess gasped as he pinched her finger tighter in the pliers' toothed grip. "Me." The pain cut off her breathing and made her eyes water.

Ethan released her finger and took a step back to study her, the specimen of his curiosity. "I would have picked the dog."

"And spared yourself." Her finger throbbed with the kind of pain she couldn't stand to look at.

"Possibly, but that's not why. Not mainly." He enjoyed philosophizing with an audience for his dark ruminations. The novelty excited him. "I would want to see it done. It's hard to take anything in when you're in pain."

She stared past Ethan at Shakti. One of her paws twitched. It was the first movement she'd seen. Jess's heart ached.

The corner beside Shakti was empty. Dan had disappeared.

The overhead light came on and Jess pushed back against the chair, blinking rapidly, the sudden change throwing her into a momentary state of shock.

"I want to see what I'm doing." Ethan grabbed her wrist and pulled. Jess made a fist and tried to hold her hand against her chest, but he yanked, forcing her muscles to yield, demonstrating his superior strength. Jess struggled against the chair, yanking her right hand until the handcuff cut into her wrist, while Ethan held her left arm extended away from her. "I don't have to play with you *now*. There's this nice yellow puppy on the table over there, and she won't struggle while I take my time with her." Jess forced herself to settle into the chair and stared at him defiantly, despite the tears on her cheeks. "That's better. Relax your hand." He shook her by the wrist until she uncurled her fingers. He took hold of the index finger and turned it for inspection. "Tsk-tsk-tsk. This nail is already looking a little purple. I'm sure it's only a matter of time before it falls out." He lifted his face to meet Jess's gaze with his own cold gray eyes. "We'll just help it along."

She turned her head away from him. Her body tensed and sweat leaked from every pore in anticipation of the pain he was about to inflict upon her. The pliers pinched the tip of her finger as Ethan sought the rim of her short nail.

He paused his grasping. "I could give you something to bite on. Maybe a bullet, so you don't bite your tongue." Jess didn't respond. "I promise," a note of mirth crept into his voice, "you won't have to worry about the lead poisoning."

Jess kicked her leg out to the side and brushed his shin. He yanked her head backwards by her hair. The chair back dug into her skull and she blinked at the ceiling. Ethan brought his head down beside hers. She felt his breath on her ear. "Try anything else, and I'll work on the dog while you watch. Then I'll give you the same treatment it got. You know, I took human anatomy last semester. We dissected cats, because they're anatomically so similar to humans. It's the same with dogs. So when I cut out your dog's tongue, you can imagine me cutting out your tongue. When I slice into its intestines… well, you get the idea." He breathed heavily against her skin, moving the soft hairs at her neckline. "Tonight, I'm more interested in a psychological question than a physiological one." He paused to stare at his specimen. "For all intents and purposes, is that dog your child?"

He straightened up and looked Jess in the face again. "Given that you're willing to be subject number one…" He opened and closed the pliers so the pincers clicked against each other. "…just so you don't have to watch what I *am* going to do to your dog, suggests…but why state the obvious?"

He grasped her finger in the pliers and squeezed. Jess grunted and looked away. Her heart felt like the pliers had clamped down on it as well. Ethan dug his thumbnail into her palm as he worked the pliers off the pad of her finger and over the tip, until he gripped only the narrow white half-moon of nail. Sweat poured off of Jess. She squeezed her eyes shut. *This is for Shakti. This is for Shakti.*

Ethan pulled.

Jess screamed.

The front door banged open, followed by the back door, its lock shattering the frame where it pulled free. A gust of wind rushed through the shotgun house like a hurricane, blowing against Jess so that she leaned almost out of the chair. The wind moaned and growled and suddenly changed direction, blowing from the back of the house to the front. Jess opened her eyes, squinting against the squall of dirt and debris swirling through the passageway.

Chopin blared from the CD player, as though the wind had turned the volume all the way up. The pianist's hands must have moved frantically, the left hand racing up and down the keys while the right pounded out chords or plunked notes over the rapid rise and fall of the left hand. Something pinned Ethan against the shelves with the cluster of candles he'd arranged around the wine bottle behind him, his feet off the floor. He kicked the shelf, shaking its contents. Glassware fell over and dropped, shattering under Ethan's feet. Jess smelled burning before she saw a plume of smoke rise above his shoulder. He kicked harder. A pile of old *National Geographic* magazines slid to the side, knocking over a Mason jar full of buttons. It rolled onto the floor, broke and spilled its contents. Ethan screamed, a noise high and shrill that caused Jess's heart to stick in her chest then hastily resume its frenzied beat. He fell away from the shelves onto all fours, onto the broken glass beneath him. Flames spread across his back, eating the fabric of his tight shirt, taking with it his body hair, scorching his skin and all that precious DNA. The candles that had surrounded the CD player and wine bottle lay on their sides, one of them still lit, the flames licking the wax circumference, blackening it and causing fresh drips to cascade onto the shelf. Chopin's music pounded, one crescendo after another. The music came from everywhere so loudly it hurt Jess's ears.

Ethan stood, his latex gloves torn by the glass shards, blood from his palms and knees escaping too quickly to be contained. Their eyes met only briefly, and he sprang for the door like a sprinter from the starting block. Jess moved to follow, but the handcuff forced her back onto the chair.

He can't get away.

The crossbar on the chair snapped and Jess stood up, free. She looked at Shakti unconscious on the table, saw movement. A wind circled the room, extinguishing all the candles. Trails of carbon rose from each wick.

Dan stood beside the table and placed his hand on Shakti's shoulder. He gave Jess a slight nod. She grabbed the Glock and ran out the back door after Ethan.

Jess rushed off the deck and across the train tracks into the woods. She didn't know where Ethan had gone, but with his back smoldering it would be toward water.

A bright moon and stars helped to light the way, despite the thick canopy of tree cover overhead. Jess dodged branches and leapt over soggy, rotted logs, the ground squelching under her feet. She nearly ran into the water when the trees broke, and she found herself on the bank of a small pond. Jess searched the area while trying to listen for some sound other than her own panted breath, her panicked thoughts.

Frogs. She heard the peeps and croaks of hundreds of frogs singing their night song. And somewhere in the woods, a great horned owl hooted. A small splash, probably a fish jumping, drew Jess's attention and she scanned the surface of the water, looking for the moon's reflection on the ripples' crests. She found something else.

Across from her, only twenty yards or so, a long slithering creature pulled itself up onto the leaf-littered shore. Jess thought it was an alligator the way it dragged itself from the water, then her mind made sense of the sight. Ethan must have ran into the pond and, realizing Jess was chasing him, half-swum half-slithered across it to the other side.

Ethan turned, crouching on the bank across from Jess, and looked directly at her. She felt his eyes, his hatred fixed on her as she pointed the gun at him. He launched from his squat into the tall sedges at the water's edge, disappearing between their stalks.

"Shit!" Jess ran. Mud filled in the tread of her tennis shoes and made her slip, but she kept to her feet and rounded the pond, focused on the edge of the forest, looking for the path that Ethan would have taken to get to the

river.

Jess. Jess. The frogs called her name. She imagined it, of course. She found the break in the trees and rushed forward, determined to get to Ethan before he disappeared into the Mississippi.

Something felled Jess like a wrecking ball taking down a house of Legos. The blow knocked her backwards out of the forest and she lay in the mud on a bed of bent and broken canary grass. She struggled to prop herself up, to get gravity on her side again.

Jess! Jess! It was more insistent, almost real.

Ethan stepped out from the tree trunks and stood over her with arms raised, a gnarled branch held high, ready to come down upon her head. She kicked her feet, trying to get purchase on the slippery ground and scoot away.

"Jess!"

Ethan looked in the direction of the voice. Beckett. Thank God. Jess lifted her hand from the mud and pointed the gun at her attacker. Ethan looked back down at Jess, his mouth a smirk, his eyes glimmering with malice. He had time to land a good blow or two before her rescuer arrived, and a good blow or two would be enough to bash her brains out. Jess's arm trembled and she brought her left hand up to support the right, keeping her damaged index finger out of the way. She watched his face, his dark eyes with their cold, expressionless alligator's stare, as she squeezed the trigger, taking up the slack. Ethan's eyes dropped from Jess's face, saw the gun, and widened. His mouth opened into a loose O. She pulled the trigger. It fired with a flash of red and a single percussive explosion that silenced everything else. The recoil jerked her hands up and she gritted her teeth against the stabbing pain in her shoulder. Ethan dropped to the ground, the branch falling with him. The owl took flight, shaking an old pecan tree's upper branches as it spread its wings and rose above the clearing. The stinging smell of gunpowder reached Jess.

"Police!"

Shouting and crashing through the trees, the wet undergrowth, slogging across the marshy edge of the pond. Jess listened to everything around her, the first croak of a frog, hesitant after the crack of the gun interrupted its song, Ethan's sucking and gurgling, the heavy footfalls of boots slapping wet ground. "Jess." It wasn't Beckett's voice. Who? Martinez. The gun pointed at the treetops. It had grown heavy and the muzzle shook from tremors that started in her shoulders and extended through her outstretched arms and into her hands.

Everything around her snapped and popped on the same level as her ears as help rushed in. And then they stopped moving. Her rescuers surrounded her. Her trembling increased.

"Jess," Martinez said her name like it was something solid, something she could reach for. He appeared above her, his body long like the trees that surrounded them, his face lit enough by the moon and stars to read the calm professionalism, the switching off of adrenaline, or at least its suppression, long enough to deal with her. "Jess," he said it softly now, looked down into her eyes, then reached slowly toward the gun. He took hold of it, and with his other hand uncurled Jess's fingers and removed the weapon from her hands. Jess let her arms drop and cried out at the pain in her shoulder and chest and hand.

With the gun out of her hands, law enforcement moved quickly. Johnson and a uniformed deputy went around Jess to check on Ethan. Another deputy swept the area with his flashlight.

"How do you feel?" Martinez knelt beside her.

"Shakti."

"She's fine and an ambulance is on the way. Now how are *you*?"

"I hurt. He hit me with a branch and..." Jess held up her left hand.

Martinez motioned to the deputy with the flashlight and he shined it on her hand. Martinez whistled. "Damn. You're going to lose that fingernail."

"He was pulling it out. Me or Shakti he said."

"And you picked you." He shook his head like she'd made a dumb choice.

Johnson appeared next to Martinez, standing above him, another tree in the forest. "How is she?"

Jess was about to answer she was fine. In a world of pain, but fine, but Martinez answered first. "She shouldn't walk. He whacked her with that branch, so there could be internal bleeding." Jess hadn't thought of that.

"That guy's not walking either. Lung shot."

"Too bad." Martinez said.

Johnson called a deputy to him. "Hurry back to the road and get the medics. Tell them what we've got and help them find us. Fast." The deputy nodded and was gone. "You just hang on. We'll get you out of here as fast as we can," he told Jess, then returned to stand over Ethan.

"I shot him in the lung?" she asked Martinez.

He reached a hand toward Jess's, but instead of taking it in his own, he lifted the loose end of the handcuff. "How the hell did you get out of the junk shop?"

"Dan."

"Dan." He shook his head again. "I should have known." A patch of moonlight shone on his face and his dark brown eyes showed a compassionate interest otherwise hidden by his well-worn persona.

"Dan held him against the shelves by the CD player until the candles caught his shirt on fire. And Dan broke the chair so I could get up."

He rolled his eyes. "I do not know how I'm going to explain that one."

"How about telling the truth? It's my story, after all, not yours."

Martinez lifted his face to look at the sky above them and ran a hand through his hair. "Nobody's going to believe your story."

"Do you have a better one?"

"I'm fine," Jess insisted. "I mean, I'm not fine, but my spine is fine. I can move my toes. See?"

"Sweetheart," the medic carrying the head of the backboard spoke, "that's the adrenaline talking. Once it wears off, you'll feel differently."

"Differently how? Like more pain? Because I already have pain. I have *plenty* of pain."

The medic shook her head, but didn't comment. They came to a stop and then the foot of the board lifted, tilting Jess toward the medic at her head. The medic at her feet grunted and Jess bounced and jostled. "We're going over a big log here," Jess's rescuer explained as she lifted and tilted the head of the board. Jess gasped at the fresh throb in her shoulder. "Sorry, sweetie. I'm trying to be gentle."

The medic was right. As Jess's adrenaline subsided, her pain came into acute focus. Jess winced at every new bump and jostle on the trail. Besides which, mosquitos had found her and she was, in fact, a smorgasbord for the annoying little bloodsuckers. Being strapped down, she couldn't even swat them away. Jess stopped talking and stared straight overhead at the patterns of light and dark where the moon and stars shone through the forest canopy.

I am being carried out of the floodplain. I am surviving. "I am surviving" seemed as good a mantra as any, and she repeated it for the rest of her ride.

They emerged from the trees and carried Jess around the junk shop. She knew where they were by the eaves of the shotgun house. They stepped under open sky and onto the shoulder of the River Road. They passed one ambulance and carried her to another.

She heard Ethan's pained gasps and looked as far to the side as the strap across her brow would allow. She caught a glimpse of him on a gurney, a medic holding an oxygen mask over his face while another delivered an injection.

A thought formed in her mind that she did not allow to take the shape of words. The lack of words, however, did not prevent her knowing it. If she had allowed herself the indulgence of words, they would have been: *I wish I had killed him.*

Martinez jogged over to Jess as the medics began sliding her into the rig. "Hang on, guys," he said. The medics stepped back from the gurney and he smiled down at Jess. He kept his hands folded in front of his abdomen, but his eyes offered her a kind of friendly touch in their stead. "You did good."

"Shakti?"

"Dave took her to a vet he knows. Got her to open her clinic special."

Movement caught Jess's eye and she gazed past Martinez to the front of the junk shop. "Dan's on the porch."

Martinez looked at the porch. "What's he doing?"

Dan stood with his hands on the railing. He was a nice-looking man, and Jess suddenly wished she had met him that day she stopped by the café, so that she could have known him even the smallest amount before all of this. "Watching. But I think...I think he's satisfied. We got his killer." A deputy carrying an evidence collection kit walked past Dan and into the junk shop, oblivious to the presence there. Jess looked back at Martinez. "Victor, I know where the hands are. Dan wants his wife to get his wedding ring back as soon as possible."

Chapter Forty

JESS COULDN'T HELP her impatience. While the doctors X-rayed and scanned her for damage, her body turned black and blue. Her right shoulder took the brunt of the blow from the tree branch and was deeply bruised. As much as the blow hurt, it had been relatively weak, meant to drop her, which it did well enough. Had she not had the gun in her hand, Jess had no doubt Ethan would have crushed her skull.

She had only just been parked in a room. The neck collar was thankfully gone, her spine declared healthy. She had deep bruises and would be sore for weeks, and the fingernail would turn black and fall off, but all things considered, she was fine. Beckett rushed into the room. "Jess." He moved to embrace her and she tensed, made a guttural sound. He stopped himself before making contact, straightened up, looked her over for the first time, then lifted his hands. He held them over her, hovering near her head, then tentatively placed one against her brow. "Are you...?"

"I'll be all right."

He leaned down and kissed her, and it was the best thing that had happened to her all day.

Beckett sat at her bedside. He moved to take her hand and stopped, stared at her bandaged fingers—the left hand had been reduced to a sort of lobster claw with bandages and tape holding her wounded index finger to her middle finger—then he went to place a hand on her shoulder and stopped, stared at the purple swath under her collar bone. Jess used her good hand to slide the neckline of the hospital gown up toward her neck. "Do you want anything?" Beckett asked. "A cup of tea maybe?"

Jess shook her head. "I want to see Shakti. She should see me when she wakes up." Jess tried to sit up and exclaimed as a jolt of pain shot through her shoulder. She gritted her teeth. "Why are we still here? They said I'm all right."

"Aren't they keeping you overnight?"

"Bull shit." She swung her legs off the edge of the bed. "Where's my clothing?" A plastic-handled bag sat on one of the visitor's chairs in the corner, its sides bulging. Beckett reluctantly passed her the bag.

Jess discovered new layers of awkward movement as she unsnapped the handles and reached inside. She pulled out her shorts. They were damp and covered in mud. "Oh…" she said, disappointed.

Martinez knocked on the door even though it stood wide open. Behind him moved a stream of activity, hospital personnel coming and going from the nurses station, where phones rang and computers hummed and a light board received a signal from each of the patient rooms. Though it was past visiting hours, there seemed to be plenty of civilians roaming the hallway, too. "Hello." Martinez came in and stood beside Beckett.

Beckett offered him his hand to shake. "Thanks for getting Jess out of there."

Jess turned and punched the call button near the head of her bed. She stared past Beckett and Martinez at the nurses station, watching as one of the nurses glanced up at the board, saw her light, and stood. By the time the nurse came around the station and crossed the corridor to enter Jess's room, she bore a pleasant-enough smile.

The nurse wore scrubs covered in Snoopy doing his Snoopy dance, flying his doghouse, and wearing his Joe Cool getup. "How can I help you?" she asked.

"I need some clothes. Does the gift shop sell t-shirts or sweats or something?"

She looked confused. "Are you cold? I can…"

"No. I'm leaving. My shorts are dirty and my shirt's not even here."

The Snoopy nurse nodded slowly and looked at Martinez, his badge visible on his belt, then at Beckett who stood with his arms folded, watching

Jess. Neither of them offered her any help. "Your shirt was cut off of you, and..." she picked up Jess's chart from the end of the bed and flipped the cover back, "...it doesn't look like you've been cleared for discharge."

"Forget it." Jess dangled the shorts in front of her with one hand and, sitting on the edge of the bed, lifted a foot to slip it through the leg hole. She got her other foot in the shorts and yanked them up underneath her hospital gown using only her right hand, wincing with each tug. Beckett looked worried. Martinez looked like he was stifling laughter. "What do you guys charge for this thing?" She pinched the hospital gown with the fingers of her right hand.

"I could check with billing in the morning," Snoopy nurse said, "but now I'd like you to get back in bed."

"Tell you what. I'll bring it back in the morning. That way nobody has to sweat it. It'll be like it never left."

"Jess..." Beckett used his concerned voice, hinting that she was being unreasonable.

She chose to ignore Beckett's warning and looked hard at Martinez, locking her eyes on his. "He's here. Isn't he? That little shit's in this hospital."

"Yes. But we've got officers guarding him and Johnson is there right now. He can't hurt you or Shakti."

"You get me out of here right now or I will find him and I will hurt him. I swear to God." Jess caught a glimpse of Snoopy nurse's shocked face before she turned and hurried out of the room.

"Jess, he's in custody. He's going to pay for what he did to you and Dan and Shakti. We've been to his house. We have the hands. We have you. There is no way he's going to get away with anything."

"Do you swear?" Jess felt something on her arm and looked down to discover that Beckett had reached out to her, put a hand there to soothe her. She'd been so amped up, she couldn't even feel his touch. The realization softened something in her. She met Beckett's gaze and found it so familiar, so comforting. She anchored herself in the blue of his eyes. "I would like to leave this place. I would like to see my dog now."

Martinez turned toward the door and then back to face Jess. "Yeah. All right. Go see your dog. Get some rest. I'm going to come by your house tomorrow to get your statement. All right?"

Snoopy nurse hurried back into the room with a doctor behind her. "Ms.

Vernon," he said, "what can I do for you?"

"You can discharge me."

Beckett drove at what seemed a leisurely pace to Jess. It wasn't leisurely, but it was cautious. Plenty of deer roamed the area at night and they drove county roads flanked by fields between the Rice County Medical Center and the Pepin Animal Wellness Shelter. Jess could barely contain her anxiety. This thing with Ethan wouldn't be over until she knew Shakti was all right. And she couldn't be certain it would be over even then. She rested her head against the window and enjoyed the cool stream of air conditioning blowing along the glass before reaching her face. When the vibrations of the van got to be too much, she sat up, then sank her head against the seat's headrest.

"We're almost there," Beckett said.

"Thank you."

Beckett glanced at her. "For what?"

"For everything." Everything included making a run to her house for clothes while the doctor cleared her to leave the hospital. She reached across the center of the van and put her hand on his arm, her bandaged fingers sticking out, fat with wrappings. "I don't know what I'd do without you."

"You…" He smiled, the glow of his dashboard instruments casting a faint green tint across his skin. "Yeah, I don't know either."

Everything above the waist throbbed and ached. The pain meds they'd given her in the hospital were wearing thin already. Jess had a bottle of Tylenol with codeine in her bag, but she wasn't supposed to have any for a couple hours.

Beckett rolled into Pepin, another river town about six miles south of Skoghall. All of these towns started at the water's edge and expanded inland. Pepin was a right triangle with the river the long edge and Main Street running away from the water, perpendicular to it, just like in Skoghall. Dave's friend, the veterinarian, lived at the apex of the triangle. Beckett drove down Eighth Street, past quiet houses with porch lights burning. Being the outskirts of town, the houses were newer, built in the 1950s and later. Rusted trucks and SUVs parked in front of single stall garages too small to house them. Fishing boats decorated yards alongside fake deer and garden pinwheels. On one front stoop, a man stood in his underwear facing the street, the tip of a cigarette burned red as he inhaled, then disappeared as he lowered his hand. Jess glanced at the clock, 2:00 a.m., and she wasn't even tired. She felt like she'd had a double espresso and the crash was coming.

Beckett pulled off the road into a wide gravel driveway in front of a doublewide trailer home. Dave's pickup stood next to an old Jeep with a PAWS logo and phone number on the side.

Dave opened the door as they approached. "You're a sight for sore eyes, Jess."

"So are you, Dave." She smiled. "Thank you for bringing Shakti here."

He nodded and ushered them into the reception area. "This way." They went past a couple of exam rooms and back into the heart of the clinic, full of equipment and cabinets and counters stocked with medical supplies. Shakti lay curled in a corner, her nose tucked underneath her tail, eyes shut tight, but her ears twitched at the sounds of their entrance.

Jess rushed to her, dropping to her knees and reaching to put her arms around her dog. The pain in her shoulder and chest stopped her from embracing Shakti. Shakti lifted her head and licked at Jess's face, wagged her tail weakly, then put her head back on her paws and whined. Jess leaned further down to kiss the top of her head before looking up at the people who surrounded them.

"Jess, this is Cassie." Dave introduced a tall woman in a white doctor's coat, blue jeans, and a pair of Birkenstock sandals.

"Hi, Jess." Cassie had a warm smile, a round face, and lovely green eyes. Shaggy blonde hair fell to her broad shoulders. "I hear you've been through…" She paused to consider her words. "Okay, I know this is an understatement, a lot tonight."

"Yes." Jess situated herself on the floor beside Shakti and stroked her head. "How is she?"

"Whatever type of sedative she was given has knocked her out for quite a long time. The effects are similar to what I see with a general anesthesia. She has been conscious for a couple of hours and wanted to move on her own. That's why she's on the floor."

Jess nodded.

"She hasn't got her coordination back yet. I think she'll be all right, since she's made it this far. She did vomit. I collected a sample of both her blood and vomit, so if the cops want to run a tox screen, we've got it."

Dave stood next to Cassie, practically beaming pride.

"Thank you. I'm just going to sit with her."

Cassie nodded. "I think I'll go put the kettle on."

"I'll help you," Dave said.

As Cassie and Dave left the room, Jess tilted her head back to lean it against the wall and let her eyes close. She was aware of Beckett settling on the floor beside her and resting his hand on her thigh. And then she fell into the sleep of the exhausted.

Chapter Forty-One

SHAKTI CURLED ON the bathmat, her chin on her paws, eyes half closed, but her ears remained alert to everything around her. Jess lay in a bath full of Epsom salts to soak away some of her soreness. Beckett sat on the closed toilet seat beside the claw foot tub, pitcher in hand. He dipped it into the tub, then poured a stream of warm water over Jess's head, working the shampoo suds out of her long, dark locks. They had hardly spoken since leaving the veterinary clinic. Jess was too tired for words, and Beckett—bless him—seemed to understand. Tenderly, he smoothed a hand across the top of her chest where the tree branch had struck, giving her a long, purple bruise. "Jesus, Jess," he said breathlessly. Jess closed her eyes and sank against the back of the tub.

Shakti sprang to her feet at the sound of the doorbell, a growl in her throat. Beckett and Jess looked at each other.

"I don't know," Jess said, then, "oh…Martinez."

Beckett nodded. He rubbed Shakti's head and neck. "It's all right, girl. It's a friend." He left the room to go get the door, and Shakti watched him leave. She looked over her shoulder at Jess, eyebrows raised.

"Come on, Bear. You can help me get dressed." Shakti dropped her rump into a sit, but kept her eyes trained on her mama as Jess carefully climbed out of the tub. "It's all right. Nobody's ever going to hurt you again." She stood on the bathmat and rubbed Shakti's soft head. The dog relaxed her face into a grin and allowed her tongue to fall out from between her teeth.

Toweling off was harder than she'd expected with her shoulder bruised and tight. Jess dressed and let her hair drip down her back as she carried her towel downstairs, Shakti on her heels.

The smell of coffee greeted Jess as Beckett poured the water over the grounds. Shakti stopped short when she saw Martinez, and the fur over her shoulders lifted. Martinez dropped to one knee and held his hands out to Shakti, smiling. "Hey there, Shakti," he said. "Remember me?" Her hackles dropped and she sprang to greet him with most of her old enthusiasm.

Jess sighed. "I'm so glad to see that."

"Me, too," Martinez said as Shakti put her paws on his knee and raised herself to lick his face.

"Honey," she addressed Beckett, holding out her towel, "can you dry my hair? I can't really reach up with this arm."

Beckett wrapped her hair in the towel and squeezed it out for her.

"Well, if that isn't the picture of domestic bliss," Martinez commented.

"Maybe if I weren't all bashed and bruised."

They moved to the dining room, and Martinez placed a recorder on the table between them. He needed to hear Jess's story in its entirety. "Where do I begin? At the bar?" She looked at Shakti. "With her disappearance?"

"Start at the beginning and tell me everything."

It was a long story; long enough that Beckett made them scrambled eggs and toast in the middle of it, as well as another pot of coffee. While he cooked, Jess and Martinez took Shakti outside. She sniffed around the sugar maple, did her business, and came back to Jess's side. "She's spooked."

"Give her time. I bet she'll be back to normal in a week."

"Will I?" Jess looked at Martinez.

"Do you want an answer? Because I'm not a shrink."

"But you've seen stuff like this before. You've seen people get hurt."

"Not like this, Jess. Your case is special. Besides, I deal with the crime, the body, not ongoing care for the victims."

"Right." Jess sighed. "I feel like putting up a giant fence with great big curls of razor wire along the top." She scanned the tree lined boundaries of her yard, the old barn she had big hopes for, and considered the wildlife she knew hid in those trees. "I bought this house because I loved it, and now my sanctuary has been violated. Ethan came onto *my* land and took *my* dog. Will the desire to hurt him back be gone in a week?"

"Maybe, if you follow your dog's example, but I doubt it."

"So in your experience…"

"In my experience, people hang on to stuff until it eats them full of holes."

Jess reached down to rub Shakti's shoulders and look out at her yard. She'd claimed it as her own after setting Bonnie to rest, believing nothing could ever disturb her happy home again. Those first months here were remembered by the footprint of the old smokehouse and the scar at the base of her sugar maple, a triangular wound with blackened edges that curled in on itself called a cat eye, a name given it by loggers. There was no such marker left by last night's adventure, but it was no less real, no less painful.

"Am I going to have to tell you all of this again at the sheriff's office?" Jess asked, ready for a new topic of conversation.

"Yes, but not necessarily the entire story. I'm trying to decide if the psychic stuff is too weird to include."

"It's weird all right, but it's what happened."

Beckett pushed the screen door open and stuck his head outside. "Come on, you two. Breakfast is ready."

After Jess had finished her story, Martinez asked Beckett questions about his involvement.

"After I got Jess's message," he said, "I tried calling you, but you weren't answering."

"I was in the interview room with two of the suspects," Martinez said clearly, the recorder still rolling.

"So I tried Dave. I tried to call and text him a bunch of times, before he finally picked up his phone."

"He was in the interview room with his cousin, the father of Erick Matheson, at the request of the father."

"So what happened then?" Jess asked Martinez.

"When Dave heard Ethan had you and Shakti, he went for Erick's throat. Told him if his friend hurt one hair of that dog's head…" Martinez glanced at Jess.

She smiled, reached down to find Shakti under her chair. "I'll have to thank Dave for that."

"Did you have to stop Dave?" Beckett asked.

"Stop him? That was the moment that cracked the suspects—and their parents." Martinez said with a hint of amusement. He picked up the recorder, rewound it slightly, checked it, and pressed record again. "And then Investigator Johnson and I headed to Skoghall to find you."

"What's going to happen to that psycho?" Jess said.

"We'll charge him with everything we can, which is a lot, but not as much as it should be."

"How do you mean?"

"The girl killed Dan before Ethan got there to cut off the hands. And Shakti is a dog, so kidnapping laws don't really apply. What he did to your finger, Jess, helps us a lot, actually. It shows he had the intent and the desire to torture a human."

"He *did* torture a human," Beckett said, pointing at Jess's hand. "That is torture."

"Okay, guys. All this attention to my finger is making me realize how much it frickin' hurts. I need my pills."

Keeping her bandaged finger out of the way, Jess struggled to open the bottle of pills. She could tell both men present were eager to help, but she wanted to do it herself just to figure out how much she would need Beckett in the coming days. As wonderful and willing as he was, she didn't want their relationship to be about her convalescence and his nursing skills. Once she'd swallowed her pills—just knowing they were on their way into her system made her hurt less—Jess addressed Martinez. "How did you end up in the interview room with Erick and the girl that late in the evening?"

"The law never sleeps, Ms. Vernon." He turned his water glass as though examining the condensation forming on its sides. "You know your revelation about the lipstick tube?"

Of course she did.

"I managed to get a warrant for the girl's lipsticks and any other lipsticks in the house. I expected to find quite a few between her, the sister, and the mother, but apparently they don't believe in makeup. The parents don't anyway. The daughters both had a stash of cosmetics hidden in their bedrooms. I don't know if the father was more upset we were poking around his house or that his girls had makeup." Martinez shook his head. "I thought my papa was bad. This guy is bottled rage.

"So, I started with the red tube," he continued, "just like you said. She hadn't bothered to clean it out. I could see the traces of white powder inside it. I sent it to the lab with a rush order and as soon as it came back, which was at the very end of the day, Johnson and I picked up our suspects."

"What was the powder?" Beckett asked.

"Diazepam," Jess said. "I asked Ethan last night. Erick's mother has panic attacks and the pills came from her."

Martinez nodded, "Which is bad news for Erick. He's not going to get off lightly after providing the pills that caused this whole mess."

"What do you mean *caused* it?" Jess rubbed Shakti's ears while listening to Martinez.

"You know how Dan was such a nice guy, but attacked the girl? She slipped the drug into his drink thinking it would sedate him and cause mild memory loss. Then Ethan and Erick would come in and do whatever they planned to do to him—I'm sure Ethan planned to kill him all along. But Dan was one of those rare people and had a paradoxical reaction to the drug. Instead of sedating him, he went berserk. She gave him a high dose mixed with alcohol. So he really wasn't himself when he followed her to the junk shop."

"That is so...so...what a waste." The loss flabbergasted Jess. "Those stupid kids! What the hell were they thinking?"

"Well," Martinez said, "that's what we're still figuring out. We know Ethan was the leader and coerced the other two into participating in his plot. But what any of them wanted to accomplish, I'm not sure. I think they all had their own reasons for getting involved."

"What about Ethan?" Beckett asked, his tone grim.

"That kid is a psychopath. He's organized, he's charming, he's possibly the scariest perp I've encountered so far in my career. I have no doubt that if we hadn't caught him, he would have become a serial killer. I think he might have gotten away if you hadn't been involved," Martinez caught Jess's gaze and held it. "You may have saved a lot of lives by helping to put him away now."

"Then I guess it was all worth it." Jess's voice cracked, betraying her attempt at sincerity. It was worth it, wasn't it? If what she went through saved others, prevented this kid from becoming a serial killer, then it must have been worth it. Maybe she'd be convinced of the fact tomorrow.

"Why do you think he would have gotten away?" Beckett asked.

"I think he would have stopped after he had the hands and waited to see how this turned out, bided his time until the next victim came along. But there was something about you, Jess, that he couldn't resist going after."

"Lucky me," she scoffed.

Martinez shrugged. "I'm sorry. I know this isn't what you want to hear, but the candles and music were a form of seduction."

"You're right. I don't want to hear this."

A woman with straight brown hair, very girl-next-door cute, came out of the café and stood in the middle of the garden, looking lost. A bench sat beside the path nearby and she put a hand out like she needed to find something to hang onto. Her body began to fold on itself, knees and hips bending, every part of her sinking toward the ground. And then she found the bench like it had never been there before, and with a sideways lurch seated herself upon it. Jess didn't know if the woman wanted company, but to stand nearby and pretend she hadn't witnessed this collapse felt wrong, like contributing to one of the ills of society so often despised and so seldom corrected. So she walked over and sat down beside the woman.

"Are you all right?"

The woman looked at Jess, startled, her eyes wet. "I...um...I don't know what I'm doing here."

"I feel that way all the time," Jess smiled.

"What do you do about it?"

"If I wait long enough, something occurs to me and I go with that."

The woman nodded her head. They were similar in age and build, both brunettes. She kept her head bowed and Jess knew something inside her had broken. "I wanted to see this place," she said to her lap. "But now I don't know what for. What can I get from it? It all looks so *normal*." She gestured across the garden toward the ice cream parlor and bakery. "They're happy. They're eating ice cream and pie."

"It's inconceivable, isn't it?"

The woman wore two wedding bands, a lady's set with a princess-cut diamond on her ring finger, and a man's band on her index finger. She turned the band around her index finger like it was a newly acquired and still self-conscious habit.

"Samantha?"

256

She nodded and wiped fresh tears from her cheeks. "How did you know?"

Jess hesitated, then decided to be honest. "I've met Dan."

She looked up, startled, her expression hopeful. "How?"

Jess glanced over her shoulder, wondering who was near. Only strangers licking the drips from their ice cream cones, enjoying the last days of summertime freedom. School would be starting in a matter of days, then the weather would turn, and Miss Grundi would close up her shop for the winter and fly south, an Arizona snow bird. Jess almost smiled at the simple pleasures of those around her, but of course, she couldn't when Samantha sat beside her; Samantha, whose grief was only beginning. Jess found Samantha staring at her bandaged fingers and held up her hand to show them off. "The man who killed Dan did this to me."

"You're," her face widened with a mixture of shock and recognition, "the other victim."

"Is that my official title? The other victim? I suppose I am that, but I prefer to think of myself as the hero." She faltered, felt herself blush. "I mean only that if I think of myself as a victim, it's something I'll have to live with. With what was done to me. I'd rather focus on the fact that I survived."

Samantha looked at her husband's wedding ring, turned it around her finger again.

"I'm sorry. I don't know what to say now."

"It's all right." She lifted her face to meet Jess's gaze. "I'm glad you survived. You can tell me what happened. Investigator Martinez told me some things, but I feel like there's something he hasn't told me. And I think I came here to find out what that is."

Jess had felt Dan's presence before, and now that she was willing to acknowledge him, he became visible, standing behind his wife. He placed his hands on Samantha's shoulders and leaned forward to kiss the top of her head. When his lips touched her, she lifted her head, her eyes glistening and her mouth round with a subtle surprise.

"Dan just kissed the top of your head. He's standing here with you, his hands on your shoulders."

Samantha placed her hands on her own shoulders and stared at Jess.

"I don't do this. I don't... I don't even know what it's called—give readings or something. But I recently became able to see spirits. I know it sounds crazy, but that's how I know Dan. I never met him before he died."

Samantha gasped, a sort of hiccup. Her hands remained on her shoulders while the wheels turned in her brain. Jess waited for her to react, expecting to be called a liar, charlatan, fraud. Samantha finally closed her mouth and looked up, over her own shoulder at her husband. She looked back at Jess. "That makes sense to me. I don't know why. I just *feel* like he's here. I feel warmth." She patted her shoulders with her hands. "Can you talk to him?"

Jess nodded. She turned on the bench so she faced Samantha and looked at Dan standing behind his wife. Jess heard the words, "Kiss the baby." They repeated in her mind's ear. "He's saying kiss the baby. He wants you to tell her that her daddy loves her, every night."

Samantha nodded and wiped fresh tears from her cheeks.

"He's showing me a picture now, but it doesn't make any sense. It's a maze. A big one. And now a bull? A bull in a maze?" Jess paused. She closed her eyes and felt a warm sense of security pass through her body. "He wants you to know it will take care of you."

Samantha gasped and pressed a fist to her mouth. "I know," she said. "I know what it means."

Jess went to sleep on her back. If she lay on her right side, her shoulder ached. And on her left, her hand risked getting mashed by her bedfellows. So on her back she remained the entire night with her left hand resting across her abdomen. Shakti lay on her right side, her spine against Jess's ribs, the crown of her head tucked into Jess's armpit. The dog snored lightly. Beckett slept on Jess's other side, his body curled toward hers so that his nose nestled in her hair and his hands gently held her arm above the elbow. Nesting between them, Jess had felt a renewed sense of security and had gone to sleep grateful to be in her own bed in her own home.

The sun now shone through her bedroom window, a gentle wash of dawn's light. Birds twittered outside in the sugar maple.

Jess's eyes moved beneath their lids. Her brows pinched and released. She muttered something incoherent.

Isabella stood beside the bed and watched Jess sleep. She touched Jess's brow. "We shall be the best of friends," she said, "forever and ever."

Acknowledgments

Thanks to my family and friends for love and encouragement, especially Mathia, Mom and Dad, Alexia, Laura, Nico, Susan, and Wendy. I am grateful to Pepin County Sheriff Joel Wener for sharing his time and expertise with me. Investigator Martinez would not be as real without Sheriff Wener's input. Also, I first heard of the Coleman Bros. from him. Thanks to Terry Mesch for opening the Old Courthouse Museum and the original jail to me. A big thank you goes out to David W. Nance for photographing double barrel shotgun houses in New Orleans for my cover. I am also grateful to Richard Greelis, Heidi Steffens, and Nico Taranovsky, the first readers of *Dark Corners in Skoghall*. They provided the kind of feedback that ensures a better book reaches readers. I am thankful for Minnehaha Creek, where Seva and I walk to stretch our legs and our imaginations.

About the Author

Alida Winternheimer lives in Minneapolis, Minnesota. When she is not writing, editing, or teaching, she likes to kayak on local lakes. She also bikes, bakes, and feeds animals.

Alida and Seva, the inspiration for Shakti and Bruno.

If you enjoy The Skoghall Mystery Series, please check out Alida's other novel, *A Stone's Throw,* and don't forget to leave a review online.

Look for Book Three of The Skoghall Mystery Series, *Don't Get Stuck in Skoghall*, in 2016.

Please go to www.alidawinternheimer.com/book to find more information about Alida and her work.

Send Alida a note at alida@alidawinternheimer.com.

DON'T GET STUCK *in* SKOGHALL

SHE SCREAMED AT him. She was always screaming at him lately. "So what is she to you? Just another mid-life crisis, I suppose."

"More like a mid-life wake up call," Dick shot back. "I'm through, Carole." God, it felt good to say it. He'd been so afraid to tell her how he really felt. Well, not really that, the telling, but the repercussions that were sure to follow. Divorce. She'd make sure it got ugly. They'd have to liquidate property. She'd expect alimony for the rest of her life—good God. Dick rolled his eyes at the thought. He'd need another attorney now. Dick began running through his list of contacts, noting those who were in a position to recommend one. Despite all these new complications, he felt free for the first time in years. Big snowflakes twirled and danced as they made their descent to earth. A sign from Heaven that everything would be all right for Dick.

"What do you mean you're through?" Her voice went shrill whenever she got upset. It was a sound that had aggravated Dick for half of his life.

"Through. Done. Finished." Carole's cheeks had reddened in the cold. No wonder. She drove out from the Cities in a fashionable, unlined, short-waisted wool jacket with autumnal leaves embroidered on the lapels and cuffs. Was it embroidery? Or appliqué? Dick could never keep that sort of thing straight. It mattered to Carole, and if he got it wrong, if he called embroidery appliqué, she corrected him like he was some kind of moron.

They stood on the edge of a storm. A great big beautiful winter storm, the likes of which the region hadn't seen in over five years, not since global warming made the Upper Midwest a temperate climate. Sixty degrees in November. Preposterous. And more than disappointing: disastrous. When folks as far north as Ely had to truck up to Canada to play in the snow, economies collapsed. Here it was Thanksgiving weekend and Dick finally had something to be grateful for.

"What are we doing here, Dickie?" Carole gestured, raising her hands to her sides like maybe he could explain it.

"You drove, Carole. Hell if I know what we're doing here."

Carole had arrived at the cabin earlier than anticipated, and Dick hadn't finished cleaning up. When she saw the wineglass in the sink with the lipstick print on the rim, she snatched it up and threw it at him. It was so obvious, maybe he wanted to be caught after all. She fled the cabin, and Dick followed her like a fool. Hadn't twenty-seven years of marriage taught him anything? This wasn't her usual fly-off-the-handle dramatics. She had proof, albeit shattered on the kitchen's tile floor. That's why he followed her out to the car, left the front door open, the fire in the fireplace roaring, and jumped in the passenger side as she backed out. He'd never expected her to leave the driveway.

But she did. She sped down the bluff and raced up the River Road with Dick white-knuckled, doing his own screaming in the passenger seat. She'd always preferred washable mascara, and now, lit by the dashboard lights, she looked like a ghoulish raccoon. The first fat snowflakes appeared in the headlights. She turned hard onto Skoghall's Main Street and screeched to a stop beside the community garden. She jumped out of the car and rushed into the dark enclave of dormant flowerbeds and leafless trees. Dick chased her to the dead end, here on the footbridge over the spring. A light above the café's door lit them under the dazzling winter sky.

"Carole," he said, holding his hand out, palm up, "when's the last time you caught a snowflake on your hand and looked at it?"

"What?" she spat out the word. "Dickie, you're a ridiculous man."

"Look." He lowered his hand and pointed at a perfectly shaped snowflake resting on the pad below his middle finger. "See the prongs? The structure? Right there, you can see it with the naked eye."

"I'll give you naked," she muttered.

"Snow has been like miniature chips of ice lately, like hard, jagged lumps of stuff. But this…" He raised his hand closer to Carole's face. "This is perfect. It's like the snow we grew up with. A real flake."

"You're a flake." Carole pressed her thumb to the snowflake, melting it between them. "You cheated on me, Dickie. And now you tell me you're through." She sniffled, but was it a show of emotion or just the cold making her nose run?

The snow came harder now and would be piling up. With the temperature dropping fast, the roads would freeze and the lakes would follow. The region had thrived for more than a hundred years because of winter sports, and Dick's grandfather had vision. He capitalized on the move away from fishing shacks constructed with scrap lumber and old doors to slick, prefabricated models with added comforts. "Even on the bitterest of winter days, you'll sit pretty in a Pratney Ice House." Pratney Ice House, Inc. was in the red for the third year in a row, and this storm—it might as well have been dropping flakes of gold.

"Come on, Carole. Let's go back to the house. We'll have some brandy and talk this through."

"But…" she sniffled again, "you want a divorce?"

"Don't you?"

"No." Carole had brought her purse out of the car with her. Dick hadn't really noticed it. It didn't even make sense for her to have it, other than force of habit. He noticed it now as she reached her right hand across her body to grab the handles and swing it upward. She put her shoulders into it and rotated at the waist. Her golfing coach would be pleased. The bag, a $2600 Prada tote in caramel, made of calf leather in Italy, with a flat bottom fitted with brass feet to keep it off the floor—something Dick had always teased her about, calling it her luggage—arced upward from Carole's hip toward his chest. The hard bottom caught him squarely in the sternum. He rocked back on his heels and flailed his arms. The bag caught him under the chin next and knocked him backwards. Dick felt the footbridge's railing pressing into his back. He grabbed for it. Snow made the wooden handrail slick, hard to grasp. And then the bag came down from above and slammed into his face, the straight edge of that bottom cracking the bridge of his nose. He bent over the railing in a way he never would have imagined his body could bend. His feet slid out from under him and he flipped backwards.

The fall covered a short distance, not even enough time to grasp what was happening. His backside hit the water first and his head struck a weathered paddle of the waterwheel. A bit of hair and scalp came free, stuck to a splintering of the board. The cold of the water caused him to gasp for air—a reflex, one he knew the dangers of, being an ice fisherman, but one he had not trained to prevent in the recent years of mild winters and warm lakes. If he had not struck his head… Or if he had not gasped for air as he sank into the spring, filling his lungs with icy water…

Carole leaned over the railing, her hands gripping the soft leather of her purse's double handles. She had to stand on tiptoe to look down at the dark spring that had so quickly taken her husband. "I want..." she paused to catch her breath, to watch the fresh snowflakes cover the handrail where Dickie had tried to stop his fall, "you to die and make me a rich widow."